Stephen Wentworth's kisses were sweet, warm, and playful.

He kept his hand on Abigail's side, just inches from her breast. She liked that he was bold but not presuming, familiar without harrying her into intimacies beyond what she was prepared to share.

The whole business became so engrossing that Abigail forgot this kiss was meant as a rehearsal or a test case, forgot she was being hounded by an arrogant marquess. She forgot much that badly needed forgetting. Instead, she recalled that she was not yet an old woman, and not simply an inquiry agent with a reputation for thoroughness and discretion.

Lord Stephen drew back, and urged Abigail against his side. "You offer me a challenge," he said, his hand smoothing over her hair.

The warm glow within died, for all that the embrace was cozy. "This plan was your idea, my lord, and I'm not *that* hard to kiss. You aren't exactly conventional in your approach, but I suppose I can manage further displays of affection if I must." She was blustering, trying to ignore the disappointment she felt.

For him the kiss had been an experiment, while for her it had been...

A revelation.

PRAISE FOR GRACE BURROWES AND THE ROGUES TO RICHES SERIES

"Grace Burrowes is terrific!"

—Julia Quinn, #1 *New York Times* bestselling author of the Bridgerton series

"Sexy heroes, strong heroines, intelligent plots, enchanting love stories.... Grace Burrowes's romances have them all."

—Mary Balogh, *New York Times* bestselling author

"Grace Burrowes writes from the heart—with warmth, humor, and a generous dash of sensuality, her stories are unputdownable! If you're not reading Grace Burrowes you're missing the very best in today's Regency Romance!"

—Elizabeth Hoyt, *New York Times* bestselling author

THE TRUTH ABOUT DUKES

"Burrowes takes her series to new heights with this tender, turbulent romance."

—*Publishers Weekly*, starred review

A DUKE BY ANY OTHER NAME

"All of Burrowes's secondary characters shine with wit and personality, and her sensitive development of two characters living with disabilities in the unaccommodating

Regency era is particularly notable. This sparkling romance does not disappoint."
—*Publishers Weekly*

"A standout in the historical romance subgenre but is also a powerful story all on its own... Highly recommended."
—*Library Journal*, starred review

FOREVER AND A DUKE

"Another smart story from popular Burrowes. Fans of Amanda Quick and Brenda Joyce's Cahill mysteries should enjoy this."
—*Booklist*

"Delightfully geeky and warm... an excellent continuation of a very strong series."
—*Publishers Weekly*

WHEN A DUCHESS SAYS I DO

"An unusual pair of smart and worldly but reticent lovers; a modern sensibility about themes of consent, class, and disability; and a surprising and adventurous plot make Burrowes's latest Rogues to Riches Regency satisfyingly relatable nerdy escapism... will warm readers' hearts to the core."
—*Publishers Weekly*, starred review

"Readers will root for these two wary people as they learn to trust each other with their foibles and their truths. With revealing dialogue, games of chess and subtle sensuality, this romance sings." —*Bookpage*

MY ONE AND ONLY DUKE

"Skillfully crafted and exquisitely written, Burrowes' latest is pure gold; a brilliant launch to a promising series."
—*Library Journal*, starred review

"Burrowes is a writer of towering talent."
—*USA Today* Happy Ever After

Also by Grace Burrowes

The Windham Brides Series

The Trouble with Dukes

Too Scot to Handle

No Other Duke Will Do

A Rogue of Her Own

Rogues to Riches Series

My One and Only Duke

When a Duchess Says I Do

Forever and a Duke

A Duke by Any Other Name

The Truth About Dukes

HOW TO CATCH A DUKE

A Rogues to Riches Novel

GRACE BURROWES

FOREVER

NEW YORK BOSTON

Forever

Hachette Book Group

1290 Avenue of the Americas, New York, NY 10104

read-forever.com

twitter.com/readforeverpub

First Edition: April 2021

Forever is an imprint of Grand Central Publishing. The Forever name and logo are trademarks of Hachette Book Group, Inc.

The publisher is not responsible for websites (or their content) that are not owned by the publisher.

The Hachette Speakers Bureau provides a wide range of authors for speaking events. To find out more, go to www.hachettespeakersbureau.com or call (866) 376-6591.

ISBNs: 978-1-5387-5383-5 (mass market). 978-1-5387-5384-2 (ebook)

Printed in the United States of America

CW

10 9 8 7 6 5 4 3 2 1

To those fighting the good,
hard fights

Acknowledgments

I have had such wonderful fun writing the Rogues to Riches stories. When Leah Hultenschmidt, my editor, said to come up with a series completely unconnected to any of my previous efforts, I was at first stumped. Then I bethought myself, "What is the absolute opposite of a polished, privileged duke? I know: a convicted murderer from the slums!" Then I smacked myself, because *that'll never work*...except it did. My heartfelt thanks to all the readers who've enjoyed the Rogues to Riches series right along with me, and to Leah, and the great team at Grand Central Forever who took *that'll never work* and turned it into a half dozen happily-ever-afters. Thanks, from me—and the Wentworths!

HOW TO CATCH A DUKE

Chapter One

"I have come to ask you to murder me, my lord." Miss Abigail Abbott made that announcement as calmly as if she were remarking on the pleasing composition of a still life with apples.

"Miss Abbott, good day." Stephen Wentworth struggled to his feet so that he might offer his visitor a bow. "While it is my greatest joy to accommodate a lady's pleasure *wherever* that quest may lead, in this instance, I fear I must disappoint."

Miss Abbott had earned Stephen's notice from the moment he'd met her several months ago. May she ever bask in heaven's benevolent light, her unexpected call at his London abode renewed his delight simply to be in her presence.

"You are the logical party to execute this errand," she went on, pacing before the library's hearth as if he hadn't spoken. "You'll see the thing done properly, and you are in line for a dukedom. A man so highly placed will face few repercussions should he be charged criminally."

That the butler had shown Stephen's guest into the library was a breach of etiquette. Miss Abbott should have been received in the formal parlor, which faced the street and thus afforded a lady's reputation greater protection.

Bless all conniving butlers. "Might we sit, Miss Abbott? My knee is—as it were—killing me."

She glowered at him down the length of her magnificent nose. "I importune you to commit homicide, and you jest."

In actuality, she'd demanded that he commit femicide. Rather than refine on vocabulary, Stephen used his cane to gesture at a comfortable wing chair set before the blazing fire. He waited until Miss Abbott had seated herself before he settled onto the sofa.

"Your faith in my criminal abilities is flattering, Miss Abbott, but my family takes a dim view of violence toward women—as do I. I cannot, alas, accommodate your request."

She popped out of her chair and stalked across his new Axminster carpet, gray skirts swishing. "And if I were a footpad trying to snatch your purse, a brigand menacing your person? Then would you send me to my reward?"

She moved with all the confidence of a seasoned general preparing to fight for a righteous cause, though her attire made for very odd battle finery. Stephen had never seen her dressed in anything but gray frocks or dark cloaks, and the severity of her bun would have done credit to a particularly dour order of nuns.

Everything about Abigail Abbott was intended to disguise the fact that she was a stunningly well-built female with lovely features. Such attributes made her merely desirable, and Stephen had come to terms with desire years ago—for the most part.

What fascinated him about Miss Abbott was her wonderfully devious mind, and how her penchant for guile waged constant warfare with her unbending morals.

"Why would a professional inquiry agent with very few unhappy clients need to die?" Stephen asked. "From what my sister has said, your business thrives because you excel at what you do."

Miss Abbott had been a very great help to Constance up in Yorkshire. To see Miss Abbott in London was both a lovely surprise—to see her anywhere would be lovely—and worrisome. If the Creator had ever fashioned a woman who did not need or want any man's assistance, for anything, Miss Abbott was that formidable lady.

"My situation has nothing to do with my profession," Miss Abbott replied, resuming her seat. "Might you ring for a tray?"

"Is that how you go on with your lovers? Issue commands couched as questions? *Sir, might you apply your hand to my—*"

"My lord, you are attempting to shock me." Her expression was so severe, Stephen was certain she was suppressing amusement. "As a dilatory tactic, this is doomed to fail. I am nearly impossible to shock, and also quite hungry. A tray, if you please. In more genteel circles, this is called offering a guest sustenance. Hospitality, manners. Need I explain further?"

"Tug the bell pull twice," Stephen said, gesturing again with his cane. "I have been taken captive by the sofa. *You* are being dilatory, madam, evading a simple question: Why must you die? I would be desolated to think of a world without you in it."

He offered her the God's honest truth, at which she sniffed.

"You are doubtless desolated eleven times a day." She gave the bell pull a double yank and sat back down. "I am not asking you to rid the world of my presence in truth, though I must convincingly appear to die. I have some means, and I can make my way from England easily enough once I've been officially expunged from the race."

"My dear Miss Abbott, had you wished to terminate your existence in truth, you would have done so by now. Never for a moment did I think you expected me to actually take your life."

A scintilla of the starch suffusing her spine eased. "I should have been more clear. I know you are not a killer."

"I am, as it happens, though that's old business." Old business she should at least be warned about before she awarded Stephen any points for gentlemanly conduct. "I generally avoid violence if I can do so without compromising my honor."

"And when you cannot?"

What an odd question, and an excellent example of why Stephen delighted in this woman's company.

"I keep my affairs in order and make sure my family remains untroubled by my actions. If your work has not forced you to flee for your life, then who has inspired you to take the grave step of asking for my help?"

Miss Abbott stared at her gloved hands, then consulted her pocket watch, which looked to be a man's article, heavy and old-fashioned. As stage business went, the watch was badly done, because the ormolu clock on the mantel was in plain sight and kept perfect time.

Stephen let the silence stretch, unwilling to trick Miss Abbott into any admissions. She'd resent the manipulation, and besides, she was tired, hungry, and unnerved. To take advantage of her in a low moment would be unsporting. Far more interesting to put her back on her mettle, and engage her when she could bring her usual trebuchet of logic and the boiling oil of her asperity to the battle of wits.

The tray arrived, and without Stephen having to ask, Miss Abbott poured out. She apparently recalled that he liked his tea with a mere drop of honey. She used far more than a drop in her own cup, and made short work of two toasted cheese sandwiches and an entire sliced apple.

"Don't neglect the shortbread," Stephen said, sipping his tea.

"You're not eating, and the food is delicious."

"Not much appetite." Stephen had an enormous appetite, but a man with an unreliable leg ought not to push his luck by carrying unneeded weight. He was nowhere near as well disciplined when it came to his mental appetite for solving puzzles.

Still, he had learned some manners, thanks to the ceaseless efforts of his family. He waited until a mere half sandwich remained on the tray before he resumed his interrogation.

"Have you committed a crime?" he asked, starting with the usual reason people shed an identity.

"I have committed several crimes, as do most people in the course of a week. You, for example, are likely behind on the longbow practice required by the Unlawful Games Act of 1541. Very bad of you, my lord, considering how much interest you take in weaponry."

A footman came for the tray, and Miss Abbott's look of longing as he departed made Stephen jealous of an uneaten half sandwich.

"We will not be disturbed again," Stephen said. "For you to resort to sixteenth-century legislation for your obfuscations means, my dear, that you are very rattled indeed. Miss Abbott—Abigail—you are safe with me, as you knew you would be. I cannot help you if you refuse to apprise me of the nature of the challenge before you. Who has presumed to menace you?"

She had taken off her gloves to eat. She smoothed them against her skirts now, one glove atop the other, matching the right and left, finger to finger.

Why was the one glove resting atop the other vaguely erotic?

"I have apparently angered a peer," she said. "Infuriated him, though I haven't wronged him that I know of."

Why come to the brother of a *duke* for aid unless…? "A *marquess* is after you?" They were few in number, particularly if the Irish and Scottish titles were eliminated from consideration. "An English marquess?"

"I think so."

"You know so, but how do you know?"

She tucked the gloves away into one of those invisible, capacious pockets sewn into women's skirts.

"Do you promise not to repeat what I tell you, my lord?"

"You are exhausted and afraid, so I will overlook the insult you imply."

Her head came up, like a dominant mare sensing an intruder in her paddock. "I am *not* afraid. I am vexed past all bearing."

She was terrified, and that was such a rare prospect that Stephen himself became uneasy. "Give me a name, Miss Abbott. I cannot scheme effectively on your behalf unless you give me a name."

She had the prettiest gray eyes. All serious and searching, and those eyes were worried. That some fool had given her cause to fret vexed *Stephen* past all bearing. He'd not enjoyed a rousing fit of temper for ages, and the pleasure of putting a marquess in his place appealed strongly.

"You won't believe me, my lord."

"If somebody told me a mere marquess had blighted the confidence of Miss Abigail Abbott, *that* I would find hard to credit. The ranking imps of hell could provoke you to brandishing your sword cane, and for the massed armies of Britain you might slow your stride a bit. St. Michael the Archangel flanked by the seraphic host could inspire you to a respectful pause. But a marquess? A lowly, human marquess?"

Her hands bunched into fists. "He has tried to harm me, twice. Before he tries again, I will simplify matters by having you commit an arranged murder."

Like an arranged marriage? "Who is this pestilence of a marquess?" Stephen mentally began sorting through Debrett's. This one was too old, that one too young. Several were on the Continent, a few were simply too decent or too arrogant to resort to intriguing against a female of common origins.

Women were easy to ruin, and a female inquiry agent with a tarnished reputation would be ruined indeed.

"Lord Stapleton," he said. "He's an idiot. Arrogant, wealthy, nearly ran off his own son, God rest the earl's randy soul. Stapleton has made his widowed daughter-in-law's life hell. You needn't die. I'll kill Stapleton for you and the world will be a better place all around. Shall I ring for another tray? You're still looking a bit peaky."

Lord Stephen Wentworth displayed a strange blend of chilling dispassion and surprising graciousness. Abigail hadn't spent much time with him, but her observations suggested his intellect worked like the mechanism of an automaton—ruthless logic turned mental gears unimpeded by sentiment. If a marquess was attempting to murder somebody who hadn't committed any particular crime, then murdering the marquess was both just and advisable.

That taking a life was illegal, immoral, and contrary to Abigail's values did not seem to occur to his lordship, or trouble him if it did. Then too, Stapleton hadn't precisely attempted murder—yet.

"You cannot kill a peer of the realm, my lord, though I am touched by the offer." Abigail was also unnerved that Lord Stephen would so easily guess the identity of her nemesis.

"You are appalled at the very notion, even as you tell me this man has twice attempted to do you harm. His bloodthirsty behavior is merely vexing while my gallantry appalls you. Female logic at its unfathomable finest. I need details, Miss Abbott, and I suspect you need another tea tray."

And there was the odd flash of consideration, at which Lord Stephen also excelled. "You attempt to confuse me. Spouting offers of murder one instant and proffering more sandwiches the next." Abigail could eat more than most farmhands and still be hungry. Trust Lord Stephen to sense that unladylike trait and remark upon it.

"Can you be confused by sandwiches? Good to know. The bell pull, Miss Abbott. Thrice."

She rose to comply, because with Lord Stephen one chose one's battles—and she was hungry. The inn fare on the Great North Road had been unfit for feral dogs, and stagecoach passengers seldom had time to finish a meal, in any case.

"Do you promise you won't kill Lord Stapleton?" Abigail remained on her feet to ask that question, which was petty of her. Lord Stephen was cursed with an unreliable leg. To stand for any length of time pained him, according to his sister, and walking a distance took a heavy toll. With this man, though, Abigail would use every means available to gain and keep the upper hand.

Bad enough she needed his help. Worse yet if she could be befuddled by a plate of warm, toasted cheese sandwiches that had cheddar dripping over the crusts and smelled of butter with a hint of oregano and chives.

"If I did finish the old boy off," Lord Stephen asked, "would you spank me for it?" He batted his eyelashes at Abigail, such an absurdity she nearly burst out laughing.

"I suspect Bow Street would see you punished were you to murder the marquess, and I don't want their inconvenience on my conscience. I simply need to be left in peace and allowed to go safely on my way."

The discussion paused again as two footmen wheeled in an entire trolley of comestibles. One fellow lifted the lid of a tureen, and the scent of a hearty beef barley soup wafted to Abigail's nose. The other footman set a second tea tray on the low table, except that the offerings also included a pot of chocolate, a carafe of claret, and a mug of cider.

"Would miss care for anything else?" the footman asked.

"What else could I possibly...?" She left off speaking as the footman ladled a steaming serving of soup into a delftware bowl.

"Lemonade?" Lord Stephen suggested. "A syllabub, a posset, orgeat? Three tugs on the bell pull means the kitchen is put on full alert. Battle stations, present arms, forced marches to the pantries and wine cellars. Tell Thomas your inmost culinary desire and he'll convey it directly to Cook."

Only a very wealthy man had the resources to put a kitchen on full alert at a moment's notice. Abigail had made discreet queries into the extent and sources of Lord Stephen's fortune, and the sums he was said to possess were nearly as staggering as those attributed to his ducal brother.

"The available offerings are more than sufficient," Abigail said, as the footman set out cutlery on a tray and added the bowl of soup, thick slices of buttered toast, and a spicy mug of hot mulled cider.

"That will be all, gentlemen," Lord Stephen said. "Though please have the fires lit in the blue suite."

Abigail noted his lordship's presumption, but she wasn't about to take issue with his high-handedness until she'd done justice to the soup, a baked potato stuffed with bacon and brie, and an apple tart drizzled with some sort of raspberry-flavored cream.

As she finally, finally ate her fill for the first time in days, Lord Stephen arranged his booted foot on a hassock and leaned his head back against the sofa cushions as if—harmless old thing that he was—he'd doze off in the presence of a lady.

"I am being rude," Abigail said. "I know I ought not to eat so much, and that I'm supposed to make polite conversation while I clean my plate—my plates—but I don't take you for a high stickler."

"I can be a high stickler," his lordship replied, slouching lower against the cushions without opening his eyes. "I take very firm exception to marquesses who threaten my favorite inquiry agent, for example. Such fellows could end up facing me over pistols on the field of honor, whereupon their odds of survival are abysmal. Have another tart."

She should decline, but the tarts were magnificent. Warm, sweet, rich, and spiced with cinnamon in addition to the raspberry drizzle.

"Will you share one with me?"

He opened his eyes. "You are trying to cozen me. Pretending we're friendly enough to share a tart before you toss my hospitality back in my face without giving me a scintilla of the information I request. Then you will make your way through the dangerous streets of London to some poky little lodging house run by a grouchy widow. She will overcharge you for a thin mattress on a short cot and demand your attendance at morning prayers. Have the second tart, Miss Abbott."

On principle, Abigail could not capitulate. "Only if you share it with me."

"Then serve me one quarter, and pour me half a glass of cider."

He sat up, pain flitting across his features. Lord Stephen spent so much effort being naughty and disagreeable that his looks probably went unnoticed, but they were interesting looks. Like his siblings, he had dark hair and blue eyes. His build was leaner than that of the other Wentworths, though his shoulders were powerful and his air more self-possessed.

The Wentworth siblings had been born to direst poverty, with an abusive gin-drunk for a father. That much was common knowledge. The oldest sibling—Quinton, now His Grace of Walden—had finagled and scrapped his way into the banking business, where he'd made a fortune.

And that was before an ancient title had meandered and staggered down familial lines of inheritance to add old consequence to new wealth.

Lord Stephen, the duke's only brother, was heir to the title and to at least some of the wealth. Their Graces had four daughters, and Lady Constance maintained that the duke and duchess were unwilling to add to the nursery population when Her Grace's last two confinements had been difficult.

Lord Stephen limped badly, often using two canes to get about. The limp ought not to slow the matchmakers down at all—in fact, it made their quarry easier to stalk—but the naughtiness and sour humor were doubtless more difficult to overlook even in a ducal heir.

All of which made Lord Stephen the perfect accomplice to a murder of convenience. Nobody would trifle with him, if indeed anybody ever suspected him of the crime.

Abigail served him a quarter of the second tart—a largish quarter—which seemed to amuse him.

"You will accept my hospitality for the night," he said, "and I will brook no argument. The staff seldom has an opportunity to spoil anybody but me, and they have grown bored with my crotchets. The laundry is heating your bathwater, the kitchen will make you up a posset, and before I go out I will select a few lurid novels to entertain you as you rest from your travels."

"And if I'd rather stay with the grouchy widow at the poky lodging house?" She would not. Self-indulgence was Abigail's besetting sin.

Lord Stephen took a bite of tart, which drew her attention to his mouth. Had she ever seen him smile? She'd seen him happy. He'd taken the time to explain to her the mechanism in his sword cane, conveying a child's delight with a new toy over an elegant spring lock set into a sturdy mahogany fashion accessory.

Not the cane he was using now.

"If you'd rather stay with the grouchy widow, then London's footpads could well render your death a truth rather than a fiction. Times are hard for John Bull, Miss

Abbott, and thanks to the Corsican menace, an unprecedented number of humbly born Englishmen have grown comfortable with deadly weapons. Such a pity for the civilian populace who can offer no employment to the former soldier."

Abigail had occasionally spent time in London, but she was nowhere as familiar with the capital as she was with the cities of the Midlands and the north. Besides, London was growing so quickly that even somebody who'd known the metropolis well five years ago would be confused by its rapid expansion.

"I will stay one night, my lord, because I am too tired to argue with you." And because she longed for a hot bath, clean sheets, and a comfy bed rather than a thin mattress in a chilly garret.

His lordship set down his fork, most of his sweet uneaten. "You will stay with me, because I can keep you safe. What I cannot do is keep you company." He shifted to the front of the couch cushion and, using the arm of the sofa and his cane, pushed to his feet. "I will see you at breakfast, Miss Abbott, when you will present a recitation of all the facts relevant to the marquess's attempts to discommode you. The house is festooned with bell pulls owing to my limited locomotion. One tug summons a footman, two a tea tray, and you've seen the results of a triple bell."

He moved away from the couch carefully. Cane, good foot, bad foot. Cane, good foot, bad foot.

"Is there nothing to be done?" Abigail asked, gesturing with her cider toward his leg.

He didn't answer her until he was at the door. "I've

consulted surgeons, who are loath to amputate what they claim is a healthy limb. The problem is the knee itself, which was both dislocated and broken, apparently. I was young, the bones knit quickly, but they weren't properly set first. I fall on my face regularly and resort to a Bath chair often."

Hence, the bell pulls hung a good two feet lower in his house than in any other Abigail had seen.

"And yet, you say you must go out. It's raining, my lord. Please be careful." She wanted to rise and assist him with the door, but didn't dare.

"Enjoy your evening, Miss Abbott, for surely there are no greater pleasures known to the flesh than a soaking bath, a rousing novel, and a good night's sleep." He bowed slightly and made his way through the door. Before he pulled the door closed behind him, he poked his head back into the room. "Finish my tart. You know you want to."

Then he was gone, and Abigail was free to finish his tart—and to smile.

Chapter Two

Babette de Souvigny slurped her tea. "You know how it is with most of the fancy gents, Marie. *On your back, poppet, there's a love.* Heigh-ho, righty-o! Three minutes later he's buttoning up and leaving a few coins on the vanity."

"What that approach lacks in charm, it makes up for in brevity," Marie Montpelier replied. "This is wonderful tea."

"Lord Stephen gave it to me."

To Stephen, dozing in the bedroom adjacent to this conversation, Babette—given name Betty Smithers—sounded a little perplexed by his latest gift.

"What's he like?" Marie asked. "His lordship, that is."

An interesting pause followed, during which Stephen told himself to get the hell out of bed and take himself home. Abigail Abbott expected him to be awake and sentient at breakfast, and only a fool would cross swords with that woman on less than three hours' sleep.

"Lord Stephen is different," Babette said. "Take this tea, for example. What lordling brings his light-skirts a tin of excellent tea? How did he know I'd appreciate that more than all the earbobs in Ludgate? The tea merchants don't trot out the fine blends for the likes of us."

"The earbobs are mostly paste," Marie replied. "Did he bring you these biscuits too?"

"Aye. Had his footman deliver me a basket. I never had such glorious pears, Mare. I'm saving the last one to have with the chocolates he sent me. If you'd told me a pear could make right everything ever wrong in an opera dancer's life, I'd have said you were daft."

Another slurp.

"A man with glorious pears must be making up for a lack of glory in other regards, Bets."

Marie had been with the opera five seasons. Stephen had steered away from her practiced smiles and knowing glances. Babette was new to the stage and had retained some generosity of spirit on her recent trek down from the Yorkshire dales.

Stephen had endured the usual round of cards at the Aurora Club, then caught the last act of the evening's opera. Escorting Babette home had led to an *interlude*, and now—at three in the morning—Babette was having tea with her neighbor. Very likely, Marie had just bid good night to some wool nabob or beer baron.

"If you mean in bed," Babette replied, "Lord Stephen is a handful."

"A mere handful?" Laughter followed, the sort of laughter women shared only with one another. Stephen liked that variety of mirth and was happy to be its inspiration, though he really should be getting dressed.

"Not that sort of handful," Babette replied. "He's demanding, inventive, and relentless, is the only way I can describe it. You know how we sometimes flatter the menfolk?"

"Feign pleasure, you mean?"

Stephen felt a twinge of pity for Marie, who mentioned her subterfuge with no rancor whatsoever.

"He doesn't put up with that, Mare. He has a way of insisting that there be no faking, no pretending, and that's unnerving, it is. Goes along with the scrumptious pears and the rich chocolates. Lord Stephen deals in a kind of blunt honesty that wears me out as much as his swiving does."

Women spoke a dialect Stephen didn't entirely understand, though he sensed Babette was not offering a compliment to his sexual prowess. She wasn't insulting him either, but she was blundering perilously close to an insight.

Should have left fifteen minutes ago.

"I hate it when a man lacks consideration," Marie said. Porcelain clinked, suggesting she was serving herself more tea. "Some of them have more care for their horses and lapdogs than they do their women."

A sad truth.

"Lord Stephen is frightfully considerate. He holds doors for me, holds my chair, as best he can with his canes and all. He never hurries me into the bedroom, and he never rushes away as if a hand of cards matters more than a fond farewell."

"Betty, you know better." Marie's tone was pitying rather than chiding. "You let a man have your heart, you're doomed. Look at poor Clare. A babe in her belly, naught but another few weeks of dancing left to her, and where's her lordling? Off shooting grouse in Scotland. She'll be lucky to survive the winter, and he promised he would marry her."

Clare Trouveniers had been under the dubious protection of Lord Alvin Dunstable, known as Dunderhead to his friends. Stephen made a note to send Dunstable a pointed epistle and to slip Clare some coin.

"Lord Stephen doesn't have my heart, not yet," Babette replied. "It's a near thing, though. You know what he does that just unravels me, Mare?"

"Pays well?"

"Of course he pays well, and he puts the money in my hand, and tells me how to invest it. His brother owns a bank, you know."

"His brother owns half the City. Does Lord Stephen bring you flowers?"

"Flowers are predictable. Lord Stephen isn't predictable."

That observation was inordinately gratifying.

"He'll be predictably married before too long," Marie observed. "His brother's wife was just delivered of yet another girl child. That's four girls, Bets. I do love it when Providence refuses to bend to the will of the Quality."

That observation—about Stephen having to marry—was inordinately disquieting.

"He doesn't do what you think he'll do," Babette replied. "Take the last biscuit. We have rehearsal in the morning. You'll need to keep up your strength."

That Babette continued to dance when Stephen paid her well enough that she could put away her ballet slippers bothered him even as it earned his admiration. Men were fickle, fate was a mercurial old beldame, and bad luck was inevitable. To wit, Jane's fourth child was indeed yet another girl.

Though Stephen was helpless to do anything but adore his nieces.

"You are perilously fond of your lordling," Marie said, sounding as though her mouth were full of biscuit. "He doesn't strike me as a man to inspire fondness. Cold eyes, never a wrinkle on his Bond Street finery. His canes are worth more than my poor papa's life savings, God rest his soul. Have you ever heard Lord Stephen laugh? Does he snore? Does he forget where he put his sleeve buttons?"

"He smiles."

What had laughing or snoring to do with anything, and who in his right mind would misplace gold sleeve buttons?

"He smiles like I smile at this butter biscuit, Bets, like he's about to demolish something or someone and relishes the prospect. He's fought duels, you know."

"Men do. They don't typically linger after an encounter with an opera dancer, don't cuddle up with her like she's a warm hearth and he's a weary soldier."

A cup hit a saucer with a definite *plink.* "Betty Smithers, what have I told you about cuddling?"

There were rules about cuddling?

"You break it off with Lord Stephen," Marie went on. "The sooner the better. If you crooked your finger at Framley Powers, he'd be sniffing at your skirts in an instant. Powers is rich."

"He's nearly twice my age and silly."

"You're barely twenty. No cuddling, Bets. No cuddling, no pet names, no foolish notes that can be used to blackmail you if you ever turn decent. You show up for rehearsals and keep dancing until you've enough put by to open a shop. Those are the rules."

And sheaths, Stephen wanted to add. *Always make the blighter use a sheath.* He'd sent Babette a trove of expensive Italian sheaths in a fancy box, though he knew to always bring his own to any encounter. An enterprising mistress with a sharp needle could easily conceive her way to a generous pension.

A gentleman was honor bound to support his offspring, but he needn't sprinkle progeny across half of London. Then too, Stephen would not visit bastardy on any child if he could avoid it.

"I will never have a shop," Babette replied tiredly. "Name me one dancer who's earned enough to open a shop. Clare will end up sewing herself blind for some modiste, her baby farmed out to a wet nurse who'll kill the poor thing with the black drop. When Lord Stephen holds me..."

"Babs, don't."

"When he holds me, I feel like the most precious, dear, cherished woman in England, Marie. His hands are warm, and he does this thing.... He squeezes my neck, not hard, but firmly, and every ache and pain from rehearsals, every worry and woe, just drains right out of me. He rubs my feet, Mare. My ugly, aching feet. Then he rubs my back, slowly, all the time in the world, like caressing me is his greatest joy. His hands are inspired, and far more than the swiving, I crave that tenderness from him."

Thundering throne of heaven. No man should hear such a confession. Duncan, Stephen's cousin and erstwhile tutor, had once mentioned that the ladies liked a bit of petting. Stephen liked a bit of petting, saw no harm in it, and had added a few little gestures to his amatory repertoire.

Abruptly, departing the premises became an urgent necessity. Departing London itself had gained appeal as well, if not England, but then, there was Miss Abbott, tucked up in Stephen's blue guest suite.

In the next room, a chair scraped. "Betty, we are friends, as much as anybody in this idiot business can be friends. Get free of Lord Stephen before he destroys you. He won't mean to, you won't blame him, but he'll ruin you all the same. He'll ruin your ability to be happy even if he doesn't put a babe in your belly. Don't argue with me, for I must be off to bed if I'm to dance before noon. Thanks for the tea and biscuits. Don't be late for rehearsal, especially not because you fell back into bed with the likes of him."

A door closed, none too softly.

Stephen remained stretched on the mattress, eyes shut, when what he wanted was to bolt for the door right behind Marie. Eavesdroppers supposedly heard no good of themselves, though Babette had had only positive things to say about her lover.

Stephen wished she'd complained instead. He stole all the covers, he never sent smarmy epistles, he had a vile temper, and he insisted on keeping his canes within reach even when making love. Surely those were noteworthy shortcomings?

A weight settled on the bed a few minutes later. Dancers could move silently, but Stephen had sensed Babette's approach. She was fastidious, and the aroma of the rose soap he'd purchased for her preceded her under the covers.

"There you are," he muttered, when she tucked up against his side. "Wondered where you disappeared to. I should be getting dressed."

Her hand drifted down the midline of his belly. "One more before you leave?"

He'd make her oversleep and be late for rehearsal if he lingered, which he was in no mood to do in any case, despite the ever-willing attitude of his male flesh.

"Alas for me, I must away," he said, trapping her hand in his and kissing her fingers. "You've worn me out."

"You wear yourself out." Babette stroked his chest. "Did Marie wake you?"

"I thought I smelled her perfume. Was she here?"

Babette withdrew her hand. "How is it you know her perfume?"

"She's keeping company with the Hormsby pup. He buys cheap Hungary water and pours it into pretty bottles, then claims he has it blended just for his current *chère amie*."

"That is awful. Must you rush away?"

"As if I could rush anywhere." Stephen dredged up a sigh. "Hand me a cane, if you please?"

Babette obliged and helped him dress, all the while chatting about the latest drama among the corps de ballet. She was restful company, and Stephen would miss her. He missed them all, the restful ones and the tempestuous ones, and he hoped they missed him too—but only a little and for only a short while.

"The sky is nowhere near light enough to ride in the park," Babette said, smoothing her fingers over his cravat. "Do you truly have to leave? I could show you what I know about riding crops."

She was a Yorkshire shopkeeper's daughter whose father had lost his military contracts when peace had been declared on the Continent. As far as her parents knew, she was toiling away for a tea-and-tobacconist in a decent London neighborhood, and happy to send most of her pay home.

"You have no business knowing anything about riding crops," Stephen said, assessing his appearance in the cheval mirror. "And I outgrew my curiosity about the English vice before I gained my majority." A person in constant pain wasn't distracted, much less aroused, by applications of a birch rod to his backside, but Stephen had experimented with erotic pain for a time nonetheless.

One wanted to be thorough in one's investigations.

"You look splendid," Babette said. "I'm not just saying that."

"I look splendid, until I'm required to saunter along, all lordly nonchalance. The second cane rather destroys the fiction." On good days, he could make do with one cane. Good days were rare when he bided in London.

"You look splendid to me when you're not wearing anything at all," Babette said. "Shall I wait for you after Friday's performance?"

Now came the hard part, the part Stephen hated and was so adept at, but had already put off for too long. "Did I mention I'll be leaving Town shortly? Hand me my hat, would you?"

Babette passed over a high-crowned beaver. "Leaving when?"

"Possibly by the end of the week. You can catch up on your rest." He tapped the hat onto his head, then gave it a tilt. Not quite rakish, but a nod toward style.

"How long will you be gone?"

Stephen started for the door, his progress slow. Upon rising, he often overestimated his mobility because his knee hurt less. Pain, by contrast, kept him careful.

"I'm not sure how long I'll be gone. I'm heading north to avoid the Little Season, and the ordeal of making my way to my country dwelling is sufficiently taxing that I dread the return journey. I might not come back to London until next spring."

That had been his plan before Miss Abbott had arrived, looking haunted and weary.

He made it to the door, then paused, waiting for Babette's response to his announcement. He preferred a rousing farewell argument, complete with recriminations and curses, and maybe even a stout blow to his cheek. The lady was entitled to make such a display, and the verbal beating assuaged his conscience.

"This is good-bye, then," Babette said. "I will miss you."

She was so young and so dignified, Stephen nearly did bolt out the door.

"You will not miss me," he said. "You will consider

yourself well rid of me, but I did buy you a small token of my esteem in the hope that you will recall me fondly."

He withdrew a folded paper from the pocket of his coat. He'd been carrying this particular paper for several weeks. Preparation was critical to victory in any battle, especially the battle to maintain his reputation for savoir faire.

"What's this?" Babette said, eyeing the paper.

"It's not a bank draft," Stephen said. "If you need blunt, I am happy to pass some along, and if you should find yourself in an interesting condition, you will most assuredly apply to me before you pursue any rash measures, Babette. Promise me that."

She smoothed a crease on his sleeve. "I'm not in an interesting condition. I take precautions, because the sheaths aren't reliable."

"I meant if you *ever* found yourself in an interesting condition. My solicitors know how to reach me, and you know how to reach them. Your word on this, please."

She nodded. "Did I do something wrong? Is that why you're tossing me over?" Such vulnerability lay behind the ire in her gaze.

"Yes," Stephen said, leaning against the door and mustering a scowl. "Yes, you have done something I cannot countenance. If you must know, I am growing too attached to you, and that will not serve. I have no time for maudlin sentiment or fawning displays, but you threaten my resolve in this regard. I hope you're pleased with yourself, because German princesses and the most celebrated of the *grand horizontales* in Paris haven't accomplished the mischief you've caused."

Babette looked a bit less crestfallen. "You're becoming *too attached* to me?"

"A man needs his dignity, Babette." That qualified as an eternal verity. "With your sheer friendliness, your affection, your laughter...you put me at risk for foolishness. Better to leave before you set your hook and while we are still friends, wouldn't you say?"

She finally took the paper. "What is this?"

Stephen put a gloved hand on the door latch. "You can read it for yourself."

She opened the paper before he could make his escape. "This is the deed to a tea shop, my lord. *You bought me a tea shop?*"

The shop, the inventory, and the articles of the clerk who'd been working there for the past two years. The enterprise was operating at a healthy profit too, and Stephen had topped up its cash reserves and inventory as well.

"Bracelets as parting gifts show an execrable lack of imagination, and the pawnbrokers take ruthless advantage of anybody trying to hock such baubles. A tea shop will generate income and give you an option if you're ever injured in the course of your profession. There's a price, though, Babette."

She tucked the deed out of sight. "What price?"

"You keep the terms of our parting to yourself. Say you inherited a competence from an auntie or that a friend of the family willed you the means to buy the shop. Keep my name out of it. Put it about that I'm off to the grouse moors when I quit Town. Grumble at my pinchpenny ways and tell everybody I'm a bad kisser."

She peered around at her rooms, which were far more comfortably appointed than they had been several months ago. The carpet was Savonnerie, the drapes Italian brocade. The tea service was Spode—not antique, but certainly pretty.

"You are a splendid kisser, my lord."

"If you insist on lavishing such compliments on me, I really must be going."

Babette put her hand over his on the door latch. "You will drop in to buy tea from me from time to time?"

He'd more likely send a spy, at least until she was walking out with some worthy fellow. "You intend to keep the shop yourself?"

"I'll give notice at rehearsal tomorrow and speak to Clare about coming to work for me. She can dance for only a few more weeks."

An inordinate sense of relief followed that announcement. "Perhaps I'll look you up when I return to Town, but don't think we can resume where we left off, Babette."

"My name's Betty. Betty Smithers, purveyor of fine teas and sundries."

"Betty," he said, brushing a kiss to her cheek. "Be well and say grumpy things about me."

She grinned. "You're an awful man who has no sense of humor and no eye for jewelry."

"Just so," he said, lifting the latch. "And I make you late for rehearsal with my endless selfish demands on your person. You are well rid of me."

Stephen left her smiling by the door. By the time he'd retrieved his horse from a sleepy groom in the mews, his relief at a friendly parting was fading. He liked Babette, of course, and was fond of her, but then, he liked most women, and was fond of all of his lovers.

Years ago, he might have been capable of risking his heart for the right woman, but life had taken him in other directions, and romantic entanglements didn't number among his aggravations, thank the heavenly powers.

Miss Abigail Abbott didn't number among his aggravations either. She was more in the nature of a challenge, and Stephen prided himself on never backing down from challenge.

Chapter Three

"You did ask us to wake you at seven, miss," the maid said. "Shall I come again in an hour?" She was clean, tidy, and cheerful, like every female domestic Abigail had met in Lord Stephen's abode. The men were also clean, tidy, and cheerful, and the lot of them moved about with more energy than was decent.

Morning sun slanted through Abigail's window, and elsewhere in the house what sounded like three different clocks were all chiming the seventh hour—in unison. The result was a major triad—*do-mi-sol*—and the effect unusual, to say the least.

"I'm awake," Abigail said, sitting up and flipping back the softest quilts ever to grace the bed of mortal woman. "Barely. Oh, you've brought tea. Bless you." No toast, no croissants, though. No hope of escaping breakfast with his lordship. But then, Abigail had come here precisely to secure his lordship's assistance, hadn't she?

"Shall I help you dress, miss?"

"I can manage, thank you."

"I'll come back to make up the bed and see to the hearth. Your frock is hanging in the wardrobe, and Lord Stephen awaits you in the breakfast parlor."

Well, drat the luck. Abigail had been hoping to enjoy at least a plate of eggs before she negotiated with his lordship. She ought to have known he'd not simply accede to her plan.

"I'll be down directly." Good food and rest had fortified her, and finding that the hem of her dress had been sponged clean and the skirts ironed added to her sense of well-being. She downed two cups of tea as she dressed and tended to her hair.

By the time she joined Lord Stephen in the breakfast parlor, she had resolved to tell him the version of the truth she'd concocted during her journey south.

"Miss Abbott." He rose. "The sun rises to illuminate your beauty. I trust you slept well."

He could not know how his levity wounded. "I slept soundly, my lord. And you?"

"I am rested. Help yourself to the offerings on the sideboard. I'd serve you, except handling two canes and a plate is beyond me."

Walking into the breakfast parlor was like walking into heaven's antechamber. The windows admitted bright morning light, the scents of toast and butter graced the air, and the room was warm at a time of year when most households were parsimonious with coal. His lordship sat not at the head of the table, but along the side closer to the hearth. Though the day was sunny, autumn had arrived, and a fire crackled on the andirons.

"I am entirely capable of serving myself," Abigail said. "Have you been out riding already?" Lord Stephen wore riding attire, and he wore it well.

"I enjoy a hack on dry mornings. You are welcome to join me tomorrow if you like to ride."

Time on horseback was a rare pleasure. Abigail's cart horse was biddable enough under saddle, but his gaits were miserable, and his sidesaddle manners nonexistent.

"I haven't a habit with me." *And I won't be here this time tomorrow.*

"A pity. Would you care for tea or chocolate?"

His lordship was a gracious host. Abigail took the place to his left—sitting herself at the head of the table—and settled in to enjoy a fluffy omelet, crisp bacon, buttered toast, stewed apples, and her very own pot of chocolate.

"Your breakfast buffet is impressive," she said when her plate was empty but for one triangle of toast. "Is this the prisoner's last meal before you put her on the rack?"

"I am profoundly relieved to know you are feeling more the thing. To see you in less than fighting form daunts a man's faith. Do you prefer to acquaint me with the facts of your situation in here, or shall you take your cup of chocolate with you to my study?"

Abigail wanted to see his study. From the outside, Lord Stephen's home was just another staid Mayfair façade, but inside, no expense had been spared to create a sense of order, beauty, and repose. The art on the walls—northern landscapes full of billowing clouds and brilliant blue skies—was first rate. The spotless carpets were decorated with fleur-de-lis and crown motifs that suggested an antique French provenance.

And yet, the house was also stamped with his lordship's personality. A mobile of lifelike finches and wrens hung over the main entrance, and the slightest breeze made the birds flit about. The transom window was a stained-glass rendering of roses and butterflies that left dots of ruby, emerald, and blue on the white marble floor.

Stylized gilt gryphons had been wrought into candelabra, and a carved owl—the symbol of Athena's wisdom—served as the newel post at the foot of the main staircase.

Lord Stephen led the way down the carpeted corridor, his progress brisk for all he relied on two canes. Abigail trailed after him, sipping chocolate and frankly gawking.

So many winged creatures for a man who had trouble with earthbound locomotion.

"You pretend to admire my landscapes while you concoct a taradiddle," Lord Stephen said when Abigail had closed the door to his study. "Your tale will include enough elements of truth to be convincing and enough fabrication to obscure your secrets. It won't wash, Miss Abbott. I can hardly help you defeat Lord Stapleton if you keep me in the dark."

The study had a vaulted ceiling across which a fantastic winged dragon trailed smoke and fire. The image was startling for its novelty and also for the peacock brilliance of the dragon. How many solicitors and business associates had sat all unsuspecting beneath the dragon's fire and fangs?

"A beautiful rendering, isn't it?" Lord Stephen said, gesturing Abigail to a wing chair. "At night, when firelight illuminates the ceiling in dancing shadows, that dragon seems more real than my hand in front of my face."

"What's his name?" Abigail asked, taking the indicated seat.

"Why do you assume the dragon is male?" Lord Stephen remained standing as he posed the question, the picture of tall, muscular English virility and a testament to Bond Street's highest art.

An illusion, or the real man? And that smile...his smile was sweet, playful, and warmhearted, the opposite of how his mind worked.

The conundrum of his mental processes, charm juxtaposed with calculation, fascinated Abigail. She was counting on his calculating mind to keep her physically safe, while the charm imperiled her heart.

"I assume the dragon is male," she said, "because most violent destruction is rendered by male hands, is it not?"

His lordship sat and propped his canes against the arm of the chair. He carried a matched set, softly gleaming mahogany, elegantly carved with leaves and blossoms. Either cane could knock a man dead with a single blow if wielded with sufficient force.

"Violent destruction or effective protection?" his lordship mused. "You have come to me for the latter, apparently, while I'd prefer to indulge in the former. Out with it, Miss Abbott, and not the embroidered version that flatters your dignity. How do you know Stapleton is after you, and what motivates him?"

Abigail finished her cup of chocolate—she would not be hurried even by Lord Stephen Wentworth and his pet dragon.

"The first incident escaped my notice until the second occurred. My companion keeps a dog. A smallish terrier sort of fellow with a mighty bark. She says we are safer thanks to Malcolm's vigilance, while I maintain we simply get less sleep. In any case, Cook was preparing a roast for our Sunday dinner and because cheaper meat tends to be tough, she typically marinates any large cuts for some time before they go into the oven."

That much was truth and Lord Stephen looked as if he accepted it as such.

"I received a fancy bottle of burgundy as a gift," Abigail went on. "The note accompanying the bottle suggested a former client was making a gesture of appreciation, but the signature was a single letter—*R*. I have several clients from whom the bottle could have come, so I thought nothing of it."

Lord Stephen propped his chin on his fist. "One of those would be my brother-in-law, His Grace of Rothhaven?"

"Precisely, and His Grace is a generous and thoughtful man. A fine bottle of wine sent on the spur of the moment would be like him or like your sister."

"Do go on."

"After the prescribed time, the roast went onto the turnspit, and Cook set aside a bowl of burgundy marinade thinking to use it to baste the meat. When her back was turned, Malcolm got to the bowl and began to slurp up the contents. The dog regularly consumes ale. A few swallows of wine ought not to have laid him low, but he was asleep within minutes."

"Asleep?"

"Cook used a feather to bring up the contents of his stomach. He survived."

Lord Stephen traced the claw-foot carved into the head of one of his canes. "Are you fond of dogs?"

"What has that to do with anything?" Abigail was very fond of dogs and cats and of her stalwart cart horse, Hector. Had Malcolm suffered permanent harm... "Malcolm is a dear little fellow, for all he's terribly spoiled."

"We dear fellows enjoy being spoiled, Miss Abbott."

"Malcolm nearly died because his bad manners go unchecked."

"Did he? I ask if you care for the dog because I'm trying to discern motive. Was somebody trying to poison you, your companion, and your staff—because a roast would feed the whole household—or merely trying to frighten you? Did the perpetrator know you allow your dog kitchen privileges, and was poison involved, or had the burgundy gone off somehow and the whole business is merely an unfortunate culinary accident?"

"I dismissed it as such. My dimensions are much greater than a terrier's, and poisoning a marinade is an unreliable way to administer an effective dose of many drugs. My companion, however, is a more diminutive specimen, though how could anybody know we'd use the burgundy for a marinade? If we'd consumed the wine directly, as a good burgundy deserves, the results might have been different."

"Does your companion have enemies?"

"Not that I know of, but allow me to continue." This part of the tale, the attempted harm, was more of the simple, truthful part, and the part Lord Stephen must be made to focus on. "I did not connect the poison and Lord Stapleton until his second call upon me. He believes I am in possession of some letters and asked me for the return of them. I declined to accommodate him for reasons having to do with client privacy."

"Commendable," Lord Stephen murmured, though Abigail had the sense he was mocking her. The letters terribly compromised the privacy of two parties, so her description was somewhat true.

Not entirely false, anyway.

"His lordship showed up on my doorstep on Monday well before sunrise, and he had two very large footmen with him. The hour was so early that the household should still have been abed."

Lord Stephen's caresses to his walking stick ceased. "As the lot of you might have been if you'd been drugged?"

"Precisely. Everybody partakes of a Sunday roast in most households that can afford a roast. A dose of somnifera or whatever the offending substance was, and we'd simply be slower to rise the following morning. Sunday is also the day when two maiden ladies are most likely to allow themselves a glass of good wine as a digestive following the weekly feast."

The fire had been lit in this room as well, suggesting that cold aggravated Lord Stephen's injured leg. Abigail found the warmth delicious, particularly after spending days and nights on a crowded, stinking coach.

Lord Stephen tipped his head to the side, considering Abigail with an owlish look. "Tell me about the letters."

He would ask that. "They are predictably personal, between people who ought not to have been corresponding."

Abigail was not blushing. She was too angry to blush. She picked up her empty cup, then set it down.

"Miss Abbott, have you been indiscreet?" His lordship's tone was merely curious. If he'd made a jest of the situation, Abigail would have coshed him with his expensive cane.

"I did not write those letters, your lordship. Stop speculating. The marquess wants them, he's not entitled to them, and he's apparently willing to go to extreme measures to retrieve them."

A little silence bloomed, while Abigail could nearly hear the gears whirring in his lordship's busy mind.

"Tell me more about those extreme measures. You said Stapleton has made two attempts to do you mischief. A case can be made for poison, though it's a weak case and shades more toward drugging you ladies to enable a thorough search. Something more serious inspired you to seek out my assistance."

Abigail rose, not to escape Lord Stephen's scrutiny, of course, but to better organize her thoughts. "I travel about for my clients. It's part of the job. For one client, I began taking the coach from York to Allerton every Tuesday. Round-trip, that's often six or eight hours, longer if the roads are bad."

"Why subject yourself to such misery?"

"The case paid well. I attended a weekly meeting of a knitting group, gathering intelligence for an inheritance situation."

"I do envy you the variety of challenges your profession entails."

Lord Stephen seemed to mean that, though nobody should envy a woman hours and hours on English public conveyances.

"Coach travel is cheaper for those on top of the coach," Abigail said, "but outside passengers are rarely female. I dress as a man for the coach rides. I can get the cheaper fare, and I'm less likely to be identified as Miss Abigail Abbott of Cockcrow Lane, York."

Lord Stephen's brows rose. "You wear trousers, waistcoat, boots, the whole bit?"

"Complete with pocket watch and hat. I put my hair in an old-fashioned queue and wear it under my coat. Because of my size, I pass for a man easily." A boon, that. Truly, having the dimensions of a plow horse had been a benefit in any number of situations.

"So there you were," his lordship murmured, "bouncing along topside, probably sharing a flask with your fellow passengers and discussing the latest racing form, and then what happened?"

They'd been discussing some pugilist or other. "Highwaymen stopped the coach, your lordship. No less than six armed and masked men on very fine horseflesh, towing a spare mount. They had exquisite firearms—Mantons, if I'm not mistaken—and dressed rather better than highwaymen ought to."

"Noticed that, did you?"

"They also took nothing and spoke like exponents of public school. They simply demanded to see the lady travelers. The passengers were all made to get off the coach while the brigands inspected the parcels on the boot and beneath the seats. Then they let us go on our way. The two female passengers were wearing wedding rings worth a bit of blunt, and one of the inside dandies had a pocket watch well worth stealing."

"But the brigands wanted only you."

"I believe your blue spectacles saved my life." The first time Abigail had seen Lord Stephen in disguise, he'd been wearing blue spectacles and impersonating a down-on-his-luck tinker.

"You recalled my blue spectacles. Miss Abbott, I am touched and impressed, and you, my dear, are being less than forthcoming. Tell me the rest of it."

Abigail was not his *dear* and she had no intention of telling him the *whole* rest of it, so she served up the morsel she'd saved back for purposes of gratifying his lordship's vanity.

"They had a likeness of me," she said. "About the size of a miniature, maybe a little larger. They compared the two lady travelers to the likeness, and thank heavens neither woman resembled me. They were both also too petite to be me."

Abigail sank back into her seat, that last admission not exactly comfortable.

"Do you know what I think when I consider your fair form, Miss Abbott?"

"The question of your opinion of my physique has never crossed my mind." Though it had kept her up for a moment or two last night, and possibly on a few other nights.

Abigail sorted men into two categories: tall enough, and *the rest*. The rest were disappointingly numerous, and she took many precautions not to unduly offend them.

Lord Stephen, for all his numerous faults and annoying tendencies, was *tall enough*.

"When I behold you," he replied, "I think, ye gods, if only I had the ability to waltz with such a magnificent creature. We would turn every head in the room, and should I stumble, which I am wont to do regularly, she could easily catch me up in her arms and put me right. You could do it too, without a thought. How I adore that about you."

Now, when it mattered not at all, Abigail felt heat creep up her neck, suffuse her ears, and fill her cheeks. She hadn't blushed in years, but less than a day under Lord Stephen's roof, and she was as pink as a blooming carnation.

"Quakers eschew dancing, my lord."

"I am not a Quaker, Miss Abbott." No sooner had Stephen spoken than he grasped the significance of her comment. "*You* are a member of the Society of Friends?" This was bad news. Quakers were an appallingly virtuous lot, much given to probity, reform, and philanthropy.

"I am not, but my parents were born into the Quaker faith, and my father raised me according to its precepts."

"And what would the Friends think of you strutting about the countryside in breeches and top hat?" The image would not leave Stephen's mind. That lusciously curved backside in trousers, that abundant bosom trussed up in a waistcoat…

He shifted in his seat, crossing an ankle over a knee.

Such pre-occupations always befell him after he'd parted with a *chère amie*. He became both sentimental and randy, a dangerous combination.

"My appearance when I am on a case is nobody's business but my own," Miss Abbott replied. "When I visit my Quaker relations, I observe the courtesies any lady ought to show her aunts, uncles, grandparents, and cousins."

"You thee-thou them and call everybody by their first names?" *Would you call me Stephen if I asked you to?*

"They are family, all the family I have, so of course I use informal address and plain speech. Might we return to the problem at hand, my lord?"

His own words came back to him from their previous conversation: *Sir, might you put your hand on my...*

"You were the one dissembling, Miss Abbott. Tell me more about these letters that have Lord Stapleton attempting to kidnap you."

She sat up very straight. "As letters go, they aren't very remarkable. There are about two dozen."

"Somebody fancied himself in love."

She glowered at him. "And why do you assume the author was male, my lord? Women fall in love every bit as foolishly as men do."

The asperity in her tone so soon after breakfast could not be explained by fatigue or hunger.

"No, Miss Abbott, women do not typically make asses of themselves on anywhere near the grand scale men achieve in matters of the heart. Ladies are generally sensible creatures compared to the louts who father their children. Women have a care for the next generation, whereas men usually have a care for nothing more pressing than their next pint of ale, though I'll grant you, exceptions abound. My brother is sensible to a fault, and he's also a man very much in love."

"You see that as a paradox?"

Stephen shook a finger at her. "None of that. We will not plumb the abyss of philosophy. The letters, if you please. Who wrote them to whom, and why would Stapleton want them?" *Why would Stapleton believe they'd been left in your care?*

Stephen had a theory, though he was reluctant to share it with Miss Abbott. She was an inquiry agent, and thus no innocent where human foibles were concerned, but she was a *Quaker-raised, lady* inquiry agent.

"The letters, as you can imagine, my lord, shade in the direction of *billets-doux*. They are not recent, and they were not written by Stapleton himself or by anybody with whom Stapleton or his late marchioness might have been entangled, from what I can gather."

Whenever Miss Abigail Abbott folded her hands in her lap and pretended demure fascination with the carpet, she was hiding information. The carpet was currently on the receiving end of a thorough inspection.

"You are doubtless protecting a client as you prevaricate," Stephen said, "but let me share what I know of the situation, and you might feel free to be more forthcoming. Stapleton's late son was a charming bounder, but let it not be said that the Earl of Champlain was a difficult husband. He and the fair Harmonia had a thoroughly civilized marriage."

Miss Abbott turned her inspection on Stephen. "What does that mean?"

"To put it in the parlance of my youth, they comported themselves like a pair of minks. Lord Champlain indulged his amorous impulses wherever he pleased, and her ladyship had a number of gallants. I'm sure Champlain and his countess also gave the matter of securing the succession due attention from time to time—I believe he left a son behind, after all. Champlain and his wife were certainly cordial when they encountered one another socially."

Stephen had reason to know the friendliness between the earl and countess had been genuine. They hadn't been a love match, but they'd reconciled themselves to their parents' machinations with good grace, good humor, and the occasional shared good time.

All very civilized.

Miss Abbott looked like she needed to pace again, and how Stephen envied her that habit.

"How do people live like that?" she asked. "How do they cavort from bed to bed, behaving—as you say—like beasts in rut? I have seen too much evidence of this nonsense to doubt your recitation, and such goings-on are not limited to the high and mighty. Nonetheless, I am unable to reconcile myself to the notion that something so precious and intimate can be undertaken as casually as sharing a glass of punch."

Beneath the predictable distaste of a gently reared lady lay a hint of true bewilderment at marital infidelity. Perhaps that was the Quaker upbringing peeking through the inquiry agent's pragmatism?

"Miss Abbott, the earl and his lady were very likely betrothed while still in leading strings. Champlain was heir to an ancient title and a vast fortune. He was not in the habit of denying himself."

"You knew him?"

Stephen set his cane aside, though still within reach. "We were acquainted. He was no worse than many of his ilk, and that he and the countess were not possessive of each other was hardly unusual among the peerage. Lord and Lady Champlain considered themselves forward-thinking."

Miss Abbott rose and struck off across the carpet, and as much as Stephen liked watching her move, he wasn't as comfortable with her poking about his private domain.

"This is not a variety of forward-thinking of which I can approve." She leaned over his worktable. "What are these?"

"Plans for a firing mechanism that will be less susceptible to heat and humidity."

She picked up a diagram and held it about a foot from her nose. "You design *guns*?"

Did she but know it, she'd brought up an abyss into which Stephen could fall for days on end. "I design them, manufacture them, distribute them, and sell them. Britain cannot seem to enlarge its empire without doing so at gunpoint."

"Hence the impropriety of that enlargement." She put down the schematic and stalked around the table, bootheels rapping even through the thickness of the carpet. "I disapprove of the munitions trade."

Stephen pushed to his feet, though his knee screamed in

protest. "I disapprove of people who raise perfectly healthy children and forbid them to dance. We can debate that topic later, when we've figured out why Stapleton would need those letters so desperately, though I'm fairly certain I know."

Finely arched brows drew down. "You do?"

"One of Lady Champlain's lovers was apparently of a literary bent. Some fool mentioned her ladyship's indiscretion to Stapleton, and now, having no wife to talk sense to him, the marquess is darting about like a March hare. He is determined to retrieve the evidence of his daughter-in-law's peccadillo, even to the point of kidnapping you. We will need a list of the gentlemen who have employed you since Lady Champlain spoke her vows."

An hour of sleep at Babette's, then another hour upon returning home was plenty enough to refresh Stephen's mind, but he'd been going short of sleep too much lately. His knee protested loudly, and yet he stood, hands braced on a single cane, while Miss Abbott peered at the signature on the landscape behind his desk.

"Who is Endymion de Beauharnais? Is he related to the late empress?"

The change of subject was much too welcome. "He's the same fellow who painted my dragon. Very English." Also breathtakingly handsome and an absolute dunderhead in matters of the heart. "He's quite talented, unlike you, who are sadly lacking in the thespian's ability to dissemble. You know who wrote those letters. You know why Stapleton thinks you have them."

Stephen made a careful circumnavigation of the wing

chair, and collected his second cane. The rooms in this house were large, which made for safer perambulations when a cane had to be used even indoors. The furniture was bunched in well-spaced groups, and the carpets were tacked down along every edge.

"I might know," Miss Abbott said. "I can certainly make the list you describe, but none of this is effecting my demise, which is the reason I sought you out, my lord. If Stapleton thinks I'm dead, he'll stop trying to drug me and kidnap me."

"I refuse to kill a woman who is being unfairly menaced," Stephen said, "not because I am averse to violence—violence has many uses and justifications—but because a staged death will not solve your problem."

Miss Abbott's chin came up, and Stephen realized he'd blundered across her Quaker upbringing again. Quakers had no patience with violence generally, hence their distaste for the munitions industry. The lot of them hunted game, though, and many a Quaker fortune included arms money from generations past.

"Don't give me that look," Stephen said. "You carry a sword cane." A man's sword cane, which she could manage because of her height and the confidence with which she sailed through life.

"For defensive purposes only."

"That cane will not defend you against Stapleton's next attempt on your person." Stephen was seized with a sudden curiosity about the fragrance Miss Abbott preferred. She struck him as a lemon verbena sort, all tart and bracing, not that he had any business even wondering about such a thing.

"Nothing will keep me safe if his lordship is determined to find me, hence the necessity for me to die."

"I'll not have your death on my conscience, or I won't if I ever locate my conscience. For God's sake, why are you wearing that execrable rosemary scent? A hedgehog would not be flattered by such an olfactory—"

Fate, the nemesis of all who aspired to effective insults, intervened as she so often did in Stephen's life. Her meddling took the form of a wrinkle in the carpet, a cane tip slipping ever so slightly, and Stephen losing his balance.

Fate, though, had for once shown herself to be a benevolent intercessor, for Stephen went toppling straight into Miss Abbott, and Miss Abbott caught him in a snug and sturdy hold.

Abigail was surprised to find her arms full of Lord Stephen Wentworth. He was no wraith, and she needed a moment to get a firm hold of him.

"Steady there, my lord."

His face was mashed to the crook of her neck and shoulder, and his cane had gone toppling. In the few moments necessary for him to find his balance, Abigail perceived all manner of curious details.

He wore a divinely complicated fragrance. Floral and spice aromas intertwined to delight the nose and beguile the curiosity. The scent was doubtless blended exclusively for him, and he'd very likely designed it himself.

The lace of his cravat was a soft, silky brush against Abigail's décolletage, an intimate and disturbing sensation. What sort of sybarite used blond lace on a cravat that wasn't intended to be worn against the skin?

More disturbing than either of those perceptions was Abigail's sense that for the merest instant before he began sorting himself out, Lord Stephen had rested against her, lingering on purpose where he should be mortified to be.

Could he possibly have engineered this mishap, and, if so, why?

"My apologies," he said, bracing a hand on the table and standing straight. "And my thanks for your timely support. If you'd please hand me my cane?"

He was all genial good humor, as if thirteen stone of handsome lord went flying into the arms of unsuspecting ladies every twenty minutes or so. Abigail scooped up his cane, passed it to him, and retrieved the second cane as well.

"These are not sword canes," she said, peering more closely at the one she held. "And yet they would make effective weapons."

"Sword canes are more useful out-of-doors, where I have room to swing and thrust. For indoors, a cudgel is the better option, or two cudgels."

She passed over the second cane, which was sturdy indeed. "Why must you go about armed even in your own home?"

He used both canes to maneuver to a couch arranged along the inside wall. "You don't ask about my unsteady balance. Thank you for that. If you wouldn't mind sliding that hassock—"

Abigail gave the hassock a shove with her boot. The thing would have been hard to move for a man using two canes.

"How often do you fall?" An impolite question, but then, Lord Stephen was not a polite man, and he'd already reported falling "regularly." He was mannerly when it suited him, and Abigail suspected he was kind to those he cared for. He would never tolerate a slight, and never leave a debt unpaid.

That he occasionally went sprawling offended her on his behalf. He wasn't *nice*, but in his way, he was honorable, a far more worthy virtue in Abigail's opinion.

"In my youth, I toppled over constantly. Boys do not carry canes, and I hated that I was different. I'd forget where I put my canes, leave my room without them. For my Bath chair, I spewed maledictions too vile to blight a lady's ears. I was not reconciled to my fate, and thus everybody around me had to suffer as well."

He rubbed his knee as he spoke, which required that he bend forward rather than rest against the cushions.

"Shall I remove your boots?" Abigail asked.

"You'd play footman for me?"

"I will remove your boots so you don't get dirt on the hassock."

He left off rubbing his knee. "Do your worst. My boots aren't as snug as some. They can't be or I'd never endure their removal."

His boot in fact slipped off easily. It wasn't much larger than one of Abigail's men's boots, though the calf was longer. The second boot was a trifle more closely fitted. She set them both within his reach and took the place beside him.

"Does massage help?"

"Yes, but Miss Abbott, I must forbid—damn it, Abigail. That's not fair."

She'd wrapped both hands around his knee and made the same smooth, slow circles he'd used. "That you have a bad knee isn't fair, and if the knee has become unreliable, the ankle and hip are likely in pain as well. Am I pressing firmly enough?"

He flopped back against the cushions, gaze on the ceiling. "My dragon's name is Abigail. I've been waiting for inspiration to name her, and lo, the appellation fits."

"You are trying to make me blush. Flattery is pointless, my lord. The joint isn't quite as it should be, is it?" Not that she was well acquainted with the particulars of a man's knee bones.

"You have a gift for understatement, Miss Abbott. Allow me to offer a reciprocally understated observation: Ladies do not apply their hands to the persons of ailing gentlemen. Desist, if you please."

He was protesting for form's sake, bless him. "You are not ailing. You were injured, long ago. How did it happen?"

He gave her a peevish look. "My father decided in a drunken rage that a boy with a bad leg would be a more effective beggar than one who could scramble out of range of Papa's fists. He later intimated that stomping the hell out of me was an accident. I was the accident, and his violence toward me was quite intentional."

Abigail kept her hands moving in slow, steady strokes, though Lord Stephen's recitation upset her. "I try not to take cases involving children. Such matters can provoke me to an unseemly temper."

"Abigail, please stop. You need not exercise your temper on my behalf. I had my revenge."

She ceased massaging his knee but remained on the sofa beside him. "Good. A man such as your father deserves a thorough serving of retribution. That he spent coin on gin instead of providing for his children was his shame, not yours, and that he'd do violence against his own small son…"

Would that she was merely blushing. Instead Abigail felt tears welling. They were not for Lord Stephen, or not exclusively for him. They were for fatigue, and homesickness, old lost love, and all of the children who could not be protected from horrid fates.

"I miss Malcolm." The stupidest words ever to escape from a woman's mouth.

"Miss Abbott…Abigail, please don't cry." A linen handkerchief so fine as to be translucent dangled before Abigail's eyes. "You must not cry. I had my revenge. I killed the old devil, so nobody need ever cry for me again."

She took the handkerchief, which was redolent of his exquisite scent. "You don't fool me, my lord. Your father needed killing—my Quaker family would disown me for that sentiment—but I killed my mother, and I know taking the life of a parent is a difficult wound for a child to heal regardless of how it happens."

Chapter Four

As a youth, Stephen had occupied himself with deciding which day had been the worst of his life. The day he'd killed his father had not made the list. The day his father had smashed his knee hadn't either. At the time, a very young Stephen had shrugged it off as just another beating from old Jack Wentworth. Slower to heal and more painful than others, but all in a day's suffering.

The day he'd fallen face-first into the grass of Berkeley Square while trying to manage two canes and deliver an ice to a viscount's blushing daughter was on that list. So was the day Quinn had been marched to the scaffold for a murder he hadn't committed. What had been Abigail Abbott's worst day, and why did she weep for the company of an ill-mannered terrier she didn't even own?

"Did you slip some rat poison into your mother's gin?"

Stephen asked, surely the least genteel question a gentleman had ever asked a lady.

She looked up from his handkerchief. “You laid your father low with rat poison? Very enterprising of you, my lord.”

Nobody had ever referred to Stephen as enterprising in quite those admiring tones. “I was lame, eight years old, and my sisters’ sole protection. Jack was making arrangements to…making arrangements for them I could not countenance. Quinn had gone off somewhere to earn coin, and I had to make do. Quinn was old enough to fend for us, but he lacked the legal authority to take us away from Jack. I remedied the situation as best I could.”

Nobody else outside the family knew this story. Duncan, Stephen’s cousin, had the basic facts, but Stephen didn’t discuss what he’d done with even his siblings. Better that his sisters not know how close they’d come to dwelling in hell itself, better that Quinn never learn of it.

“You saved your sisters’ lives,” Miss Abbott said. “And that is understating the matter.”

To hear the words spoken with such conviction, by a female as decent and estimable as Abigail Abbott, was unsettling.

“Tell me about your mother.” Stephen kept the query general rather than ask specifically how the lady had died.

“I killed her simply by being born. She survived a month past my arrival, but she never stopped losing blood.” Miss Abbott sniffed at Stephen’s handkerchief and bowed her head. “I was too big.”

Those four words held a world of sorrow and despair.

Also a world of injustice. "You were not too big. Babies are whatever size the Almighty decides they should be, and I have it on the authority of no less person than Jane, Duchess of Walden, that her smallest baby gave her the worst trouble in childbed. The larger brats seemed to have some sense of how to go about the business, but the littlest one was contrary. She still is, in fact."

Miss Abbott's profile belonged on some martyr of ancient renown. "But the midwife said..."

Clearly, nobody had ever walked the formidable Miss Abbott through some basic reproductive facts.

"Is this why you haven't married?" Stephen asked. "You punish yourself for biology you had no power to change? Do you know who ought to be examining his conscience? The rutting fool who got your mother with child. Women do not conceive absent the involvement of some fellow or other, unless you'd have me believe divine intervention occasioned your existence? You do know where little dragons come from, don't you?"

She swung her gaze on him like the port authority swiveling harbor cannon on an enemy fleet.

"Why haven't *you* married, my lord? You are in line for a dukedom, you are *a gun nabob*, and not hard to look upon. Surely if one of us is behindhand matrimonially, you are."

Stephen rejoiced to see the glitter of battle returning to Miss Abbott's eyes, rejoiced to earn her upbraiding. That she'd light upon the sad reality of his situation was entirely convenient to his plan.

"You and Her Grace will get on famously, Miss Abbott. She likes you. My entire family will second your opinion that I am *behindhand matrimonially*, and in a variety of other regards. This is precisely why you must give up on your plan to die for Lord Stapleton's convenience."

Miss Abbott folded his handkerchief and rose, stuffing it into a pocket. "Stapleton will not stop, my lord. Nothing less than a permanent end to me will suffice to ensure my safety."

Why was she so confident of that conclusion, and what exactly had been in those letters?

"Stapleton bides here in London at present, and yet he had the ability to set six ne'er-do-wells on your tail in godforsaken Yorkshire. He nearly managed to have your household drugged, if we accept your version of events, and that took both careful attention to your circumstances and a ruthless exercise of power. Do you suppose he won't have your corpse dug up, Miss Abbott?"

Grave robbers were a sad fact of life. Miss Abbott's expression said she hadn't calculated on Stapleton retaining their services.

"And what if," Stephen went on, "you *die* and his search for those letters goes on? Does your companion suffer his wrath? Is Malcolm's well-being imperiled again? You, being ostensibly dead, could not intervene to protect them. I surmise that if you had the letters, you would have surrendered them, but for two things: A client asked you to keep them safe, or client privacy means you cannot surrender them. That also means you aren't at liberty to destroy the letters. Destroying yourself won't destroy the letters."

Miss Abbott took the seat behind Stephen's desk. "You really can be quite detestable, my lord."

"Nonsense. You have been anxious, exhausted, concerned

for your household, and had nobody with whom to think the situation through. A half-daft, wealthy marquess makes a formidable foe. What you detest is being out-gunned and out-maneuvered by him."

She tapped a fingernail against his blotter, like a cat switching its tail. "I hate that too, but I cannot carry on my business expecting every coach I climb onto will be stopped and searched, and every roast I serve will be poisoned. Dying will at least stop the attempts on my person."

She was magnificently stubborn, and that quality was probably why she had so many happy clients.

Stephen, however, had learned to be stubborn as a matter of survival, and now he would be stubborn for her sake as well.

"The attacks will stop," he said, "only until Stapleton figures out that you are not, in fact, deceased. What of your family, Miss Abbott? Will you leave them to grieve your passing with no explanation? They will inherit your personal goods, I'm guessing, and Stapleton might well turn his attention in that direction. A passel of peace-loving Quakers up against a man who resorts to armed criminals and poison. How well do you think your thee-thou aunties and grannies would fare against such odds?"

"You would like them," she said, balancing the point of his favorite silver letter opener on the tip of her finger. "Their unwillingness to use force of arms means they are ingenious about other means of persuasion."

"If you'd like to put your feet up on my desk, please feel free." Stephen could picture her like that, at ease, feet up, her grand decorum for once set aside.

She put down the letter opener, shoved out of his chair, and returned to his side on the sofa. "I would not risk my family for anything. You know that, which is why you are herding me into a corner of your choosing. I do not appreciate the manipulation, my lord, so let's just hear your brilliant plan for thwarting Stapleton's mischief."

"Kiss me."

Her scowl was thunderous. "That is not a plan, my lord. That doesn't even qualify as a jest."

"And eau de napping hedgehog is not an enticing fragrance, Miss Abbott. If my plan is to have a prayer of working, you must be able to suffer proximity to my person."

Wariness joined the disapproval in her eyes. "I am proximate to your person now."

"A salient fact." Stephen sat up enough to brush his lips over her cheek, then pulled back to survey her reaction. "That went rather well. If we're to be engaged, you must weather at least that much affection from me, and it appears you are up to the challenge."

Oh, damn. Now she was looking bewildered. "You are eccentric. I know that. I counted on that. A near genius, in the opinion of many, but a difficult man. I wanted exactly that sort of help when I came here, and now you are kissing me and spouting nonsense. I had best be going."

He caught her hand rather than let her fly into the boughs over a mere peck on the cheek.

"Miss Abbott, be reasonable. Stapleton is a marquess. He has breached the citadel of your home. He has sent his minions against you. He thinks you are a mere lady inquiry agent, a member of an obscure profession and one not much respected except by those needing your services. Your family, while doubtless dear to you, has no resources equal to Stapleton's, *but I do*."

He had her attention. God bless a woman with a rational mind.

"Go on."

"Stapleton will not expect you to recruit an ally whose standing exceeds his own, whose wealth exceeds his own, whose connections in Yorkshire and elsewhere exceed his own. Ally yourself with me, and you are safe."

She studied their joined hands. Her hands were nearly as large as Stephen's, but oh, they were so much more lovely. She cared for her hands. When dressed as a man, she doubtless had to wear gloves, or those pale fingers and tidy nails would give up the game.

"You spoke of an engagement, my lord. Why would a duke's heir choose a Yorkshire nobody for his duchess?"

Did she truly think of herself as a nobody? Stephen knew for a fact that at least one duke and duchess had relied upon her good offices to solve a very, very delicate matter.

"Let us consider the practicalities, Miss Abbott. I must marry, but I was born in the gutter."

She looked him up and down. "You have overcome your origins rather handily."

He kissed her knuckles for that. "In your opinion, which I value highly, but not in the opinion of the matchmakers who matter. I cannot dance, I cannot walk in the park, I cannot amble along the wooded paths of Richmond, and otherwise ingratiate myself with the darlings making their debuts each year."

"You can play cards, you can make witty conversation at formal dinners, you can—" Miss Abbott waved a hand.

"I can engage in the activities leading to procreation?"

Her expression became wonderfully severe. "One surmises you can—and do."

"One surmises correctly. I am not, however, considered a good catch. Impecunious viscounts can out-court me, and because I can never overcome the circumstances of my birth or the limitations of my disability, that will always be the case."

Miss Abbott disentangled her fingers from his. "So you'll bow meekly before your fate and marry an Amazon of humble origins?"

"The Amazons were warrior queens, to a maiden. Quakers are bankers, and His Grace of Walden, being a banker himself, has all manner of Quaker associates. You are from the north—from my home shire, as it were. My family thinks highly of you, which is no small accomplishment, and you will be an original in the Mayfair drawing rooms. You might even—I blush to suggest it—*enjoy* being my intended."

This speech was coming off all reasonable and businesslike, but Stephen waited for Miss Abbott's reply with inordinate anxiety. That Stapleton hadn't succeeded thus far was due to chance. Stephen had reason to know that the marquess was as stubborn as he was arrogant, and he was very arrogant.

Miss Abbott considered Stephen's boots, which she'd set neatly next to the sofa. "You do not suggest a real engagement."

"I would not presume on your future to that extent." The most honest, humble truth he'd ever offered a lady.

"Kiss me," she said, half turning to face him. "Kiss me as if you're stealing a moment with the woman you love. Make it convincing so I'll know what to expect should such a performance ever be needful."

In some dimly functioning rational part of his mind, Stephen concluded that Miss Abbott doubted her desirability. Either he inspired her to question that conclusion or he'd have to find some other scheme for keeping her safe.

If she found his advances distasteful, she could lay him out flat with a single unwelcoming shove. That thought brought him some comfort—she'd lay out flat *any* man whose advances she found distasteful.

Stephen did not want to come up with another scheme, and he did want to kiss her.

Very much. In his present state—randy and sentimental and all that—stage kisses were a stupid idea. But then, he had desired Abigail Abbott from the moment he'd set eyes on her, he esteemed her even more than he desired her, and she was an addled goose to think herself anything less than delectable.

"Very well, then," he said, taking her hand, "convincing, I shall be."

"A woman that size does not simply disappear." Honoré, Marquess of Stapleton, stated that observation calmly. He never raised his voice with subordinates, and Tertullian, Lord Fleming, was a subordinate in every regard.

Fleming was a mere earl's heir, his family's fortune

barely qualified as modest, and his intellect was similarly limited. He was loyal, and he longed to marry Stapleton's widowed daughter-in-law. Harmonia was, of course, free to remarry wherever she pleased, provided her son remained in the care of his doting grandpapa.

For the sake of the Stapleton succession, Stapleton would hound Miss Abbott to hell's front door, if necessary.

Fleming stood at attention, though he'd never bought his colors. "Miss Abbott has been known to wear disguises, my lord."

"I am aware of that. She's a professional snoop, but we must out-snoop her, mustn't we?" Two searches of her home had yielded nothing. Not so much as an overdue bill from a greengrocer.

"She might simply have gone to her covert, my lord. Just because she hasn't been seen doesn't mean she isn't at home, tatting lace or embroidering handkerchiefs."

Fleming disapproved of this whole venture. He had a softhearted view of women and probably kissed his dogs when nobody was looking. He would be putty in Harmonia's hands, and happy, devoted putty.

"Abigail Abbott wouldn't know what to do with an embroidery needle if you threaded it for her and..."

A tattoo of heels on the parquet foyer had Fleming's head coming up.

"Fleming, attend me. You may join Lady Champlain upon the conclusion of our interview and not before. Harmonia never goes out this early in the day."

Fleming assumed parade-rest posture—chin up, hands behind his back. "Perhaps Miss Abbott doesn't have the documents, my lord. Some time has passed, after all, and paper burns easily."

"Does it? Does it truly?" Stapleton sat forward, linking his hands on the desk blotter. "Paper burns easily. Well, I had no idea. Thank you for enlightening me, Fleming. You put my mind at ease. I will simply trust that some very sensitive information has been twisted into spills and sent up Miss Abbott's chimney. That makes perfect sense, paper also being expensive and her means being limited."

A flash of impatience showed in Fleming's eyes. He was the typical English lordling, flaxen-haired, tall, full of his own consequence, and none too bright. For Stapleton's purposes he was an adequate resource. Fleming had enough standing to be treated deferentially by lesser mortals—by hired footpads, for example—and enough native wit to execute most tasks without immediate supervision.

Most tasks, apparently not all. And the blighter was besotted with Harmonia, or with what he perceived her settlements to be.

"Your lordship must consider that we're on a goose chase," Fleming said. "Perhaps if you'd see fit to share with me the nature of the documents, I might have a better chance of retrieving them."

Stapleton had the odd thought that if Miss Abbott had been tasked with retrieving the letters, she would not make excuses or let inane flirtations distract her from the goal. She'd see the thing done and done right—drat the woman.

"Your job is not to find the documents." Fleming would doubtless read the letters, which Stapleton could not allow, hence the necessity of resorting to less literate subordinates for searching Miss Abbott's abode. "Your job is to find a woman who'd stand out in a company of dragoons. Perhaps you are in need of spectacles, Fleming. The dratted creature is impossible to miss."

Stapleton knew he was being petty, but he preferred proper ladies, all sweet and diminutive with just enough guile to be interesting. A Brobdingnagian such as Miss Abbott was contrary to the natural order, towering over men who substantially outranked her. Had she the docile nature of a beast of burden, her proportions would not rankle so, but she was half a foot taller than Stapleton. She would only affect docility in service of some stratagem such as she had used to entangle Stapleton's hapless son.

Champlain likely hadn't known what had hit him, poor lad.

Fleming strode for the door. "I will instruct the men to maintain vigilance over her residence in York and keep an eye on the usual posting inns. I thought we might also set a watch here in London, my lord, at Smithfield Market at least."

There you go, thinking again. "Why would Miss Abbott flee straight to the very place where I await her capture?"

Fleming paused, not quite turning, his posture conveying impatience. "Because she is canny as hell, and London is the last place you'd think to look for her?"

"Perhaps we should set a watch in Timbuktu and Calcutta, then. I hear the American wilderness can swallow up even giantesses. She would be daft to come to London."

"She could be here already, my lord, and you none the

wiser. Once she disappears into the stews, you'll never find her."

This show of spirit would have been gratifying were it not so nonsensical. "In the stews, where the average female is about four feet tall, Miss Abbott will stand out like a maypole. She's not in London, I tell you. Now, be off with you until you have something more encouraging to report. Harmonia is in the blue salon entertaining some portraitist. Try not to make too great a fool of yourself. Her ladyship genuinely grieved for Champlain, and as far as I know, she's not looking to find his successor yet."

Fleming bowed curtly and withdrew, leaving Stapleton to consider the prospect of Miss Abigail Abbott in London. The Romans had had a saying about even a blind dove finding the occasional pea. Perhaps a footman sent to loiter about Clerkenwell's coaching inns might not be a bad idea—though Stapleton would never admit as much to Fleming.

Abigail had never in her entire interesting life commanded a man to kiss her. Lord Stephen had spoken the truth, though: She was weary of flight, bewildered, and not herself. She'd noticed Stephen Wentworth the moment she'd set eyes on him, noticed his watchfulness and the way his family kept their distance rather than intrude on his privacy.

Then there was his height and general air of substance. Nobody trifled with this man, and for Abigail, that sense of self-possession was more attractive than all the artfully styled tailoring or graceful pirouettes in Mayfair.

He began his flirtation with her hands, which were as

outsized as the rest of her. In his grasp, her fingers felt fragile and if not exactly petite, at least feminine. He planted a kiss on her palm, holding her hand open, then laying it against his cheek.

He watched her eyes while he did this. If he was looking for signs of repugnance, he was doomed to wait forever.

"Do that again."

Being Stephen Wentworth, he did not obey her command. Instead he pressed his lips to Abigail's wrist.

"Was that *your tongue*?" she asked.

"Mmm."

He did it again, and Abigail's insides began leaping about like a flock of starlings at a fountain. Just when she would have told him to cease his teasing, he desisted and moved closer.

"Your hair," he said, tracing the line of her brow with his thumb, "doubtless falls to your hips. I want to see it down, want to see you wearing nothing but these glorious tresses."

"These naughty love words are not kissing, my lord." But oh, the images he brought to mind. The sensations, the longings...

"Haste is the enemy of pleasure, Abigail, and if I cannot pleasure you with my kisses, then I am a failure as a man."

He touched his mouth to the corner of her lips, which had the maddening effect of making Abigail go still, the better to aid his aim on the next attempt. But he, of course, knew exactly what he was doing and only teased at the other corner of her mouth.

"You will drive me daft, sir."

"Good. We are making progress."

The hint of smugness in his tone collided with a thought: Abigail need not sit demurely while Lord Stephen toppled her self-control with practiced skill. He was a mortal if formidable man. His self-restraint could be toppled too.

She slid a hand inside his riding jacket, around the lean warmth of his waist. She urged him closer and felt the surprise of that boldness go through him.

Now they were making progress. When he would have inflicted another one of his off-center kisses on her, she shifted, so their mouths lined up squarely. She anchored her free hand in his hair and held him still while she learned the taste of him.

Stephen Wentworth's kisses were sweet, warm, and playful. He gave new meaning to the term *nimble tongue*, and he kept his hand on Abigail's side, just inches from her breast. She liked that he was bold but not presuming, familiar without harrying her into intimacies beyond what she was prepared to share.

The whole business became so engrossing that Abigail forgot this kiss was meant as a rehearsal or a test case, forgot she was being hounded by an arrogant marquess. She forgot much that badly needed forgetting. Instead, she recalled that she was not yet an old woman, and not simply an inquiry agent with a reputation for thoroughness and discretion.

Lord Stephen drew back, and urged Abigail against his side. This resulted in her head on his shoulder, his arm encircling her. She rested her palm over his heart, which beat a steady and slightly accelerated tempo.

"You offer me a challenge," he said, his hand smoothing over Abigail's hair.

The warm glow within died, for all that the embrace was cozy. "This plan was your idea, my lord, and I'm not *that* hard to kiss. You aren't exactly conventional in your approach, but I suppose I can manage further displays of affection if I must." She was blustering, trying to ignore the disappointment she felt. For him the kiss had been an experiment, while for her it had been...

A revelation.

He cradled her cheek in his palm and pressed her face gently to his chest. "You are enthralling to kiss, and God preserve me from convention in any but the most traditional endeavors. Give me your hand."

He possessed himself of Abigail's hand. The next thing she knew, her palm was pressed to his falls, and to the hard column of flesh therein.

"Men get this way frequently," she said, though few men got this way on quite such an impressive scale, at least in her limited experience. "It means nothing. What is your point?"

She removed her hand, and he wrapped her fingers in a snug grasp.

"Abigail, I do not *get this way* frequently, not anymore. One learns to manage one's impulses lest one make a fool of oneself. I can appear to court you in all sincerity, steal kisses that I will genuinely treasure, disport with you in secluded alcoves and honestly resent any intrusions. You should know this before you embark on any subterfuges with me."

He was trying to tell her something, to posit a thesis

delicately. Abigail was too bothered with conflicting emotions and bodily sensations to properly dissect his words.

"You are attracted to me?" she asked.

"Need you make it a question?"

The slight testiness of his response, the evasiveness, suggested an extraordinary possibility: This gloriously intelligent, handsome, shrewd, wealthy, titled, and clever man was unsure of his own appeal. The test had been not of his ability to appear the doting swain, but of her willingness to appear doted upon—*by him.*

Abigail would ponder the why of that conclusion later, but in the easy rhythm of Lord Stephen's caresses and the patience with which he awaited her reply, she accepted that Stephen Wentworth was even more complicated than she'd realized, and not what he appeared to be.

He was more, much more, than an arrogant London lord with a penchant for solving mechanical questions.

"You will forgive my befuddlement," Abigail said, snuggling closer. "I am unaccountably muddled."

He squeezed her in a half hug. "Got you stirred up, did I?"

"Don't sound so pleased with yourself." He sounded, in fact, relieved.

He kissed the top of her head. "Don't sound so *dis*pleased with yourself. Women have needs. As it happens, I delight in meeting those needs."

"Nobody needs to be kissed." She was arguing in part for form's sake, and in part because it seemed to amuse his lordship. Also because—no harm in being honest—she did not want to leave this couch or leave Lord Stephen's comfortable, almost friendly embrace.

"Abigail dearest, we all need a little kissing, cuddling, and cavorting. Proving that to you shall be my fondest challenge."

Abigail closed her eyes, savoring the rare comfort of another's animal warmth, the utter relaxation Lord Stephen's touch encouraged. Even as her body quietly hummed with pleasure, her mind faced an uncomfortable truth.

She could pose as the object of Lord Stephen's affections. She could easily reciprocate his overtures and enjoy his attentions. That playacting would complicate the whole business of the letters, even as it sheltered her from Stapleton's mischief.

The greater problem was the role Abigail would be inhabiting. She would be impersonating the woman she could never be, the woman Lord Stephen Wentworth loved with his whole, complicated, magnificent, devious heart.

Lady Mary Jane Christine Benevolence Wentworth was perfect, her tiny fingers and toes all present in the proper numbers, her face the envy of Botticelli's cherubs. In sleep, her mouth worked in a pantomime of suckling, as if even her dreams were of nurture and security.

"Welcome, my lady," Stephen said, cradling the baby against his heart. "I am your uncle. I will counsel you in the difficult diplomacy of having older sisters. I claim two such siblings, and they are formidable. I am proud to say that your older sisters are terrors, in no small part thanks to my inspiring influence."

Mary Jane had three older siblings, all robust, clever, darling young ladies, full of the well-loved child's high spirits and lively curiosity. Their papa and mama—Quinn and Jane—ruled the nursery with loving firmness, and unlike other titled parents, spent considerable time with their children.

"You have chosen well," Stephen whispered. The nursery had a pair of rocking chairs next to the hearth, and in this setting—and in this setting only—a chair that rocked made sense to Stephen. "I taught Hannah how to pick a lock, and she'll soon need clocks to take apart. Elizabeth makes up stories for me." The baby—meaning the third youngest, who was no longer the baby—had yet to manifest her special gifts, but Stephen suspected she'd be highly musical.

He was helpless not to love them, and the little beggars took shameless advantage of his weakness. They loved him back, indifferent to his lurching gait, his tendency to play with their toys, and his frankly nasty outlook on humanity in general.

"You lot ruin all my theories," he murmured, rocking the baby gently. "Curmudgeonliness becomes impossible with little princesses galloping the corridors of their kingdom and flying down the banisters." Though sorrow was ever at hand when the nieces were present.

Stephen could not chase Quinn and Jane's offspring, could not grab them about their sturdy middles as Quinn and Duncan did to hoist them onto the stair railings, could not take them on his shoulders when they began to tire in the park. He could put them up before him in the saddle, but only if an obliging groom lifted the child for him.

"You will not have cousins of me," he murmured against

the baby's downy crown. "I told your sisters the same thing. Look to Althea and Constance for that madness." Or to Duncan and Matilda. Duncan was a cousin to Stephen and Quinn, and Duncan, like Quinn, seemed capable of fathering only females.

"Whom he spoils shamelessly," Stephen added. To the casual observer, Duncan appeared all serious and academic, but put an infant in his arms and he was about as scholarly as fairy dust and spotted unicorns.

"The Wentworth menfolk are easily besotted," Stephen said, more quietly still. "See that our womenfolk have more sense than that, for I will call out any young swain who offers you dishonor."

The nursery door creaked open, and Stephen prepared to hand the baby over to her mother or father. A mere nursery maid would not be able to pry the child from his arms, for Jane's labor had been difficult, and the infant's survival a domestic miracle.

Quinn settled into the second rocking chair. His temples sported a few threads of silver, and he was within hailing distance of his fortieth year. Jane said he grew only more handsome—about which Stephen had no opinion—but clearly, Quinn grew happier with each passing year.

About which, Stephen was torn.

"Promising her ponies and peppermints?" Quinn asked, leaning his head against the back of the chair.

"Promising to kill anybody who brings her dishonor."

"That's my job, though Jane will usurp that honor from both of us. Why are the children always so good for you?"

Because I love them. Of course, Quinn and Jane loved

their children, but Stephen never envisioned having progeny of his own—what sort of father couldn't carry his own toddler up to the nursery at the end of the day?—and thus Stephen's love was gilded with desperation.

These children had to be happy, they had to thrive, or he would go mad.

"The children are simply children," he said, "and that wonder bedazzles me whenever I behold them." The girls were the antidote to Stephen's memories, tonic for the constant pain of a leg that would never be straight or strong.

"You are a fraud, Stephen Wentworth." Quinn pronounced sentence gently. "You travel the world leaving a trail of lordly disdain and casual brilliance. You build heavy artillery and small arms, you destroy any business that you take into dislike, but in your heart, you were meant for domesticity."

The baby sighed, the softest, most contented exhalation ever to soothe an upset uncle.

"I am about as well suited to domesticity," Stephen said, "as you are to be a duke."

Quinn's gaze shifted from Stephen to the baby. "Jane says I've grown into the title, and my duchess is never wrong. She sent me to retrieve yon hooligan, and when it comes to Her Grace's whim, I am pleased to step and fetch."

Stephen's every instinct clamored to keep the baby close and safe, to guard her from even the loving attentions of her own parents, and yet, he could not safely rise with the child in his arms.

He could not manage the baby, a cane—much less two canes—and a door latch.

This limitation, previously acknowledged mostly in the abstract, had consumed his awareness since he'd kissed Abigail Abbott that very morning.

He passed the child to her father. "Perhaps you'll have better luck with the next one."

Quinn cradled his daughter with the practiced ease of a father of four. "Wee Mary and her sisters are all the luck I could ask for, Stephen. I will not subject my wife to child-bed again. Jane was in agony for the better part of two days. Only her great fortitude and determination brought about a happy result, and even if she is willing to risk another pregnancy for the sake of the succession, I am not."

Truly, Quinn had become a duke, for he delivered that blow in the most casual tones, rising easily to tuck his daughter against his shoulder.

"Jane will change your mind." A desperate hope.

"Jane changed my mind last time and this time, and my capitulation nearly killed her. I will not be talked around again, even by Jane."

Jane's fixity of purpose made Toledo steel look like so much crumpled tin. Quinn, however, was the one force of nature whom Jane could not and would not cozen, cajole, or command when he'd settled on a course. Stephen did not understand how marital differences were resolved between two such people, but he did know that trading Jane's life for a male child was no bargain at all.

"Is the duchess receiving?" Stephen asked, gathering up his canes. Some women still observed the tradition of forty days lying in. With previous confinements, Jane had begun short excursions from the house in less than half that time.

"Jane will want to see you," Quinn said. "Give us half an hour, and join us in our private parlor."

"You will allow me to buy that child a pony," Stephen said, trying for a light tone. "If I can't teach her to shoot or smoke or drink, I must be permitted at least that boon."

"You can teach her all of those things, but it still won't make her or any of her sisters male, Stephen. Reconcile yourself now to the fact that you will be the next Duke of Walden." Quinn opened the door, and who should be on the other side but Duncan.

"Another man seeking to call upon my daughter," Quinn said. "Alas, her mother has summoned her. You can keep Stephen company as he contemplates his gloomy fate. He'll be a wealthy and powerful duke one day, poor sod."

Quinn left, closing the door quietly in his wake. Stephen remained in the rocking chair and Duncan took the seat Quinn had vacated.

A silence ensued, broken only by the soft crackling of the fire in the hearth. Jane ordered wood burned in the nursery, declaring that wood fires were better for the children's lungs than coal. That was only one of the myriad decisions required of her as a parent, and Jane made them with the confidence of an experienced general bivouacking over familiar terrain.

Duncan had powers of contemplation that rivaled the sagacity of the ancients. He and Matilda had traveled to Town from their Berkshire estate in honor of the nursery's newest arrival. For years, Duncan had been Stephen's constant companion, first as a tutor, then as a traveling companion. Matilda had come along and spoken for all of Duncan's waltzes, as it were.

"You haven't been out to see us for months," Duncan said. "Are you in love again?"

Another man might have asked how the crops were faring, how the harvest went on at the Yorkshire properties. Duncan had faced demons that made Jack Wentworth look like a passing inconvenience. Prying into Stephen's non-existent personal life thus passed for small talk with Duncan.

"I gave up falling in love when I turned five-and-twenty. Put away my childish things, as it were. When will you and Matilda have a son?"

"Never."

Et tu, Duncan? "The Almighty has given you those assurances?"

"I am older than Quinn, and Matilda has a year or two on Jane. We are well blessed with our two girls and refuse to court disaster by asking for more. You will make a fine duke."

Nothing frightened Duncan. His sangfroid was equal to highwaymen, irate dukes, squalling infants, and self-destructive adolescents. He'd studied for the church and drew on a well of moral fortitude Stephen could only envy. Duncan had taught a surly, adolescent Quinn to read. When Stephen's mind had been caulked shut with rage and despair, Duncan had pried it open with books and riding lessons.

Stephen would cheerfully die for Duncan, and Duncan would never allow him that privilege.

"I will make a terrible duke," Stephen said. "I am bad-tempered, enthralled with commerce, frequently in company with opera dancers, and unable to waltz."

Duncan set his chair to slowly rocking. "Dukes keep company with whomever they please, they generally own vast swathes of commercial property, and have been known to be difficult. Ergo, it's that last—the waltzing—that renders you unfit for the title?"

Well, no. "Go back to Berkshire."

"Matilda is having too much fun doting on the older girls, and that leaves the field clear for me to dote on my own offspring. What is it about the title that truly bothers you, Stephen? You have many of the attributes that should characterize the nobility. You are wise, tolerant, hardworking, loyal to friends and family, and kindly disposed toward humanity in general. You will be an asset to the Lords precisely because you were not born to privilege. You are already a reproach to the cits who use their wealth only for their own indulgence."

"An occasional charitable donation is expected of the wealthy. Quinn would thrash me if I were to neglect that duty."

Quinn would never thrash him. Once, long ago, Stephen had pilfered a currant bun—the most delicious, delectable, delightful currant bun ever to be consumed by a famished boy. Quinn had learned of the misdeed and swatted Stephen once on the bum. The pain had been nothing, but the reassurance to Stephen, that his older brother would not allow him to slip into a criminal life, had been inordinate.

"Perhaps I should have stolen more currant buns."

"You would make a fine felon," Duncan said. "You would execute your crimes without getting caught, inspire loyalty among your subordinates, and keep order in the ranks."

"You make me sound like some sort of regimental authority." And how Stephen had envied all those young men buying their colors.

A log fell on the hearth, sending a shower of sparks up the flue. "The military and the better-organized street gangs have much in common. That many of our returning soldiers now belong to those gangs emphasizes my point. What stops you from taking up a life of crime is the guilt. You know what it is to be a victim, thus you refuse to victimize others."

"Truly, Duncan, a return to Berkshire on your part would be appreciated. I'll squire Matilda and the girls about, and you can go back to reading the Stoics. I have a houseguest."

Duncan's chair momentarily stilled, then resumed its slow cadence. "You have acquaintances from all walks of life. What makes this houseguest different?"

"Miss Abigail Abbott is unlike any female—any person—I've encountered. She has no patience with guns."

"And you love them. I'm sure that makes for rousing philosophical arguments. This is the inquiry agent from York whom Constance and Rothhaven hired?"

"The same. Miss Abbott kept Con's secrets for years, never gave up on the goal, and eventually met with success. I admire that."

"Having an entire regiment's worth of tenacity, you would find such persistence admirable. Why is this woman your guest?"

She had nowhere else to turn. Stephen knew what that felt like too. "She has provoked the wrath of the Marquess of

Stapleton. She sought my counsel regarding the best means of thwarting him." Duncan had kindly omitted the obvious lecture: Bachelor lords did not house female guests who arrived without benefit of chaperonage. Bachelor lords did not socialize with inquiry agents of common origins.

Bachelor lords, in other words, were a lot of useless prigs.

"The marquess has a reputation for self-importance," Duncan said. "I believe he and Quinn are on opposing sides of the child labor law debate."

In Stephen's opinion, children did not belong in the mines or factories. They belonged at school, and at the sides of parents or mentors engaged in trades, crafts, or some family enterprise. Quinn shared that viewpoint, having been worked without mercy as a boy and paid next to nothing.

"Stapleton wants some letters Miss Abbott has. She is bound by conscience to safeguard them." Or was she? Stephen had begun to wonder who exactly had those letters.

"You cite the conscience of a woman who goes through life essentially as a professional fraud. She finagles secrets from those who don't even know they have them, disguises and misrepresents herself, and takes coin to spy at keyholes. What is it about her that draws you?"

The clocks elsewhere in the house chimed the quarter hour. One was an instant behind the others.

"The footmen have been lax," Stephen said. "The clock in the family room was wound at least an hour later than the others."

Duncan held his peace, at which he was damnably talented.

"Miss Abbott has a conscience," Stephen said. She still suffered guilt over the moment of her birth, for example. "She managed Con's business without once taking advantage of the situation."

"And now Miss Abbott needs help. She cannot bide with you, Stephen. Her reputation will not withstand that impropriety."

"I'm here to ask Quinn and Jane to extend their hospitality to her."

Duncan rose and added a log to the fire. He could do that—rise, move the fire screen, grab a length of wood from the basket, lay it amid the flames, and replace the screen—without once having to consider his balance. He could do nearly everything without considering his balance, and how Stephen envied him such sure-footedness.

"When Matilda showed up on my doorstep," Duncan said, "frightened, famished, and friendless, I had no choice. Gentlemanly honor was the fig leaf I draped over my actions—damsels in distress and so forth—but Stephen, I *had* no choice. She beat me at chess, she thought I was intelligent, she admitted an attraction to a man who'd eschewed all bodily entanglements. She took me captive, utterly and forever, and if you lot had told me to turn my back on her, I would have instead turned my back on you."

Such effusions from Duncan, the soul of intellectual dispassion, were unprecedented. Stephen had told Duncan to at least consider the proprieties where Matilda was concerned and had got exactly nowhere.

"Your point?"

"You never ask anybody for anything, but you are

imposing on Quinn and Jane for the sake of this inquiry agent. That says a lot."

"It says I can't keep a decent female under my roof without her reputation suffering."

"It says you will do for her what you would never do for yourself."

"Observe propriety? Really, Duncan, I am not the outlandish boy who careered all over Europe with you. I am to be a bloody duke, after all."

Duncan ambled for the door. "And a duke who intends to secure the succession must have a willing duchess, and that, my friend, is why you so dread taking up the title. I look forward to meeting your Miss Abbott."

"Go back to Berkshire."

Duncan paused, hand on the door. "What you dread to do beyond all else is *ask for help*. If Miss Abbott inspires you to such humility, she is surely the stuff duchesses are made of. Mind you don't muck this up, Stephen. The right duchess only comes along once in a fellow's life."

Duncan slipped through the door, leaving Stephen alone to contemplate missing letters, irate marquesses, and family obligations.

Try as he might to focus on those topics, his thoughts kept wandering, back and back again, to kisses much too passionate to be entirely for show.

Chapter Five

"You have agreed to play the part of my intended," Lord Stephen said. "All manner of speculation will start once the gossips get word of my interest in you. Your reputation must be above reproach, and thus you will accept Their Graces' hospitality."

Abigail stalked up to him, and to his credit he did not flinch or step back. "Where was your concern for my reputation when you consigned me to the blue suite two nights ago, my lord?"

The last she'd seen of him, he'd been off to pay a call on his family yesterday afternoon. He had not come home for dinner, and he'd avoided her at breakfast that morning. She'd barged into his study in search of something to read—something besides lurid novels—and found his lordship peering at the plans spread out on his worktable.

He patted her arm. "Inactivity makes you cross, or

perhaps your female humors are troubling you. I don't care *that*"—he snapped his fingers before Abigail's nose—"for polite society. They would have cheerfully hanged my brother and let a titled potwalloper go free. My concern is for your safety."

Abigail *was* cross, and inactivity *did not* sit well with her. That Lord Stephen would make a decision without consulting her rendered her positively furious.

"According to you, I am safe here. I do not want your family burdened with my problems."

He peered down his nose at her. "Have trouble asking for help, do you? That shows a serious want of humility. What would your Quaker relations say to this display of hubris, Miss Abbott?"

In their last conversation, she'd been *Abigail*, *my dear*, and *dearest* to him. "My Quaker relations would say I come by my *self-sufficiency* honestly. They disowned my father, *read him out of meeting*. He was a master gunsmith, raised to excel at his trade before the Friends took such a dim view of it. Papa had no other skills with which to make a decent living, so he turned his back on his faith community."

"As you turn your back on both guns and your father's religious affiliations. Might we sit? I've been out and about already today, and a respite would be appreciated."

Abigail caught a whiff of his lordship's luscious fragrance and moved away. "You need not ask my permission to sit, my lord. Sit whenever you please."

He remained standing, regarding her, both of his hands resting on the head of his cane. This one looked to be of oak—more easily worked than mahogany and still quite heavy.

"You value self-sufficiency, Miss Abbott. I value every semblance of normal, able-bodied gentlemanly behavior I can manage."

Abigail sat on the sofa, a poor choice given the memories she had of it.

His lordship came down beside her. "What is the real reason you are reluctant to dwell with Their Graces?" He rested his foot on the hassock, which Abigail took to be a concession to his limitations.

"If Stapleton was willing to poison me once, he might try poison again. If he set brigands looking for me once, he might do that again too. Their Graces have children in the nursery—a newborn, for God's sake—and you expect the duke and duchess to take on the burden of me and my troubles."

His lordship propped his cane between them and began rubbing his knee. "Have you any siblings?"

"My father never remarried. My mother was the love of his life."

"Whom you killed, with malice aforethought, being an entire eight pounds or so of villainy at the time of the crime, and so on and so forth. I recall the particulars. Allow me to enlighten you regarding that blessing known as the sibling bond, at least among Jack Wentworth's offspring, though for all we know, Quinn isn't related to the rest of us."

"His Grace of Walden is a legitimate bastard?"

"We can't be sure. His poor mama was already carrying when she married Jack, and she married somewhat down, suggesting Jack was a husband of convenience. He also treated her miserably, sending her into an early grave and reviling her ever after for her faithlessness."

His lordship shared this extraordinary confidence casually, and yet, Abigail knew why he did it. He was informing her, in a roundabout way, that she wasn't the only one with family secrets and sorrows. As if an inquiry agent needed reminding of that.

"His Grace of Walden might not even be your brother?"

"The College of Arms doesn't care. Quinn is the legal and legitimate offspring of Jack Wentworth, and more to the point, a brother is as a brother does. Quinn saved our lives, over and over. We would have starved without the wages he earned, or worse, we would have succumbed to Jack's meanness without Quinn to show us how to manage. Althea took much of the brunt of Jack's temper, but we all came in for our share."

"Let me see to your knee," Abigail said, setting his cane aside and moving closer.

"My cane, please."

"Your leg hurts. You should rest it."

"Abigail, please put my cane where I can reach it." His tone was civil—barely.

She passed him his cane. "Only the one today?"

"When I go out, I try to manage with one."

"And then you pay for your pride." She began the slow, smooth massage he seemed to favor.

"Harder," he said, leaning his head back against the cushions. "That knee only understands a firm touch."

She dug in with her fingers, which earned her a sigh.

"Exactly like that. Ye gods, I might not let you stay with Quinn and Jane after all."

"You are not *letting* me do anything, my lord. I've asked for your help. That does not put you in control of me. Finish your explanation regarding your siblings."

"If my family learned that I was in difficulties, and I did not turn to them for aid, they would be hurt. I have hurt them enough. In my youth, when I could not lash out with my fists, I lashed out with words. I broke antique vases. I threw food I would have sold myself for a few years earlier. I was impossible, and only Duncan's monumental patience and even greater stores of academic guile stopped me from the worst of my foolishness."

"What is academic guile?"

Lord Stephen closed his eyes. "When you meet him, you'll understand. Life is a logic puzzle to Duncan, and guiding my self-destructive impulses into creative directions became his defining challenge. Duncan's virtue is so stern as to be nearly invisible, but nobody loves more fiercely than he. I owe him my life. I owe Quinn, Constance, and Althea my life. I owe Jane my soul, and my nieces my heart. Please say you will stay with Quinn and Jane."

The truth was, Abigail could not bide with Lord Stephen for any length of time and still be accepted by decent society. Lord Stephen might produce a fictitious maiden auntie to serve as a nominal chaperone for a sum certain, or he might allude to an equally fictitious distant family connection between him and Abigail, but tongues would inevitably wag.

The Quality were nothing if not hypocritical.

"If you can assure me that your family will be in no danger, I will stay with them."

Lord Stephen opened his eyes. "Quinn is filthy, reeking rich, and as suspicious of his fellow man as only a gutter whelp who has come up in the world can be. He's seen Newgate from the top of the scaffold, and been betrayed by fancy employers since his earliest youth. If you come across a titled family in financial distress, they probably hate Quinn Wentworth, because he either cut off their credit or refused to lend to them altogether."

And *this* was the dukedom Stephen would inherit? "Walden is conscientious about his family's security?"

"He's fanatical about it and has tasked me with measures to safeguard the ladies in particular. Every Wentworth conveyance is a rolling fortress of my design, the footmen are all skilled with firearms and knives, which I've fashioned for ease of concealment. We employ a lowlier variety of domestic than most households, because we want the sharpest possible eyes looking out for us. My sisters typically carry weapons, as do I, and the children never go abroad without a platoon of guards."

Abigail's Quaker relatives would shudder with horror at lives lived in anticipation of violence. "My uncles would say the price of endless wealth is endless fear."

"So they've sold all their worldly goods, given away the proceeds, and taken up a life of carefree penury? I can assure you, Abigail, the price of poverty is also fear, along with disease, misery, despair, starvation, and death."

Would Stapleton kill her for the letters? Abigail did not know and would prefer not to find out.

"I will stay with your family. If I'm to be credibly passed off as your intended, that only makes sense."

Lord Stephen caught her hand in his. "But you had to put me through my paces, lest I begin to think you anything less than deucedly independent. It's better now."

His grip was warm and firm, reminding Abigail of another firmness. "I beg your pardon?"

"My knee. It's better. Thank you."

Something about his smile was a little too cheerful. "No, it isn't. You are dissembling. I have no patience with liars, my lord, and if I'm to impose on your family, please assure me that we will be honest with them about the nature of our dealings."

His kissed her fingers. "They will know what's afoot, the better to keep you safe."

More glib assurances that Abigail did not entirely believe. "What's the real reason you are sending me away?" The part about turning to his family for aid was true, as was the bit about safeguarding Abigail's person and her reputation.

And yet, she'd bet her favorite sword cane Lord Stephen was prevaricating about *something*.

"I know why you are so fond of that terrier, Malcolm," his lordship said. "You are both persistent to the point of foolishness."

"Persistence gets results."

His lordship winced as he lowered his foot from the hassock. "Truer words...How soon can you be ready to accompany me to the ducal residence?"

He was in a hurry to get rid of her, probably having

second thoughts about the whole scheme. "I am nearly ready now. I have but the one satchel, and packing that will take me five minutes." She rose, wanting to be away from the man who apparently wanted to be away from her.

Lord Stephen extended a hand to her, and Abigail realized that she was to help a gentleman to stand, a reversal of the usual social convention.

"Don't get all hedgehoggy on me," he said, pulling himself to his feet. "You turn up prickly at the least provocation. I am trying to keep you safe, outflank Stapleton, and preserve decorum."

Never in the history of masculinity had a man's scent been so delectable. Abigail batted aside that awareness and studied her reluctant host.

"Preserve my reputation? I'm an inquiry agent. I haven't all that much reputation to safeguard. And if you must know, my virtue in the technical sense was jettisoned as useless baggage years ago."

Lord Stephen's gaze went to the dragon frolicking across the ceiling. "The precious resource I seek to preserve by putting your person at a slight distance from my own is *my sanity*, you daft female. I slept exactly not at all last night, and I haven't had such a close acquaintance with my own right hand since I was sixteen years old."

He stood near enough that Abigail could see the flecks of gold in his blue irises. Some rare breeds of cat had eyes like that, azure intensity gilded with promises of lethal force.

"What has your right hand to do with—?"

"I give up." He appeared to address his surrender to

the dragon, and then he wrapped an arm around Abigail's waist and kissed her.

Stephen had tried the opera, and he'd tried locking himself in his idea room. He'd had a few tots of brandy, though inebriation and unsteady pins were a foolish combination, so the brandy had been of limited use.

He'd finally repaired to his study to partake of the strongest soporific he possessed, the steward's monthly reports from the Yorkshire estate. Even that drastic measure hadn't chased away memories of kissing Abigail Abbott.

She took hold of a fellow and kissed him into submission, and the novelty of that, the sheer relief of being confidently handled, had captured Stephen's imagination as no mechanical puzzle ever had.

Self-gratification hadn't eased his desire one iota, and kissing Abigail again was rank folly, but she was soon to be ensconced in the Wentworth family fortress, where folly could not intrude. Surely a farewell kiss was permissible?

"The scent of you," she murmured, wrapping Stephen in her arms. "You drive me witless. I can't bear—" She fused her mouth to his, and all over again, Stephen was awash in desire and madness.

"I dreamed of you," he said. "You breathed on me and I went up in flames." In the last reaches of his thinking mind, where reason despaired and mischief rejoiced, Stephen knew that nothing could come of his attraction to Abigail Abbott.

When he'd spiked Stapleton's guns, Abigail would go back to her inquiry business and Stephen would resume—

She ran her hand over his falls, her touch every bit as sure as it had been on his stupid knee. An even more brainless part of him leaped at the pleasure of her caress.

"You are so wonderfully bold," he whispered, "and I am so hopelessly willing. I can keep you safe from Stapleton, and Quinn and Jane will keep you safe from me."

Abigail subsided against him, though gently. Stephen had kept hold of his cane, Abigail had kept hold of him. The whole kiss had progressed without Stephen once worrying about his balance.

"You might have been kissing me to distract me," she said, "but you weren't."

Hence her bold caress. Ah, well. "Distract you from what?"

"Whatever objective you are truly intent on. You have guile too, my lord."

He could have stood there embracing her until the seasons changed, except that the sofa was calling to him, as was the temptation to lock the door.

"Perhaps you are distracting me, Abigail."

She pulled back to study him. "Your kisses are enticing. When you call me Abigail, in that slightly chiding, slightly confiding tone, I lose a piece of my self-control. Nobody addresses me by my given name. I am Miss Abbott, even to my companion."

He smoothed his hand over her shoulder, just for the pleasure of learning her contours. "I hear a fellow call out to Lord Stephen at the club, and I think: Who let some damned nob in here when I'm trying to enjoy a quiet meal with another inventor?"

She smiled at him, the first such benediction Stephen could recall from her. "I wonder if anybody ever feels entirely themselves?"

"You can be yourself with me."

Her smile dimmed into something more complicated. "Thank you. I trust you will do me the same honor—of being yourself with me."

"You enjoy the company of barbarians? Perhaps this is the result of dwelling in proximity to the Scots." The Scots did not deserve Stephen's humor. They were better physicians, more skilled inventors, and wiser philosophers than their southern neighbors, and they brewed up hellfire in a glass which even their elderly ladies consumed as if it were Christmas syllabub.

"I enjoy the company of a gentleman with a lively mind and sweet kisses," Abigail said, stepping back. "You are a very bad influence, my lord."

"Happy to be of service, and might I add, you have a similarly salubrious effect on my own overly taxed self-discipline."

The moment had turned, becoming superficial and wary. Stephen wanted to drag Abigail back into his embrace and kiss her senseless—or drag her to the sofa, where kissing would be the tamest aspect of their exchange.

"Shall I fetch my satchel?" she asked.

"Please. I'll have the coach brought around. Jane is expecting you, and she has Matilda—Duncan's wife—to abet her schemes where you are concerned. When I left yesterday, they were conferring about fabric."

Abigail stepped away. "Fabric, my lord?"

"I told them you prefer subdued colors and no flourishes. You aren't quite dressing plain, Abigail, so don't attempt to hide behind Quaker eccentricities at this late date."

"I compromise," she said, leaning over to sniff at a bouquet of roses on the windowsill. "I need pockets for my work, but I eschew the ruffles, lace, and flounces most ladies indulge in. I wear no jewelry and own nothing of brocade or silk."

Embroidery, then, was fair game, and velvet wasn't out of the question. A watch for her bodice might be allowable, or nacre hairpins.

"I will leave the wardrobe questions to you and the duchesses."

Abigail straightened. "Matilda is a duchess too?"

"Maybe not now in the strictest sense, but she's the widow of some pumpernickel duke, and she is the equal of any duchess I know. You will get on well with her."

"They will try to fancy me up."

Stephen maneuvered himself away from the sofa and hassock. "They've been trying to fancy me up for years, all to no avail. To have a fresh challenge will do them good. Before I throw you to the lionesses, though, I did have a few questions for you about the letters Stapleton is so keen to get hold of."

Abigail's gaze went from guarded to absolutely composed. "Questions, my lord?"

"Why does Stapleton want them so badly? Whose letters are they, and what do they contain that makes his lordship so nervous?"

Abigail started for the door. "I'll fetch my satchel, and

we can have this discussion on the way to your brother's house. There really isn't much to tell."

She swished through the door, leaving Stephen with a fading cockstand and a sense of disappointment as much of the heart as of the body. Abigail was planning to lie to him, though she apparently needed a few minutes to rehearse whatever Banbury tale she was preparing to spin.

This suggested she did not entirely trust Stephen, which was prudent of her. His courtship of her would be for show, while his desire was very much the genuine article. Even he wasn't sure what to make of that puzzle.

The blasted, bedamned letters were the aspect of the situation Abigail hadn't sorted out to her own satisfaction. She'd kept possession of them as a reproach to herself, proof of where mad impulses and foolish dreams could lead the unsuspecting. Now she had to explain them to a man whose intelligence was outstripped only by his curiosity.

And ye gods, by his kisses. Stephen Wentworth knew exactly where and how to touch a woman so she became focused exclusively on him. On his words, on the pitch of his voice, on the stillness he used as effectively as he used his hands. On the slow brush of his lips across her cheek, the heat of his palm along her shoulders.

"That is not why I came to London." Abigail took stock of her reflection in the cheval mirror positioned in the corner of her bedroom. She wore the same gray coach dress she'd worn upon her arrival, but it had been brushed, sponged, pressed, and otherwise refreshed.

The dress hadn't changed, but the blue velvet bed

hangings, blue brocade curtains, and fancy floral carpet gave the ensemble a borrowed luster. Then too, Lord Stephen's house had the high ceilings common to the dwellings of the wealthy. The result was more wall space on which to hang expensive art and, in summer, a cooler room.

A tall woman benefited from chambers built on a grander scale, complete with floor-to-ceiling curtains and yards of bed hangings. She looked less out of proportion with her surroundings, more of a piece with good taste, elegance, and comfort.

A maid rapped on the doorjamb and joined Abigail in the bedroom. "Excuse me, miss. Jake's here to take your valise. Himself awaits you in the porte cochere and himself does not deal well with idleness. Jake, get in here."

Standing for any length of time doubtless aggravated Lord Stephen's leg.

A lanky young fellow in sober livery came through the door and offered Abigail a cross between a nod and a bow. She passed him her satchel, took up her sword cane and reticule, and followed the maid down the steps.

"I hadn't realized this house had a porte cochere."

"We have tunnels too, and priest holes, and hidden passages. His lordship is clever like that, and this is not his only London residence. He moves about, never biding in one place for long."

The maid showed Abigail to the side entrance, where his lordship waited, looking impatient and handsome beside a gleaming town coach.

A rolling fortress, he'd said, though the vehicle was also beautiful. Black lacquered panels were trimmed in red, crests adorned the door and boot, and the coachman and grooms all wore black-and-red livery.

"I have never traveled in such style."

"And I have never known a woman for whom five minutes actually meant five minutes. You impress me, Miss Abbott. In you go."

A footman held open the door, and Abigail climbed inside. She took the rear-facing seat out of habit, and Lord Stephen took the forward-facing seat.

"Miss Abbott, you are playing the part of a future duke's sweetheart and you are to be the guest of a duchess. Stop acting like a maiden auntie or paid companion." He patted the tufted red-velvet seat cushion at his side. "I don't bite. I do nibble on occasion when offered certain delicacies."

Abigail switched seats, which in this roomy conveyance was easy. "Stop being naughty."

"You like it when I'm naughty, and I love it when you are naughty."

His teasing was preferable to being interrogated about the letters. "I kissed you once to ensure we could support the fiction of a romance between us, and a second time because you caught me unaware." He hadn't been playacting the second time, but what *had* he been up to?

"What excuse will you make for our third kiss, because I very much hope there will be a third kiss?"

So did Abigail. "My justification for further familiarities will be that I am out of the habit of kissing overbearing louts and the business wants some practice."

His lordship thumped the roof once with a gloved fist and the coach rolled smoothly forward.

"Which overbearing lout had the pleasure of relieving you of your virginity?"

He would ask that. "Relieving me of my ignorance, you mean? I can hardly recall. To whom did you surrender yours?"

He smiled—fondly, damn him. "Her name was Jenny O'Neill. She was four years older than I, a goddess wearing a tavern maid's apron and a siren's smile. I learned to spend an entire hour on a single tankard just for the pleasure and torment of watching her flirt with the other fellows."

The coach was delightfully well sprung, traversing the cobbles as smoothly as a barge crossed a calm lake. "You weren't supposed to answer that question, my lord."

"I will always answer your questions, Miss Abbott."

"Did you break her heart?" Abigail hadn't meant to ask that. She was merely trying to put off any discussion of the letters.

"She broke mine, gently, sweetly, as all hearts should be broken the first time. I make it a point to stop by her inn when my travels take me back that direction. She has a pair of little boys now, and her husband worships her and the boys equally, else I should have to have a stern word with him. They are trying for a daughter and I expect they will succeed."

Abigail caught a hint of wistfulness beneath this cheery recitation. "*Her* inn?"

The shades were drawn, doubtless to protect Abigail's privacy, but she could see Stephen's eyes well enough. He sent her a bland look.

"I might have bought the place for her. *I can hardly*

recall, it was so long ago. Shall I tell you about the handsome blighter who stole your heart?"

"You will air your suppositions whether or not I want you to." His lordship's mood was hard for Abigail to read, which he doubtless intended.

"He was handsome, because only a man with a bit of arrogance would have the balls to approach you."

"Language, my lord." And whatever did he mean?

"You ride atop stagecoaches with ne'er-do-wells and drovers. My language does not shock you. This man, though, whom you can *hardly recall*, was above your touch too, or you would never have given him the time of day. He was no tame Quaker lad. He instead embodied what a sheltered Quaker miss would consider forbidden fruit."

"I am not a Quaker miss." The Quakers wouldn't have her, not for one of their own. Good heavens, her dresses had pockets and she carried a sword cane and she wasn't meek and peaceful and pious.

Nor did she wish to be. To be a bit more conventional might have been nice, though.

"Your lover was from a good family," Lord Stephen went on, "maybe even a titled house. He was close enough to real consequence to trifle with somebody he considered of a lower order and know he would not be held responsible. He was all golden charm and lazy promises—he was doubtless an acolyte of Sartoris and probably gave you a bauble or two that you dared not wear. He had sense enough to win your heart. We must commend him for that one instance of good judgment, though he then broke your heart, for which I should call him out."

"He did not break my heart, and you cannot call him out." The wretch was dead, and his passing had occasioned all manner of confused emotions for Abigail. "I have no patience with guns, my lord, lest you forget."

"Well, I can't very well duel with swords, can I? My opponent would be felled by mirth when the first riposte sent me arse over ears into the dirt. I no longer duel, in the ordinary course, though for a time I indulged."

The coach swayed around a corner and slowed.

"Indulged? And have you since realized masculine pride isn't worth dying for?"

His lordship propped his foot on the opposite bench and idly rubbed his knee. "Masculine pride is not worth *killing* for, though I might set a brace of ruffians on the prancing dandiprat who broke your heart, Miss Abbott."

Abigail's lover had been a prancing dandiprat. Lord Stephen's aim was deadly accurate in that regard. Her lover had also been gorgeous, exquisitely attired, and—this was also true—the embodiment of everything a pious Quaker girl ought not to esteem. He'd been vain, decorative, hedonistic, a slave to fashion, and self-indulgent to a fault.

And he hadn't even given her baubles she could not wear. He'd entrusted her with a pocket watch that kept bad time. Even so, he had fulfilled some need in Abigail for rebellion, though she would not admit Lord Stephen had handed her that insight.

"The prancing dandiprat has gone to his reward, and this is all none of your business."

His lordship paused in his knee-rubbing and peered at Abigail. "Is that how he broke your heart? Swilling bad ale or taking a stray bullet in a duel? Does an old shade own your affections?"

"We were no longer involved at the time of his death, and, no, a bullet did not end his life. He was simply taken before his time by happenstance and bad luck. Tell me about your family. I've met them, but I don't know them."

Stephen cocked his head. "That is the clumsiest attempt to change a subject this side of an occasion of royal flatulence. The ruddy prickster was married, wasn't he? He was married, you were his delicious little secret, and he neglected to inform you that he would never make good on all his saccharine promises. It's as well he's dead, because I do not countenance lies told for amatory gain."

How had this conversation happened? "I am nobody's delicious little anything. Tell me about your family."

"Tell me about the letters, Abigail. Why does Stapleton want them?"

"I have no idea. They are love letters that do not identify the party to whom they were sent. They are several years old and not particularly inspired. I have read them, and I saw no state secrets, no royal scandals, no discussion of stolen treasures. They are quite dull, actually." And once upon a time, she'd thought them so precious as to deserve memorization.

"Have you read many love letters, then?"

Doubtless not as many as *he* had. "I have been employed on several occasions to retrieve embarrassing correspondence. One must read the letters to know whether they are the epistles one was hired to find."

"My, my. The Quakers failed spectacularly with you, didn't they?"

"They failed my father. What are the names of your nieces?"

He removed his foot from the opposite bench. "The newest one is Lady Mary Jane Christine Benevolence Wentworth, and she's about the size of half a bread loaf. Jane labored for two days, and I gather Quinn was with her for most of it. They are like that—not at all high in the instep in the things that matter."

He prattled on about his nieces, upon whom he clearly doted. He would make a devoted and patient father, and be the sort of papa who knew exactly how to discuss a difficult topic with a child. No helpless retreats into scripture when common sense was wanted, no vague allusions to celestial mysteries when some blunt biology would do.

His daughters would know where little dragons came from before genteel ignorance could be used against them.

"We arrive," Lord Stephen said as the coach took a slow turn some moments later. "Jane will sweep you away from me before I so much as find a hassock for my foot, so allow me to pass along a parting thought."

"A warning?" Abigail had met the Wentworths when she'd been in Lady Constance's employ. Lady Constance—Her Grace of Rothhaven, rather—now bided with her duke in the north, her case having been successfully concluded.

"What I have to say is not intended as a warning," Lord Stephen replied, "but you will hear it as such."

The coach came to a halt, and the coachman shouted a greeting.

"Speak your piece, my lord."

"I do not lie for anybody's convenience, Abigail, including my own. I will court you to draw out Stapleton because you asked for my help and because I will enjoy the game. When I kiss you, that is not a performance. I like you, I desire you, I delight in sharing intimacies with you, and my actions in that regard are in complete earnest."

He spoke calmly and quietly, no teasing, no insouciance in his tone. Would that he had been jesting.

"I never took you for a charming bounder, my lord." The words were inadequate, unworthy of his display of courage, so Abigail tried again. "I am supposed to say thank you, put my nose in the air, and act as if such honesty is vaguely distasteful. I should pretend that I tolerate your advances because men cannot help themselves when females are willing, and it all means nothing as long as Stapleton believes the playacting."

"Kisses should never be meaningless."

Not exactly. Kisses should mean as much or as little to one party as they did to the other. If nothing else, Abigail had learned that much from her foray into worldly peccadillos.

"Your kisses are not meaningless, Stephen Wentworth. I have asked you to enter into a deception with me, and I am grateful for your aid, but I delight in sharing intimacies with you as well."

He unlatched the coach door and pushed it open. The footman let down the steps and moved aside.

"I have two objectives, then," Lord Stephen said, gathering up his cane and passing Abigail hers. "I must inspire you to like me, and I must also aid you to thwart Lord Stapleton's mischief. Which of the two will be the greater challenge?"

Abigail descended from the coach rather than reply, but she knew the answer, for she already did like Lord Stephen—far too much.

Chapter Six

"You left me there for *three days*," Abigail muttered before Stephen had even given the gelding in the traces leave to walk on. "Three days with little more than a note from you."

"Did you miss me?" Stephen had missed her. Had missed their verbal swordplay, missed the sight of her, and even missed the tattoo of her confident stride on his carpets. Learning the identity of the varlet who'd broken her heart had become a mental puzzle box, one that distracted him from frustrated lust.

She twitched her skirts away from the fender. "I missed making progress regarding Lord Stapleton. He's biding here in Town, by the way. You were right about that."

"That is a new frock," Stephen said, clucking to the horse. "Quite fetching. I told you the duchesses would take you in hand." The ladies had apparently compromised, for this dress was blue-gray rather than Miss Abbott's preferred dreary slate. The cuffs bore a tiny border of light blue embroidery, and the buttons were nacre.

Understated, but not nearly plain. *Bravo, Duchesses.*

"Your womenfolk are, as you say, formidable. Why didn't you remind me that Her Grace of Walden is nearly as tall as I am?"

"Because your height is immaterial?" he said, turning the horse down a quiet alley. "Because Jane has so many other delightful qualities that her statuesque proportions hardly bear mention? Have you made me the list I requested?"

Stephen had sent Abigail a note, unable to go three entire days without any communication between them.

"I have the list with me. I came up with the names of about a dozen clients who have London connections, but I don't see why those people are relevant."

Stephen had been curious about her lover, of course, and had concluded that if she had been disporting with a fashionable courtesy lord, she would have most likely met him in the course of a case. Hence, her London-based clients were of interest.

"People who hire Yorkshire inquiry agents don't expect to find those agents driving in Hyde Park at the Fashionable Hour," Stephen said, which was true enough. "You must be prepared to encounter your former clients, and I must be aware of who they are the better to dote on you convincingly when we meet them. I don't suppose the author of your *billets-doux* has family in Town?"

"What is this?"

Stephen had passed her a parasol. "I didn't think

Matilda would have time to drag you about on a shopping expedition, so I took it upon myself to safeguard your complexion. Open it."

"My complexion is not...that is, thank you, my lord. This is too personal a gift, though."

"Then don't tell anybody how you came by it."

She untied the blue satin ribbon holding the parasol closed. "But you bought it somewhere, and the modiste's work will be recognized. Because I haven't shopped at her establishment—this is quite pretty."

The parasol was made of silk rather than lace, the shade somewhere between pewter and silver. Neither tassels nor beading adorned the rim, though three bands of flowery blue stitchwork ran around the border.

"This is elegant," Abigail said. "Tasteful without being showy. I like it."

But do you like me? The question bothered Stephen inordinately. "I was afraid you'd find it too un-plain."

Abigail opened the parasol and propped it over her shoulder. "Plainness can become vanity. When people use a lack of ornamentation to call attention to their own piety rather than to the world's vanity, the exercise takes on the wrong significance. I choose subdued fashions the better to blend in and not call attention to myself, also because I want my clothing to last."

Stephen brought the horse to a halt, because the alley was blocked by a phaeton that canted off to one side, its left wheel cocked at an angle.

"You have no personal objection to wearing colors?" he asked.

"None at all, other than valuing modesty generally. I doubt I would wear jewels even if I could afford them, though."

Alas, no bracelets or earbobs. But then, bracelets and earbobs showed a dreadful lack of imagination. "What do you have against jewels?"

"Jewels are a means of hoarding wealth and being ostentatious about it. When veterans beg in the street and children must toil in the mines to avoid starving, such displays are unseemly."

The owner of the phaeton was standing beside his conveyance, arms akimbo, whip in hand. He was young—Stephen would put his age at less than twenty—and he had a perfectly matched pair of dappled grays in harness. No tiger was on hand to hold the horses, though perhaps the tiger had been sent to retrieve a wheelwright.

"You've lost a cotter pin," Stephen said, drawing his gig closer to the disabled vehicle. "Not a difficult repair."

"Beg pardon," the fellow said, bowing and tipping his hat to Abigail. "I've lost a what?"

"The cotter pin," Stephen said, wrapping his reins around the brake so he could gesture with his hands. "It holds the wheel to the axle without impeding rotation. If you have something of stout metal, about four inches long and half an inch thick, you can make do well enough to get back to your mews."

The young fellow looked glum. "I haven't any such thing, and my brother will kill me. This is his phaeton, and I didn't precisely ask permission before taking it out. Why does nobody fix the potholes in London's streets?"

"That would cost money," Stephen said. "Miss Abbott, might you surrender your parasol?"

She passed it over and Stephen unscrewed the handle from the shaft. "This might do," he said, brandishing the handle. "You will have to hold the phaeton steady so the wheel isn't bearing weight when you thread the pin through the axle."

The young man looked baffled, which meant Stephen would have to climb down and show him, an awkward undertaking with no groom to hold the horse, pass Stephen his cane, or otherwise prevent a fall.

"Miss Abbott, might you take the reins?" She was a competent whip, at least in the wilds of Yorkshire.

She studied the damaged vehicle and stepped down from the gig. "I believe I can manage, my lord." She stripped off her gloves and left them on the seat.

Stephen passed her the parasol handle, which had a good four inches of straight steel shaft above the curved end.

"What is she about?" the young man asked.

"She is making sure you live to see your majority."

"This will work," Abigail said, peering at the axle. "Let's be about it, sir. I will lift the phaeton, and you will hoist the wheel onto the axle. Then you slip this"—she held up the length of steel—"through the holes in the axle."

The repair took less than a minute, with Abigail holding the phaeton just high enough off the ground that the owner could fit the wheel on straight and thread the parasol handle through the hole bored in the axle.

"We still need something to stabilize the makeshift pin," Stephen said. "If the axle wobbles too much it can shear off the pin, and you're stranded all over again."

Abigail climbed into the gig unaided. "Your cravat is made of silk, my lord, and silk is exceedingly strong. If knotted tightly..."

"I cannot go about in public without my neckcloth, Miss Abbott."

She gestured at the youth standing beside his conveyance. "If linen will do, then why not use his?"

"Good idea. Lad, knot your neckcloth around the axle and the parasol handle so the lot is snug, and then walk your cattle—and I do mean walk—back to their stable. Do not put the weight of your fashionable arse upon the bench—walk your horses like a groom would walk them. If anybody asks, you tell them the nearside gray is going a bit off."

"That is a capital notion." He tipped his hat to Abigail again, and bowed to Stephen. "My thanks to you both. All's well and all that, right?"

Stephen saluted with his whip and waited until the phaeton had clattered out of the alley.

"I have never encountered a parasol with a steel handle," Abigail said. "Where did you say you bought it?"

Damn and blast. "I made it."

"You *made* me a parasol?"

"Not precisely. I am experimenting with designs, toying with the notion that a parasol can serve more than one function."

She pulled on her gloves. "Such as carrying a scent bottle or vinaigrette in the shaft?"

Small scent bottles were typically about the size and shape of a fat cheroot. "Something like that. You did that boy a significant service, Abigail." She'd hefted the phaeton like it weighed no more than a velvet muff, a feat Stephen could have managed only at peril to his balance.

"He was in the way and nobody save you was on hand to gawk at my outlandish behavior. *You* made that parasol?"

Stephen stopped the horse short of the end of the alley. High garden walls provided privacy on both sides, and the plane trees had enough leaves left to obscure the gig from any second-story windows.

"I made that parasol. I like adding cleverness to existing designs." That much was true.

She examined the stitchery around the rim of the parasol. "You sew a very pretty seam, my lord."

She was paying him a compliment rather than mocking him.

"I could not have lifted that damned phaeton, Abigail."

"I could not have designed a parasol with any practical uses, my lord. Shall we to the park?"

"In a moment."

First, he kissed her. Kissed her because she liked his pretty seams and his un-fussy, un-plain parasol, kissed her because she'd helped save a young man from mortification, kissed her because he could not do anything more than kiss her and shouldn't even be doing that.

"I don't normally go about impersonating a hostler," she said when Stephen drew back. "The poor young man seemed utterly helpless. I gather you were not mortified?"

"I am impressed at your generosity of spirit, Abigail." At her pragmatic disregard for appearances, at her ingenuity when it came to using a cravat to secure wheel and axle.

She kissed him, a ladylike little peck on the cheek that drove him wild. "To the park, my lord. The day is fair and I've a mind to show off my new finery. Most worldly of me, but there you have it."

Stephen gave the reins a shake. "I have just now this moment come upon a new use for the handle of a parasol."

"What would that be?"

"French letters. A lady ought to be able to carry discreet contraception on her person, nobody the wiser. The handle of the shaft would have to be rectangular, like a pencil box, and the mechanism stout, but what do you think? Would it sell?"

He was improvising, and making a complete hash of matters, as usual.

Abigail made a sound halfway between a sniff and a chortle, then she punched Stephen on the arm and laughed outright, and soon Stephen was laughing with her.

"His lordship doesn't drive young ladies in the park anymore." Duncan offered that observation staring down at the empty drive, where not ten minutes past, Stephen had tooled away with Miss Abbott up beside him. They made a handsome couple, though Stephen would have demanded satisfaction if Duncan had rendered that compliment aloud.

"If Stephen wants time alone with Miss Abbott," Quinn replied, "he'll observe the proprieties, and that means driving with her in the park in an open vehicle at a decent hour."

Duncan let the curtain drop. "Because he cannot walk

with her in the park. He has nightmares, about being pushed in his Bath chair by unseen hands that shove him over the brink of a precipice."

Quinn had been unaware of Stephen's nightmares. Quinn was not, in fact, as well acquainted with Stephen as he should be. A difference in ages was partly responsible—he and Stephen were more than a decade apart—but so too was a difference in temperament.

"Stephen finds London misses insipid," Quinn said. "They are not complicated enough for him." Quinn, by contrast, had been awed by fine ladies as a young man. More fool he.

Duncan prowled the length of the library. He had overseen the development of the collection, and had doubtless read every volume on the shelves. Quinn liked books well enough, but only because his duchess enjoyed having him read to her at the end of the day.

"You have it all wrong, Quinn." Duncan wound up a music box Stephen had made for Jane. "Stephen thinks himself too wicked for the sweet young things. He's afraid he'll make some joke, some little aside, and betray his upbringing. Add to that his inability to stand up with them, to even sit comfortably for long periods, and he's like a cat in a kennel. His options are to remain in the shadows or stir the pack to violence."

"They are young ladies, Duncan, not starving wolves." Quinn's daughters would be among those young ladies all too soon. Elizabeth was already jabbering about putting her hair up and letting her hems down and she was still a little girl, for God's sake.

"The heiresses and matchmakers are of the same ilk as those who sent you to the gallows, *Your Grace*. What do we know of Lord Stapleton?"

That was Duncan, always focused, always thinking, and protective as hell where Stephen was concerned. "Should our duchesses join this conversation?"

"They are closeted in the sewing room. Miss Abbott's wardrobe needs attention if she's to be courted by a ducal heir."

That bothered Quinn—the courtship that wasn't supposed to be a courtship. "Stapleton and I butt heads in the Lords," he said. "Jane is adamantly opposed to children doing factory labor, especially in the heavy industries. Stapleton maintains that a poor child should become inured to hard work early in life, the better to accept God's will and make a contribution to the improvement of the realm. Children who don't work are parasites in his estimation."

The music box played a rendition of Mozart's Sonata in C, a confectionary piece Elizabeth banged away at by the hour. Quinn had grown to detest it, though he'd never admit that to his daughter.

Duncan closed the lid of the music box and the contraption went blessedly silent. "Stapleton had only the one son if I recall?"

"Champlain, who went to his reward shortly after his own son was born. Stephen knew Lord Champlain and was among Lady Champlain's many admirers for a time."

"Stephen finds married women likeable." Duncan set the music box in the middle of the reading table. "They are not interested in his prospects, according to him. He said Lady Champlain's chess was so bad as to be interesting. I think he felt sorry for her because Champlain was such a bounder."

Stephen seldom operated out of pity, at least not when he could be caught at it. "Could that be why Stapleton is in such a lather? His son misbehaved and left written evidence that Miss Abbott now possesses?"

"Few people care if titled sons misbehave," Duncan said. "Stephen and I first encountered Champlain in Paris, where he was quite the bon vivant. According to Champlain, his papa sent him to the Continent precisely to indulge his frivolous inclinations. He and Stephen had a few adventures, about which I did not inquire."

"Bordellos?"

"The French are more tolerant of certain predilections than we English."

Duncan was former clergy, and the habit of primness died hard. "You think he and Stephen were lovers?"

"I did not inquire and neither will you, unless Miss Abbott, of all the ironies, has evidence of Stephen's indiscretion and has earned Stapleton's wrath as a result."

Blast and bedamned. No wonder Duncan hadn't suggested the ladies join them. "You and Stephen traveled on the Continent years ago. Why is Stapleton taking up the matter now? Maybe *Stapleton* committed the indiscretion or one of his mistresses did." The old boy hadn't remarried, which was odd, when the succession rested on the shoulders of one young child.

Duncan took the seat behind Quinn's desk, and Quinn

thought, not for the first time, that the wrong Wentworth had been made the duke. Duncan could inherit the title, if Stephen left no male issue and predeceased him.

Duncan—like all Wentworth menfolk, apparently—did not want the title, but he had the requisite gravitas, and more to the point, he would wield the power of the title for good ends.

"I am loath to suggest it," Duncan said, "but somebody had better thoroughly interrogate Miss Abbott. Is Stapleton prone to violence?"

"We are all prone to violence under the right circumstances." Quinn certainly was. "Stapleton dotes on his grandson, he provides well for his daughter-in-law, and he is civil enough when he and I meet. We disagree as reasonable gentlemen often do."

Duncan took up a quill pen, twiddling the feather between his fingers. "Perhaps Stapleton's problem is commercial. Most people who advocate working children and the poor to death for the sake of God's holy plan have commercial interests. Mines, foundries, mills. What do we know of Stapleton's investments?"

"I'll put Ned and Jack to researching that question, and by this time tomorrow, we will know who sews Stapleton's underlinen, whether he pays his bills on time, and the exact hour he last visited his mistress."

"You will keep Stephen informed?"

Quinn would keep Jane informed. "The question should be, rather, is Stephen keeping us informed, and if not, what secrets is he guarding?"

Duncan looked pained. "He is entitled to his privacy,

Quinn. Your motives for sending him touring with me weren't entirely academic."

"You're right. My motives where Stephen was concerned were desperate, and in some regards, they still are. We will speak with Miss Abbott, and Stephen will insist on being present when we do."

"The duchesses will insist on being present. One wishes Althea and Constance were on hand as well. They know Miss Abbott better than we do."

"Shall I send for them?"

"Let's confer with Stephen first. If we bungle this, he will never ask for our help again. You do not want a blunder of such proportions on your conscience, and neither do I."

Hyde Park was a magical oasis of clean air, open space, autumnal verdure, pretty lanes, and quiet. York, true to its medieval origins, had nothing quite like it, and Abigail was enthralled.

"In spring," Lord Stephen said, "the vehicles jam the pathways, and all the young swells on horseback flirt their way from carriage to carriage."

"Are you among those young swells?"

"I was, for a few years. I am no longer flattered by the overtures of women willing to hold their noses and marry me in hopes of wearing the Walden tiara. Every time Quinn and Jane have another baby girl, I feel the wolves stalking closer. Horse, stop pulling at the bit or we will have words."

The horse slowed to a walk.

"Did somebody break your heart?" Abigail asked. "Somebody other than your darling Jenny?"

"Half of Mayfair, a quarter of Paris, and about one-third of Berlin. By the time I reached Rome, I was a sadder and wiser fellow. I took to keeping company with widows and married women because they could be trusted. Married women and a few flirtatious fellows. Are you horrified?"

"No." More than one client had retained Abigail to secure and destroy evidence of such liaisons. "Is that why you haven't married? You prefer men?" She would be disappointed in a purely theoretical sense if that was the case.

"This is not the sort of conversation I envisioned us having, Abigail."

"Then tell me to mind my own business and bestir yourself to flirt with me. We are here to be seen, are we not? We could also discuss the list of my clients with London connections, but I doubt that will be a productive conversation."

A swan glided along on the still water of the Serpentine, cutting a path through the leaves dotting the water near the shore. The time of year was pretty but melancholy, and Abigail was abruptly homesick for York. She was in Hyde Park, driving out with one of the most eligible bachelors in England, wearing a truly lovely dress for the first time in ages.

Using the time to discuss old cases was pointless and just plain wrong, though Lord Stephen's worldly sexual adventures weren't an ideal topic for such an outing either.

"I have promised you honesty," Stephen said, "and the healthy male form honestly delights me, and so have a few healthy males in particular. I mentioned the painter to you—Endymion de Beauharnais. He's everything I'm not. Athletic, artistic, charming, beautiful, socially deft. I am a skilled draftsman and something of a flirt, but that man can make dragons fly and dowagers simper. I like him very much, though when it comes to the actual passionate part..."

He steered the horse around a bend in the path, and London might have been magically transported a hundred miles away. The quiet was deeper here, the sunlight more golden.

"I found intimate congress with men worth a casual investigation," Stephen went on. "I find parasols, guns, poisons, cannon, lifts, anatomy, locomotives, canals, codes, alchemy, locks, clocks... I find much interesting. Endymion was genuinely attracted to *me*—a nearly incomprehensible notion, I know—while I was mostly tired of earls' daughters groping me under the card table. My darling Jenny will always hold a place in my heart, while Andy... I am fond of him. In answer to your question, I do not *prefer* men in the sense you allude to, but I have enjoyed a passing hour or two with a specific few fellows."

And Abigail sensed Stephen would tell her if his interest was more than avid and lusty curiosity. That degree of honesty was attractive, also troubling.

He steered the gig up onto the verge, which was carpeted with fallen leaves. "I have shocked myself."

"I can keep a confidence, my lord. My livelihood depends upon it."

He drew the horse to a halt. "I have shocked myself because I do not part with confidences ever—at all. That business with de Beauharnais.... I was eighteen, he was twenty-two. Sophisticated men of the world, or so we thought ourselves. I don't discuss it, don't think of it, don't bring it up when he and I share a meal, which we do every few months. I've never so much as hinted about it to Duncan even when in the dregs, and Duncan has seen me in the dregs many a time."

A gust of wind stirred the carpet of leaves, a dry, chilly sound, though the sun was warm and the grass a lush green.

"I have not been entirely forthright with you," Abigail said. She had deliberately misled him, which had cost her the past three nights' sleep.

"Are you married, Abigail? Are you Stapleton's runaway marchioness? His illegitimate daughter? He's a tiny cockerel, but my own father wasn't nearly as tall as I am. Please tell me you aren't married."

Lord Stephen seemed genuinely distressed, and Abigail was genuinely ashamed. "If I had a husband, would you put aside our sham engagement before it's announced?"

"No, but I'd keep my lips and hands to myself. The occasional determinedly straying wife has overcome my gentlemanly scruples—I've admitted as much—but your vows would be genuine and sincere. You would not stray. You might deal severely with a husband who disappointed you, but you would not stray."

"I am not married, but neither do I deserve your good opinion of me."

"I will be the judge of that. Whatever frolic or wrong turn you've kept to yourself, you'd best out with it. Quinn,

Duncan, and the duchesses are doubtless conferring, and they will have questions for us. We need some leverage over Stapleton, and if he has leverage over you... Well, forewarned and all that."

Why can't we be just a couple in love enjoying a pretty autumn day? Why must we be two people with complicated pasts and no future?

"The letters Stapleton wants," Abigail said, "I've read every one. I have nearly memorized them."

"I admire your thoroughness."

"Thoroughness has nothing to do with it. I was a fool."

Lord Stephen picked up the reins and stared off into the trees. "Did you steal the letters? Steal them for a client, perhaps?"

"I had no need to steal them. They were sent to me, and they belong to me. Stapleton has no right to them." No right to cut up her peace and wreak havoc in her life.

His lordship propped his boot on the fender. The breeze stirred again and a shower of freshly fallen leaves twirled to the grass. He said nothing for a long moment, then sent Abigail a faintly puzzled glance.

"*Champlain* was your lover. That sniffing hound charmed his way under your skirts, put his false promises to you in writing, and now Stapleton thinks to destroy the evidence of his son's rutting. Was there a child, Abigail?"

She shook her head.

"Abigail?" Stephen spoke her name gently as he tucked an embroidered handkerchief into her hand. "The damned bounder is dead. I can't call him out, and I no longer duel. Talk to me."

He slipped an arm around her shoulders, a shocking presumption in public, no matter how secluded the path, and Abigail leaned into him.

"I was so happy. Champlain had promised to have a very important discussion with me as soon as he returned from his latest trip to the Continent—a discussion of highly personal matters, he said. Champlain called himself Mr. Richard Champion when I knew him, the man of business for a great lord whom discretion forbade him to name. I was too overjoyed to question anything he did or said. Everything I'd ever wished for—a devoted husband, a family, a home of my own—I was to have it all, at last. I was about five months along when he returned from Paris. He wrote to me, but I wasn't to write to him, so I told him in person. I expected him to share my joy and have the banns cried."

"I take it back. I will kill him even if he's already dead. I knew Champlain, I know his widow. He could have plundered any number of willing citadels. He should not have trifled with you."

"Oh, he *loved* me. Said so himself, wrote the words many times. I only learned he had a wife after I'd conceived. He loved his wife too, and would never give her cause to regret their marriage. But what did it matter that he was married when he would cheerfully *set me up* in my own establishment and make sure the child wanted for nothing?"

"I hope you hit him, Abigail. I hope you kicked him right in his courtesy title."

So fierce, for a man who couldn't kick anybody. "I almost burned his letters. *Mon petit agneau chéri* and *Mein liebstes Häschen*... As if I could be anybody's dearest little lamb or favorite bunny rabbit. I should have burned them. I lost the baby a month later. A stillborn boy."

The words were simple, the emotions complicated. She had eventually been relieved not to face endless scandal, not to visit illegitimacy on her firstborn. But the relief had been tiny, belated, and guilty—also vastly outweighed by sorrow.

"You kept the letters to punish yourself, didn't you?" Stephen stroked her shoulder, as if they had all the time and privacy in the world. "You kept them as a reproach, and you became an inquiry agent because you wanted to preserve other young women from having to pay for trusting the wrong man."

Perhaps she had. Abigail had never considered her motivations, beyond keeping a roof over her head and maintaining her independence.

"Champlain died within two years," she said, "and destroying the letters seemed overly dramatic. They are mostly travelogues of his gallivanting on the Continent. Fine beer here, excellent wine there, an impressive violinist at some comtesse's chateau. That should have told me something."

Stephen hugged her, a quick squeeze about the shoulders, then took up the reins. "He was a shallow, vain, overly indulged heir. They are thick on the ground and a disgrace to the peerage. I am sorry about the child, Abigail. You grieved that loss irrespective of Champlain's stupidity."

Nobody had consoled her for the loss of the child, nobody had even known of it until this moment—nobody except Champlain and a grim-faced, taciturn midwife.

"I grieve," Abigail said, as the horse toddled on. "I grieve, but I don't rage as much as I used to."

"That's like my knee," Lord Stephen said. "The damned thing won't get any better, and it probably will get worse. Bloody unfair, pardon my language, but there's nothing to be done about it. I sulk and rage, then get on with the next experiment, not that a bad knee and a lost child are of the same magnitude. Did you name the baby?"

"A stillborn child cannot be baptized."

The gig tooled along through the pretty afternoon, the gleaming surface of the Serpentine winking through the trees. Like Lord Stephen, Abigail had shocked herself by reposing this confidence in another.

"I named him Winslow Trueblood Abbott. Trueblood was my mother's maiden name." Abigail had never spoken her son's name aloud before, never written it except on the walls of her heart.

Stephen collected the reins in one hand, and linked the fingers of his free hand with Abigail's. "That is a fine name, very Quaker and upright. I like it. Any boy would be proud to have such a name."

The park was deserted, save for a young woman feeding the waterfowl. Abigail was sitting too close to Stephen, clutching his handkerchief, and holding hands with him too. They might have been mistaken for any besotted couple, except the situation was worse than that.

She liked him. She *trusted* him, and she liked him enormously.

Chapter Seven

"I'm having my portrait done." Harmonia, Lady Champlain, made that announcement at breakfast, the only time she was reliably in her father-in-law's company. Lord Stapleton came to the nursery occasionally, and she served as his hostess at formal entertainments, but the marquess was a busy, busy man.

And a right pain in the arse too, to quote his late son.

"I suppose it's time," the marquess said, folding over the newspaper and laying it flat beside his plate. "The boy has long since been breeched. A portrait with his mama ought to be hung in the gallery. Pass the toast."

Harmonia was the entire length of the table away from her father-in-law, but he expected her to step and fetch like an unpaid scullery maid. When Champlain had been alive, he'd been able to jolly her past her frustrations with Stapleton. Champlain had been a fellow traveler on the journey to wrest pleasure from the dull business of waiting for Stapleton to die.

How was it Harmonia could miss such a frivolous, self-indulgent husband more each year? She aimed a smile at the liveried footman standing at the sideboard—Wilbur, and a lovely fellow he was too—and Wilbur set the toast rack at the marquess's elbow.

"I can ask de Beauharnais to take on a second commission," she said, "of me and Nicky, but I am having my own portrait done first."

Stapleton looked up from his steak. "You aren't exactly in the first blush of youth, Harmonia. Why memorialize the ravages of time?"

When the marquess peered down his nose like that, he looked like an arrogant ferret. "I am barely six-and-twenty, sir. You are twice my age, and you had your portrait done last year." De Beauharnais had pronounced the result flattering and workmanlike, for he was too much of a gentleman to criticize a fellow artist.

Endymion was nothing if not diplomatic, which was why Harmonia—who was closer to eight-and-twenty, truth be told—wanted him doing her portrait. That, and he doubtless needed the money.

"I could remarry," Harmonia said, pouring herself a second cup of chocolate. She ought not to indulge—her dresses were still larger than they'd been before she'd carried Nicky—but joys in her life were few, and a cup of hot chocolate was prominent among them.

"Remarry?" Stapleton chewed his steak. "Yes, I suppose you could. Remarry whomever and wherever you please, in fact. Marry an American. They're a lusty bunch, I'm told. The boy stays with me, though. The boy will always stay with me."

Stapleton's authority over Nicky was not quite absolute. Champlain, bless him for an occasional flash of rebellion, had proclaimed before witnesses that Nicky was to grow up under his mother's loving guidance, and in her household. He'd specified in his will that during Nicky's minority, Harmonia was to have a London residence if she so desired, but he'd failed to spell out details other than that. Stapleton was the child's guardian, and thus Stapleton held the legal reins.

Harmonia loved her son to distraction, but much more of Stapleton's dismissiveness and meddling and she would be tempted to do Papa-in-Law an injury.

"I'm taking the carriage out this afternoon," she said. The weather was still fine enough to enjoy a day of shopping and paying calls.

"No, you are not. I have committee meetings to attend. Where's the butter?"

"Beside the toast." Stapleton was being petty, forcing Harmonia to either remain at home on a sunny day or take the second coach and advertise to all and sundry that Lady Champlain was a tolerated fixture in her father-in-law's household.

"Don't frown, Harmonia. It emphasizes your wrinkles."

"I have dimples, not wrinkles." Champlain had assured her of that many times.

"Whatever they are, they are unattractive. If you insist on behaving disagreeably, perhaps you ought to remove to the dower house."

The dower house was a moldering wreck on the Yorkshire dales. The dowager marchionesses of Stapleton went there to die in peace. Harmonia had been forced to spend the entire Season at the family seat in Yorkshire, because Stapleton had decreed that Nicky ought to learn to appreciate the ancestral pile from a young age.

"During Nicky's minority," she said, "I am to have the use of a London property of my own, should I decide to leave Stapleton House. The settlements are quite clear on that, and so was Champlain's will."

Stapleton put down his knife and fork and patted his lips with his table napkin. "Shall I have the solicitors find you a house? A woman dwelling alone won't need much space."

Meaning, a mother forbidden to live with her son. "And what would you do for a hostess, my lord? All those political dinners don't plan themselves, and you would have a very hard time without the gossip and rumor I collect on your behalf. As you've aged and become unable to manage the grouse moors and hunting parties, your reliance on my intelligence has only increased."

Harmonia never felt so much like a whore as she did pouring out for the wives of other peers, particularly the political wives. They all played a game, exchanging opinions on fashion while subtly conveying questions about this bill or that report. A question could hide a potential concession on an important vote, while a smile might signal acquiescence in some complicated exchange of favors.

The whole tedious, fraught dance bored Harmonia witless, but political gossip was her only means of exercising any influence over Stapleton. For the sake of Nicky's future, Harmonia would pour oceans more tea and preside over hundreds more gossipy dinners.

"I can still sit a horse, Harmonia," Stapleton muttered, finishing his ale. "And I've seen enough of Yorkshire of late. I really am considering opening up the dower house. Nicholas will be ready for public school in a year or two, and your role in his life will all but end. What Champlain saw in you, I do not know."

Nicky would not be among the poor little wretches sent off to Eton to starve and shiver his way through a brutalized childhood masquerading as an education.

"Champlain left explicit instructions that his son was not to be sent to public school until age thirteen at least. Nicky is to have governesses until age six, then tutors and governors acceptable to me. I have already begun considering candidates for the tutors' posts. Pass the toast, my lord. If you are not having any, I would like some."

Stapleton rose. "The choice of tutors will ultimately be mine, though you are free to interview whatever handsome young men you please. A reducing diet might do you some good, Harmonia. Nobody likes a woman running to fat."

"Champlain liked me because I am not mean, possessive, vain, or greedy—I was a refreshing change from the company to be had under this roof, in other words. I valued many of the same qualities in him, though how he came by them, I do not know. I wish you a lovely day, your lordship."

She saluted with her cup of chocolate, because even Stapleton would not argue with his late son's express wishes while a footman stood by. Champlain had been a terrible husband in many regards, but he'd been a good friend and—bless him, bless him—a loving father.

When Stapleton departed—without bowing to the lady of the house, of course—Wilbur brought Harmonia the toast and butter and laid the newspaper beside her plate.

"Will you and his little lordship be having a picnic for your nooning, my lady?"

"What a lovely idea. I believe we shall. Please send word to the nursery and have Nanny join us. If Mr. de Beauharnais should call, you can show him to the garden as well."

The worst part of being a widow wasn't the political nonsense, and wasn't even Stapleton's nasty, pinchpenny attitude. The worst part was the loneliness. Champlain had abandoned her for weeks at a time to swive and drink his way across France or the Low Countries, but she'd had his returns to look forward to and her own amusements to divert her.

Perhaps it was time to find another diversion—well past time—and if Stapleton wanted his steady supply of political gossip and tattle, he'd save his complaints and insults for his long-suffering mistress.

"We were seen in the park the other day," Stephen said, "and word of your arrival in London will doubtless reach Stapleton shortly."

Abigail looked well rested to him, but then, she was attired in a dress of soft rose velvet, a cream shawl wrapped around her shoulders. The color and cut of the dress flattered her and hinted subtly at her curves. She seemed at home in the Walden family parlor, Jane's big black Alsatian canine reclining at her feet.

"That's good, then, that we were seen?"

"The sooner the gossip begins, the sooner Stapleton will know you've dodged his snares in York." *I missed you.* Stephen settled into the place beside her on the sofa and resisted the impulse to take her hand. "How are Quinn and Jane treating you?"

"Splendidly. Matilda is giving me chess lessons, and Elizabeth is making me the heroine of her next great literary adventure. I grew up with only my father—visits to extended family were awkward and few—and having all these friendly people around... I envy you your family, my lord."

"They are good folk."

Abigail stroked the dog's head, and Wodin, being a shameless beggar where female affection was concerned, sat up and put his chin on Abigail's knee.

"He knows I miss Malcolm," she said. "Dogs are such comfortable companions."

And walking a dog on a pretty day would be a pleasant outing for a lady and her doting swain, except Stephen could not manage a cane, a leash, and a rambunctious beast, much less all of that and a lady on his arm.

"You should know that Champlain's widow is biding here in London along with Stapleton. Harmonia likes Town, and her son is also under Stapleton's roof."

Abigail's caresses to the dog's ears paused. "Harmonia?"

"Lady Champlain and I are acquainted. I was counted among her *cavalieri serventi* at one point."

"What is she like?"

How in flaming perdition to answer such a question? "She's pragmatic, tolerant, not-bad-looking if you prefer petite blondes, a devoted mother, sometimes funny, and occasionally bitter."

Wodin put a large paw on Abigail's knee. She gently replaced it on the floor. "You like Lady Champlain."

"I do. You probably would too." *If her husband hadn't abused your trust, got you with child, and broken your heart.* "I've been meaning to ask you something."

Abigail went on petting the dog, who seemed to be grinning at Stephen. "Ask."

"Where are the letters?"

She rose, leaving Wodin looking bereft. He settled to the rug, his chin on his paws, ten stone of poor, abandoned puppy.

"I don't know."

Of all the answers Stephen could have anticipated—stuffed into a mattress, sent to the Quaker aunties, held in a safe, buried in the garden—*I don't know* had not been among them.

"I beg your pardon?"

"I had them for years. For a time, I read them nigh daily. Sometimes, I would take them out and hold them, trace the handwriting, sniff them, and imagine I caught a hint of Champlain's scent, but I moved past that. Then I'd read them on the anniversary of the day I lost the baby. The anniversary of my father's death, my mother's death. I stopped crying every time I read them. I stopped reading them all from start to finish, and instead browsed one or two...."

Abigail stood by the bow window that overlooked the garden, tall, straight, dry-eyed, while Stephen absorbed what she wasn't saying.

She had known repeated, grievous loss. She had not simply given her heart to Champlain, she had fallen for him body and soul. If Stephen lived to be a hundred and wrote letters to every woman he'd ever admired, none of those ladies would treasure his words as Abigail had treasured Champlain's maunderings.

A fine wine, a talented violinist… mere travelogues with some smarmy endearment appended for form's sake, and Abigail had counted those letters among her most precious possessions. What would it be like to so thoroughly claim a woman's allegiance that even casual notes became holy relics?

"When did you last see the letters?" *And won't you please come sit beside me again?*

"I had them in the spring," Abigail said, turning her back on the window. "I know I had them in April, because the baby died in April and I read over the last letter to mark the occasion."

"Did Champlain know you'd lost the child?"

"He did. He sent me a bank draft after our last… after we argued. A sizable sum. I was insulted and never deposited it. A week after I miscarried, I sent it back with a few lines of explanation. He did not reply, which I considered decent of him. By then I wanted nothing to do with him, and within two years, he was dead. I learned later than he'd left a child behind, a very young, legitimate son."

"Champlain sent you a bank draft." Abigail had said that almost casually.

"Yes, a substantial amount."

Stephen had always struggled with his temper, particularly in adolescence, when other boys were gaining height and muscle, and he was becoming yet more awkward and visibly unsound. He had enough experience containing his rages that he could speak somewhat calmly.

"Champlain bestirred himself to spend three minutes affixing his name to a piece of paper. A bank draft. Does a *bank draft* check under a boy's bed at night to make sure Old Scratch isn't lurking there to steal an unsuspecting little fellow away in his sleep?"

Abigail's expression had become wary. "I beg your pardon?"

"Does a *bank draft* explain to a lad that some words, no matter how much swagger they convey, are never used before the ladies?"

"My lord?"

"Does a *bank draft* read tales to a boy of brave knights on their destriers or magical unicorns whose horns can cure all ills? Does a *bank draft* give a child affection, love, a sense of his place in the world? A *bank draft*. Bloody hell."

Abigail regarded him from a distance of several yards across a sea of consternation. "I would think that a man raised in want of coin would value financial responsibility in a parent."

"You were insulted by that bank draft," Stephen retorted, "because you know that coin alone does not raise a child. Quinn used to leave his wages with Althea. He'd sneak around to wherever we were begging or make stupid bird calls outside the window until she could slip away. We'd have food for a few days. Lucky us."

"You consider yourself unlucky to have an older brother taking an interest in your welfare?"

A logical question, but what did a lame boy know of logic? "He left us with *Jack Wentworth*, Abigail. Time after time, he'd scuttle away, back to his grave digging or his footman's job, knowing that Jack was using his fists and worse on us. I begged Quinn to take me with him, but he said to stay where I had a roof over my head, to stay and look out for my sisters."

Begging for food had never been half so corrosive to Stephen's soul as begging Quinn not to go, begging him to take them with him.

"And you held up your side of the bargain," Abigail said. "You plainly took your sisters' welfare to heart in a way your brother could not. Quinn provided the coin, you provided the safety, though I shudder to think of the toll that arrangement took on such a young and defenseless boy."

Abigail was so refreshingly practical, and her view of the matter—Stephen doing the part Quinn could not—hadn't occurred to him previously. He'd reconciled himself to having committed murder, but in a situation where nobody dared interfere with a habitually violent father, perhaps that constituted a child's form of self-defense?

A merciful God might see it thus. Perhaps. Maybe.

"I would do it again," Stephen said, "if I heard Jack making the same plans for Althea and Constance, I'd do it again in a trice. Quinn was off somewhere on a job that was expected to last weeks. I planned to drink the poison myself at first. If Jack would sell my sisters to a brothel, what fate would he plan for me? Then it occurred to me that the poison might have another use."

And what a wicked, hopeful thought that had been. "I recall gazing at the gin bottle in its place of honor on the windowsill, the light shining through the blue glass, obscuring the color of the contents. Jack was not a delicate drinker. He guzzled in quantity. Althea and Constance were out, unaware of the danger, and there I was, alone with my conscience and a quantity of rat poison." Not a perfect solution, because rat poison did not take immediate effect.

But a solution nonetheless.

"How fortunate for your sisters that you did not go off into service with your brother."

Fortunate for them. Althea had likely figured out the sequence of events, but she'd never mentioned it, and neither had Stephen.

He'd recounted the whole to Abigail, along with all the sordid details. *What* had got into him? "Suffice it to say that bank drafts do not impress me when paternal duty is at issue, and this digression is hardly relevant to the instant topic. When did you realize the letters were missing?"

And can we please forget I ever mentioned Jack Wentworth?

Abigail drew the shawl up around her shoulders, though the day was mild. "I first realized the letters were gone in June," she replied, clearly willing to leave the topic of patricide behind. "Another anniversary—my father's death—and at first I thought I'd misplaced them. I asked my companion about them. We searched the entire premises and found nothing. The staff professed ignorance, and they've been with me for years, so I believe them. Nothing else, not so much as a hairpin, has ever gone missing."

Stephen patted the cushion beside him, wanting Abigail closer for reasons that didn't bear examining. "We must think this through. How do you know Stapleton didn't take them?"

"Because his attempts on me and my household were later in the summer. I have wondered if one of his subordinates didn't steal the letters with intent to blackmail the marquess." She settled beside Stephen, cozily close. "But why hold them this long? Stapleton is wealthy, and he could pay handsomely for a lot of old drivel."

Stephen did take her hand and Wodin visually reproached him. "*Are* they drivel?"

"I have seen enough love letters to know Champlain was no Byron."

"Nonetheless, Stapleton is apparently concerned they will fall into the wrong hands and reflect badly upon the late earl." Though that explanation bore further thought, because Stapleton himself was no Puritan and never had been. Nobody expected strict fidelity of a wealthy, married peer or his charming son.

"I can pretty much reconstruct the letters," Abigail said. "If I've seen something in handwriting, I can often recall it exactly. In my profession, such a skill comes in handy, and I read the letters many times."

"Don't admit that ability to anybody else. Quinn will hire you to spy on other banks for him."

"I think your brother dislikes me."

Stephen resisted the urge to kiss Abigail's knuckles and settled for wrapping her hand in both of his.

"Quinn is like that hound. He looks fierce, and he can be fierce, but it's mostly appearances. He gets down on all fours in the nursery and roars like a bear for the children's entertainment. When Jane is expecting, Quinn rubs her feet and her back by the hour. He reads treatises on childbirth, though he does not like to read anything that's more words than figures."

To honestly praise Quinn's role as head of the family was a relief. Quinn had clearly learned from Jack's awful example, and that was some consolation.

Abigail patted Stephen's knee. "Your brother is protective of you. He showed me your old room."

What the hell? "And?"

"You had read more books by age eighteen than I have seen in my life."

"When a fellow spends most of his time in a damned chair, reading happens."

"Walden admires you for your book learning. He doesn't understand how anybody could devour that much knowledge, and he respects you for it."

Abigail no longer wore her rosemary hedgehog scent. Jane must have put a stop to that. The new fragrance was soft, gardenia with a citrusy top note and a cinnamon finish. Complicated, warm, feminine...perfect for Abigail Abbott.

"Quinn *said* he admires me?"

"The admiration was in his voice, in his gaze as he peered around at shelves and shelves of books, some in

German, some in French, many in Latin. He said you are a mechanical genius. I was flattered to be allowed into the sanctum of your adolescence and found two books on poisons that I would like to borrow."

"You may have them, of course. Quinn is a financial genius, by the way. He reads the paper, stares off into space, moves money around, and the money has babies and grandchildren and great-grandchildren. I am more pragmatic, investing in the inventions that I know will be of use."

Abigail withdrew her hand. "You made a portable cannon that could swivel three hundred and sixty degrees. Walden showed me the plans."

Just what a lapsed Quaker lady did not need to see. "I've also patented firing mechanisms, safety triggers, bullet molds, rifling processes, bomb designs, cranes, lifts, folding stairways...some of it's useless, some of it's lucrative. Might we get back to the letters?"

"You are quite enterprising. Walden was warning me."

Enterprising was good, wasn't it? "Subtlety is not Quinn's style. His warnings are blunt, sincere, and unmistakable. What would he be warning you about?"

"Not to trifle with you, not to try to make a pretend engagement into something it cannot be."

God spare me from meddling siblings. "What if I'd *like* to be trifled with? What if you'd like a bit of trifling in return? We are adults, Abigail, and I'm a first-rate trifler. One of the best in the realm. I *like* trifling, and because one doesn't need two good knees to go about it, I've made something of a study of trifling in all its glorious permutations."

She patted his bad knee, which was not well advised when the subject under discussion was *trifling*.

"You have such a keen wit. I like that about you."

He kissed her cheek. "I am not jesting, and Quinn was not threatening. He was meddling. He thinks he's being subtle, but he's about as subtle as Wodin introducing himself to a cured ham. So I read a lot of books. What sort of woman is impressed with that?"

This time, her pat was more of a stroke along his thigh. "I am. I love books. I love that you used your disability as inspiration for the nurturing of your intellect."

Love. Abigail Abbott had used the word *love*, and in connection with Stephen's accursed knee. Perhaps the infernal letters of doom had best stay hidden for a good long while.

"You developed your inquiry business on the strength of a young woman's rotten experience with romance. I don't like that, but I admire it."

Wodin rose and put his chin on her knee again.

"Does he want to go out?"

The bloody dog wants to steal you away from me. "He can go out whenever he pleases. I fashioned a swinging door off the pantry, like a hinged portcullis. Constance's cats and Wodin are free to visit the garden as they need to. Please tell me the rest of what you know about the letters, Abigail, or I will succumb to the lure of my impure thoughts."

Her next stroke along his thigh—a caress, really—began an inch higher. "Impure thoughts?"

His thoughts regarding Abigail were both pure and

impure. She'd lost a child, for God's sake, grieved in solitude, and climbed from a pit of sorrow to fashion a life on her own terms. She solved other people's delicate problems with a combination of cunning, tenacity, and discretion.

That she was as physically attractive as she was formidable created a tangle of esteem, desire, curiosity, and some vague yearning Stephen could not name in any language.

"Lustful thoughts," he said, petting her knee. "Naughty, delicious, naked, wild, lascivious, hot, erotic...Trifle with me, Abigail, please."

He was growing aroused, under his brother's roof, the parlor door open, and the damned dog giving him censorious looks.

"I want to be alone with you," he muttered, stealing another kiss. "I miss you. I dream of you, and any minute, my darling sister-in-law will march in here, a pair of smirking blond footmen pushing the tea cart behind her. I will die a thousand deaths of frustrated longing while swilling scandal broth and getting biscuit crumbs on my cravat."

Abigail gave his knee the most luscious, maddening *squeeze*, and then sat back. "Now is not the time or the place for your courting nonsense, my lord. We face a conundrum."

Where to swive without being interrupted was always a puzzle. "We do?"

"If I don't have those letters and Stapleton doesn't have them, who does? How did that person obtain them, and what will he do with them? Why steal the letters in the first place when they are merely sentimental effusions, years old, and they don't even mention me by name?"

When Stephen fell, he usually experienced a moment of knowing he was toppling before the hard reality of the cobblestones or floor connected with his person. That instant of rage (to be sent sprawling again), dread (cobblestones hurt, carpeted floors weren't much better), and resignation lasted a small eternity.

So too, when Abigail sat back, all polite composure and logical pronouncements, did a small eternity pass.

Stephen's body grasped that yet another occasion of arousal was about to end in disappointment, even as his mind acknowledged that the situation with the letters was troubling.

Between those reactions lay the truth in his heart: He desired Abigail Abbott. She was formidable and luscious. Her touch was lovely and bold, she wasn't put off by honest arousal, and she had reposed her darkest secret into Stephen's keeping.

What smacked him as abruptly as landing on hard cobbles was the reality that he would die for this woman. She had heard his worst confessions, taken them quite in stride, and even seen his decisions in a compassionate light.

He would lay down his life to keep her safe, and, more than that, he would kill for her too.

"Stapleton is tithing to the Temple of Venus in the person of Ophelia Marchant," Ned Wentworth said. "He plays his games in the Lords, and he haggles with the trades, but I couldn't find any evidence that he is being blackmailed."

As best Abigail could tell, Ned Wentworth wasn't a Wentworth by birth, but he had in common with the family a practical approach to life's seamier challenges. He was dark-haired, slim, and of an age to be recently down from university. His attire was natty to the point of dandyism, while his gaze held the shrewdness of a young man who'd matriculated in a hard school.

"Gaming debts?" Lord Stephen asked.

"He's too busy fleecing John Bull in the Lords to sit about his clubs dicing," Ned replied.

Various Wentworths were lounging about the library, Their Graces on the sofa, Duncan and Matilda on a love seat. Stephen had the reading chair by the fire, his foot on a hassock, while Ned had the seat behind the desk and Abigail the second reading chair.

"What about recent disruptions of routine?" Abigail asked. "Is his mistress of long-standing? Has Stapleton changed where he attends divine services? Does he no longer go to the theater, or has he discharged any staff?"

"You are thorough," Ned said, "and those are good questions, but we don't have all the answers yet. I can tell you Lady Champlain and Lord Stapleton don't get along, don't occupy the same box at the opera. One of our fellows chatted with Stapleton's head maid over a pint. Stapleton is threatening to dispatch her ladyship to the north again after she spent the Season at the family seat, but the settlements say she must be housed in London if she so desires."

"What of her ladyship?" Abigail said, getting up to pace. "Has she undertaken any new relationships lately, does she have debts, could she be expecting a child?"

The duchesses exchanged a look.

"My professional activities don't permit me to shy away

from human foibles," Abigail said. "Somebody has those letters, and Stapleton has decided that now—years after Champlain's death—the letters have significance."

Stephen had put Abigail's situation to his family in plain terms, saving her the recitation: Champlain had implied a promise of marriage, though Abigail hadn't realized he was dissembling until it was too late. Champlain's letters had gone missing several months ago, and Stapleton had started attempting to steal them from about the same time. Stephen had omitted mention of a child, for which Abigail was grateful.

If anybody thought Abigail an idiot for succumbing to Champlain's charms, they were too well bred to show it.

"Do you have copies of any of the letters or can you recall portions verbatim?" Duncan Wentworth asked. "Sometimes codes can be secreted in the most innocuous-sounding prose. When Stephen and I traveled on the Continent, we were approached several times with requests to carry sensitive documents, though they were always described as reports, testaments, or simple correspondence."

Stephen stuffed a pillow under his knee. "Duncan would not allow me to involve myself in any intrigues. I could have been a dashing spy, but, alas for me, my self-appointed conscience objected." He lounged in his reading chair, not a care in the world, when twenty minutes earlier he'd been declaring himself the best trifler in all of England.

I will miss him. Abigail set that thought firmly aside, and focused on Duncan's suggestion. "You think Champlain was involved in some matter of national security?"

Stephen was hard to read, Walden nearly impossible to read, and Duncan's self-possession put sphinxes to shame.

"I have no idea," Duncan replied. "Stephen described his lordship as a fribble, but a good spy would know how to impersonate a fribble."

Abigail considered what she knew of Champlain. "He *was* a fribble, the genuine article. No clandestine operative intent on the king's business would have dallied with a gunsmith's daughter."

Ned spoke up from behind his desk. "Guns are items of interest to most governments. Was your papa a gunsmith or, like His Pestilence here, a designer of weapons?"

Stephen blew Ned a kiss. "No need to be jealous of my tinkering, Neddy. I will never be the pickpocket you are."

Ned threw a glass paperweight at Stephen's head, which Stephen caught with one hand. Something interesting passed between them, part affection, part threat.

"My father," Abigail said, "could do simple clock repairs or fix a broken clasp on a bracelet, but he was a gunsmith, not an artificer. The mechanisms of handguns have evolved quickly in recent years. He preferred to work on the fowling pieces and long guns because the hardware hasn't changed as much. Many a squire still carries a Brown Bess. Who are the most frequent callers at Lord Stapleton's house?"

Ned consulted a list. "He has political dinners from time to time, a lot of fat, bleating Tories. Socially, Lady Champlain makes the usual rounds. Lately she's been inclined more toward the artists and poets, and the staff says she's to sit for a portrait for that fop de Beauharnais."

"Enough, Ned." Two words, casually rendered, from His Grace of Walden. "*That fop* did Her Grace's portrait, and I rather like it. I'd have him do yours except you can't sit still long enough. What do we know about security at Stapleton's town house?"

"I can answer that," Stephen said, "having been a caller on many occasions. The staff is on the older side, probably hired in the late marchioness's day. The butler likely saw Queen Anne crowned, and the house isn't exactly a fortress."

"Now you're a second-story man," Ned muttered. "St. Nicholas, pray for us."

"The garden wall is about five feet high," Stephen went on, tossing the paperweight back to Ned. "The windows on the north side of the house are overdue for a good glazing. Our Neddy could be in and out in half a tick."

"A quarter," Ned said. "The cook doesn't lock the kitchen door in case the tradesmen show up when she's kneading the bread dough or stirring a pot of porridge first thing in the day. The head maid says Cook has a follower, meaning the grocer's boy probably comes mooning about after the household's abed."

"I won't have crimes committed on my behalf," Abigail said. "We needn't contemplate any housebreaking. Stapleton doesn't have the letters, or he didn't two weeks ago."

"You don't know that," Stephen replied, lifting his foot off the hassock. "Stapleton might have them and believe there are more. He might have stolen them from you and suspect you stole them back, when instead one of his political detractors has them. We need to take a closer look at his lordship's domestic situation."

Abigail cast a look at the duke and duchess, expecting Her Grace of Walden to object to housebreaking. Their Graces were *holding hands*, and the duchess was sitting close enough to the duke that their joined hands rested on her thigh.

"We also need to go to the opera," Lord Stephen said, pushing to his feet. "Stapleton favors the opera. Jane, does Miss Abbott have suitable attire for Friday night's performance?"

Ned rose as well. "I hate the damned opera."

"Language, Ned," Her Grace murmured. "Miss Abbott will be appropriately dressed for an evening engagement."

"Neddy, if you'd rather not attend," Stephen said, "I will escort Miss Abbott unassisted. Stapleton should have word by now of her arrival in London, and I don't want him getting any untoward ideas."

"I have an untoward idea," Ned replied.

Stephen smiled. "I knew I could count on you."

"No housebreaking," Abigail said, though clearly her words were falling on deaf male ears. "We have no reason to believe Stapleton has the letters."

"We aren't looking for the letters," Ned said. "We're looking for why he's desperate to get his manicured, beringed paws on them."

"Lady Champlain does not favor the opera generally," Stephen said, "and she stays in when Stapleton attends—you are not to seduce her, Ned. She has gallants aplenty for that. I must take myself off for a spot of contemplation. Miss Abbott, I'd like to escort you on a round of the shops tomorrow. You'll want your own pair of opera glasses."

Abigail had no intention of spending a single farthing on opera glasses she would use only once. "What time should I be ready, my lord?"

"Walk me to my coach, and we'll sort that out."

That was about as subtle as Wodin's enormous paw on her knee. Abigail excused herself and accompanied Stephen down the steps to the main foyer.

"Ned doubtless knows what he's doing, but I have no wish to impose on your time, my lord, and no interest in enriching Mayfair's shopkeepers."

Stephen took her hand, hung his cane on the edge of the sideboard, braced his back against the wall, and pulled Abigail in close.

"To blazes with the rubbishing shopkeepers, Abigail. To blazes with Stapleton, and if Ned makes sheep's eyes at you one more time, to blazes with him too. You're driving me mad, d'you hear me? Mad."

Then he fused his mouth to hers, wedged his bad knee between her legs, and drove her mad too.

Chapter Eight

"This is half of them," Abigail said. "I can't promise I've recalled them word for word, but I've read them dozens of times. Much of the language is verbatim."

Stephen accepted the copies of the letters and all they represented. "I promise they are safe with me. May I show them to my family?" He tucked them into an inside pocket, though he longed to read them. He would rather keep Abigail's secrets to himself, but only a fool would muddle on without the aid of keen minds eager to help.

"Read them first, then decide. You look splendid."

They held this exchange in the foyer of Quinn's home, for the hour had come to accompany Abigail on a shopping expedition. The outing was for show—Stephen hated shopping and suspected Abigail wasn't much for idling about in commercial venues either.

"I am supposed to look besotted." He'd spent five minutes

choosing a cravat pin and eventually settled on plain gold. "Somebody waits in the carriage whom I'd like you to meet."

Her gaze grew wary. "Not another one of your sneak thieves in dandy's clothing?"

"Neddy is not a sneak thief. He's a loyal and highly skilled family retainer, and I was so jealous of Quinn's affection for him I nearly shot young Ned in the leg. Quinn hugged him, just the once, when Ned was a boy, and I happened to see it. I should not have been spying—Ned would die of mortification if he knew I'd caught that moment—but I was overcome with jealousy."

Stephen was also babbling, prattling like the nervous suitor he almost was.

Abigail took down a cloak from a hook. "My father always had fine words for the ladies who came into his shop. They wore lovely bonnets, had fetching reticules, or were in quite good looks, while I—striving endlessly to learn his trade without even the respect an apprentice is owed—was invisible."

Stephen took the cloak from her and managed to drape it over her shoulders without setting aside his cane.

"Which do you suppose does more damage," he asked, "a violent parent or a parent who treats a child like an invisible servant?"

He fastened the frogs of her cloak, and—glorious moment—she allowed him to perform that courtesy.

"I feel conspicuous in colors," she said, frowning at her reflection in the mirror over the sideboard. "But Her Grace has an eye for fabric, and velvet is durable. Who is this friend I'm supposed to meet?"

Her cloak was brown, for pity's sake, the plainest color Stephen could think of that flattered her coloring, and the richest velvet he could purchase on short notice. The garment had a mere dash of red and purple embroidery on the collar.

"I have brought a gentleman to make your acquaintance," Stephen said. "He comes from good family, and his betters have put the manners on him. He will also safeguard your person at times when I cannot."

Abigail pulled on her gloves. "You insult your brother's footmen. I don't so much as sit in the garden without two of them keeping me in sight at all times."

Stephen would thank Quinn for following orders, or thank Jane. "Footmen cannot sit adoringly at your feet while you read salacious novels by the hour."

Abigail glanced around, then pressed a kiss to Stephen's cheek. "You are so naughty. I adore that about you." She took a straw hat from the sideboard but didn't put it on.

"One tries." Stephen opened the door and Abigail sailed through ahead of him. She took his arm when he joined her at the top of the portico's steps and let him escort her to the coach waiting under the porte cochere.

"I miss you," she said, staring at the coach door as she donned her straw hat. "I watch Their Graces, always touching each other. I see Duncan sitting with an arm around Matilda's shoulders. Your family is affectionate and I..."

They hadn't always been affectionate. Far from it. "And you?"

"I have regrets," Abigail said. "Introduce me to your friend, and let's be on our way."

Stephen sent up a prayer, opened the coach door, and stepped back. "Hercules, come."

The beast descended with all the dignity of a duke, his plumed tail waving gently. He sniffed at Stephen's hand, then at Abigail's, then sat as if he awaited the formal introductions that must follow with any new acquaintance.

"*This* is your friend?" Abigail said. "*This* splendid fellow is your friend?"

Hercules panted gently at her side, his enormous head coming to her hip.

"He's a Danish-bred mastiff, sold to me by an earl's son who has a way with canines. Hercules can impersonate a lapdog or an imperial guard, depending on your commands."

Abigail scratched Hercules behind the ears, and Hercules sent her an adoring look. "He's not a lapdog. Gentlemen usually give ladies fussy little lapdogs."

Well, blast and bedamned, Stephen had got it wrong, then. "One doesn't want to be predictable, Abigail, and one does want you to be safe. A lapdog can bark, true enough, but Hercules can take down an intruder. The command is 'Take down,' followed by 'Hold.' His leash manners are impeccable, and he has all that *sit, stay, shake*, and *roll over* nonsense well in hand—or in paw?"

Hercules flicked him an annoyed glance. Reciting commands when twelve stone of noble hound was busy at his flirtations was apparently not the done thing.

Abigail took off her glove, the better to bury her fingers in newly washed fur. Stephen's footmen had threatened to give notice over that job.

"He's really quite splendid," she said. "I love his name. It suits him."

"You don't mind that he's a little big for a lapdog?"

Abigail left off petting her puppy. "I *love* him. I love that you thought of my safety, that you have found a companion for me whose quiet good nature is apparent even on a few minutes' acquaintance. Thank you."

She kissed Stephen's cheek, and if he'd been able to dance a jig, he would have. "You like him, then?"

"I adore him. Nobody gives me gifts, nobody worries about me. I must consider a reciprocal display of affection, for we are a courting couple, are we not?"

They were, and they weren't. "Be honest, Abigail. Willow Dorning always sends his dogs off on trial, and if the canine doesn't suit the owner or the owner doesn't suit the dog, he takes the beast back."

Abigail leaned close. "Hercules is *my* dog now. You cannot have him back, not even when this business with Stapleton is over. A little somnifera would not have slowed Hercules down one bit, would it?"

She aimed that question at the dog, who appeared to reward her faith in him with a toothy smile.

"He's yours," Stephen said. *I am yours too, if that matters.* "Shall we leave Hercules here to get acquainted with Wodin?"

"I suppose we should, but what an impression he would make on the shopkeepers."

Stephen signaled a groom. "Take him around to the back garden, please, and a bone to gnaw on wouldn't go amiss."

Abigail watched the dog trot off, her expression more wistful than one panting, drooling canine deserved. "I will treasure him all of his days, my lord. He is the most thoughtful gift I've ever been given."

Stephen opened the coach door. "Then clearly the wrong people have been giving you gifts. Let's be off."

She climbed in and took the forward-facing seat, a minor victory. Stephen came down beside her and thumped the roof with his fist—once, because a sedate walk would give them a longer period of privacy than a brisk trot.

"I'd like to deposit your letters in my safe before we make our obeisance to Bond Street," he said.

Abigail set her hat on the opposite bench. "They are only approximate copies, my lord."

"If they should fall into the wrong hands, that won't matter. Are we shopping for anything in particular? Handkerchiefs, gloves, scent bottles, or fripperies?"

Abigail took his hand, as if that was simply how couples comported themselves when sharing a coach.

"I have no need for fripperies." She shifted closer. "I love that dog, Stephen Wentworth, and I have missed you."

He'd parted from her less than twenty-four hours ago. They were alone, she was tucked up beside him, and he had missed her too.

He wrapped his arm around her and gently pushed her head to his shoulder. "You must humor me. A gentleman buys his lady-fair fripperies. You could use a spare sword cane, I trust?"

She sighed, she snuggled closer, and Stephen's heart eased in a way he could not describe.

"A new sword cane would be lovely. I was thinking of asking you to design one for me."

He kissed her temple, and launched into a discussion of features necessary for a lady's sword cane to be both attractive and serviceable. By the time they reached his town house, they'd had two arguments and four kissing spells, and he was even more hopelessly in love.

Also as hard as an ironwood sword cane.

Running from the Marquess of Stapleton had seemed like a solution to Abigail, but what sort of future did an inquiry agent have if she couldn't solve her own case? She had agreed to this shopping expedition because she wanted Stapleton to know she was in London, and also—heaven help her—because she wanted to spend more time alone with Lord Stephen.

"The porte cochere isn't only for privacy, is it?" she said, as Lord Stephen handed her down from his coach. "It's to keep the cobbles dry for when you alight."

"Both objectives are important," he said, offering Abigail his arm.

She liked his escort. Whether his bad knee prevented him from hauling a lady about or he was inherently tactful when handling a woman, he had the knack of keeping pace without interfering with Abigail's progress.

"Duncan said you are a demon on horseback. How does that work with an unreliable knee?" She was making conversation lest her mind turn back to their last kiss. Stephen had slipped a hand beneath her cloak to rest his palm against her belly, an oddly intimate touch.

"I love to ride," he replied, holding the door for her. "I love the speed and power and motion."

"But one must put weight in the stirrups at least some of the time." The foyer was deserted, and Abigail made no move to take off her cloak because she wanted Stephen to do that for her.

"The problem isn't putting weight on my knee," he said. "The problem is the joint itself. The horse stabilizes the joint laterally so it never gives out. The bones or ligaments or whatever can't slip to the side when I'm gripping the horse with my legs. My knee for once can support me because the horse supports my knee. I find all this talk of anatomy somewhat…" He fell silent while he undid Abigail's frogs and slid the cloak from her shoulders.

"Somewhat…?" she asked, setting her hat on a hook.

"Somewhat *stirring*." He set his hat and gloves on the sideboard. "I think not of a great, hairy horse, but of a knee—your knee. Of my hand stroking your knee, and what manner of derangement turns the knee into a source of venereous inspiration?"

"Venereous?"

The house was quiet, suggesting the servants were belowstairs or perhaps on their half day.

"Venereous," Stephen replied. "That which excites or stimulates sexual desire."

He stood close enough that Abigail could have stroked her hand over his falls. She didn't dare. "You wanted to put my letters into your safe."

"The safe." He ran a hand through his hair. "Letters. Lest

we forget. This way." He stalked off down the corridor, his cane striking the carpet with particular force.

Abigail followed, noting, not for the first time, the breadth of Stephen's shoulders and the taper of his hips. His clothing was exquisitely well made, but then, so was he. His older brother was more heavily muscled, while Stephen was both lean and strong.

"The safe is in the most prosaic of hiding places," he said, leading Abigail to the study, "in plain sight."

He closed and locked the door, withdrew the letters from his inside coat pocket, and approached a longcase clock built into a corner of the room. He set his cane against his desk and opened the middle compartment of the clock, where nothing but chains or weights should have been. The compartment concealed a combination lock on the face of a steel box.

"Where are the clock parts?" Abigail asked.

"The weights drop behind the safe. There's exactly one-half-inch clearance." He spun tumblers and turned the handle, and the safe opened with a soft click. "I put another safe behind that portrait over the fireplace, and I leave a little money in it, but nothing of any import. Everybody puts their safes in the chimney wall. Can't blame a cracksman for looking there."

"But you didn't want to be predictable. Is there a third safe?"

He stashed the letters inside, shut the door, spun the tumblers, and closed the clock panel. "Abigail, you are a constant source of delight. The house has a total of five safes. Two are decoys, and one only Quinn and I have the combination to. I suspect a gunsmith's daughter could open at least three of them, given enough time."

He was smiling at her with approval and affection.

"I would rather not spend the next hour getting into your safes, my lord. I'd rather plunder treasure of a different sort."

He blinked. "The shops. Right. I am your humble—Abigail?"

She had stepped closer, mindful that he wasn't holding his cane. "*You*," she said. "I want to plunder you."

"Plunder...me."

"Your person. I want to enjoy your intimate favors. This is not a real engagement, and when it ends, I will go back to being York's most boringly dressed inquiry agent, while you..."

"While I?"

She passed him his cane. "While you resume the life of a duke's genius heir, flirting with all the merry widows and straying wives, making fortunes in all the wrong industries, and hiding treasures where nobody will find them. A little trysting with me ought not to impose too much on your busy schedule until you can resume your usual diversions."

He caught her hand when she would have stalked off across the room, for he appeared to regard her proposition with something less than enthusiasm.

Perhaps that was for the best.

"Abigail." He kept hold of her hand. "Is this what you want? An illicit affair with a scapegrace lordling who can't even manage to promenade around a ballroom with you?"

When did anybody, ever, ask Abigail what *she* wanted? "If you aren't inclined, you need only say so, but your kisses have been convincing, and you tell me that honesty characterizes—"

He braced his cane across her bum, grasped an end in each hand, and pulled her closer. "I want you. I want you until I am insensate with longing, until you haunt my dreams and preoccupy my waking thoughts. I had to toss myself off in the damned coach on the way to fetch you. That came out wrong."

"I know what you meant." And the image of him, falls undone, cock rampant, all that velvet, leather, and lace luxury around him while he… "Shall we find a bed?"

Sexual congress did not require a bed, but Abigail would have few enough opportunities to be intimate with Stephen Wentworth. Some awkwardness was unavoidable. Nonetheless, she wanted their memories to be sweet, not of itchy carpet or a hard desk.

"We have a bed," Stephen said, easing the pressure of the cane against her backside. "The sofa folds out, like the benches of a traveling coach, only more commodious." He crossed to the sofa, bent down and released some sort of latch, then gave the bottom cushions a yank. The sofa flattened out into a sizable bed.

"*Et voilà tout*. Shall I undo your hooks, or will we go about this dressed?"

He probably knew eighteen different ways to copulate without removing a single stitch—the wretch.

"We have time. Why not dispense with some clothing?"

Stephen closed his eyes, hands braced on his cane.

"Abigail, you are a woman after my own heart. Come here."

She crossed her arms.

"*Please*, rather. *Please* come here that I might be your lady's maid and finally, finally get my hands and lips and tongue on the luscious abundance of your breasts."

He did more to arouse her with words than Champlain had done with his entire repertoire of loverly overtures. "*Please* suffices. You needn't lapse into erotic flights."

Stephen wiggled his fingers at her. "No second thoughts, Miss Abbott, and one doesn't lapse into flights. One soars. More accurately, two will soar into flights and raptures."

"Such humility about your amatory skills." Abigail crossed the room and turned her back to him. She expected to feel deft fingers undoing her hooks, but nothing happened.

"My lord?"

"I am marshaling my self-control. If a stray bit of tinder were to land on my imagination right now, the Great Fire would be a mere glowing coal by comparison."

Something was afoot with all this prolixity. Not shyness, exactly, but self-consciousness, perhaps?

"My hooks, Stephen, and my stays. Be about it, please, or we will have to go shopping when we could be cavorting instead."

She barely felt his fingers brushing at her nape as he undid the back of her dress. Her stays loosened without any of the usual tugging.

"You have the hands of a safecracker," she said, turning. "Allow me to reciprocate." To stand around in loosened stays and an undone dress in the middle of the day was peculiar and naughty. Abigail liked the daring of it, and made a production out of removing Stephen's cravat pin and sleeve buttons, then his watch and fob.

"Why do you wear silk cravats?" Most men preferred starched linen, though the silk was exquisite to the touch.

"Several frolicsome relationships ago, the other party had a taste for being bound when I used my mouth..." He tipped his chin up, as if consulting with the dragon on the ceiling. "She liked to have her hands tied during certain intimate acts. I could not countenance rope against a lady's wrists, so I took to wearing silk cravats."

Abigail drew the cravat from around his neck. "I see."

"You don't, but if the Deity is merciful to a man about to sin as boldly and joyously as he possibly can, you will soon."

She unbuttoned his waistcoat and shirt, and pushed his coat from his shoulders. "I should take off your boots."

A frisson of wariness flickered in his eyes. "*We* should take off *our* boots, unless you'd like to be rogered while you wear stockings and boots."

Abigail considered it. "Not this time." She pulled the draperies closed on both windows, then shimmied out of her dress and laid it across the desk. Next, she sat on the sofa and unlaced her boots. All the while, Stephen merely watched her, and she ignored the bulge displacing the line of his falls.

"What?" she asked.

"You, sashaying around my study in your shift, boots, and stockings. You are very bold."

She bent to unlace her boots. "And you are shy."

He shrugged out of his waistcoat and pulled his shirt over his head. "Me, shy? My family would be overcome with hilarity to hear that description."

Abigail set her boots aside, undid her garters, and rolled down her stockings. "I want to kiss you, want to shove you to your back and run my hands all over you, but if I stop for that now, I will never get you out of those breeches." She rose from the sofa and held out her hand. "Boots, Stephen."

He sat and held out his bad leg to her first, then the other one. "When we go shopping, I will buy you some chemises that do more to inspire a man's imagination. Every trousseau needs a few dainty negligees and wedding night—"

Abigail straddled his lap and kissed him into silence. They would never have a wedding night, but they could have a consummation. When she sensed hesitance in Stephen's kisses—not delicacy, but a hesitance—she desisted.

"Abigail?"

"I'm marshaling my self-control, and you are being a goose, my lord."

"More of a gander, actually."

"Ganders don't care what their knees look like," she said, standing, "and I don't care what your knee looks like."

He peered around at his study, which now resembled a theater dressing room. Abigail's stockings were draped over the back of the reading chair, her dress adorned the desk. Stephen's waistcoat and shirt were half falling off the bookshelf, and his coat graced the reading table.

"The knee is ugly," he said. "I've tried ignoring it, but then the lady eventually catches sight of the scars, and she's horrified, so I've tried keeping my breeches on, and that limits the opportunities. There's always waiting for dark and moonless nights, but—I hate this."

"You hate being imperfect." Abigail knelt and started on the buttons of his falls. "I'm none too keen on some of my shortcomings either. My breasts are different sizes. I never noticed, until Champlain kindly pointed it out to me."

"He *pointed it out to you*?"

She finished with his falls. "He made something of a study of the matter, and even wanted to measure…It's all ridiculous. Do men go around measuring their cocks?"

"Some of us, figuratively if not literally. Promise me you won't run shrieking for the carriage?"

Abigail wrapped her arms around him and pressed her cheek to his bare chest. "I won't run shrieking to the carriage."

"There's something else. About my canes."

She swiped her tongue across his nipple. "Hmm."

"I can't…you know…unless my cane is within my reach. That feels lovely."

She teased him for a moment, long enough to get herself stirred up—more stirred up—then she sat back. "I will take off my chemise when you remove your breeches."

"Dear God, Abigail, that's rather…Oh, very well. You first."

He'd risen to her challenge, but she had expected no less of him. Taking off her chemise was harder than she'd thought, though. Perhaps one lost the habit of physical intimacy, or perhaps one learned the price of folly. Abigail remained kneeling before Stephen and drew the shift over her head.

"The right one is larger," she said, looking down at her bare breasts.

"Nonsense. They are both perfect."

If Stephen's expression was any indication, they were. "Champlain was an idiot," Abigail said. "Thank you for illuminating that fact. Your breeches, Stephen. Now."

He stood, put a hand on her shoulder, and used her for balance as he stepped out of his breeches and kicked them onto the reading chair.

When she'd risen to stand next to him beside the sofa, he took her hand and bowed. "Miss Abigail Abbott, may I make known to you Lord Stephen Wentworth, in all his abundant natural glory, and more than a bit aroused. Will you please come to bed with me?"

She wrapped her hand around his shaft, which was arrowed straight up along the midline of his taut, muscled belly. "Yes. Yes, absolutely, I will come to bed with you."

"Don't you want to inspect my knee?"

"No. Stephen, I do not want to inspect your perishing knee."

He pulled her close and fell with her straight back onto the sofa.

Stephen did not normally make a fuss about taking off his clothes. He was usually too eager to get to the part about mutual pleasure and bone-deep satisfaction. Abigail Abbott, however, had ambushed him.

He hadn't been able to manufacture subdued lighting, a big bed that sat low enough that no steps were needed to climb into it, a perch for his canes, and other accommodations that freed him to focus on frolicking. Instead he was sprawled on the pulled-out sofa in a room full of ledgers and correspondence, sunlight finding its way through the cracks in the curtains.

Abigail crouched over him, her breasts a soft wonderment against his chest. "There's a name for this," she said, nuzzling his neck. "When the female is atop the male. I forget what it is."

"You will forget the day of the week, if I acquit myself properly. The term for it is happiness, at least for the male. I want to be inside you."

Oh, that was gracelessness incarnate, that was.

She nipped his ear. "One did get the impression you were interested in making my intimate acquaintance. Guess what I want?"

To have me inside you. "To have the size of your breasts compared by a man with science running in his very veins." A trickle of science, next to a roaring torrent of lust.

Abigail brushed her sex over his cock, and the roaring torrent threatened to overflow its banks.

Get hold of your damned self, bucko. Show the lady some consideration. Stephen palmed Abigail's breasts and she ceased sucking on his earlobe. His next foray was to trace the curve of her hip and stroke his hands over her bum. She sighed, her breath breezing past his ear.

She liked to be petted. Thank the heavenly powers, Stephen could work with that.

"Let's get comfortable, shall we?" He elbow-walked himself over the cushions so the sofa could serve as a proper bed and tugged Abigail down beside him. "There's a quilt..." He hooked the blanket with his good foot and dragged it up within reach. "Wouldn't want you taking a chill."

He'd no sooner arranged the quilt than Abigail had a knee resting on his thighs and a hand drifting across the hair of his chest. She was gently pinning him down—as if he might totter off to do a spot of naked accounting when she wasn't looking?

"Now what?" she asked.

"Now we get to know each other. I'm ticklish." He took her hand and placed it right beneath his ribs. "I suspect most people are, but you can reduce me to begging if you tickle me here. What about you?"

"I won't tickle you if you don't want me to."

"Good to know." She sounded in complete earnest, and Stephen's desire ebbed the tiniest bit. He tried again. "I like to sleep with a window open on even the most bitter nights. If a window is locked, I can't crawl out of it." He'd never told that to anybody. Duncan hadn't remarked it in all their travels, probably considering a cracked window just one more among numerous eccentricities.

"I sleep with a window open in summer, I suppose."

The lady who'd been so eager to get Stephen into bed had retreated somewhere behind a locked window. Why?

"Abigail, what's wrong?"

Her hand remained right where it was, no happy explorations to the south. "Nothing. I like that you use my name."

Stephen plumbed the depths of that admission and came up with a few possible insights, none of them reflecting well on the late Lord Champlain.

"I like that we are to become lovers, Abigail." He wrapped his arms around her and wrestled her over him. "Kiss me, please."

She obliged, and by slow degrees and sweet caresses, he felt the passion rising in her once more. Her breasts were sensitive, and he'd just graduated from teasing her nipples with his fingers to indulging that same pleasure with his mouth when she gave his cock another delicious caress with her sex.

"Whenever you please," he said, lifting his hips to move with her. "You choose the moment, Abigail."

She sat back, and he died a little, though the chance to behold her was lovely.

Her expression was thoughtful as she casually circled the tip of his cock with her index finger. "Champlain would be done by now. Dressed and one boot out the door, tossing a string of stupid pet names at me over his shoulder."

"As a wise woman once said, Champlain was an idiot. Lovemaking with you is worth savoring, Abigail. I will tarry on this sofa all afternoon if you'll allow it." *All week, all year.* Stephen traced the curve of her jaw, then her brows, wishing he could make her smile, loving that she wasn't pretending jolliness for his sake.

She caught his hand and kissed his palm. "I'm sorry. I hadn't thought to bring memories to bed with me, but then..." She curled down against Stephen's chest, the sweetest gesture of trust a woman had ever bestowed on him.

He stroked her hair, searching in vain for some sophisticated witticism that would ease the moment.

No such witticism obliged him, but he had to give her something. Had to. "I want joyous memories with you and for you, Abigail. If now is not the moment to make them, then please stay with me and let me hold you, for that will be delight enough to fill my heart."

He let his hands wander, over her neck and shoulders, across her chest, along the individual features of her face. He at first feared he'd made a terrible hash of the situation. What woman wanted a mere cuddle when she'd invited a man to be her lover?

Abigail turned her head the better to move into his touch, though, and hope replaced uncertainty.

She truly, *truly* liked to be petted. He started there, making a slow inventory of every bone in her back, then moving to her haunches and the firm musculature of her fundament.

"Up a bit," Stephen whispered, patting her bum.

She obliged and he turned his attention to her luscious, perfect breasts and the nipples peaking so sweetly beneath his fingertips. She moved against him, a slow, sinuous reawakening of desire that was both more delicate and more insistent than her previous caresses.

"I want…" She dragged her sex along the length of his cock.

"Have what you want, Abigail." A watchful, hopeful corner of his awareness realized that she needed to hear her name. She needed him to call her home to her own joy.

"Please, Abigail." He took himself in hand and used

his cock to stroke her intimately. She closed her eyes, and Stephen glossed his thumb over intimate folds. "Say you'll have me."

She opened her eyes, took his wrists, and pinned his hands to the pillows. "Yes."

The next two minutes were the most hard-fought battle for self-control Stephen had ever waged. Abigail pressed herself down over him in slow, rocking increments as she held his hands fast beside his head. He could have wrestled free—probably—but why on earth would he want to?

"Move, I beg you," he whispered when she'd hilted herself on his arousal. "However you please, but, Abigail, please *move*."

She moved—moved his whole world and the moon and stars beyond. He had the sense she was exploring the boundaries of her own pleasure while she enlarged his. He'd experimented with delayed gratification, with toys, bindings, drugs, and odd positions, but none of that was half so arousing as the knowledge that Abigail was taking her pleasure of him.

This lovemaking proceeded at her whim and wish, and his great honor was to be her attentive escort on the journey.

She hitched closer and her undulations quickened. "I like this."

"Good. I love it."

She smiled down at him, the loveliest sight he'd ever beheld. "So naughty."

Well, yes, he was naughty, and she liked that about him, so he matched her thrusts and then raised the stakes. She apparently liked that too, because she bundled in close, and Stephen wrapped his arms around her, the better to drive her 'round the bend.

And that, of course, drove him 'round the same bend, until they were a single magnificent creature, writhing across a glorious firmament of pleasure and panting in a shared rhythm.

Abigail subsided against his chest, even as echoes of passion communicated themselves from her body to Stephen's cock. He used his waning arousal to send her off again, and that nearly sent him off again, which was not biologically possible.

But this was Abigail, and anything was possible.

"You are so good at being wicked," she whispered some moments later.

"Not wicked." *Loving.* "Attentive, inventive, possibly inspiring. Please, not wicked." He kissed her cheek and pulled the blanket up over them.

"We'll make a mess."

Stop, he wanted to say. *Don't let the world take you away from me so soon.* "This is an old sofa. Don't be like those fools who can't linger in a lovely moment. Have a little nap. Dream of me, and when you awaken, I might be hard inside you again, making your dreams come true."

He'd never quite managed that feat before, but it was a delicious fantasy. Abigail looked as if she wasn't sure whether he was teasing.

He wasn't sure either.

She eased away from him and curled up against his side. "You nap too."

Lovely idea, lovely woman. "I will be here when you wake up, Abigail," he said, spooning himself around her. "I will be right here." Unlike a certain courtesy earl who'd apparently had the bed-manners of a stud colt.

She took Stephen's hand in hers and wrapped it around her middle, settling his palm over her breast. "See that I don't waken alone."

She dozed off, her breathing becoming soft and slow, while the dragon on the ceiling appeared to smile down upon them. Stephen remained awake, mentally sifting through the puzzle of how to convince Abigail Abbott to become his duchess.

His truly, forever, one and only duchess.

Chapter Nine

"This is serious."

Quinn's duchess sounded serious, and Jane looked serious as she watched two enormous dogs get to know each other in the afternoon sunshine.

"They're playing," Quinn said. "Becoming acquainted. They seem quite compatible." The new dog, Hercules, was the larger of the pair, also the younger and more willing to frolic. Wodin was trying to stand on his dignity and even mustering an occasional growl for form's sake, but when Hercules went gamboling off among the hydrangeas, Wodin woofed and gave chase.

Much rustling in the bushes ensued, as well as some barking.

"I don't mean the dogs are serious," Jane said. "I mean that Stephen would procure *that* dog for Miss Abbott is serious."

If any member of the Wentworth family could inspire Jane to frowning, it was Stephen. "My brother is generous," Quinn said. "That's one of his three fine qualities, but don't ask me what the other two are."

Jane gave him a *your-wife-is-not-impressed* look over her embroidery hoop. She'd brought her workbasket out to the back terrace, and Quinn had brought some draft bills to read, though he wasn't making much progress with them.

"Stephen is loyal," Jane said. "He's hardworking, he's kind."

"Kind? The man who seeks to patent a repeating pistol is kind? I grant you Stephen is loyal, but Wodin is loyal and causes much less drama." Quinn loved his brother, truly he did, but he did not *understand* Stephen. From a young age, Quinn's challenge had been to find paying work, no matter how filthy or miserable. He'd dug graves, he'd carried night soil, he'd worn livery and toadied to the wellborn. His pride hadn't mattered half so much as his ability to keep his younger siblings fed.

He no longer labored with his hands, but he worked long hours both at the bank and in the House of Lords. Stephen had been injured too early in life to have any experience of brute manual labor. He tinkered and sketched and flirted his days away, coming up with brilliant mechanical devices as more of a hobby than a vocation.

"Wodin is a canine," Jane said. "I hadn't realized he's lonely."

The dogs emerged from the hydrangeas, both tails waving happily. Wodin nipped at Hercules's shoulder, and Hercules dodged off down the garden path.

"Wodin is..." Wodin gave chase, looking much younger than he had five minutes earlier. "Why do you say that?"

"Look at him, Quinn. He's acting like a puppy. He's not watching you to make sure you are watching me. He's being a dog."

Hercules chose that moment to lift his leg on a rosebush.

"What else would he be?"

"A bodyguard. Stephen keeps his distance from Wodin."

Stephen again. Stephen, who for some reason found the prospect of taking a wife and starting a family unfathomably burdensome. Quinn was losing patience with his brother's delicacy, because it wasn't as if Stephen had the sexual habits of a monk.

Far from it. "Stephen is vain about his appearance," Quinn said, "and dog hair does not comport with a dandy's notion of acceptable turnout."

"I never took you for a dunderhead, Quinn Wentworth, but consider that your brother requires a cane for locomotion."

"He does, and sometimes he uses two, though they are generally weapons in disguise. What does that have to do with buying Miss Abbott a canine coach horse?"

Jane jabbed her needle into a corner of the pillowcase she was working on and set aside her hoop.

"Dogs don't understand about canes. Wodin might cross a room to come to my side and accidentally knock Stephen over. Something as casual as jostling Stephen's cane can send him to his knees. I've seen it happen."

So had Quinn. "When Stephen falls, I'm torn between wanting to put him in a Bath chair for the rest of his life and wanting to kill whoever so thoughtlessly bumped his elbow."

"And how do you think Stephen feels?"

Quinn avoided wondering how Stephen felt. Stephen had barely survived his adolescence, so given was he to histrionics. Only Duncan's timely intervention with a great lot of book learning and scientific twaddle had distracted Stephen from his self-pity.

"I think Stephen feels resentful when he takes a tumble. Any man would."

Jane closed the lid of her workbasket. "No, Quinn. Any man would feel *ashamed* to go sprawling to the cobbles while his family looks on. A two-year-old can walk upright with reasonable assurance. Not Stephen Wentworth, but he hasn't given up trying."

"Stephen is determined. I'll grant you that."

"How generous of you."

Jane was by nature sensible and kind. She did not resort to sarcasm often, which suggested to Quinn that he was Missing The Point.

"Jane, have mercy. What subtlety am I not seeing where Stephen is concerned?"

"Spend a day in a Bath chair, Quinn. Force yourself to carry two canes at all times. Trip on the bank steps while half of London is passing on the walkway. Though you are smart enough to take firsts in every subject, pass up Eton and Oxford because you can't manage the steps, can't manage the schoolyard brutality. Can't manage the mud. You think Stephen is so different from you, but he's not."

"He's proud." All the Wentworths were proud, and God

be thanked for that, else London society would have eaten them alive.

"He's proud, and he's stubborn. His stubbornness makes your determination look like... What are those dogs doing?"

Wodin was trying to hump Hercules, who apparently wasn't interested in playing that game. "They're deciding who's in charge. Finish your thought about Stephen." Because whatever point Jane was making, Quinn had the sense that it could help him solve the puzzle that was his only brother.

"Stephen lives in constant pain. You do not. Stephen lives with constant humiliation. You do not. Stephen would die to protect you, while you want to put him in a Bath chair so he doesn't suffer any more public falls. You tell Ned you're proud of him every chance you get."

"I *am* proud of Ned. The damned lad should have been transported by now, but he's as upright as any Methodist."

"And Stephen should be dead. He should have given up or consigned himself to the solution Jack Wentworth chose, blaming everybody and everything for his miseries when he was sober enough to make that effort."

"Stephen is honorable." Quinn made that admission slowly. Why was it an admission, and a reluctant one?

"How did Jack Wentworth die, Quinn?"

What an odd question. "Bad gin. It was bound to happen. I was working on a fishing boat that summer, gone for two weeks at a time, and Jack apparently went on one bender too many. Why do you ask?"

Jane watched the dogs, who were back to sniffing and

frisking about. "You should ask Stephen about that time. Hercules seems like a very sweet dog."

Some leap of female logic had occurred. Stephen, oddly enough, might have been able to follow it. Quinn could not.

"Stephen bought him from Willow Dorning, purveyor of fine canines. The beast is certainly well trained."

"But the dog is huge," Jane said. "Stephen would not have purchased such a pet for Miss Abbott if he intended to spend a significant amount of time with her."

"He should have bought her the typically irksome lapdog, but Stephen must be original in all regards. Miss Abbott seemed pleased."

Miss Abbott was another mystery. Quinn had never met a woman so self-possessed and *mannish*. And what exactly did an inquiry agent *do*, anyway?

"She was pleased, but she did not understand that Stephen gave her such a dog only because Stephen sees his path and hers diverging."

Truly, the conversation had become confusing. "It's a sham engagement, Jane. When Stapleton has been flushed from his covert and the business with the letters sorted out, Miss Abbott will go back to whatever she does, and Stephen will resume his patronage of opera dancers."

Jane left off watching the dogs. "What do you think Stephen and Miss Abbott are doing right now, Quinn?"

He thought back over the breakfast conversation. "Shopping for gloves? Picking out fans?"

"She has no use for fashionable accessories. He hates crowded walkways and fawning clerks."

Hence, the publicly besotted couple had…"That is damned fast work, even for Stephen. I might have to have a word with him, Jane. Miss Abbott is nominally under my protection, and Stephen is a strutting cocksman, canes or no canes."

"When has Stephen ever asked us for anything, Quinn?"

"He doesn't have to ask. We all hop to anticipate his needs."

"Did he need to travel up to York this spring to keep an eye on Althea for us?"

"He was restless."

Jane rose and leaned across the table. "Did he *need* to assist Rothhaven and Constance with their situation? Did he *need* to travel out to Berkshire in the winter mud and slush when Duncan and Matilda were in such difficulties? Did he *need* to come armed to the party when you and your old friend the *viscountess* were having a rather dangerous reunion?"

Jane never threw that situation at Quinn, and she wasn't exactly throwing it at him now.

"I've conceded that Stephen is loyal."

"He's loyal, he's brave, he's fierce, and he's in love with Abigail Abbott, but he won't offer for her. If I had given birth to a boy, even one boy…"

She subsided into her chair, and Quinn reached for her hand. "Never say that. Never *ever* say that. You and the girls are my entire happiness, and I wouldn't have it any other way. Tell me what to do regarding Stephen and Miss Abbott, and I'll do it, and the perishing title can go hang for all I care."

She kissed his knuckles. "I do love you, Quinn, and if I knew what to do about Stephen and Miss Abbott, I'd be doing it."

Quinn linked his fingers with Jane's. "You let them scamper off on a shopping expedition and declined to send Matilda as their chaperone. I'd say you're abetting the cause of true love rather vigorously."

Jane brushed her thumb across his palm. "But will that be enough? Stephen might get up the courage to offer for Miss Abbott, but very few women of modest birth step into the role of future duchess if they have any sense."

Quinn kissed her wrist. "Being my duchess has been hard, I know. I would not be a duke were you not my duchess, Jane. I'd be just another titled nincompoop with too much money. I showed Miss Abbott the room Stephen used to have."

Jane came around the table and subsided into his lap. "Clever of you, Quinn. I accepted an invitation to the Portman ball on Stephen's behalf."

"He never attends social gatherings if the occasion requires dancing."

"For Miss Abbott's sake, I believe he will."

Days of travel, worry, and upheaval caught up with Abigail, for she didn't simply nap in Stephen's arms, she slept deeply. When she awoke feeling warm, relaxed, and *safe*, Stephen was—true to his word—still ranged along her back, a cozy blanket of semi-aroused male.

"I did dream of you," she said, returning his hand to the place over her breast. "You were playing fetch with Hercules."

And Abigail had been there too, as had a small boy in short pants. The scene had been domestic and prosaic in her dreams, but its recollection was painful.

"Hercules knows a lot of tricks," Stephen said, "and he's young. He'll keep you company for years to come."

"Do I detect an offer from you to keep me company, my lord?" His arousal was becoming more apparent, and Abigail had no wish to rise, dress, and resume the pretenses her situation called for.

"One doesn't like to impose," Stephen said, kissing her nape. "But if offered a choice between lingering with you for another half hour or visiting a milliner, I must admit the bonnets come a distant second."

Abigail rolled her hips back against him. "For me as well."

Stephen took that for the invitation she'd intended and lazily toyed with her breasts, then explored yet more intimate flesh, all the while rocking gently against her. By the time he eased into her heat, Abigail was ready to pin him to the mattress and have her way with him once more.

"I want to be on top again," she said, reaching behind her to draw Stephen's hips close. "This is too cozy, too…" *Too sweet and easy and relaxed.*

"Hush," Stephen said. "We can play St. George and the dragon again next time."

That was the vulgar term for the position Abigail sought, the only one where she maintained the dominant posture.

"I considered waking you like this," Stephen said, "but I didn't want to cheat you of rest. I also considered bringing myself off, but—selfish brute that I am—this is infinitely better."

"You didn't sleep?"

His hand drifted up to gently palm her breast. "I did not want to miss a moment of your company."

By the time he'd finished with her, Abigail was lying prone, a pillow under her hips, and Stephen draped over her, in the fashion of a pair of lazy beasts. The pleasure had been nearly unbearable as a result of arriving at the end of a slow build, for Stephen refused to either hurry or relent.

He knew what he was about, the wretch, and Abigail was coming to suspect that Champlain had *not* known what he was about. Stephen produced a handkerchief from Abigail knew not where and tucked it between her legs, then rolled to his side.

"You have worn me out," he said, "but fear not. Given present company, my humors should be restored within the quarter hour."

Abigail lay over her pillow, enjoying the glow of wanton abandon. Lovemaking had never left her so utterly boneless and at peace before.

"Do you fear I'll leap up and desert you for the shops?"

Stephen lay on his back, Abigail on her belly. He appeared to feel as great a sense of repletion as she did, if the slumberous calm in his gaze was any indication.

"You will abandon me," Stephen said, "though probably not for the shops. You will return to finding missing nieces and errant husbands, retrieving incriminating letters, or confronting embezzling clerks. Does lovemaking build up your appetite? For food, that is?"

"What will you abandon me for?" Abigail asked, though where the courage to posit the question came from she did not know. Perhaps from Stephen himself.

"You think me a fribble," he said, reaching over to caress her cheek. "I enjoy fribbling, but I'm also a consultant to the military on all manner of weapons design questions. I am tinkering with steam power for naval vessels, and I am fascinated with locomotives. Steam could be used for everything from sending packets back and forth to Calais—no more waiting on the tide and wind—to reducing the manual labor involved in purse seining. I'm also fiddling with a lift that can be built on to the outside of an existing building, rather than requiring internal renovations."

The small of Abigail's back began to protest her position, so she pulled the pillow from beneath her hips and shifted to her side, taking Stephen's hand in her own.

"Do you support any charities?"

"A dozen or so, mostly to do with returning soldiers, or families whose soldiers did not return. Many of the veterans need medical attention, and I'm not a doctor. I can hire doctors, though, and order them about and build surgeries and clinics for them. The Scots are the closest we have to competent medical practitioners in Britain, so I tend to employ them if I can."

Abigail tucked closer. "What of children? Are you active in children's charities?"

"I run two orphanages for the offspring of soldiers. They want more attention than I can give them, but the children seem happy and well cared for. I pop in unannounced whenever I'm in London, and have my eyes and ears among the urchins."

Abigail would love to pop in with him and see him consorting with his little spies. "You are no sort of fribble whatsoever."

"I'm a ducal heir. We apparently have a reputation to uphold as decorative bon vivants. You never did tell me if you're hungry."

Abigail was hungry. Starving for the company of a man who chatted in bed, took his time with lovemaking, and quietly supported more charities than any five dukes combined.

"I am a bit peckish," she said, mostly because Stephen had to be famished. "I would not want to put the staff to any trouble."

"It's half day," he said, sitting up, "and my employees are well compensated for tolerating my eccentricities regarding mealtimes. I also look in on the kitchen unannounced."

"Eccentric, indeed."

And so dear. Stephen was the most attentive lady's maid Abigail had ever encountered, using his pocket comb to tidy her hair and making short work of her ribbons, hooks, and laces. He required no assistance dressing, having developed methods of donning his clothing that let him either sit or use one hand while balancing on sturdy furniture.

All too soon, he was again the natty gent, and Abigail was a lady attired for an outing to the shops. When she would have left the study for the kitchen, Stephen stopped her with a hand on her arm.

"A hug for courage," he said, drawing her close. "And for gratitude. Thank you, Abigail. I will dream of this interlude when I'm a curmudgeonly old relic, and the memory will make my heart that of a young and happy man."

She hugged him back, hard, and blinked away foolish tears. All too many of her encounters with Champlain had ended with a quick kiss and him telling her to "tidy up and take care." He'd disappear for days or weeks, then show up again, all smiles, ready for another quick trip to the nearest hayloft.

And she, being young, stupid, and desperate for a man's notice, had gone with him willingly.

"Food for the soul having been attended to," Stephen said, stepping back and taking her hand, "let's find some food for the body. One doesn't attempt a mercantile sortie on an empty belly."

He knew his way around the kitchen, and waved off the single scullery maid on duty. He directed her to take her work into the garden, and she seemed happy enough to gather up her bowl of peas and go.

"That one," he said, "was plying the horizontal trade until six months ago. You never saw a woman happier to peel potatoes. Ham or beef on your sandwich?"

"Neither. Cheese and butter will do. Do you prefer cider or ale, or should we make a pot of tea?"

"Cider this time of year is a good choice. Were your people the sort to boycott sugar?"

"Absolutely, and I still buy sugar sparingly and only from Indian sources."

Stephen was at home in this kitchen, knew where the

knives and bread loaves were, handled the cheese parer competently, and managed to move about with a cane in one hand and plate in the other.

He brought a tray stacked high with sandwiches to the plank table in the center of the kitchen. "I suspect," he said, "that reducing English consumption of sugar just allowed more enslaved labor to be devoted to tobacco, rum, and coffee, all of which lend themselves to habitual consumption, and were more impervious to boycotts."

"Do you hold property in the West Indies, my lord?" Abigail would protest if he did, but would she flee his company and take her chances with Stapleton?

"Certainly not. Jane is a preacher's daughter. She has strong views on abolition, as do I. Quinn's favorite political cause is getting young children out of the mines. He labored like a bullock as a boy, and because he was a boy—albeit a large boy—he was paid a pittance compared to what a man was paid for the same work. Pass me that mug."

Abigail slid a mug of cider to his side of the table. "For what we are about to receive, we are humbly grateful. Amen." Abigail's Quaker relatives frowned on recitation of grace as a rote exercise, while Abigail liked the comfort of a simple expression of gratitude.

"Amen," Stephen murmured, "and for the company in which we receive it too." He nudged her foot under the table with his boot and saluted with his cider.

She was lost. Utterly, entirely lost. The lovemaking was wonderful, but this casual affection, this friendliness and honest joy in her company . . . she had been infatuated with Champlain, and with the notion of being in love.

Stephen Wentworth was stealing her heart, and she was helpless to prevent his larceny.

"Stapleton opposes any child labor reforms," he said, taking a sip. "He and Quinn oppose each other frequently on various committees. If I were a better brother, I'd stand for a seat in the Commons and support Quinn's issues in the lower house."

The food was good, hearty and plain. The cider was cold and fresh, and Stephen's willingness to discuss politics an unexpected treat. Quakers were pacifists, and they did not hold office, but they could be intensely political.

"What stops you from taking a seat in the Commons?" Abigail asked.

He sent her a peevish glance over the rim of his mug. "The actual sitting. The job entails hours and hours of it, far into the night, and my backside honestly can't tolerate the inactivity. Then there's standing to make speeches, another activity at which I do not excel—the standing. I can speechify as well as the next man."

"You could still back a candidate or two, if the right man came along."

His lashes swept down. "This is good cheese, don't you think?"

Subtle, that was *not*. "How many seats do you control?" And, yes, the cheese was wonderful.

"About a dozen, not enough to do any damage, just enough to keep me well informed and make a spot of trouble for the occasional nabob or marquess. Quinn can't be allowed to have all the fun. Are you fortified sufficiently to plunder the shops with me?"

"Let me finish my sandwich, and then you may dragoon me wherever you please."

"Careful, Abigail. You could find yourself flat on your back on this table." He looked to be considering it too, all dangerous and steamy.

"Or you might find yourself flat on *your* back, my lord." She reached for her cider, but Stephen caught her hand.

"I adore you," he said. "From the bottom of my heart and a few other parts of my anatomy, I adore you."

What on earth was she to say to that? "I am flattered and fortified, and you are…"

He brushed his thumb across her palm. "Yes?"

"You are not a fribble, my lord. Your attempts to impersonate one fail utterly with me. You are no fribble at all. Let's start with a toy shop."

He, of course, knew exactly where the best toy shop in London was, and clearly, the proprietor knew Lord Stephen as a frequent and devoted customer. Abigail browsed, she did not buy, while Stephen chose a number of items for his nieces. He knew each child's likes and personality, and for the baby he bought a storybook.

Which he would, of course, read to her. Of that, Abigail was certain. They were leaving the shop, and she was about to enlarge on her previous description of him—*not a fribble* had been a cowardly dodge, after all—when Stephen patted the hand she'd wrapped around his arm.

"Look sharp, Miss Abbott," he said quietly. "Do you see the four-in-hand idling across the street?"

The boulevard was broad, but the coach in question was impossible to miss. Four matched grays were in the traces, and the coach itself was painted silver-gray with gold trim. The livery on the coachman and groom was purple.

"Those are Stapleton's colors," she said. "I don't recognize the man at the window."

"That fine specimen is Tertullian, Viscount Fleming. His papa the earl is in wretchedly good health, and Flaming, as he's known, hasn't found a lady willing to shackle herself to him. He is entirely Stapleton's creature and may have designs on the fair Harmonia."

Did anything happen in London that Stephen was unaware of? "And he's watching us," Abigail said, repressing a shudder. "What do we do?"

Stephen leaned close, as if confiding a delicious secret. "We figuratively tell him to bugger himself."

He straightened, smiled, tipped his hat at Lord Fleming, and sauntered down the walk with Abigail at his side.

Harmonia's own dear god-mama had termed her goddaughter's looks "middling pretty." Mama had been even less complimentary. Champlain had married Harmonia for her settlements and for her earnest assurances that she would not interfere with his "manly pursuits."

He'd appeared vastly pleased with those assurances and offered Harmonia reciprocal promises to ignore her "little adventures" as well.

She'd been vastly disappointed at his cavalier attitude and had entered into holy matrimony determined to make Champlain so jealous he'd stop his philandering and declare his undying love for her.

He'd declared her a capital good sport and gone frolicking

off to France. Or the grouse moors. Or Brighton. Or God alone knew where. Harmonia had coped as best she could, developing skills appropriate to a future marchioness and taking lovers when her mood was particularly low.

One of the skills she'd found indispensable was the ability to eavesdrop on the marquess. Stapleton had his fingers in many a pie, from mining ventures to legislation that protected his mining ventures to trysts with his current mistress, and all manner of political intrigues. For Stapleton, socializing was an ancillary activity to manipulating politics for the betterment of himself and his titled cronies.

When Tertullian, Lord Fleming, strode up the walkway apparently intent on paying yet another call on Stapleton, Harmonia decided to have a listen. Fleming was heir to an earldom and had a dull, dutiful view of life that might recommend him to Stapleton, but Harmonia found Fleming's company tedious. He wasn't a bad fellow, but he was already going a bit portly about the middle, and he smelled of bay rum. Bay rum, according to Mama, was a sure sign that a man lacked imagination in bed. Harmonia had tested the theory on three occasions, and, alas, Mama had been right.

A fit of pique had inspired Harmonia to mention remarriage to the marquess, and that had been a mistake. She would not put it past Stapleton to choose her next husband, and make marriage a condition of remaining part of Nicky's life.

Blast all meddling men to perdition anyway.

Harmonia took herself to the pink parlor and lifted the carpet that covered a vent in the ceiling of Stapleton's office. The vent kept the office below cooler in summer and afforded a view directly down onto Stapleton's enormous desk all year round. Champlain had showed her this spy-hole and several others, may he rest in peace amid well-endowed nymphs.

"I tell you, she was on the arm of Lord Stephen Wentworth," Fleming nearly shouted. "I know Miss Abbott at sight by now, and Lord Stephen is hard to miss. He can't walk proper, and he's even taller than she is."

Stapleton remained at his desk, fingers steepled, while Fleming paced before him. Papa-in-Law was a small man in both senses of the word. He'd married a lady whose stature exceeded his own, and Champlain had taken after his mother's side of the family. Stapleton remained seated as much as possible, wore heeled slippers even when dancing and lifts in his boots.

"How did Miss Abbott get from York down to London without your men spotting her en route? She rather stands out in a crowd."

"She was doubtless in disguise," Fleming said, pausing before the portrait of the late marchioness. "She does that sort of thing. She might have been hobbling along bent over like an old crone or even have been dressed as a man."

How wonderfully devious of Miss Abbott.

"But the fellows you set to watch for her were supposedly a sharp-eyed bunch, Fleming. Now you tell me this woman is strutting about on the arm of *Lord Stephen Wentworth* in the middle of Mayfair?"

"His family hails from Yorkshire. Maybe he and Miss Abbott know each other from up north."

Stapleton remained silent, tapping his steepled index fingers against his lips. Fleming was supposed to squirm and fret as the silence lengthened, but he mostly seemed annoyed.

"You promised to smooth the way for me with Lady Champlain," Fleming said. "I've wasted plenty of coin and time in a nearly criminal pursuit on your behalf. You still haven't told me what this is all about, and I have yet to so much as stand up with Harmonia."

"That's *Lady* Champlain to you."

"*She* said I could call her Harmonia, and she fluttered her fan as she said it."

Stapleton's hands dropped to the blotter. "What's that supposed to mean?"

"I don't know, but m'sister claims the ladies use their fans to say what can't be said in polite conversation."

Lord Stephen Wentworth knew the languages of the fan, glove, flower, and parasol. He was a better flirt sitting in his Bath chair than Fleming could be in his most inspired moments. If Miss Abbott was keeping company with Lord Stephen, she had good taste in escorts.

Troublingly good taste.

"Lady Champlain is the pattern card of decorum," Stapleton said, "as any proper widow must be if she wants to remain a part of her son's life. She will attend Lady Portman's ball."

That was news to Harmonia. Lord Portman was young, Whiggish, and always spouting off about reform. His family had an old title, and the previous generation had married new money. Papa-in-Law had no time for Portman or his ilk.

"You're telling me I'll have an opportunity to stand up with her?" Fleming asked, facing the desk.

"You might. Her Grace of Walden has come safely through another confinement—a fourth girl, may the Almighty be thanked for small favors—and that means Walden might not attend. Lord Stephen will likely have to carry the family standard because Portman and Walden are as thick as a pair of drunken drovers when it comes to the blasted child labor bills. If Lord Stephen is smitten with Miss Abbott, he'll escort her."

Fleming leaned across the blotter, hands braced on the desk. "Lord Stephen has a reputation for dueling first and ignoring all questions. I am not kidnapping Miss Abbott from a Mayfair ballroom. Not for you, not even for the promise of marriage to Harmonia."

Papa-in-Law gazed off across the room. "I never said the objective was to kidnap the woman. The objective is to inspire her to surrender some letters, and that apparently requires a pointed, face-to-face discussion. She must have a price, and she can't possibly know what the letters are worth. With whom is she staying?"

"I only caught sight of her an hour ago. How should I know where she's biding?"

Stapleton rose, but went only so far as to prop a hip on the corner of the desk. This was another ploy to mask his lack of height, to ensure that he never went literally toe-to-toe with taller men.

"Miss Abbott comes from Quaker stock," he said. "She's not wealthy, and she charges only modestly for her snooping services. She's probably staying with some widowed third cousin or in a boarding house run by a Quaker goodwife. Start looking in those sorts of places. She doubtless has the letters with her, and she's probably planning to call on me to discuss them."

Fleming went back to studying the marchioness. "What if she's given the letters to Lord Stephen for safekeeping?"

Oh, dear. Papa-in-Law's face turned the shade of a ripe pomegranate.

"Why would she do that?" he asked. "Stephen Wentworth is nothing but a randy, tinkering, lame ornament. He and his brother should have been consigned to the mines in childhood, and the entire peerage would have been spared the embarrassment the Walden title has become."

Fleming lifted the stopper from a decanter of brandy on the sideboard and sniffed. "The navy buys cranes from Lord Stephen, and the army won't approve a new rifle pattern without asking his opinion first. He'll become the next duke in all likelihood. You might dismiss him, Stapleton. I do not."

Well, well, well. Fleming wasn't entirely dunderheaded, for all he wore bay rum. In Harmonia's opinion, Lord Stephen was every bit as formidable as his ducal brother, though his lordship did a creditable job of playing the part of a frivolous heir.

And—Harmonia was well informed regarding such matters—Lord Stephen was a devilish good kisser with more stamina in bed than any lame ornament ought to have.

A woman looking for a prospective second spouse did not account that a detail, though Stephen Wentworth was too shrewd for her taste. The damned man noticed everything and kept too much of his thinking to himself.

"Find Miss Abbott," Stapleton said. "That's the next step, and I rely on you to take it."

Fleming let the stopper fall back into the decanter with a *clink*. "I rely on *you* to insinuate me into Lady Champlain's good graces. You have thus far disappointed me, my lord, and my patience will soon be at an end. I bid you good day."

"She's at home," Stapleton called as Fleming marched for the door. "Her ladyship can receive you now."

Not if I'm waiting for Endymion de Beauharnais to call, I can't.

"My sister expects me to drive out with her this afternoon," Fleming said. "Perhaps we'll encounter Lord Stephen and Miss Abbott in the park."

"Give them both my cordial regards, and find out where the hell the woman is staying. She's kept the letters from me long enough."

Fleming looked, if anything, amused at that pronouncement. "I will call on Lady Champlain tomorrow. You need not join us." He bowed—ironically?—and withdrew.

Stapleton returned to his desk and took out pen and paper. Harmonia went to the window and watched as Fleming and de Beauharnais exchanged polite bows on the walkway. They chatted for a moment, a study in gentlemanly contrasts.

Fleming was stolid, plain, and apparently dogged, though wellborn and a conscientious brother. De Beauharnais was gorgeous, talented, a commoner, and interesting company. Watching them converse, Harmonia felt a sense of sympathy for Champlain's wandering eye. He'd wanted everything—a wife, a lover, adventure, another lover, the familiar company of his fellows, the management of his own wealth, the inane ritual of drinking away the dawn in a duck blind or galloping half-inebriated after a fox. He'd sought to live every second of his life.

Not to hide in empty parlors listening at vents.

Harmonia's goal in life was to see that Nicky had the same opportunities Champlain had had, though she hoped her son also possessed a bit more sense by the time he was enjoying those opportunities.

De Beauharnais bowed again to Fleming and jaunted up the porch steps, using his walking stick to rap on the door.

Harmonia really ought to remarry. She needed an ally who could take on Stapleton and best him easily. Perhaps de Beauharnais would have some ideas. He knew everybody and knew a few interesting little secrets too. Best of all, he knew how to make a lady smile and how to keep his mouth shut about the lot of it.

Stephen could not recall the last time he'd been so purely pleased with life. Abigail in a toy shop was a revelation. Beneath her pragmatic, self-contained veneer lay a female who'd not been cosseted or flirted with half enough. She'd turned the pages of pretty storybooks one by one and marveled at the softness of a doll's hair. A child-sized tea set put longing in her eyes, and Stephen knew she was thinking of his nieces.

The moment she'd spied Stapleton's damned coach, the softness and wonder had gone straight out of her, and

Stephen had been forced to all but drag her away from the scene.

"Shall we tool over to Berkeley Square for an ice?" he asked, then regretted the question. The protocol at Gunter's was for the adoring swain to fetch his lady her treat. If she also wanted a glass of lemonade, Stephen would have to make two trips from the shop to the coach, or to the benches under the maples where happy couples could turn a few spoonfuls of sweet into half an afternoon's flirtation.

"I would like to pay a call on Lord Stapleton," Abigail replied as Stephen held the coach door for her, "and ask him some very pointed questions about housebreaking, drugging, and attempted kidnapping. He frightened me. I hate him for that."

Hate, for a woman raised with Quaker values, was very, very strong language.

"Stapleton frightens a lot of people," Stephen said, handing Abigail up into the coach. "He's a nasty, manipulative, arrogant little sod, and he uses his wealth to conduct his schemes with impunity."

Stephen settled beside her on the forward-facing seat, used his teeth to pull off his glove, and took Abigail's hand. Why he liked touching her so very much, he did not know. Casual affection toward a lover was a pleasant commonplace, but his craving for contact with Abigail was of a different order.

He thought more calmly when he took her hand.

As he had lain in bed with her, mesmerized by the rise and fall of her breathing, his mind had wandered to why he and Quinn were so un-brotherly toward each other. Stephen did resent Quinn for leaving him in Jack Wentworth's care, but he also resented that Quinn had been *able* to work.

Was resenting Quinn simply a habit? Was that what this horror of becoming the duke one day was really about? Or was the problem a fear that Jack Wentworth's shade would have its revenge if Stephen had children?

Such questions had eluded his notice, much less his attention, prior to becoming Abigail's lover.

"You are removing my glove," she said, once again all starch and vinegar. "My lord, what are you about?"

"I like touching you. Fleming rattled you. Perhaps petting me will settle your nerves."

The coach rocked as the groom climbed up to the box.

"Do you suppose Fleming has the letters?" Abigail asked. "If Lord Fleming is in Stapleton's confidence, he might well have stolen them for his own purposes, then made a great show of pretending to search for them at Stapleton's behest."

Stephen rapped on the roof, and the coach rolled forward. "We are back to the *why* of this whole mess. Stapleton likely wants the letters to ensure Champlain's reputation remains untarnished by proof that he trifled with a decent young woman. Why would Fleming want the letters?"

"To blackmail Stapleton."

Stephen considered putting the tip of Abigail's third finger in his mouth—and discarded the notion. Sex in a moving coach was enjoyable enough, but Abigail didn't need that from him now.

"Fleming is in expectation of a title," Stephen said. "He's not given to deep play, drunkenness, wild wagers, or scandal. The only thing Stapleton has that Fleming might want is influence with Lady Champlain. Harmonia is pretty, very sociable, and a devoted mother. She's had plenty of time to be a merry widow, if that's what she wants, and managing Stapleton must have grown tedious by now."

The more Stephen considered the idea that Fleming sought to impress Lady Champlain, the more it seemed to fit the available facts—almost.

Abigail took off her other glove and clasped Stephen's hand between both of hers in her lap. "You think her ladyship might look favorably on a fellow who destroyed evidence of her late husband's infidelity? What if it's Lady Champlain whom Fleming seeks to blackmail with the letters?"

The knuckles of Stephen's right hand rested perilously close to the juncture of Abigail's thighs. That three or four layers of fabric lay between his flesh and hers interfered with his imagination not one bit. That he'd made love to Abigail twice in the past several hours was also of no moment.

He wanted her again, while she wanted to plant Stapleton a facer.

Stephen longed to plant the marquess a facer as well, but only after locking himself and Abigail into a commodious bedroom for a month or two.

Stephen rapped on the roof twice, directing John Coachman to pick up the pace. "I don't know as Champlain's widow would bother buying his old love letters. Not to speak ill of the dead, but I doubt you were his only inamorata."

Champlain had doubtless had a lover in literally every port, and Harmonia hadn't been exactly parsimonious with her favors either.

"Champlain tried to tell me that his wife had a very understanding nature," Abigail said, stroking her fingers over Stephen's knuckles. "He said they had a modern marriage."

"You take a dim view of modern unions?"

"I most assuredly do. The mischief I have seen between people who vowed to love and cherish each other beggars description. Hurt feelings, drama, children caught in the middle, family members taking sides or not speaking to each other, vast sums spent in retaliation for minor slights. You and your brother might not have the warmest affection for each other, but your family at least treats its members with loyalty and good faith."

Abigail was so fierce, sensible, and passionate. How dare Stapleton or Fleming or *whoever* disturb her peace?

"Whatever is afoot with your letters, Abigail, we will get to the bottom of it. Berkeley Square approaches. Have you considered sharing an ice with me?"

She let go of Stephen's hand and peered out the window. "You are taking me to *Gunter's*?"

"You sound like Bitty, though my niece is growing like a beanstalk and we will shortly have to find her a new nickname. Her favorite flavor is barberry."

Abigail let the window shade drop. "You gave me the best, sweetest puppy ever. You are taking me to Gunter's. You bought out half that toy shop and told Lord Fleming to . . . to take himself to Coventry."

To bugger himself. "Figuratively," Stephen said. "I would like to hear you use naughty language, Miss Abbott." To whisper it in his ear.

The coach rolled to a halt and Abigail pulled on her gloves. "I will dream of you tonight, when I'm alone in my bed. Perhaps I'll dream up some naughty talk. But I must ask you, if this is how you go about showing a pretend interest in a lady, what would your genuine courtship entail?"

"My interest is genuine, Abigail."

She smiled and gathered up her parasol and reticule. "But your courtship is not. I would love a vanilla ice. What is your favorite flavor?"

My favorite flavor of treat is Miss Abigail Abbott.

Chapter Ten

"De Beauharnais." Harmonia curtsied.

Her guest bowed. "My lady, a profound pleasure as always."

Endymion de Beauharnais was one of those rare people with whom nature had been lavishly generous. He was a bit over average height, but not so tall as to create awkwardness on the dance floor. His proportions were a tailor's fondest dream, from broad shoulders to a trim waist and an equestrian's muscular legs. His hands were those of an artist, while his features invited the eye to linger and delight. Straight blade of a nose, periwinkle blue eyes, defined chin....

And his *lips*. Harmonia set great store by a man's lips. By what came out of them—de Beauharnais was witty, tolerant, and well educated—and by how he applied them to a lady's person. De Beauharnais had been gifted with a full mouth, a warm smile, and a way of bussing a lady's cheek that made Harmonia feel about sixteen years old.

"I've brought some sketches for you to look at," he said, brandishing a satchel. "Your portrait has been much on my mind."

"Mine too, of course. Shall I ring for a tray?" In Harmonia's experience, artists rarely turned down free food.

"A tray would be appreciated. Was Lord Fleming calling upon you?"

If only de Beauharnais were asking out of something other than politeness. "Fleming and Stapleton are conspiring over some intrigue or other. Next week Stapleton's schemes will involve a feckless viscount or a silk nabob." She tugged the bell pull twice and seated herself in the middle of the sofa. "I am expiring with curiosity over these sketches."

De Beauharnais took the place beside her but didn't open his satchel. "Fleming's call put you out of humor somehow. Your countenance shows the worry here"—he stroked his thumb down the center of her brow—"and here." His next caress glossed over the corners of her mouth.

How lovely, to be on the receiving end of a man's warm and gently flirtatious touch. "Stapleton is ever threatening to take Nicky from me," Harmonia said. "Champlain did what he could to safeguard my maternal interests, but Stapleton is ruthless, while I..."

De Beauharnais stroked his thumb across her lips. "While you...?"

"I can be ruthless, though I'm not good at it. I'm better at being agreeable while I quietly go about my business."

That approach had worked thus far, though Stapleton and his dratted meddling could prove troublesome.

De Beauharnais turned her chin toward the window, and Harmonia was reminded that he was a talented portraitist. His boldness was probably more artistic curiosity than flirtation. The notion was lowering, and Stapleton's foolishness with Fleming was worrying, and Harmonia was abruptly ready to cry.

Blast all men to Hades anyway. The tea tray arrived, sparing her from the humiliation of pointless tears.

She poured out while de Beauharnais chatted about the symbolic objects that should be included in her portrait. Should Champlain's presence be hinted at in a sketch hanging on a back wall? Ought there to be a child's rattle or storybook on a side table?

"May I tell you something?" Harmonia asked when they'd done justice to a plate of cakes and sandwiches.

De Beauharnais set aside his cup and saucer. "You may tell me anything, my lady. By the nature of our work, portraitists make good confidants. We hear more than you think, and because we are underfoot in a client's house for days at a time, we see a lot too."

No guile colored that comment, no innuendo—and no threat.

"I don't care two figs about my portrait. Well, maybe two figs, but I'm having it done mostly to twit Stapleton. He would erase me from Nicky's life if he could, and I am very much afraid he'll get away with it. I want my son to recall what I look like when Stapleton banishes me to the north again."

De Beauharnais studied her, then rose and closed the door. Prudent of him, and Harmonia purposely received guests in one of the few parlors without a vent, dumbwaiter, peek hole, or other means of spying.

De Beauharnais resumed his place beside Harmonia, right beside her, in fact. "Are you in fear for your safety, my lady?"

Was she? Harmonia hadn't wanted to face that question. "I don't trust Stapleton. My husband and I lived independent lives, but I knew Champlain would always take up for me if his father grew difficult. Now…" Now life had grown complicated, and Stapleton, as always, was at the root of the complication.

If only he could leave well enough alone and content himself with his parliamentary schemes.

"Now?" De Beauharnais prompted.

"Now I worry all the time," Harmonia said, getting up to pace. "I have done things I'm not proud of, de Beauharnais, foolish things, angry things. Stapleton can hold the lot of it against me, and I have virtually no way to return fire." No way she was *willing* to return fire.

De Beauharnais rose as well, as any gentleman would. "Stapleton's hands are hardly clean, my lady. He's what's politely termed old school, meaning a pattern card of old corruption. From his enclosure acts, to his battle against reforms in the mines, to his tendency to buy up an unsuspecting MP's vowels, Stapleton plays dirty and mean."

Harmonia drew the draperies closed, lest even the gardeners report on her to Stapleton. "You relieve my mind in a way. I know Papa-in-Law is arrogant, that he regards himself as above the law and above society's strictures, and you tell me this is common knowledge, not my fanciful imaginings. You also give me more cause to worry."

"Stapleton is dangerous, but you have allies, my lady."

"I do?"

He took her hands in his. "I am an ally, however humble. I have a few connections, and they are not uniformly humble. Stapleton needs to be reminded that you have a place in society independent of your late husband's standing. You are an earl's daughter. You were Lady Harmonia before you were Lady Champlain. You are the mother of the next marquess. Stapleton is without exception disliked and distrusted, while you are..."

I am tired. I am overwhelmed. I am stuck in my father-in-law's household if I want to see my son grow up.

"I am...?"

He kissed her forehead and drew her close. "You are charm, lightness, benevolence, feminine grace, and good things. You take on Stapleton not for yourself, but for the boy, and I admire that."

Harmonia allowed herself to be held in a pair of strong masculine arms, allowed herself to be comforted. De Beauharnais was doubtless safeguarding his blasted commission, but his handsome speech wasn't all for show, and he made sense too.

"You are saying I should resume socializing."

"Your period of mourning is long past, even second mourning is behind you. You have been missed."

That was a bit of a stretch—wasn't it? "I would like to go to the Portmans' ball on Wednesday. Will you escort me?"

De Beauharnais was apparently the sort of man who could hold a woman, stroke her back, and converse with her, all without pushing his hips at her as if her highest aspiration should be to entertain him sexually.

"Escorting you would be my honor, my lady. If you'd like to attend the Veaters' musicale, I am also available on Friday afternoon."

Old habits stirred. At one time, Harmonia had carried a calendar in her head, right alongside a copy of Debrett's and a map of weekday at-homes. She'd kept Champlain's itinerary in another mental cupboard, and Stapleton's appointments in yet another. Now, her life revolved around the nursery and enduring Stapleton's bile.

"You are a good friend," she said, stepping back. "Do you suppose I ought to remarry?"

De Beauharnais brushed the side of his thumb along her temple. "Do you *want* to remarry, or is this another ploy to spike Stapleton's guns? If you married into another titled family, Stapleton would have to tread carefully."

That thought had occurred to her, and yet… "I miss the sense I had with Champlain of being allies, de Beauharnais. My husband was a hound, a daredevil, a complete gudgeon in many respects, but he was my gudgeon and I was his wife. I tell myself that in another five years, we might have settled down into a different sort of relationship."

De Beauharnais took her hand and kissed her knuckles. "He did not deserve you."

A pause followed, while Harmonia let de Beauharnais hold her hand, though she knew this whole conversation needed to be brought back to more sensible ground.

How tired she was of limiting herself to sensible ground.

"Champlain tried to take me to bed once," de Beauharnais said, watching Harmonia carefully. "I declined his offer."

"You were one of the few, then. His flirtations drove Stapleton halfway to Bedlam, which is why I never protested them too loudly."

"You aren't appalled?"

"By Champlain's behavior? I was devastated to think I could not be enough for him, that his appetites were so voracious and worldly, and all I had to offer was boring old wifely devotion. I got past that phase, to the one where I pretended amusement and near indifference, as he kindly directed both at my peccadillos." This recitation made Harmonia sad, for herself mostly. "I should have boxed Champlain's ears. He *was* appalling."

"I declined his offer. I've accepted those of other women—and men."

De Beauharnais was asking a question, about whether this would be his last call upon her, about whether she'd withdraw her commission. Being de Beauharnais, he put the questions to her through innuendo, leaving it to her to give an answer or make light of the whole exchange.

She looked him up and down, and liked what she saw very much. An adult male, not an adolescent in a protracted frenzy of self-gratification. A man willing to develop a talent into a profession, one who took her situation to heart.

She kissed his cheek. "I am long past judging others for where they turn for pleasure and company. Let's pay a visit to the nursery, shall we? Time with Nicky always improves my mood. We can kidnap my son to the garden and have a look at your sketches there."

She needed to see Nicky, to hug him and let him restore her sense of balance. De Beauharnais had surprised her with his honesty and his loyalty. If she were similarly forthcoming with him, he might be the one appalled.

"Do you mind jaunting up to the nursery with me?" she asked.

He smiled, a purely friendly and startlingly attractive smile. "I love children. They are the most enjoyable commissions by far. To the nursery, my lady, but I will also look forward to escorting you to the Portmans' ball on Wednesday."

"I will look forward to that too." Harmonia paused before opening the parlor door. "De Beauharnais, are you acquainted with Lord Stephen Wentworth?"

"I am. As it happens, I consider him a friend. Why do you ask?"

"No particular reason. I overheard Stapleton mention him. Lord Stephen and I are acquainted, though our paths haven't crossed for some time."

And that, quite frankly, was an enormous relief.

Stephen handed Abigail down from the coach, torn between insisting that she take his advances seriously—they were lovers, for God's sake—and a hesitance to dispel her lighter mood.

He ordered a raspberry ice, Abigail chose vanilla, and she took charge of carrying their sweets out to the benches on the square. Opposite them across the walkway sat a young couple, clearly of modest means. The husband held a fat, jolly baby on his lap, while the wife nibbled at an ice.

"What do you suppose the infant's name is?" Abigail asked, stealing a bite of Stephen's treat. "She looks like a Georgina to me, little Georgie to her family."

An inquiry agent would pay attention to her surroundings, and yet, Stephen had the sense Abigail would never ignore a baby.

"Georgina, possibly, or Georgiana," Stephen said, emphasizing the first *a*, "like the late duchess. She's a merry little shoat."

The baby smacked her papa's chin, and he pulled back in mock dismay. The mother smiled at him—a tender, indulgent smile—and at her baby, whose nose she touched with a playfully admonitory finger.

Stephen had just taken a spoonful of raspberry ice when a thought chilled him from within. "Abigail."

She cocked her head. "My lord?"

"I did not..." Stephen looked around, then lowered his voice. "I did not *withdraw*."

"I beg your pardon?"

How could he have been such a heedless, rutting, idiotish, imbecilic, hopelessly stupid, inconsiderate, foolish, thundering *dolt* as to not withdraw?

"I always withdraw, or wear a sheath, or wear a sheath *and* withdraw. I did not withdraw. I cannot beg your pardon humbly enough. Do you take precautions?"

She set her spoon in her empty bowl and put it aside. "I am not entirely certain of your meaning."

"Pennyroyal tea, ginger tea. Rue can work to prevent

conception, but I don't favor it. The effective dose can be dangerous."

Abigail gazed at the gurgling baby and doting parents, her expression vaguely puzzled. "You refer to avoiding an interesting condition."

"I do. I apologize for having behaved abominably, but this is not a topic to ignore. I do not seek to become a father, but neither am I willing to be a monk. I compromise by taking precautions and resigning myself to the knowledge that, should fatherhood befall me, I will do the responsible thing."

"Your ice is melting."

My brain has melted. "You finish it." He passed her his raspberry treat. "If I use my cane to start beating myself, do you suppose anybody would notice?"

Abigail took a bite from his spoon. "Champlain and I carried on for the better part of a year before I conceived. I don't believe I'm particularly fertile, and I doubt we have anything to worry about."

"You are admirably calm, Abigail. Babies create the opposite of calm. They are noisy, demanding, regularly un-fragrant, frequently hungry..." *And dear. So very, very dear.* And any baby Stephen made with Abigail would be...the idea stopped the forward progress of all his mental processes, produced a lump in his throat, and rendered his heartbeat akin to a kettledrum.

"If I get a woman with child, decency alone dictates that I marry her, and my conscience would insist on that course as well." Particularly if that woman were Abigail. "Children matter, Abigail. My children matter to me. Or they would, if I had any." Stephen fell silent lest he descend into outright gibbering.

"Does Her Grace know of these herbs?" Abigail asked.

The family across the way got up to leave, the father holding the child against his shoulder with one arm and taking his wife's hand too. The baby smiled at Stephen over her papa's shoulder, and Abigail waved farewell to her.

"Jane knows everything," he said, blowing the baby a kiss, "but if you ask her, she will tell Quinn. Quinn will denounce me to Duncan. The whole family will know our business. I hate that." Stephen also, though, trusted his family to do their utmost to look after Abigail.

"What of Ned?" Abigail asked. "Can he be discreet?"

"Brilliant suggestion. Neddy can be discreet, and he will enjoy having me in his debt. I will send around to my preferred apothecary and have them deliver the package to Ned. I am sorry, Abigail. I am sorry and ashamed of myself."

She finished his ice, rose, and collected her empty bowl. "If you'd bring my parasol, please?"

Her parasol could double as a second cane. Stephen managed it easily, and soon they were again seated side by side in the coach.

Abigail took his hand before he could think to take hers. "I have had a wonderful day. Your plan is working. Stapleton knows I'm in London, and he will soon deduce that I am a guest of the Wentworths. We now know that Lord Fleming could be involved in Stapleton's schemes, and that is progress. I very much enjoyed the toy shop and the ices."

She was trying to tell him something, but Stephen was still too appalled with himself to parse the subtleties.

"Abigail, I have failed you. I have failed honor itself and banished myself from the land of gentlemanly sensibilities. If there are consequences—"

"I lost one child," she said, squeezing his fingers. "Despite everything, I wanted my baby, Stephen. I am not a grand lady to be brought low by a common human contretemps. I'd leave York for a time, then come back with a baby in my arms, claiming that a widowed cousin in Cornwall had succumbed to a lung fever and orphaned her husband's posthumous child. Everybody would know I'd mis-stepped, though nobody would much remark it provided I was a good mother and didn't repeat the error."

The carriage rolled along through tree-lined streets, the autumn sunshine slanting from the west. Stephen's panic gradually subsided to worry and familiar self-loathing.

He would cheerfully, enthusiastically, marry Abigail, but he would not use a baby to entrap her. "When are your courses due to start?"

Abigail sent him an exasperated look. "Is nothing beyond the scope of your curiosity?"

"We are lovers. You've seen my knee." She hadn't really. Abigail, in fact, seemed to have no particular interest in his knee at all.

"Tuesday, and I am very regular. Put this from your mind, my lord, or I will have to distract you with a few kisses."

She generously bestowed several protracted, sweet, hot, wonderful kisses on him anyway, then subsided against him for the rest of the journey home. Stephen handed her down, bowed politely to her in the foyer, and watched her waft up the steps until she was gone from sight.

"You're holding a parasol," Ned said, sauntering into the foyer from the direction of the clerks' office. "I've had my suspicions about you, your lordship. One hears all manner of rumors regarding your proclivities."

Stephen shoved the parasol at him. "If Abigail Abbott asked me to carry her reticule, her gloves, her smelling salts, and her muddy boots, I would be honored."

Ned examined the mechanism on the parasol, as if looking for a trigger device. "That woman has never needed smelling salts in her life. You, on the other hand, look a bit peaky. Knee bothering you?"

"No, actually, but I could use a favor." Stephen explained that a package would arrive from the apothecary addressed to Ned for discreet delivery to Abigail. "And before you try to pry details out of me, there's also a new twist to the situation regarding Lord Stapleton, Lord Fleming, and God knows who else."

Ned, ever one to delight in an intrigue, either took the bait or, for once in his benighted life, showed a little mercy to a fellow mortal and let Stephen change the subject.

"Sounds complicated," he said. "And if you do not marry Miss Abbott, you are a moron."

Ned could deliver a setdown as effectively as any duchess, but his comment was accompanied by a gentle, nearly affectionate, shove to Stephen's chest.

"And why," Stephen replied, "would a woman like Abigail marry a moron, pray tell?"

"Because she is a lady of singular tastes." He patted Stephen's shoulder. "Have a care, Wentworth, or I will have to show you how to properly romance a willing female."

"It's not a true wooing."

Ned snorted, flicked Stephen's cravat, and strolled off down the corridor.

"It's not," Stephen repeated, to nobody in particular. "But it needs to be."

Abigail's courses had arrived two days early, which provoked mixed and entirely pointless feelings. She distracted herself by writing out the remainder of Champlain's letters, organizing them by date.

Today finds me in dreary Auxerre, missing my darling goose desperately....

I write to my dearest sugarplum from godforsaken Tournus....

I spend this week pining for you desperately in Chaumont....

The exercise had brought her no peace and less joy. The damned man had been a philandering, selfish cad, and not much of a lover, come to find out. His geographical descriptions and affectionate effusions struck her as inane, and even insulting. Could he not have used her name? Did he forget to whom he wrote?

What did a Quaker gunsmith's daughter care for a description of vineyards she would never see or chateaus where the likes of her would never be a guest? Why had Champlain bothered writing to her at all?

"This is the last of the letters?" Stephen asked when

Abigail assumed her place beside him in his town coach and passed over the letters. Duncan, Matilda, and His Grace of Walden would take the Walden town coach to the Portmans' ball, though Her Grace would remain at home in deference to her recent travail.

"That's all of them," Abigail said, "and I can't help but feel that I'm missing an obvious pattern, such as a code or signal. Do you think Champlain could truly have been a spy?"

Stephen tucked the packet into an inside pocket of his cape and took Abigail's hand. She would rather they weren't wearing gloves, but then, she would rather they weren't on their way to a fancy dress ball.

"Champlain lacked the brains or integrity to be a spy," Stephen said. "He might have undertaken some state-sanctioned snooping out of a lust for excitement, or he might have been used by spies, but he hadn't the patriotism and nerve for true espionage."

"You knew him that well?" Abigail agreed with Stephen's characterization, though she would have added that Champlain had been charming, funny, and more manipulative than an ambitious matchmaker.

"I could have *been* him," Stephen said. "Swiving my way across the Continent, more drunk than sober, much affronted when my smallest whim was denied, foolish wagers and broken hearts on every side. Duncan and Jane took me in hand and mitigated disaster. Champlain was an improvement over Stapleton—the son was nowhere near as overtly mean as his father—but that is hardly an endorsement. Witness Champlain's mendacity toward you."

Abigail had considered the months of trysting she'd allowed Champlain, and the fact that he hadn't once brought up the issue of conception. She'd assumed he'd marry her, and he'd encouraged that assumption. He probably hadn't bothered to consider the possibility of a child, and if he had, a bank draft had been the limit of his moral compass.

"I am nervous," she said, squeezing Stephen's fingers as the coach slowed. "I have never worn such a daring ensemble." Nor had she ever felt so pretty. The Wentworths were tall, and their domiciles were built on a grand design. Somewhere in the past few days, Abigail had lost the sense of being out of scale with her species, if not her gender.

"I insisted Jane equip you with a silk shawl," Stephen said, "because I am acquainted with your modesty. Please recall that these people are terrified of you, Abigail. You might not know their secrets, but you know how to unearth secrets."

"I would never divulge—"

He held up a hand. "They don't know that. They divulge one another's closest confidences at the drop of a glove. The lowliest crossing sweeper has a greater sense of responsibility than do many of the people you'll meet tonight. They are afraid of you, and that's exactly how you want it."

Stephen had the mental agility to think in such terms. Abigail could not be quite so detached. "Will Stapleton attend?"

"I doubt it. He and Portman are usually on the opposite sides of political issues. The marquess would have been invited, of course—anybody with a title receives an invitation from anybody with a title—but I'm more concerned that Fleming will be on hand."

Stephen had a remoteness to his bearing, for all that he held Abigail's hand. Mentally, he was someplace other than the coach.

"Are you having Fleming's quarters searched, my lord?"

"Thoroughly, and Stapleton's office as well. I've already had his mistress's quarters searched, and do you know, the poor woman hasn't a genuine gemstone in her entire jewelry box?"

Abigail would never have thought to investigate the mistress's quarters. "Does *she* know that?" Like father, like son.

"I will make certain she does. If she's putting up with old Stapleton's strumming, she should be handsomely compensated. A hint or two that she's considering writing her memoirs ought to get Stapleton's attention."

"What an inspired threat. You have a gift for seeing justice done." Not skulking around on client business, but upending injustice in plain view. Abigail had never found her profession anything but interesting before, though lately…

The coach came to a halt. "I have a gift for justice rather than revenge?" Stephen asked. "Revenge is a bit more dashing than justice, don't you think?"

She kissed him before the footman opened the door. "No, I do not think. If more men of your station were concerned with justice, the Stapletons and Champlains would be much less of a problem. How do I look?"

In the light of the coach lamps, Stephen's smile was

piratical. "I asked Jane to dress you in raspberry velvet. The memory of you licking raspberry ice from my spoon has resulted in more fevered dreams than you can possibly imagine. You look gorgeous."

He kissed her, the sort of friendly kiss spouses might bestow on each other: *Best of luck, chin up, onward to victory!* But what did victory look like, when the battlefield was a chalked parquet dance floor and the combat uniform was formal evening dress?

Abigail waited in the receiving line with Stephen, her arm twined through his so that she might surreptitiously offer him support. As the ordeal dragged on, he leaned on her more heavily. All the while, he chatted with this viscountess or that half-deaf baron, introducing Abigail with a fond smile and a pat to her hand.

He was good at ignoring his own pain, good at impersonating the shallow younger son. By the time the herald announced them, Abigail was ready to shout at the nearest footman to bring his lordship a damned chair.

"I hate this part," Stephen muttered, smiling genially down at the chattering, glittering mass of humanity in the ballroom. "Blasted steps go on forever."

"We'll take it slowly, so they can all get in a good gawk," Abigail said, gathering her skirts in one hand and wrapping her other around Stephen's arm. "I have you, and I will not let you fall."

The descent was stately, to say the least. Abigail realized halfway down that the crowd was not only inspecting her, they were also staring at Stephen. He'd stopped attending any gathering that involved dancing years ago, and by Her

Grace's own report, even the duchess hadn't protested his decision.

Some expressions were merely curious, some were faintly dismissive, a few were maliciously amused. If they were laughing at Abigail, well, no matter. She'd been ridiculed since the age of eight.

If they were laughing at Stephen, she would...

They reached the bottom of the steps. "I am having a violent impulse," she said. "My family would be horrified."

"Are you horrified?" Stephen asked, still leaning heavily on her arm.

"Not by the urge to toss a glass of punch at these gaping simians. I'd like to tromp on a few toes while I'm at it and accidentally spill my supper in some laps."

Stephen twitched her shawl up higher on her shoulder. "Ferocity becomes you, my love. I have two objectives this evening."

My love. Abigail's objective was to get Stephen off his feet. "And they are?"

"First, to ensure Fleming remains among the guests as long as possible. Quinn, Matilda, and Duncan will aid me to that end."

"Second?"

"To make certain that all of society knows I am passionately smitten with you, and that I will take mortal umbrage at any who seek to do you harm."

No humor leavened his words, no hint of teasing. "Ferocity becomes you as well, my lord. In fact, I think it defines you."

He bowed over her hand. "If you continue to flatter me

so shamelessly, I will find us a deserted parlor in which to be mutually ferocious."

"Find us the card room instead, my lord." *And woe to any woman who thinks to steal you away from me.*

The crowd let them pass, though that required a few well-placed glowers on Abigail's part. By the time she and Stephen reached the card room, she was ready to break chairs over the heads of those slowing his progress.

"Don't look," Stephen said, as they waited for an elderly couple to exit the card room, "but about five yards away, near the potted lemon tree, Lady Champlain is flirting madly with Endymion de Beauharnais. At some point this evening, I should pay my respects to the pair of them."

Abigail was not nearly as curious regarding Lady Champlain as she ought to have been. As badly as Champlain had treated Abigail, he'd been a disgrace as a husband.

"Her ladyship is entitled to flirt with the entire Ninety-fifth Rifles," Abigail said, smoothing a hand over Stephen's immaculate cravat, "and I hope the lot of them flirt right back. Matilda and I will visit the retiring room sometime before supper, and you can make your bows then."

She had Stephen seated across from her at the piquet table shortly thereafter, and though he distracted her terribly with his wandering foot, with his hand under the table, and with his drollery, he'd nonetheless taken the chair with the best view of the ballroom. Abigail was confident he monitored the entire gathering, even as he won far more hands than he lost.

"Fleming doesn't have those letters," Ned said, helping himself to a half-measure of brandy. "Stapleton doesn't have them, Stapleton's mistress doesn't have them; consequently, *I* don't have them. Brandy, anyone?"

"No, thank you," Stephen replied, easing his foot up onto the hassock before the sofa. "What of the vowels?"

Ned put a stack of folded papers on the reading table. "There will be rejoicing in the lower house when these are put in the post. I thought I'd mail them from St. Giles."

The poorest and most depraved of the slums, of course. Ned's sense of humor tended toward the ironic.

"How many?" Quinn asked from farther down the sofa.

"Twenty, and that was only what I found on a cursory tour. Stapleton's safe is practically in plain sight behind a mediocre portrait of the late marchioness."

Exactly where Stephen had said it would be. "Does Stapleton have anything on Lady Champlain?"

Ned aimed a look at him, which Stephen returned blandly. "She must know better than to document her dalliances," Ned said, "though since planting Champlain in the family vault, she's apparently been a pattern card of widowed decorum. I did find some vowels for Fleming's sister." He passed those over to Stephen. "For a lady barely out of the schoolroom, she is definitely frequenting the wrong establishments."

"I could do with a nightcap," Quinn said. "Lady Champlain was quite cozy with Stephen's portraitist friend tonight. Does de Beauharnais frequently play the gallant with society widows?"

Stephen had not in fact made his bow before Lady Champlain. He'd instead lounged against a pillar under the minstrels' gallery and watched her with de Beauharnais.

The fair Harmonia might as well have been a stranger for all the emotion the sight of her stirred. Once upon a time, Stephen had delighted in her smiles and flattery, even as he'd known his role had been to ease the sting of her husband's infidelity.

If she and de Beauharnais weren't lovers, they soon would be, which raised the curious possibility that they might pass the time comparing Stephen's amorous appeal.

"De Beauharnais is a good sort," Stephen said. "Genuinely talented, though he had best not venture too close to Stapleton's notice. The marquess is enough of a titled turd to set the dogs on de Beauharnais for behaviors Stapleton's own heir indulged in frequently."

Ned brought Quinn a half-full glass and settled into a reading chair. "Stapleton is a turd covered in dog vomit. He doesn't toss so much as a penny to the crossing sweepers, says they would be better off doing *honest work* in his mines. Little blighters are terrified of the mines, and well they should be. I was less frightened of Botany Bay than I was of ending up in the mines."

Stephen massaged his leg, though it didn't hurt nearly as much as it should have. "One windmill at a time, gentlemen. How do we know Miss Abbott's letters haven't been destroyed?"

Quinn sipped his drink. "Stapleton doesn't believe they are destroyed, and that's the greater problem. How do you confront him without letters to wave in his face when he's convinced the letters exist?"

How to confront Stapleton was the consuming puzzle in Stephen's mind—when he wasn't absorbed with adoring

Abigail. Between her discreet goggling at society in all its finery and the imprecations she quietly muttered at Stephen's side, she'd made the evening delightful.

Ned set his drink aside to pull off his boots. He was dressed from head to toe in black, not a watch fob or a sleeve button glinting on his person.

"You could kill him," Ned said, setting his boots aside. "Do the whole world a favor. Stapleton struts around London, not a care in the world, and his footmen would stand idly by should a runaway fish wagon gallop directly for him."

Quinn made the predictable objection. "Jane would disapprove of murder."

"Abigail would disapprove," Stephen added, comforted by the realization. His grasp of right and wrong might be shaky, but he well knew how Abigail viewed right and wrong, and could extrapolate from there. "She's not quite a Quaker, but she frowns mightily on violence." Also on guns, and—what to do? what to do?—on the people who designed, sold, and grew rich off of them.

"No Quaker ever paraded around a ballroom looking so luscious as your Miss Abbott," Ned said.

"Fleming had to have seen her."

"That was practically the point," Stephen replied. "If I thought Stapleton meant to do her permanent injury, I'd arrange an accident for him."

Quinn was looking at him oddly. "A fatal accident?"

"Yes, a fatal accident. He's a parasite, preying on a defenseless woman, impecunious MPs, the poor, his own mistress.... My guess is, the only being in all of creation

Stapleton feels any attachment to is his grandson, hence this apparent attempt to whitewash Champlain's reputation."

Ned peered at his drink. "That doesn't feel right to me. Swells and nobs dally where they please—they are expected to dally, and as long as they look after their bastards, nobody gives it a thought. What's one more affair with an unsuspecting Quaker girl? Champlain diddled everybody from merry widows to French violinists, from what I've heard."

"If he was passing state secrets to the French violinist," Quinn said slowly, "that might imperil the succession."

Stephen left off rubbing his knee. "Say that again."

"If Champlain committed treason," Quinn said, "he could be convicted posthumously, and his son's ability to inherit anything through him jeopardized."

Quinn was on to something, but Stephen's brain was too tired—and his heart too busy missing Abigail—to pick out the threads of a theory. Treason could result in an attainted title, but did Stapleton have enough smart, determined enemies in the Lords to effect such a convoluted scheme?

"I don't think it works quite like that," Stephen said. "If Champlain committed treason, he wasn't the titleholder at the time. I'll pay a call on your friends at the College of Arms and ask them a few questions."

"I am off to ask questions of my pillow," Ned said, rising. "A fine evening's frolic, my lord." He bowed to Stephen. "The lads and I thank you for it. Oh, and you might be interested to know that Fleming is calling on Stapleton's mistress once a week."

"Busy lady," Quinn muttered, finishing his drink. "One cannot envy her her duties."

"When does she see Fleming?" Stephen asked.

"Tuesday afternoons. She keeps a calendar. Stapleton calls Monday and Thursday at two p.m. and departs at three thirty. He's never underfoot at any other time. The fair Miss Marchant also entertains a Mr. Watling, probably the paper merchant."

"Was she once upon a time an opera dancer?" Stephen asked.

Ned gathered up his boots. "Not her too, Wentworth. Does a bad knee compel you to overuse other parts of your anatomy?"

Perhaps it had. Stephen would ask Abigail what she thought of that theory, and she would probably plant him a facer for his impertinence. If she was very wroth, she might be persuaded to spank him.

"Miss Marchant and I are not acquainted," Stephen said, "but I probably know some people who are friendly with her. Go to bed, and my thanks for a job discreetly done."

"'Night, Ned," Quinn called, settling lower on the sofa as Ned took his leave. "I miss Jane."

"Poor lamb. You had to go out among the wolves without your shepherdess." Stephen shifted the pillow under his foot. "I have never longed to dance with a woman as desperately as I longed to dance with Abigail tonight. She was the loveliest female in the ballroom, and there I was, stuck at the bloody piquet table."

"Jane says Miss Abbott doesn't dance."

"Abigail doesn't know how to dance. If I had two sound legs, I could coax her into it." A lovely dream, that, and Stephen had studied the instruction books enough to know that the patterns of the waltz weren't so very complicated. "She made me copies of the letters."

"She being *Abigail*. You've read them?"

"I've read half of them, and like Abigail, I sense a pattern that refuses to emerge. Your notion about treason is intriguing, because that would affect the heir, and Stapleton is the sort whose heir matters to him."

Quinn regarded him by the light of the fire. "My heir matters to me too. How exactly did Jack Wentworth die, Stephen?"

Chapter Eleven

Between one tick of the mantel clock and the next, a series of thoughts marched through Stephen's tired brain.

Why was Quinn raising this distasteful topic now?

Why hadn't anybody raised it sooner? Jack had been dead close to twenty years.

Was Stephen protecting himself by withholding the truth, or was he protecting Quinn? Perhaps protecting Quinn's view of himself as a competent older sibling?

And the final thought: Abigail was not ashamed of Stephen for having interceded on behalf of his sisters. And if Abigail did not condemn him...

"I killed him," Stephen said. "Put a tot of rat poison in his gin. It took a while, but he eventually succumbed and everybody attributed his passing to bad drink."

"You killed him." A question lurked in that statement. Perhaps a *Why?* or an *Are you sure?*

"Jack was planning to sell Althea and Constance to a brothel, and the buyer was coming around with money at the end of the week. I knew with Jack dead you'd be summoned off whatever clerk's stool or fishing boat you were working on, because nobody wanted three more useless children depending on the parish. The neighbors kept us until you showed up."

Some emotion ought to suffuse this recitation, but all Stephen could muster was relief to be dealing in the truth.

"You put rat poison in his gin. I am..." Quinn stared at the foot Stephen had propped on the hassock. "I am...I am sorry."

Whatever Stephen might have expected his brother to say—I am disappointed, surprised, not surprised—*I am sorry* hadn't been on the list.

"I made the decision, Quinn. You have nothing to be sorry for."

"I am sorry you did not feel you could tell me this. Sorry I never thought to ask. Sorry that at the *age of eight*, you were put in the position where such a desperate measure was the logical course. You did the right thing."

The night was apparently to be full of surprises. "I took my father's life. How can that have been the right thing to do?" Stephen had never quite asked that question, but it had haunted the remains of his childhood and the entirety of his adolescence. Perhaps it haunted him still.

"Jack bragged about breaking your leg," Quinn said, "about making a *proper beggar boy* of you and teaching you *proper respect* for your sire. Do you recall the game he'd play, tossing a crust of bread on the floor and making the three of you fight each other for it?"

"You never played."

"And then you refused to play, though you were barely breeched. Constance and Althea learned to break the crust in half, and Jack took to eating the food in front of us instead. His own hungry children stood before him, ragged and shivering, and he'd eat half a loaf of bread bite by bite and laugh at us and tell us we should be out looking for work. Jane has likened him to a mad dog, one that menaces all other creatures and is deserving of a bullet to the brain."

"*Jane* said that?"

Quinn stared into the fire, doubtless seeing memories of his own childhood. "Jack was an order of evil for which not even the Bible has a description. I had planned to kill him myself, but as the most likely suspect, I hadn't devised a way to evade blame. I wasn't about to leave you three without an older brother to fend for you. How ironic, that I should end up in Newgate for murder anyway."

Stephen wanted this conversation to be over. He wanted to bury his face against Abigail's hair and breathe in her scent. He wanted in some vague way to grieve and rage, not as a small boy succumbs to a tantrum, but as a grown man rails against the world's fallenness.

The whole of York had known what a monster Jack was, and not a soul had lifted a hand against him. *A father's right*, they'd murmured. *Spare the rod*…

More remained to be said, though. "Jack threatened to break my other leg if I warned Althea or Constance about the brothel."

"He would have done it, Stephen. He would have thrown

you down a well and laughed while you drowned, if he could have got by without the money your begging brought in." Quinn was blessedly sure of that conclusion.

And—now that Stephen considered the proposition—so was he. "Jack wanted to sell me along with the girls, Quinn, but the buyer wasn't interested in a lame boy. Jack couldn't sell me as a climbing boy, he couldn't sell me as a molly boy. Other than the begging, I was no earthly use to him except as a target for his fists and his hobnailed boots. I wanted to die. I wanted a benevolent angel to strike the lot of us down, but then I thought: *Why us?* Why not strike down bloody Jack Wentworth? He hadn't lamed my brain, only my leg."

Quinn patted Stephen's leg, an awkward and unprecedented familiarity. "God be thanked for your brain, and for your stubbornness. Does Duncan know?"

"He doubtless suspects. He was so determined to see the good in me, no matter how relentlessly I showed him the bad. He wore me down, and I eventually admitted a stalemate."

And what an exhausting struggle that had been.

"Duncan will approve. We think of him as a man of logic and reason, but he's passionately opposed to blind respect for corrupt authority. Talk to him, when the moment is right. He would cheerfully kill anybody who threatened Matilda, or as cheerfully as Duncan does anything."

Duncan had become obnoxiously cheerful since marrying Matilda. He was simply subtle about it. "I have never said anything to Althea and Constance, but they probably suspect too. You will doubtless mention this to Jane, and Duncan and Matilda have no secrets."

Quinn's lips quirked. "Jane had her suspicions, and as usual my duchess was correct. The Wentworth *family* will have a secret, though. How appallingly aristocratic of us. I cannot say emphatically enough that you did the right thing and the only thing."

He grabbed Stephen by the nape, shook him gently, then brought him into a fierce, brief hug. "You know that, don't you?" he said, not letting Stephen go. "You made a hard choice, but the only choice, and one no eight-year-old should have been faced with."

Stephen managed a nod.

"Good." Quinn thumped him once on the back and let him go. "And now I will join my slumbering duchess." He rose and stretched, a specimen in his prime, and a damned fine brother. "Will you ambush Stapleton with Miss Abbott's copies of the letters?"

"I was considering something like that."

Quinn picked up his glass and set it on the sideboard. "Whatever you do, don't execute your plan without consulting with Miss Abbott first. Duchesses frown on their menfolk going off half-cocked."

"Right. Good night, Quinn."

He padded to the door but paused with his hand on the latch. "She's in the peacock apartment, and the dog sleeps in her sitting room. Damned beast you gave her will soon eat its way through Smithfield Market."

Babies had a way of disrupting the most prosaic of marital routines, and the smaller the baby, the worse the disruption. Jane had no sooner returned from a nocturnal visit to the nursery and lain down in the ducal bed than the mattress shifted—or so it felt. She might well have been sleeping for an hour.

"Missed you," she murmured, feeling her husband's weight settle beside her. "Was it awful?"

From the earliest months of their marriage, Quinn had been sparing with words and lavish with physical affection, at least in private. Jane usually fell asleep with Quinn spooned at her back and woke curled against his side.

"The evening was long without you," he said, moving closer. He rested his head on her shoulder. "The baby was asleep when I looked in on her."

"Sleeping off her latest banquet."

Normally, Quinn would offer at least a cursory report: Some retired admiral had been in his cups before the dancing opened, a dowager countess had been accused of cheating at cards. He kept track of the trivialities because often, those *on dits* had financial repercussions and his banks served many titled families.

"Is Stephen all right?" Jane asked, for polite society had doubtless remarked Stephen's presence with more curiosity than compassion.

"Stephen is…" Quinn sighed, the sound profoundly weary. "Stephen is…Hold me, Jane."

Never in more than a decade of marriage had Quinn asked that of her. She threaded an arm under his neck and pulled him close.

"Quinn, are you well?"

"I am heartsick for my brother."

Jane waited, because surely even Quinn would embellish such an admission.

"All these years," he said, "I've thought Stephen spoiled—a contrary, self-indulgent, arrogant, difficult fellow who simply could not put behind him an injury that resulted in nothing more than a bad knee. Jack Wentworth scarred us all, and Stephen spent less time around Jack than any of us."

Ah, well then. In Jane's opinion, Jack Wentworth was capable of greater evil than Old Scratch himself. Mention of him would turn any conversation melancholy. Jane stroked Quinn's hair and drew the covers up over his shoulders.

"You and Stephen were discussing the past?" A difficult topic for any Wentworth.

Quinn hitched closer, and Jane was glad the candles were out and the fire was banked. This was not a conversation to have in daylight.

"All along," Quinn said, "I thought: My brother is so disgustingly smart. From the kites he makes for the girls to the modifications he's designed for his saddle, to the cannons and rifles and even a bedamned crossbow. Everything he touches is brilliant. Stephen has so much intelligence, I thought, why must he be bitter about an unreliable knee? Get the hell over it and move on. I was *jealous* of him. He can read in any language he pleases to, he's *charming*, he's *stylish*...."

Another sigh, this one a tad shuddery.

"He loves you, and you love him, Quinn. The rest can all be sorted out."

A silence stretched, while some strange tension gripped Quinn.

"The problem," he said, in a near whisper. "The problem

was never the bloody knee. What Jack Wentworth shattered was Stephen's heart."

Quinn held her in a desperately close embrace, and when Jane stroked his hair again, her thumb grazed Quinn's cheek. She kept up a slow, easy caress, until his breathing quieted, and his hold on her relaxed.

Only then did Jane admit what her senses told her must be true: Quinton, His Grace of Walden, had cried himself to sleep.

Abigail's evening had been a revelation, and not a happy one. If she'd entertained any wild fancies about eventually fitting into Stephen Wentworth's world, they'd died a waltzing, flirting, bejeweled death.

Mayfair was not simply a different strata of society, Abigail reflected as she drew the covers up over herself, it was a different world, and not one she could comprehend. The cost of the ice sculptures alone would have housed many a lamed or blinded veteran. The price of a half dozen pairs of embroidered dancing slippers would have bought many a crossing sweeper a decent pair of boots.

Stephen navigated this perfumed and silk-clad world with ease, for all he needed a cane to get around. His flirtatious ripostes had been humorous without touching the hem of ribaldry, and he knew everybody. All Abigail knew was that a Quaker gunsmith's daughter had no place among Stephen's peers.

Everybody in the ballroom had known him, and they'd approached him with the sort of nervous jocularity that indicated respect and more than a little wariness. He was at home in that jungle, and Abigail never would be.

She punched her pillow and admitted that, but for Stephen Wentworth, she would have no wish to learn how to prowl the wilds of Mayfair.

Her bedroom door opened silently and a particular, uneven tread came to her ears.

"You are not asleep," Stephen said, sitting on the bed. "And I am not tossing the rest of the night away while I pine for your company. We don't have the letters."

He shrugged out of his coat, then his waistcoat. His cravat joined the pile of clothing at the foot of Abigail's bed, then he pulled off his boots.

"Say something, Abigail. You were less than loquacious on the carriage ride home." Clad only in breeches, he moved behind the privacy screen. Even traveling that distance, he used his cane, though Abigail knew when his leg was paining him worse than usual, and that did not appear to be the case.

"Why didn't you tell me Lady Champlain is beautiful?" she asked, over the sound of her toothbrush being appropriated. "She's lovely." And slender and petite, damn her.

"She's also a good mother, not vain, and not very accomplished at games of marital revenge. Do you hate her?"

Water splashed against porcelain.

"I couldn't possibly hate her, though she probably hates me. I'm accustomed to people resenting my work, because I wreck their blackmail scheme or reveal them to be unfaithful. I'm not used to being ashamed of myself because of foolish decisions I made years ago."

"Harmonia does not hold you responsible for Champlain violating his marital vows," Stephen said, emerging from the privacy screen. "She disregarded the same promises, and didn't hold Champlain accountable either, more's the pity. I suspect she and de Beauharnais will keep company for a time. Stapleton won't allow them to marry, and for all I know they aren't inclined to marry."

Abigail propped herself up on her elbows. "I thought you said de Beauharnais…?"

"He likes some men, he likes some women. There's no accounting for taste, is there? You like me, for example."

Abigail flopped back the covers rather than admit that she'd fallen in love with such a magnificent wretch.

"Come to bed. Tell me about the letters." Because that was a far simpler topic than the dalliances of Mayfair sophisticates—also more important.

Stephen paused by the side of the bed to move the stack of his clothing to the clothespress. "Ned gave it a good try. He and his minions searched Stapleton's study, bedroom, library, and sitting room. They searched his mistress's home, and they searched Fleming's abode. No letters. Plenty of IOUs from stupid MPs, even some impressive sums owed by Fleming's sister to the wrong sorts of venues, but your letters were not to be found."

He hooked his cane on the night table, climbed onto the mattress, and sat with his back propped against the pillows.

"I am tired, Abigail."

She rested her cheek against his thigh. He'd left his satin knee breeches on, which was thoughtful of him, given that she needed to focus on the situation with Stapleton.

"I never realized," she said, drawing a pattern around his

knee, "how exhausting a wealthy life can be. The dancing alone takes stamina, and the gossiping and flirting and wagering.... The whole business struck me as a stage play put on for the amusement of the actors. A very expensive stage play."

"And your Quaker heart railed against that display." He stroked her hair. "As somebody who frequently went three days without eating in my childhood, I'm not too keen on fancy dress balls myself."

"I thought you didn't like the crowds and the dancing?"

"I loathe the whole farce. Do you have anything that bears Champlain's handwriting?"

Abigail focused on the question, though she was physically and mentally exhausted and sadder than she could recall being in years.

"I don't think so."

"An old invoice from a gun purchase? A note bidding you to meet him beneath the trysting oak?"

"I destroyed my father's business papers three years after closing his shop, and Champlain was inclined to do business in coin and show up unannounced." Then he'd expected her to drop everything, sneak away to the stable, and hoist her skirts for him. There had been occasional trinkets—a plain ivory comb, a man's pocket watch that kept unreliable time—nothing of great value.

Stephen's caresses shifted to her face and neck. "I had thought to have a forger replicate the letters you've written out, but we need a sample of Champlain's handwriting if the forgeries are to fool Stapleton."

Of course Stephen would know competent forgers. "You

will have to find some other woman to whom Champlain sent correspondence. Stephen, is something wrong?" The quality of his touch, while gentle, was distracted. The cadence of his speech less than loverly.

"I told Quinn that I killed my father."

Oh, dear competed with *And Quinn had better have taken the news well.* "And?"

"Quinn said I did the right thing. He apologized. Said I should never have been put in the position I was in."

Abigail sat up and laid an arm across Stephen's shoulders. "Now you are annoyed, because life was so much easier when you had this wall of resentment between you and the duke. He disappointed you by being decent. Wretched of him."

Stephen turned his face against her shoulder. "Have mercy, woman." His tone suggested a hint of a smile. "I will have to ravish you simply to still your tongue."

"I am indisposed." She had informed him of that by note. He'd replied with a bouquet of scarlet salvia and blue hyacinths. The first connoted consolation and was often sent to sickrooms. The second, if Abigail recalled correctly, stood for a request for forgiveness—or for regret.

Stephen took her earlobe between his teeth. "You are indisposed. I am not put off by a little untidiness, Abigail."

"You are trying to change the subject, because emotional untidiness drives you barmy. His Grace thwarted your precious fictions about his fragile pride and arrogant indifference, and now you have to like him as well as love him."

Stephen left off sucking on her earlobe and shifted down

to lay his head in her lap. "And I thought Jane was a tad too perceptive. When we marry, will you carry me over the threshold?"

"We will never marry." Abigail stroked his hair, trying not to let the heartache of that reality ruin the moment. "I truly had no idea how extravagant a society ball is. It's appalling."

"You can view it that way—the elaborate food, the gowns worn only once, the casual wagers in the card room—or you can see the beauty in it. The dancing, the music, the sartorial splendor, and laughter—also the sums transferred from wealthy coffers into those of people who work for a living. The kitchen makes certain none of the food goes to waste either. You looked lovely, Abigail, and you are a woman who deserves to dress occasionally in something other than sackcloth and ashes."

She could argue with him—nobody needed jeweled dancing slippers, for God's sake—but she didn't want to argue. She wanted to curl up in his arms and wake up in a world where nobody got in a lather about old letters, and a common inquiry agent could fall in love with a ducal heir.

"Abigail, dearest," Stephen murmured, cheek pillowed on her thigh, "have you ever had a notion to put your mouth on a man's—?"

She gave his hair a gentle yank. "Champlain kept journals."

"Journals?"

"When he'd have to wait a few minutes for me to join him in the stable, or by the side of the stream, I'd come upon him jotting in a notebook. He said he transferred the notes he took in pencil into journals, because a man's life should be of interest to his progeny."

"Not a humble sort, was he?"

"The journals will provide an extensive sample of his handwriting." Abigail traced a fingertip over Stephen's lips. "Champlain wasn't vain in the usual sense; he simply could not allow his mind to idle, so he busied himself with jottings in the odd moment."

Stephen closed his teeth on her finger, sucked for a moment, then let go. "I did not instruct Neddy to look for journals. Stapleton will have them, though, and they weren't in his safe, so they must be in his private sitting room. He'd be unlikely to keep such volumes in his library, or where Lady Champlain or a casual guest could come across them."

Stephen sat up and wiggled out of his knee breeches, extracted a handkerchief from a pocket, and tossed these items onto the clothespress. "A good forger needs some time to work, but we don't have to copy the entire body of letters. Just enough to draw Stapleton out. You might have to sit in the park reading them, and then we'll catch him trying to accost you."

"You are aroused."

He looked down at himself. "Around you, darling Abigail, this is my usual condition. One need hardly remark it and I assure you, I am capable of easing my own needs."

He was so casual about such an intimate, complicated undertaking. Or perhaps not casual—competent.

"We need to talk about the letters," Abigail said, though

she didn't *want* to talk about the damned letters. She wanted to cuddle up with Stephen Wentworth and never let him go. "Who has them? Who might have destroyed them? What if they aren't destroyed and we make copies and...?"

Stephen kissed her. "It's possible your copies are the only evidence of them. Perhaps Fleming destroyed them, perhaps somebody traded them for another twenty IOUs. Perhaps this whole business has something to do with posthumous charges of treason, of all the outlandish notions. Perhaps you should kiss me, Abigail. I truly did want to waltz with you."

She kissed him and what followed was an odd, interesting addition to Abigail's intimate vocabulary. Stephen wrapped her hand around his cock, then enclosed her hand in his own, and together, they stroked him to a quick, sighing completion.

The whole while, he kissed her and caressed her face and neck, but never once did he fondle her breasts or otherwise take liberties. She was left feeling friendly and cozy, happy to cuddle without the frustration that might have followed had Stephen been more passionate in his attentions.

Not what she would have predicted, but then, with Stephen predictions were pointless.

"Now we can have a nice sleep," he said, using his handkerchief on his belly. "And our minds can work on the puzzle of how to thwart Stapleton while we dream of candlelit waltzes and naughty kisses."

Abigail curled down to her side, more than willing to let the day finally end. Stephen wrapped himself around her and commenced rubbing her back.

"I can't keep my eyes open," she murmured.

"You have earned your rest. Go to sleep and dream of me."

She would, blast him, and though it was a poor reflection on her pious upbringing, Abigail had wished desperately that she could have waltzed with him too.

He was right, though—they needed a plan for thwarting Stapleton, and when that plan had run its course, she would return to York, and Stephen would remain in Mayfair, where he'd probably…invent the world's first repeating rifle.

"Wentworth took her to the ball?" Stapleton muttered, tapping his spoon against his teacup. "He took a professional snoop to Portman's do, paraded her before all of society, casual as you please?"

Harmonia pretended to idly rearrange the linen napkins on the tea tray, though she'd rather be anywhere but in Stapleton's study as he interrogated Lord Fleming.

"Wentworth not only paraded Miss Abbott before all of Mayfair," Fleming replied, "he did so in the company of his older brother, who chatted graciously with Miss Abbott and partnered her at whist. The Wentworth cousin and his lady were present as well, and had the duchess not recently been brought to childbed, she'd doubtless have been showing the family colors too. Lord Stephen and Miss Abbott were firing a warning shot across your bow, sir."

Stapleton took a prissy sip of his tea, then held the cup out to Harmonia. "This is too weak. You should know how I like my tea by now, Harmonia."

The marquess sat behind his desk like a lord justice at the bench. His display of pique was strategic, intended to belittle her before Lord Fleming. She considered for a moment spilling the tea *by accident* in Stapleton's lap, but denied herself that pleasure.

Papa-in-Law was angry, and when he was angry he was particularly unmanageable. She retrieved his cup and saucer and set it on the tray.

"My apologies, sir. Lord Fleming, is your tea acceptable?"

Fleming smiled at her from the reading chair. "Bitterness is an acquired taste, my lady. My tea is lovely and suits me quite well, thank you."

She subsided onto the sofa, while Stapleton's frown became a scowl. Fleming had danced an interminable quadrille with her last night, his movements correct and surprisingly graceful. She had sought solace with de Beauharnais in the garden when the dance had finally ended—and solace she had found. Lovely solace.

"Something must be done," Stapleton said. "I cannot have that woman flaunting herself before polite society. Harmonia, you will attach Lord Stephen's affections. Bed him if you have to. He's not to fall into the clutches of the Abbott creature."

Stapleton could be rude, arrogant, and blockheaded, but this...Miss Abbott was welcome to Lord Stephen, more than welcome.

"Stapleton," Fleming said softly, setting aside his teacup, "a gentleman does not address a lady thus."

"Fortunately for all concerned, Harmonia is no lady. Your sister's tendency to frequent the lowest gaming hells should have disabused you of the notion that a wellborn woman is necessarily a lady. If I tell Harmonia to bed Wentworth, she'll bed Wentworth."

No, she would not. Of all men, Stephen Wentworth would not be finding his way back into Harmonia's bed. He had been an interesting diversion, rather like a tiger in the garden was an interesting diversion. The instant he thought she was pursuing him would be the instant he refused to be lured any closer.

Besides, she'd seen Lord Stephen watching Miss Abbott across a hand of piquet. Of all the inconvenient, outlandish impossibilities, the statuesque inquiry agent had caught Lord Stephen's fancy.

She was tall enough to partner him well, whereas Harmonia…

"Is Lord Stephen your choice for Nicky's step-papa?" she asked evenly. "His standing is appropriate, he's wealthy, and he's held in high esteem at Horse Guards. His limp is the result of an injury rather than a defect of birth. He's witty, and he's good-looking. I could do much worse."

Stapleton gestured toward the tray. "Pour me another cup, and don't be impudent."

"There's more," Fleming said.

"What could be worse than that blasted woman attaching herself to a ducal heir?" Stapleton asked. He watched Harmonia pouring out, his lips pursed. "Unless she's *blackmailing* him. Wentworth is the sort to have secrets—perhaps he's a bastard, perhaps his older brother is a bastard. They both have the look of the baseborn knave, and God knows their antecedents were sordid. Miss Abbott makes her living unearthing secrets. Why would she be seen in Wentworth's company unless she coerced him into the outing?"

"She's biding at the ducal residence," Fleming said, "as a *guest*. That's not what you need to concern yourself with now."

Harmonia put the second cup of tea—strong enough to scald the rust off a rapier—on the blotter before Stapleton.

Miss Abbott was biding with the Wentworth family and accompanying Lord Stephen to his first fancy dress ball in ages. Perhaps this was, in fact, a good thing. Perhaps it was cause for rejoicing. Though probably not. Papa-in-Law was wroth, and that was always a very bad thing.

"Fleming," Stapleton began, "you have airs above your station if you think yourself capable of deciding which among endless pressing obligations I should concern myself with. A marquess, a peer of the realm whose title dates back to—"

"My house was searched," Fleming said. "I spotted Lord Stephen with Miss Abbott, and within days, my house was searched. Nothing was stolen, but I suggest you check the contents of your safe and the location of any sensitive papers."

Harmonia pretended to sip her tea, though she could taste nothing. This whole business was growing too complicated. She could only guess what Stapleton was about, and she wanted no part of it.

Stapleton left the seat behind his desk, swung the marchioness's portrait forward on its hinges, and opened the safe.

"The money's all—blasted hell. Blasted, infernal..."

Stapleton reached into the safe, though Harmonia could see plainly enough that it held only money and jewels.

No papers. *Poor Papa-in-Law.*

"You put him up to this," Stapleton said, advancing on Fleming. "You put that Wentworth jackanapes up to stealing back your sister's vowels and my entire store of leverage in the Commons."

"I wish I had," Fleming replied, pushing to his feet. "But the Wentworth jackanapes, as you refer to him, can barely negotiate a set of steps, and I have no means of making a ducal heir do anything. You have many, many enemies, Stapleton, no friends, and only a handful of paid-for allies. You had best be careful about whom you accuse of what."

Oh, that was well done. Just a hint of boredom in Fleming's tone, a hint of amusement—and a hint of threat.

And if Papa-in-Law no longer had Lady Roberta's vowels…Harmonia rose and smoothed her skirts.

"You gentlemen will doubtless wish for privacy if you're to discuss delicate matters. I'm expecting my portraitist for an afternoon sitting, so I will leave you to your plotting."

Fleming bowed cordially, while Stapleton closed the safe and positioned the painting over it.

"I am not plotting, Harmonia," Stapleton said. "The Abbott woman must be dealt with. I had thought to negotiate with her, but she's clearly intent on getting above herself. Don't be like her. Keep to your place, or I'll give you cause to regret it."

Harmonia merely stared at him. He'd apparently set Fleming to spying on Miss Abbott and Lord Stephen. He'd collected up the vowels of various MPs as a means of buying votes in the lower house of Parliament. He'd even ensnared Fleming in his intrigues by virtue of buying Lady Roberta's gambling debts.

Now he was threatening Harmonia before a witness, and not with a long holiday in the north.

She tipped her chin up, rather than let Stapleton think her cowed. "I beg your pardon, Papa-in-Law."

"What I do," Stapleton said, "I do to safeguard the boy's future. I owe him that future, and so do you."

The marquess was much given to pomposity, but in that last pronouncement Harmonia heard only weary determination, and—was she imagining this?—a hint of worry.

"I'll see you at supper," Harmonia said, curtsying. She left the study at a decorous pace and closed the door quietly behind her. The walls were too thick to make eavesdropping in the corridor possible, and besides, she'd already heard more than she wished to.

She gathered her skirts and pelted up to her private sitting room, where she changed into the flattering ensemble she and de Beauharnais had chosen for her sitting.

Chapter Twelve

"He's reading your letters," Ned said, taking the place beside Abigail on the garden bench. "Also cursing a lot and staring off into space."

Abigail moved her skirts aside to make room for Ned, though she'd rather be alone. "I assume you refer to Lord Stephen."

"In my head, he's Lord Pontifical, Lord Impossible, Lord Limping Lover...but yes, I refer to the gentleman who has stolen your heart and not set foot in the family home for the past three days."

Hercules peered up at Abigail from the flagstones. His chin rested on his enormous paws, and his eyes held the reproach of a poor wretch for whom the ball had been tossed for a mere half hour.

"I have endless privacy among the Wentworths," Abigail said, "but no secrets."

"We all have secrets," Ned replied. "I suspect his lordship has confided more than a few of his to you. Did you know he hadn't been to a fancy dress ball for years before you showed up?"

"Whereas I had never been to a fancy dress ball." Pacing would have been unladylike and rude, but the sheer, endless waiting was fraying Abigail's nerves.

"That bothers you?" Ned asked, holding out a hand toward the dog. "That you're new to the London social whirl?"

"Yes, it bothers me. I've attended a house party or two in pursuit of an inquiry, but this...this...extravagant idleness. I cannot fathom it, and I will never approve of it."

Hercules rose on a sigh and ambled over to sniff Ned's fingers.

"You think Stephen enjoys *extravagant idleness*?"

"He appeared to be enjoying himself at the Portmans' ball."

"And we know Stephen Wentworth is as transparent as Venetian glass, don't we? He hated every minute of the whole excursion. He wished desperately that he could have come housebreaking with me, but he instead kept to your side like yonder hound, guarding you against all perils."

Abigail did get to her feet and walked off a few paces. "I guard myself against all perils."

Ned studied her while he petted the dog's head. His expression put her in mind of the Duke of Walden, though Ned was no blood relation to His Grace.

"That's the real problem, isn't it?" Ned said. "You can't respect the fancy wastrels who make up the aristocracy, and your Quaker heart isn't keen on a fellow who's a genius with firearms, but the real issue is, you are too stubborn to throw in your lot with anybody, even somebody as contrary, smart, and unconventional as you are—maybe especially that sort. Would you rather have a loyal lapdog?"

Hercules craned his head back, the better to revel in Ned's caresses. Abigail felt exactly like that damned dog when Stephen touched her.

"You are impertinent, Mr. Wentworth."

"And here I thought you hadn't noticed my finer qualities, so besotted are you with his lordship." He rose, and Abigail resisted the urge to step back.

Ned Wentworth was only slightly above average height, and he was slender. He had no title, and Abigail hadn't heard any mention of Ned possessing independent means, though he was clearly well dressed, and yet...When Stephen had needed a housebreaker, Ned had apparently been able to get into, toss, and get out of not one but three dwellings in the course of a night.

Without being spotted, much less caught.

"You are wondering," Ned said, "what my agenda in all this is. I have several—a habit I picked up from his lordship. First, I am loyal to my family, because the Wentworths *are* my family. I was a boy bound for New South Wales when His Grace decided I'd make a passable tiger. I don't care how lowly the task, I was and am entirely his man.

"Her Grace put the manners on me," Ned went on. "And that was no mean feat. Duncan gave me an education, not so much by confining me to a schoolroom or deluging me with books, but by showing me how capable and articulate a well-educated man can be. Walden has wealth and influence, but Duncan will pin His Grace's ears back with a single quiet word, and devil take the hindmost."

Abigail ought to silence Ned with a single quiet word, but she was too eager to hear more Wentworth family history. Over the years she'd been employed by Lady Constance, she'd gleaned an occasional detail, and those had been filed away for recall if they proved relevant to the case.

Lady Constance's case had been solved, while Abigail's curiosity about Stephen's family had become voracious.

"And what of his lordship?" Abigail asked. "How did he earn your esteem?" For he clearly had.

"Do you know why he turned to designing firearms, Miss Abbott?"

"Because his mind works like that. He just as easily designs music boxes, stained-glass windows, lifts, puzzle tables. I've seen evidence of his cleverness all over this house."

Ned took two steps closer. "Lord Stephen cannot *march*."

"I beg your pardon?"

"He cannot *march*. He cannot slog along like the average infantryman, and even his ability on horseback can't hide the fact that he's unfit for military duty. He was denied the honorable course open to every other titled younger son when Boney was grinning at us from the coast of Normandy, so Stephen found a way to contribute without marching."

"*That's* why he makes guns?"

"He doesn't merely make guns, Miss Abbott. He looked at the whole process, from the gun-making to the shot and powder, to the rammers, and the way the men were deployed on battlefields. Britain has produced more high-quality arms, more efficiently, than at any other time in her history, and Lord Stephen Wentworth is a significant part of that achievement.

"He did the same with the heavy artillery," Ned went on, "the quartermasters' wagons, the cavalry sabers and scabbards, the navy's cranes and saws, the powder magazines.... They would canonize him at Horse Guards if they could, but here in Mayfair, our neighbors snicker at his limp."

Abigail sank back onto the bench. "War is wrong. I will never be convinced otherwise."

"And when war is brought to your doorstep," Ned said, "do you calmly hand over your women and children? Line up your menfolk to be conscripted into the enemy's army or shot? Pass along your corn and livestock to feed the enemy's populace while your own starves? Your theology is laudable, Miss Abbott—nobody *approves* of war—but you're a bit short on practical solutions."

"And Napoleon was never at our doorstep."

Ned passed her the parasol. "He was a mere fourteen miles away, across the Channel, but because Nelson sank the French fleet that's as close as he came. One sea battle away. Would you like to see more of Hyde Park?"

"You are changing the subject, Mr. Wentworth."

"That seems a prudent strategy while I am winning the argument." He cocked his head in a mannerism Abigail associated with Stephen. "As it happens, I agree with you. A hundred years of war hasn't solved a blessed thing, and it has made Britain all manner of deadly enemies. Thanks to the likes of Lord Stephen, the weapons grow more sophisticated, the slaughter worsens, and all the while, the Lords debate how long the surviving populace will be starved by the Corn Laws. We ought to be taking care of our own instead of plundering the four corners of the earth so a few nabobs can become still wealthier."

A boy who'd killed his own father to keep his sisters safe would understand war as a defensive necessity. Abigail would never change Stephen's mind on that score.

And what did it matter? Stephen needed a prospective duchess, and a lapsed Quaker inquiry agent was not that woman.

"A walk in the park sounds lovely," Abigail said, "but you aren't to bring a brace of pistols, Mr. Wentworth."

"Guns are too noisy. A well-aimed knife is just as effective, quieter, and can be thrown a thousand times. Stephen taught me that, and you do not want to stand between that man and a target when he's wielding a blade or a firearm. I'll meet you by the front door in ten minutes."

He bowed and strode into the house, leaving Abigail in Hercules's company on the terrace.

"I meant that comment about the brace of pistols as a jest," she said, stroking the dog's ears. "Ned took it seriously."

Which suggested Stapleton still posed a danger to her, and that Stephen had made no progress uncovering any clues hidden in the letters.

"Why, Miss Smithers," Stephen said, "what a fine establishment you have here."

Betty climbed down from the ladder that slid along the shelves of tea. "Tom, take yourself off for a pint, there's a lad."

The clerk had been holding the ladder and gazing adoringly at Betty's ankles. He bobbed his head at Stephen, grabbed a cap, and bolted out the door.

"You've made another conquest," Stephen said, leaning on the glass-topped counter. "I own I am jealous."

Betty dusted her hands and looked him up and down. "I thought you were leaving for the grouse moors. You haven't been sleeping, your lordship."

Stephen had slept little and badly since the Portmans' ball. "No hug for an old friend, Betty? No gesture of affection?" She looked happy, rosy, and quite at home in her shop. Stephen would not have allowed her business to fail, but neither could he have made the place a success if she wagered away all the profits.

Betty patted his lapel. "Here's my gesture of affection, *old friend*: I'll give you a ten percent discount on my best gunpowder, how's that?"

A few weeks ago, Stephen might have patted her bottom in return and bantered about giving her something for free. She was a respectable shop owner now, and thank heavens for that.

"Have you any gunpowder flavored with jasmine flowers?"

Betty glanced around the shop. "If you were tossing me over for another lady, you might have just said. You'll be taking a wife now, or you should be. Jasmine green tea is a woman's choice."

"Might we sit?" Stephen asked, because fatigue—and missing Abigail—made his knee hurt worse.

"Come into the back with me," Betty said. "Frisky Framley told Marie you were at the Portman ball, and you escorted a lady. An Amazon, but nobody knows much about her. Miss Abbott from Yorkshire. Marie heard a rumor that she's a professional snoop."

The back room was a combined office and parlor. The fragrance of tea was punctuated here with the scent of a bouquet of roses sitting on the battered desk. The blooms were fresh and the thorns had been clipped from the stems.

"Miss Abbott is an inquiry agent," Stephen said, sinking into a venerable armchair. "She has provided my family loyal service, and I have reason to believe her welfare is in jeopardy."

The kneehole desk faced the wall, papers stacked over most of its surface. Betty turned the chair to face the room and took a seat.

"You're sweet on her," she said, without rancor. "You would not escort her to a society ball unless the lady mattered to you. Who's after her?"

Abigail and Betty would get along famously. "The Marquess of Stapleton, a nasty, aging arachnid of a peer, who—"

Betty waved a hand, displaying ink-stained fingers. "Ophelia Marchant has other names for him, none of them complimentary. She's been his fancy piece for ages, but he never takes her to the theater, and hardly ever buys her a trinket. But then, she's not really earning his coin, is she?"

"Anything you know about Stapleton could be useful,

Betty. Miss Abbott had a brief affair with Stapleton's son years ago and can think of no reason why the marquess should take up against her now."

Betty worried a nail. "Did Stapleton's son marry her? Some of these dashing blades think sham weddings are quite entertaining. A sham wedding that wasn't a sham might be a lark for such as them."

"Stapleton's heir was properly married at the time." Or improperly, given the lack of fidelity on both sides of the union.

Betty wrinkled her nose. "And this lordling either lied about being married or he promised Miss Abbott his harridan of a wife was expiring of consumption. Men have no imagination." Another inspection of Stephen's person followed. "Some men. Lord Dunderhead sent Clare a very nice sum. She bought a one-third interest in this shop, though this is her day off."

"Did you invest the money?"

"Half in the cent-per-cents, like you told me. Half in a little business that employs fallen women to make parasols."

Betty was engaging in charity, in other words. "Give me the name of the parasol shop and I will offer it my custom."

"You're buying parasols now, my lord?"

"As it happens, I am, as are the womenfolk in my family. I also have a few designs involving parasols that might sell quite nicely. I am not, however, here to discuss investment opportunities with you."

"And you aren't looking to get under my skirts," Betty said, gaze speculative. "So what are you doing here?"

Guarding my dragon. "Stapleton must think that Miss Abbott knows some nasty family secret," he said. "That she's come across documents or facts that reflect badly on Stapleton. Would your friend Ophelia be willing to talk to me about Stapleton?"

Betty pushed a stool over toward Stephen's chair. "She shouldn't talk to anybody about the man who's putting a roof over her head. Rest your foot."

Stephen did, because it seemed the polite thing to do and because his knee was throbbing.

"The jewels Stapleton has given Ophelia are paste, Betty. He set ruffians on Miss Abbott in an attempt to drag her off a stagecoach, and he's searched her house at least once. Stapleton buys up vowels to extort compliance from MPs and younger sons, and now he's made Miss Abbott's life difficult."

Betty passed him a square pink pillow to place under his calf. "A mistress who gossips is soon no longer a mistress. To you it's a matter of curiosity to talk to her, but for her it's life and death to keep her mouth shut. She already sees other men on the side just to make ends meet. Stapleton cut back her allowance because he can't…he doesn't…"

Betty Smithers was *blushing.*

"His lordship can't *perform*?" Stephen suggested.

"You are awful," Betty muttered, but she was smiling. "He's useless, according to Ophelia. She's tried everything, and I do mean everything. The bindings, the whips, the elixirs, the toys…His lordship stops by for a late lunch, has a nice lie-down, sometimes fondles her bubbies a bit, then goes on his way."

Ironic. The son had been a rutting hound, the father was impotent—now. No wonder Stapleton hadn't remarried a woman of childbearing age.

"I've heard of keeping up appearances," Stephen said, "but to maintain a mistress merely for show..." No wonder Ophelia had other customers. "Does she frolic with Lord Fleming?"

"She cares for him, the fool. He'll never marry her, and he started calling on her just to keep an eye on Stapleton. Fleming is decent to her, but the men are all gents at first, aren't they? Fleming has to marry—he's an only son—and Ophelia will never be wife to a lord. Ophelia thinks Fleming will marry Stapleton's daughter-in-law, the better to manage Stapleton."

A memory intruded, of Lord Fleming leading Lady Champlain out for the quadrille at the Portmans' ball. They had made a handsome couple, with her ladyship's customary friendly smile on display throughout most of the dance.

Fleming's smile had been...possessive? Appreciative? Abigail would have the word for it, if she'd seen the couple dancing. That smile gave Stephen a glimmer of a theory regarding why Abigail's life had been turned upside down, and who was manipulating whom in the Stapleton household.

"You have been most helpful," Stephen said, lowering his foot from the stool. "How is the shop doing?"

Betty's gaze went to the roses. "I might sell it to Clare. Would you be angry with me if I did?"

Stephen pushed to his feet, though his knee offered him

profanity for making the effort. "You have caught the eye of a military man, and not a half-pay officer. He has room to keep a thriving rose garden and a glass house. He's probably widowed. Witness, he knows enough to trim the thorns from his bouquet. You like him, and that unnerves you."

"You unnerve me. How did you know he's former military?"

"The precision in the arrangement, the stems all cut at exactly the same angle, the colors chosen to match. He'll be loyal to you, Betty, and he's seen enough of life that he won't judge you for making your way as best you could here in London. Soldiers tend to be kind people, when they aren't on the battlefield." And often even when they were.

She touched a delicate pink rose petal. "He has a son, a darling little fellow. The captain adores that child. The lad's mother did not survive long after the birthing. The captain brings Tommy with him into the shop and is so patient with the boy."

Stephen had the odd sense of having been gently pushed off the stage of Betty's life. He'd thought to make a dignified exit, assuming he'd always be welcome to return for a cameo appearance, and that had been arrogant of him.

"If Clare needs a silent partner," he said, "I am happy to oblige. I'll want the name of your parasol shop too."

Betty followed his slow progress to the front of the shop. "Does your Miss Abbott appreciate you?"

"She argues with me, about guns, society entertainments, and anything else that strikes her fancy."

Betty measured out a scoop of gunpowder fragrant with

the scent of jasmine flowers. "But when she touches you, is it . . . *real*?"

"Her affection is genuine." And far too fierce for the tame label of *affection*.

Betty put the tea in a white muslin sack, tied a pretty pink ribbon around it, and passed it to him. "Then you should marry her."

"I want to, but I'm not sure she'll have me." Stephen put the tea in his pocket rather than hold it in his free hand.

Betty went up on her toes and kissed his cheek. "Good. If she puts you off balance, then she's exactly the lady you ought to wed. You are not to tell Ophelia you stopped by here."

"Of course not." Stephen bowed over Betty's hand, happy for her and her officer, and eager to discuss the conversation with Abigail.

But he was also—just a bit—daunted by the notion that Betty had so easily put him into her past. What could he offer Abigail that would prevent her from doing likewise?

Hyde Park, situated on the western end of London and thus close to the best neighborhoods, was lovely. The very air was cleaner, less tainted with coal smoke, horse droppings, and the evidence of passing fish wagons. To a lady raised in Yorkshire, the towering maples in their autumn finery were a relief, and the placid surface of the Serpentine balm to the soul.

"I'm glad we brought Hercules," Abigail said. "This is beautiful."

The park was situated next to the wealthiest neighborhoods, but open to all. Nannies with small charges toddled along the walkways, clerks and shopgirls shyly shared benches, and fine ladies walked out with their companions.

More than a few children pointed to Hercules, who trotted along at Abigail's side with majestic dignity.

"When Good King Hal stole the monasteries from the church," Ned said, tipping his hat to a passing trio of equestriennes, "he turned one of Westminster Abbey's forests into a hunting ground. In the reign of Charles I, the place was opened to the public. Ungrateful lot that we are, we chopped off his head anyway. I'd hate to think of London without its royal parks."

"I can breathe here," Abigail said. "Might we sit for a moment?" Ned was a fine escort. He walked neither too quickly nor too slowly, he didn't chatter, and he didn't make a cake of himself to the ladies he encountered along the way.

But he wasn't Stephen, and Abigail desperately wished she could be sharing this outing with Stephen, though strolling in the park with a leashed mastiff would hardly be his lordship's idea of an enjoyable errand.

"You are sad," Ned said, guiding Abigail to a bench near the water and taking the place beside her. "Or homesick?"

Heartsick? "Stephen will see a pattern in my letters that I could not see myself, and he will deduce the significance of it. He will confront Stapleton, sort him out, and I will return to Yorkshire. I am simply impatient to be home. I am also unused to relying on others to fight my battles for me."

Hercules planted himself at her feet, his chin on his paws as he watched a swan glide by.

"Trust is hard," Ned said. "For some of us, it's impossible."

Was he referring to Stephen, to Abigail, or to himself? She wasn't incapable of trust—far from it. She trusted her clients to be wary of telling her the truth, she trusted Malcolm to shed on the carpets, she trusted neighbors to be nosy, and human nature to be contrary.

Hercules rose to sitting, his gaze on the path Abigail and Ned had just traversed. A well-dressed man came up the walkway from the direction of Hyde Park Corner. He moved briskly, something about his bearing familiar.

"Do London swells typically take the air with three bully boys?" Abigail asked.

Ned casually turned his head, as if watching the progress of a nanny and her charge farther down the bank. "Bloody hell."

Language, Ned. "I know that man," Abigail said, as Hercules rumbled a warning. "I've seen him before." But he hadn't been in morning attire. He'd been…

"Take this," Ned said, shoving his walking stick at her.

"I have my own sword cane, Mr. Wentworth. That is Lord Fleming."

"That is trouble. Goddammit, Stephen will kill me, and I haven't even a loaded peashooter to wave about."

"I have a knife in my boot, a glass weight in my reticule, and a very stout hatpin in my bonnet. Hercules is trained to handle situations exactly like this. We shall contrive, and we shall do so without violating any Commandments."

Fleming approached, his escorts hanging back a few paces. They were sizable, muscular, and dressed just well enough not to be mistaken for highwaymen.

"That nasty man tried to abduct me from a stagecoach," Abigail muttered. "I have a score to settle with him."

"Miss Abbott." Lord Fleming stopped three yards off and bowed, sparing Hercules an assessing glance. "We have not been introduced. Wentworth, good day. Perhaps you'd tend to the civilities?"

"Not if you think to bother the lady, I won't." Ned fingered the handle of his walking stick, which sent looks ricocheting among the three men behind Fleming.

"We mean the lady no harm," Fleming said. "We simply want to have a civil conversation with her."

The nanny collected her charge, while the swan glided away from the bank.

"Converse," Abigail said, stroking Hercules's head, "and I will decide if your intentions are civil."

"I come to offer you my escort," Lord Fleming said. "A certain gentleman of high station would like a word with you."

The only gentleman of high station Abigail wanted a word with was Lord Stephen Wentworth.

"Here in London," she said, "I'm told a quaint custom is observed among the wellborn. They pay calls on one another. They chat over a pot of tea and discuss any number of topics—the weather, attempted kidnappings, housebreaking, that sort of thing."

Fleming's brows rose. "You admit to breaking into my house?"

Abigail stepped closer, and Hercules moved with her. "I admit to having been the *victim* of housebreaking, sir. More than once, as my companion and my entire household in York will attest. Let's talk about that, shall we?"

She itched to swing her reticule and drop Lord Fleming in his tracks. Between knives, sword canes, and the advantage of surprise, she and Ned could likely fend off Fleming's toadies, and Hercules would doubtless give a good account of himself as well.

Except…this was Hyde Park. Half of London would witness the affray and know she had landed the first blow. Gossip would take wing because the lady assaulting the fine courtesy lord had been a guest of Their Graces of Walden before she enjoyed the hospitality of Newgate.

"Let's talk," Abigail went on, "about highwaymen who ride exceptionally fine horseflesh and speak in Etonian accents. Highwaymen who steal nothing but an innocent woman's peace of mind."

Fleming seemed amused. "You have interesting fancies, Miss Abbott. You can come with us now, or I am instructed to have you arrested for housebreaking. My own residence and that of Lord Stapleton were burgled less than a week past, and we have witnesses who put you in the immediate vicinity that same night."

"Rubbish," Abigail snapped. "Monstrous fictions typical of the fevered male imagination. You yourself saw me at the Portmans' ball, which is the only entertainment I've attended."

Ned took the place at her elbow, though she hadn't heard him move. "You can't accost a lady in the middle of Hyde

Park, Fleming. That's kidnapping, last I heard. Hanging felonies play hell with a man's social schedule. Besides, you have too many witnesses here."

Fleming glanced about. "Nobody of any consequence. Walden's bastard hardly counts."

"You flatter me shamelessly," Ned replied, "but I'm afraid we cannot tarry. Tell Stapleton if he wishes to call on Miss Abbott, he should do like the rest of his ilk and send another of his catch-farts around with a card."

Fleming took a step forward, as did his henchmen, which escalated Hercules's rumbling to outright growls.

"Stapleton cannot be seen to call on his late son's fancy piece, and well she knows it."

"*She*," Abigail retorted, "can deliver a swift kick to a location that will imperil the succession of your father's title. *She* will then accuse you of having made untoward advances to her at the Portmans' ball, and *she* will make sure Lady Champlain and the Duchess of Walden are privy to all the lurid details. If Stapleton is determined to drag this situation down to the level of false accusations and public scandal, I will oblige him."

In the midst of this diatribe, a question popped into Abigail's mind: Why was Fleming still willing to do Stapleton's bidding? The gambling markers signed by Fleming's sister had been returned to him by anonymous post.

Unless *Fleming* sought to retrieve the letters? For his own purposes—who wouldn't want some sordid correspondence to wave in Stapleton's face?—or perhaps to encourage a match with Lady Champlain?

"If you don't come with us peacefully," Fleming said, "I

will see Wentworth here arrested for housebreaking. He's no stranger to Newgate, if the rumors are true. He and Walden were locked up together, in fact. Quite an example Walden sets for his progeny."

"You do me great honor," Ned drawled, "but Miss Abbott isn't going anywhere with you."

Abigail considered options while the comforting weight of her reticule rested against her leg and Hercules stared hard at Fleming.

Ned could not account for his whereabouts the night of the break-ins. He could well manufacture an alibi, and His Grace could likely see him freed, but the truth was, he'd gone on his criminal errand for Abigail's sake.

And he was a man with a criminal past, however distant, and that did not bode well for his treatment at Bow Street.

Then too, to reproduce the letters in Champlain's handwriting, somebody would have to locate the late earl's journals in the Stapleton residence, which was doubtless a sizable abode.

"You are tedious," Abigail said, rapping Lord Fleming on the chest with the handle of her sword cane. "I will accompany you to Stapleton's residence and nowhere else. Mr. Wentworth will inform Their Graces exactly in whose company I departed this park. If I am not returned to the Walden household in blooming good health by two of the clock, you will be arrested for kidnapping and the Marquess of Stapleton will be named as your accessory. Mr. Wentworth will delight in testifying against you. This lot"—Abigail sent a glower in the direction of Fleming's hired bullies—"will remain here with Mr. Wentworth."

"Miss Abbott," Ned said, most pleasantly, "might I have a word?"

Abigail rapped Fleming on the chest once more for good measure, then stepped back.

"I know what you're doing," Ned whispered, drawing her a few feet away. "Stephen will dismember me if I allow you to do it."

"I fight my own battles, Mr. Wentworth. Nothing stops you from telling Lord Stephen where the battle will be joined. Stapleton will not relent until he confronts me, and I have more than a few things I want to say to him."

"But, Miss Abbott, Abigail, the marquess does not play fair, and if anything happens to you—"

"You are very dear, but this is what I *do*, Mr. Wentworth. I untie the knotty problems and tidy up the messy ones. I know what I'm about. Tell Stephen what's afoot, send him along to Stapleton's house, and all will be well."

"This is what you do, when the issue is a straying niece or somebody's pearl necklace gone missing. These men are dangerous, Miss Abbott. They play dirty, and you know that or you would not have sought Stephen's aid in the first place."

Ned, blast him, had a point. "Can you have the carriage followed?"

"Of course, and I can make certain that Fleming doesn't have three more ne'er-do-wells lurking at his coach, but this is still the most foolish, dunderheaded, cork-brained—"

Hercules growled, and Abigail wanted to growl along with

him. "A confrontation with Stapleton is *exactly* what Stephen hoped to bring about when he dragged me to that fancy ball."

"Not this sort of confrontation."

Spare me from overly protective men. "I am leaving Hyde Park with Fleming, and a half dozen people, including you, will see me get into his coach. He is not foolish enough to harm a guest of Their Graces of Walden, much less to make an enemy of Lord Stephen Wentworth."

Ned scowled in Fleming's direction. "I will inspect the interior of the coach before handing you up, you will take the dog with you inside the coach and wherever else Fleming hauls you, and I will alert Stephen to this madness before St. Paul's tolls the quarter hour."

"Miss Abbott," Fleming called. "Are you coming with me, or do I have Wentworth arrested?"

"He can do that, Ned, but he won't physically harm me. He could have shot me from a rooftop as I returned from Sunday services if my actual end was Stapleton's objective. They must believe I know where the letters are, and that ensures my safe conduct."

"Miss Abbott," Fleming said again. "You try my patience."

"And you," Abigail said, striding up to him, "would try the patience of St. Peter himself. I will accompany you, Lord Fleming. Your dis-honor guard will remain here, and Mr. Wentworth will see me to your coach. Hercules comes with me, and if you object to those terms, I invite you to go for a swim in the Serpentine. Lord Stapleton's next caller will be Lord Stephen Wentworth, and he will do much more than try your meager patience."

Ned made a shooing motion toward Fleming's toughs, and they shuffled off in the direction of Knightsbridge, where any number of drinking establishments doubtless awaited their custom.

Abigail took a firm hold of Hercules's leash with one hand, grasped Fleming's arm with the other, and directed his lordship back to the walkway.

Hercules trotted along at her side, issuing the occasional growl. Truth be told, the dog's company did make Abigail feel ever so much safer.

Chapter Thirteen

"She was enjoying herself," Ned said, pacing the length of Stephen's office. "The damned female was meant to rule Britain, and she knows it."

"She doesn't," Stephen said, shrugging into his morning coat before getting to his feet. "Miss Abbott cannot be talked into considering the management of even a duchy. I must be off. Send a badger to tell Quinn and Duncan what you saw, and that I've gone to aid…I've gone to see if I can render any service to Miss Abbott."

And to kill Stapleton, if need be.

Badgers were the Wentworth family's network of street urchins, beggars, flower girls, and crossing sweepers. Some of them took work as bank messengers, and all of them answered to Ned. They were sharper than Wellington's scouts and expected a good deal less in terms of wages.

"A badger has already been dispatched, and I will follow

as soon as I talk sense to you. You can't just barge in on a marquess's household, Stephen. Not even you would be that bold."

"Yes, I would"—he slipped a knife into his boot and tucked another into a coat pocket—"if I thought Abigail was in immediate danger. Stapleton tried to make off with her in York, but she belongs to the Wentworths now, and the marquess will tread carefully, at least for a time. Abigail knew that, or she would not have gone with Fleming. Once Stapleton realizes she doesn't have the letters, he might not be so polite."

"These are the copies?" Ned asked, gesturing to the papers spread over Stephen's desk.

"Reconstructions, such as they are. Champlain was a nearly slavish correspondent, as if he thought his letters might be published someday to vast acclaim. He wrote to Abigail every Monday and Thursday without fail, for better than five months. Ninety percent of it is drivel."

"And the other ten percent?"

"Worse than drivel. You may read them as examples of what not to write to your lady love. If you see anything approaching a pattern, you will tell me. I am at my wit's end with the damned things."

The object of the exercise was to give Ned something interesting to do, lest dear Neddy take it upon himself to break a few heads that were by rights Stephen's heads to break.

"You think a code of some sort might be embedded here?" Ned asked, gathering the letters into a stack.

"A cypher, a signal, something." Except that only Abigail

had ever read the dratted letters, so what was the point of a hidden message?

"And you're off to challenge Stapleton to a duel?" Ned said, shuffling the letters into some sort of order.

"Abigail frowns on violence, so no. I am off to call on Lady Champlain," Stephen said. "When I showed up in Portman's ballroom, I was swarmed by matchmakers, hostesses, dowagers, and the usual straying wives and merry widows. Lady Champlain did not offer me so much as a smile during the eternity that was the ball."

"She's one of your..."

"Dear former acquaintances. I met Harmonia when she was in the mood to make Champlain jealous, and I—being an agreeable sort of fellow—obliged her."

"You are a disgrace."

"I am a charming man who enjoys the occasional interlude with a willing woman, and Champlain all but threw her at me. Said my consequence exceeded his, and she ought to like that. I am not proud of my behavior, but everybody involved was willing."

Ned folded the letters into a pocket of his tailcoat. "I do not now, nor will I ever, understand the Quality. Miss Abbott and I are agreed on that."

"Read the letters," Stephen said. "I will find out why Harmonia ignored me and see what Abigail's about with Stapleton."

Stephen knew better than to hurry—hurry resulted in falls, and falls could result in complete bed rest, not to mention days of pain and self-recrimination—but he made an efficient trip to the stables and a very quick jaunt on horseback to Stapleton's front door.

The marquess's butler was too well trained to overtly convey surprise, but he did try to take Stephen's cane from him.

"I'll keep it, if you don't mind," Stephen said. "I can see myself to the formal parlor."

"My lord, I must announce you."

"No, you must not. Her ladyship and I are old friends, and I'm surprising her."

"But, my lord, she's not in the formal parlor. His little lordship's sixth birthday is next week, and the formal parlor is being thoroughly cleaned in anticipation of the happy day. Her ladyship is in the family parlor."

"And where is Stapleton?" Stephen asked, examining his appearance in the mirror hanging on the door of the porter's nook.

"I'm sure I couldn't say, my lord. If you'll follow me this way."

A carriage rolled up to the front door, the Fleming town coach, though the crests were turned and the coachy and groom were not in livery. The chestnuts in the traces were distinctive, though, in that their white stockings did not quite match.

Fleming emerged and politely offered Abigail a hand down, which she ignored. She was in magnificent good looks, her parasol and walking stick at the ready. Hercules, regal and dangerous, panted at her side. Stephen had figured out on the ride over that her objective was reconnaissance of enemy territory. If she spotted one of Champlain's journals, she'd doubtless discreetly borrow it.

And thus commit a crime. Stapleton might not see her

tried and convicted, but he'd destroy her reputation as a lady and as an inquiry agent. That he himself had sought to commit the same crime where the letters were concerned would be utterly irrelevant from Stapleton's perspective.

Stephen made a show of organizing his cane and following in the butler's wake, until they arrived at Harmonia's private sitting room.

"No need to knock," Stephen said, slipping past the butler and lifting the door latch. "We're old friends, and I hope to surprise her ladyship." He opened the door just wide enough to gain admittance to the room and closed and locked it behind him.

"Harmonia"— Stephen bowed —"and de Beauharnais. Have you graduated to doing nude portraits now, or is her ladyship posing for a few random sketches?"

De Beauharnais had the savoir faire to smile, while Harmonia blushed and yanked up her bodice. Her figure was a trifle fuller than when Stephen had kept her company, and the added flesh looked lovely on her.

"Wentworth." De Beauharnais rose, set aside his sketch pad, and bowed. "Your timing is execrable. Her ladyship was graciously indulging my artistic inclinations."

"If you didn't want to be interrupted at your diversions," Stephen said, "then you should have locked the damned door. Harmonia, you appear to be thriving, and I mean that with all gentlemanly sincerity. A fellow could do with a spot of tea, now that you're back in your clothes. Autumn air can be so dry. Is the comely Mr. de Beauharnais the reason you all but gave me the cut direct at the Portmans' ball?"

Though that couldn't be quite right, because she'd been

more than friendly with Fleming and happy to dance with a few other gentlemen as well.

"You are quite rude to interrupt us," Harmonia said, getting to her feet. "Quite rude. I did not cut you at Lady Portman's ball, though if this is how you behave in polite company, then cut you, I shall. I avoided your company because you seemed devoted to the woman you were escorting, and introductions between her and me might have been awkward. Besides, I do entirely prefer Mr. de Beauharnais's company to yours or that of any other gentleman, and you will please accommodate my preferences by taking yourself off. Give my love to Their Graces."

The impact of this grand dismissal was undermined by de Beauharnais staring hard at a spot on the carpet while his lips twitched. The fabric of his breeches covering his manly apparatus betrayed either a misjudgment on the tailor's part or an enthusiasm on de Beauharnais's.

"You know Miss Abbott at sight?" Stephen inquired, making no move to exit the room. "Did you know Stapleton had her accosted in the park, and not two minutes ago Lord Fleming marched her right in through your front door?"

Harmonia put a hand to her throat. "Fleming pointed her out to me at the ball. She should not be here."

De Beauharnais retrieved a shawl from the chair behind the escritoire and draped it solicitously around Harmonia's shoulders.

"Perhaps we might continue this discussion elsewhere," he said, giving Harmonia's arm a pat. "Her ladyship's private parlor should be reserved for the guests whom she chooses to receive."

Oh, nicely done, and Stephen was happy to quit the fancy little parlor anyway. Champlain's journals weren't on the shelves behind the escritoire, nor did they grace the mantel or the bookshelves across from the fireplace.

"Let's retire to Stapleton's study, shall we?" Stephen said. "That is doubtless where Miss Abbott has been taken, and she needs to know that I am on hand to escort her from the premises."

Or to kill Stapleton, Fleming, the butler, and anybody else who sought to do Abigail harm.

"He's done *what*?" Quinn Wentworth spoke softly. In Ned's experience, His Grace of Walden had never needed to shout, and particularly not with Ned. The emphasis had been all the more apparent for being rendered quietly.

"Stephen's off to confront Stapleton directly," Ned said, propping a hip on the library desk. "Miss Abbott wasn't really given a choice about going with Fleming. She took Hercules with her, and I set a badger to following them. She's at the Stapleton residence, ergo, Stephen took himself off to the same location."

"We must trust Stephen," Duncan said, from his reading chair before the fire. "Stapleton isn't about to make off with a ducal heir or a ducal guest, and Stephen knows that."

Quinn rounded on him. "Stapleton had a goddamned stagecoach held up in broad daylight trying to kidnap a woman who'd never done him a moment of harm. Stapleton violated the sanctity of Miss Abbott's household. It's not Stephen I'm worried about."

Duncan nearly smiled. "There is that, and Miss Abbott is no doubt able to give a good account of herself."

Quinn ran a hand through his hair. "I wish Jane were—"

Jane strode through the door. "Jane wishes you would recall that merely because a woman has been delivered of a child does not mean her mind or her hearing have become impaired. You are in a taking over Stephen and Miss Abbott?"

Quinn grasped his duchess's hand and led her to the sofa. "I didn't want to bother you. I'm not in a taking. Dukes do not..."

Jane crossed her arms and remained standing. "Quinton Wentworth, for shame."

Ned and Duncan diplomatically found somewhere else to look.

"I would have fetched you down from the nursery," Quinn said, "but I didn't want to interrupt..." He waved a hand in the general direction of maternal delicacy.

"If you decline to interrupt every time I nurse our daughter, we will see a good deal less of each other than I prefer. Tell me what's afoot."

Duncan spoke as he got to his feet. "Might we wait for Matilda? I sent a footman to fetch her and she should be—ah, welcome, my love." Not by a raised eyebrow or a smirk did Duncan indicate that *some men* had a proper respect for their wives' counsel, but the message was conveyed by his husbandly peck to Matilda's cheek.

"Stephen has joined battle with Stapleton," Duncan said. "We are considering next steps."

Ned took up the narrative for the benefit of the ladies.

"Miss Abbott was accosted by Lord Fleming in the park. He was sent to retrieve her at Stapleton's behest. He claimed all Stapleton wanted was to speak with Miss Abbott, and she insisted that the discussion take place at Stapleton's home. Stephen suspects she is reconnoitering enemy territory, and he was in the saddle within ten minutes of learning of her decision."

"And that," Matilda murmured, "tells us all we need to know."

"Thoughts?" Duncan asked, kissing her knuckles.

"We have both a king and queen in play," Matilda said, "an unusual combination. They will likely divide and conquer, but if Miss Abbott is engaging with Stapleton, who is Stephen's target? Lord Fleming?"

"Stephen claimed," Ned replied, "that he went to pay a call on Lady Champlain."

"We are wasting time," Quinn muttered. "I don't trust Stapleton, I don't trust Fleming. I would like to trust Miss Abbott but we haven't had time to take her true measure. And as for Stephen…"

Jane patted Quinn's chest. "We do trust Stephen. He will have considered every permutation of the facts and possibilities, and he will have them all in hand."

Quinn caught her fingers in his. "And if Stapleton takes Stephen's cane away?"

Jane and Matilda exchanged a look. Ned had been deciphering such glances for several years now, and could make nothing out of them. Quinn, Duncan, and even Stephen were much easier to read, but the ladies remained a mystery. Ned suspected they remained somewhat mysterious to their devoted swains as well, and that only added to his puzzlement.

"You'd best be on your way," Jane said. "Ned will go with you as my personal guarantor that no unnecessary bravado imperils anybody I love."

Duncan bowed to his wife and released her hand. "And should *necessary* bravado arise?"

"Imperil somebody I do not love," Jane said. "Lord Stapleton's politics are disgraceful, but Quinn hasn't yet allowed me to interfere. Stapleton sends six-year-old children into the mines when his own offspring never worked an honest day in his spoiled life. Now the marquess is troubling Miss Abbott, and that troubles Stephen. We are entitled to make a show of support, lest Miss Abbott think we don't look after our own."

In other words, Jane trusted Stephen, but did not trust Stapleton.

"Gentlemen," Quinn said, "we have our orders. Let's be off."

Abigail frowns on violence. Stephen reminded himself of that guiding directive as he stalked from Harmonia's pretty sitting room down the corridor to the library. A quick inspection revealed that Champlain's handwritten journals weren't hiding in plain sight.

"My lord, you cannot run tame about this house," Harmonia said, tagging after him. "My father-in-law will take a very dim view of your behavior, and I am none too impressed with it myself."

De Beauharnais had apparently made the prudent

decision to bide in Harmonia's parlor. Alternatively, somewhere in the house a proper portrait of her ladyship was in progress.

Stephen's next objective was the formal parlor, which—true to the butler's assertion—was full of maids armed with dust mops and scrub buckets.

"You cannot do this," Harmonia said, a note of hysteria creeping into her voice. "You cannot charge in here, upend the household, and, *no*. Stephen, that is the marquess's study and even I— *You cannot go in there!*"

Stephen paused outside the door. "Stapleton has gone too far, Harmonia. He has troubled a woman I care for greatly, set his henchmen to bothering her in the park, and now he seeks to bully her into giving up personal possessions that have already been stolen from her. I won't have it. You may either join the discussion or scurry back to your pretty parlor and your pretty painter."

He expected her to flounce off in high dudgeon—she was good at that. Instead, she cast a miserable glance at the closed door.

"*She's* in there. Miss Abbott." Harmonia took four paces away, then four paces back. "She's everything I'm not. Tall, self-confident, independent, *competent*. I hate her for that more than anything else."

A niggle of intuition told Stephen that Harmonia's admission had significance beyond an insecure woman's fears.

"Harmonia, she had no idea Champlain was married. He was just another handsome customer flirting with her in her father's shop, and then he became an admirer and a lover.

The whole time, the *entire time*, he was deceiving her. If she's independent and self-assured, Champlain must take a significant part of the blame for making her distrustful and lonely too."

Abigail would smite him soundly for that conclusion, though it was nothing less than the truth.

"He lied to everybody," Harmonia said miserably, "most especially to himself."

Why did I ever think we had something to offer each other? Once upon a time, Stephen had willingly involved himself with this woman, knowing full well they were nothing more than a mutual diversion. Perhaps that had been the point.

A diversion never questioned the morality of war, a diversion never had the ingenuity to dress as a man, a diversion never confronted an aggressor who had a thousand times her social influence and ten thousand times her wealth.

"My lady, unless you want your son to turn out exactly like his father and like his grandfather, I suggest you join us in the marquess's study. Champlain's gallivanting about, wenching, and carousing made your marriage a polite misery. His behavior doesn't have to ruin your future as well."

Nor would Stephen let it ruin Abigail's future.

A raised male voice penetrated the door, the words indistinct.

"Stephen," Harmonia said, "there's more here in play than you know, and Stapleton isn't entirely to blame."

"Of course not," Stephen said, "he's hired minions and

impressed a co-conspirator in the person of Lord Fleming. His next move will doubtless be to inveigle you into trying to ruin Miss Abbott socially, which utterly clodpated maneuver will provoke Her Grace of Walden into mobilizing her legion of Valkyries against you. You will be banished to the north more effectively than if Stapleton had you bound and gagged and tossed into a coach."

A woman's voice joined that of the shouting male, her annoyance palpable through the closed door.

"Come along," Stephen said. "I won't allow Stapleton or Fleming to bully you, and Miss Abbott won't either."

"She won't bully me?"

"Don't be tiresome. Miss Abbott won't allow their lordships to bully you." He opened the door and marched in—as best he could with a cane—just in time to see Abigail wallop Lord Fleming in the knee with her reticule and a growling Hercules strain at the leash held firmly in Abigail's hand.

"Well done, Miss Abbott," Stephen said. "Next time—if Fleming is foolish enough to provoke you again—aim higher and between his legs. The targets are doubtless tiny, but I trust you to make the blow count nonetheless. Good doggy, Hercules. Very good doggy, indeed."

Abigail considered herself a patient woman, and with Stapleton, she was managing adequately. The marquess was stubborn and arrogant, but he kept his hands to himself. Fleming, however, made the mistake of attempting to take her by the arm and steer her to the sofa one too many times.

Abigail had no intention of sitting like a penitent schoolgirl while two men loomed over her and attempted to intimidate her.

She clipped Fleming on the knee with her reticule, a glancing blow that ought to smart for a time without doing any real injury. Fleming, however, was apparently not used to being thwarted, and he rounded on her with an ugly snarl, reaching for her arm again.

At some point in this exchange the door had opened, though Abigail could not take her eyes off Fleming to see who the intruder was. Stapleton was apparently inclined to let his minion manhandle a lady, which was, quite honestly, frightening. Abigail had come here for sound tactical reasons, but she hadn't counted on Fleming acting like the ne'er-do-wells he consorted with.

Hercules was about to make his opinion known regarding Fleming's rudeness while Abigail scrambled to recall the appropriate commands.

"Well done, Miss Abbott," said an amused male voice. "Next time—if Fleming is foolish enough to provoke you again—aim higher and between his legs. The targets are doubtless tiny, but I trust you to make the blow count nonetheless. Hercules, good doggy. Very good doggy, indeed."

Stephen. The relief that coursed through Abigail was unseemly. "My lord, welcome. The discussion was just getting interesting. Hercules, sit."

The dog took to his haunches, his weight a comforting presence against Abigail's leg.

"Harmonia," the marquess said, "take this disgrace to

good tailoring away, and don't come back until I bid you to. Take the damned dog too."

"We will stay," Stephen said, lounging against the marquess's desk, "and her ladyship will stay as well, because she is central to the conversation. Fleming, sit down and be quiet like yonder canine, lest Miss Abbott serve you more than a gentle tap to the knee."

Stapleton was turning the unbecoming shade of ripe tomato, but he pointed at the sofa, and Fleming subsided and commenced rubbing his knee.

"We are here to hold a thief accountable," Stephen said. "Or perhaps two thieves."

Two thieves? Abigail hadn't stolen anything—yet.

"Precisely," Stapleton said, rapping his fist on the blotter. "Somebody broke into my home and took property owned by me. That is a crime, and I intend to see the perpetrator punished."

"And you assume Miss Abbott is the perpetrator?" Stephen inquired, fluffing the silk of his cravat. "When did this dastardly deed take place?"

"Wednesday of last week," Stapleton said, "and Fleming claims Miss Abbott was seen in the vicinity of this house."

The woman who'd accompanied Stephen into the room turned out to be Harmonia, Lady Champlain. By daylight, in an old-fashioned high-waisted gown, she did not look quite as glittering and gay as she had in a candlelit ballroom. She looked, in fact, weary and worried.

"Lady Champlain," Stephen said, "you were at the Portman ball, as was Lord Fleming. Was Miss Abbott present?"

Fleming spoke first. "She was, but the dancing ended at least three hours before dawn, and Miss Abbott would have had time to effect her crimes while polite society slept all unaware."

Stephen was looking at Abigail, his head cocked at that inquiring angle. She nodded in response, though Their Graces would likely be displeased with her. Somebody had to put an end to this foolishness, and if that meant airing the truth, so be it.

"Alas for your entirely self-serving theory, Fleming, the lady was with me. I escorted her to the Walden residence, and spent the balance of the night with her. Escorted her to breakfast, in fact, and my, you should have seen the looks on the faces of the duke and duchess."

In other words, Their Graces would support Stephen's recitation, no matter the damage to Abigail's reputation.

"We're courting," Stephen said, aiming an indulgent smile at Abigail, "and the course of true love occasionally deviates from strict decorum."

"So you see," Abigail added, "neither his lordship nor myself could have trespassed on your property, Lord Stapleton. Lord Fleming, however, has no such alibi. He could well have turned down the room with her ladyship, gone for a smoke in the garden, and made free with your premises without anybody noticing his absence. Given his sister's tendency to wager, retrieving her vowels from you would have served his ends very nicely."

"How the hell could you possibly—?" Fleming began, rising from the sofa, only to sink back onto the cushions with both hands bracing his knee. "Bedamned to you, Miss Abbott, and to your quarter-ton reticule and half-ton dog."

"I am a professional inquiry agent," Abigail replied. "I need not skulk about to learn of your sister's unfortunate tendencies when they are common knowledge at the piquet tables." A slight fabrication, very slight. Stephen had been at the piquet table and he could well have known of the lady's gambling markers. "And if you had kept your hands to yourself, you would not have needed a small lesson in manners."

"Fleming?" Stapleton asked in a low voice. "Is this true? Did you feign a burglary of your own home just to disguise your perfidy toward me?"

Fleming hesitated, then sent an assessing glance at Lady Champlain. He was preparing to lie, mentally arranging prevarications, which confirmed Abigail's theory regarding his motives.

"Lady Champlain," Abigail said, "perhaps you should sit. You look quite pale. Lord Fleming's desire to propose marriage to you has clearly inspired him to foolish behaviors. You may disabuse him of his presumptions now."

"*Marriage?*" her ladyship said, as if the word had been recently borrowed from Urdu. "Lord Fleming seeks to marry me? I know we've flirted and stood up for an occasional dance, but marriage?"

"Why not?" Fleming retorted. "I am of suitable rank, you're a proven breeder, Stapleton's political influence would stand me in good stead, and you're a widow. You should be grateful that a man of appropriate rank would take you on when your settlements won't be that impressive."

"A proven *breeder*?" Lady Champlain echoed. "A proven *breeder*?"

"And you're not bad looking," Fleming added, in what had to be the most ill-advised observation a man ever made. "A bit long in the tooth, but you can still pop out a couple of sons, I'm sure. I will be diligent regarding my marital—"

Stephen waggled his cane at Fleming. "If you hold a prayer of living to ensure the succession, cease covering yourself in stupidity. She wouldn't have you if you were the last exponent of the male gender in all of creation—do I have that right, my lady?"

Lady Champlain nodded.

"So, my lord," Abigail said, "where are the letters?"

All eyes turned to regard Fleming, who had stopped rubbing his knee. "I admit I looked for them, and I admit that had I found them, I would have read them thoroughly and used them as I saw fit."

Stephen shot his cuffs, the picture of elegant male ennui. "You admit to housebreaking with intent to steal and to contemplating extortion. Your criminal acts are undertaken not to protect anybody's reputation, but simply to advance your own interests."

Fleming sat forward, elbows braced on his thighs. "My sister plays too deeply, Harmonia barely spares me the time of day, Stapleton is getting on and hasn't an heir to his influence in the Lords. The boy…Champlain's son could use a stepfather. What is so wrong about taking some old letters that simply prove what everybody knows? Champlain was a titled trollop."

A sharp crack resounded and Fleming's left cheek turned bright pink.

Chapter Fourteen

"Well done, Lady Champlain," Abigail said. "A gentleman does not speak ill of the dead." Not before the man's widow, in any case, and not when that woman had apparently had quite enough of being told what to do by the men in her life.

"Damn it, Fleming, you do have the letters," Stapleton said, rising from his chair and bracing himself on the desk blotter. "You found them, you hid them, and now some damned housebreaker has taken them. Admit it! My son's reputation, the reputation of this house, is in the hands of one of your enemies. I knew I should never have taken you into my confidence."

"But you didn't take him into your confidence, did you?" Stephen mused. "The problem with the letters isn't that they confirm Champlain's reputation as a"—he spared Lady Champlain an apologetic smile—"bon vivant, but that they prove he was kicking his heels in France at the time his son was conceived. The current heir to the Stapleton title is a cuckoo in the nest, and the letters, dated and highly descriptive of the locations in which they were written, prove that conclusively."

Lady Champlain's complexion went from pale to translucent, confirming that Stephen had deduced the *why* of the whole imbroglio. Champlain could have been the world's greatest libertine and merited only a few raised eyebrows.

Not so, *Lady* Champlain.

"You can't know that," her ladyship said, sinking onto the sofa. "Nobody can know that. I met Champlain in Paris that year, and we found a country house to rent until summer. Nobody can know…"

"We know it now," Abigail said gently.

At the desk, the marquess was silent, his gaze fixed on the portrait hanging over the mantel.

"Well, hell," Fleming muttered. "If I'd known that's why you were looking for—"

Abigail hefted her reticule. "Hush, lest I heed his lordship's guidance regarding where I aim my second blow. You are a walking verification of the theory that excessive inbreeding has rendered the aristocracy mentally unfit."

"I wanted to destroy the blasted letters," Stapleton said. "That's all I sought, to destroy them. I would have never known about them, except Champlain kept journals of his travels, for posterity, I suppose, and he noted when he wrote to whom. Her ladyship was his Sunday correspondent, Miss Abbott he wrote to twice a week. As if he feared she'd forget a marquess's heir the moment he took ship."

Would that I had. Stephen was watching Abigail, and she realized he had more to say but was waiting for her permission to say it.

"You've had Champlain's journals for years," Abigail observed. "Why set your highwaymen and housebreakers on me now?"

Stapleton, who'd aged about twenty years in five minutes, twisted a ring on his fourth finger. "The boy turns six next week. He'll soon be old enough to be interested in his father's—in Champlain's—journals. I read through them to make sure there's nothing a lad ought not to see regarding his father. The journals are surprisingly dull given my son's proclivities, but then I noticed the pattern of his correspondence, and I knew something had to be done."

"But the boy isn't your grandson," Fleming said. "Why go to all that trouble when the child isn't even your blood?"

"I didn't realize he wasn't my grandson until recently, and what does that matter? He'll be the next Marquess of Stapleton, and he's just a little boy. I want to blame Harmonia, but Champlain was…he was a difficult husband. One must concede the obvious."

Lady Champlain had regained some of her color. "Champlain wasn't a bad man, he simply had more growing up to do."

Abigail could not be so generous, but she could keep her judgments to herself. Champlain's character, or lack thereof, no longer interested her.

"I don't have the letters," she said. "Somebody stole them earlier this year. By the time Lord Fleming was plaguing me and holding up stagecoaches, I no longer had them. I had read them often enough to be able to reconstruct them fairly well, hence, Lord Stephen was able to divine the impact of the dates." Perhaps Abigail in some corner of her heart hadn't wanted to see the possibilities, but then, she'd had no idea of the precise age of the Stapleton heir. "I would like the letters back, though. They are all I have...they are mementos of..."

All I have of my son. That reality was too personal to be aired in this company—too personal, and too painful.

Stephen held out a hand to her, and Abigail took it.

"Miss Abbott wants her letters back. Lady Champlain, you will please return them."

Abigail rested against him, and perched as he was against the desk, he provided a sturdy support. The impact of his conclusion—that *Champlain's wife* had stolen the letters—frankly caught her unaware.

But it made sense. Her ladyship would do anything to protect her son, and Abigail respected that.

"You took them to safeguard the boy," Stephen said, "or perhaps to get Stapleton under control—God knows that thankless task should fall to somebody. The letters have served their purpose, Stapleton knows the slender thread by which his consequence dangles, but he also knows your own reputation will suffer should you disclose the child's origins. Give the letters back, or I will take matters into my own hands."

Abigail had missed Stephen, missed the scent of him, the hard, muscular feel of his body. She might have, eventually, suspected the petite, pretty Lady Champlain of taking the letters, but not in time to use the knowledge effectively. Knowing who had violated Abigail's household and why should have given her a greater sense of satisfaction.

"You owe Miss Abbott much," Stephen said. "You have stolen more from her than a batch of maudlin old letters. You stole her peace of mind and set in motion an interruption of the business she relies on to provide necessities. Worse yet, you imperiled her reputation. You sent her fleeing to virtual strangers for aid, and for that, she will require recompense. Give her back the letters. Now."

Abigail straightened and Stephen let her go. "I would like them back. They are my property, not yours."

A quiet knock sounded on the door.

"Enter," Stephen called.

The butler took one step into the room. "His Grace of Walden and Mr. Duncan Wentworth, to call upon the marquess." The man's voice had quavered a bit, which Abigail understood only too well.

Duncan and Quinn strode into the room, resplendent in morning attire, gold winking at their cuffs and from the abundant lace of their cravats. Both men wore boots polished to a mirror shine, and, by contrast, Lord Fleming looked frumpy and Stapleton positively mildewed.

Hercules greeted them with a few thumps of his tail, but remained at Abigail's side.

Abigail was enormously glad to see both Wentworths, not that she should have ever, ever doubted that Stephen had the situation in hand. He looked of a piece with his kinsmen, and in his casual posture, perhaps even a bit more elegant.

"Walden, Cousin." He nodded graciously. "Greetings. Miss Abbott, it appears your artillery has arrived. Perhaps somebody should ring for tea, or—given the occasion—break out the brandy. I might instruct the butler accordingly, but it is hardly my place to do so."

Stapleton glowered at his butler. "Stop eavesdropping and get thee to the kitchen."

"My letters?" Abigail said. "I will have them back now."

Lady Champlain got to her feet. "I keep them in the nursery. You may have the lot of them."

"I'll come with you," Abigail said, unwilling to let her ladyship roam free without supervision.

"That will not be necessary." Lady Champlain made a good try at looking down her nose, but for once, Abigail was delighted to be nearly six feet tall.

"Yes," Abigail said, passing Stephen the dog's leash, "it will. After you, my lady."

"I assure you," Lady Champlain said, casting a pleading look in Stapleton's direction, "you need not treat me like a common criminal. I was only trying to protect my son."

"Then you might have approached me directly and discussed the situation with me like an adult. The earl has long since gone to his reward, and I have no interest in ruining you or your son."

"Harmonia," Stapleton said patiently, "please fetch the rubbishing letters and let us be done with this."

Quinn and Duncan bowed as Abigail followed Lady Champlain to the door. Fleming rose awkwardly, standing with one knee cocked.

"Abigail." Stephen remained perched against the desk.

"My lord?"

"I named my dragon well."

His words fortified her, and she very much needed fortifying. Abigail offered him and him alone a curtsy, and followed Lady Champlain from the room.

"Stapleton, attend me. That fellow," Stephen said, pointing with his cane at Lord Fleming, "will sell you out before you can say *God bless Mad King George*. He knows your family secrets, and if you try to have him arrested for his housebreaking and coach robbing, he will implicate you thoroughly."

Hercules settled onto his haunches as if well aware that the most exciting bits were over. He insinuated his head under Stephen's hand, and damned if petting the dog didn't help Stephen restrain his temper.

Stapleton sat up straighter at his desk. "Fleming would not dare betray me. I'd call in his sister's debts, and let all of society know what a fickle and unreliable creature he is."

"Fickle and unreliable," Quinn said, studying the volumes lining the shelves of Stapleton's bookcase, "but honest in his assertions regarding your grandson's patrimony, and if I understand aright, you no longer hold the lady's vowels."

Fleming had resumed his place on the sofa, suggesting Abigail had dealt him a solid blow. "I didn't rob any coaches, and I won't say anything about the boy."

Duncan flipped out his coattails and assumed the reading chair. "You interfered with the lawful progress of a public stagecoach, which is in itself a hanging offense, no robbery required. Miss Abbott, who has a very keen eye for details, noticed your horse, your voice, and your manner of moving."

"She wasn't on the coach," Fleming retorted.

"She was dressed as a man," Stephen said, gently, for Fleming was having a trying day. His day was in fact about to get worse. "And she knows you effected at least one occasion of housebreaking, so hush while we decide what your punishment is to be. Be glad that Miss Abbott frowns on violence."

Fleming held his head in his hands, the picture of masculine despair. "I sought to offer Lady Harmonia an honorable union. I sought to safeguard the Stapleton legacy, I was only trying to be—"

"Tiresome," Stephen interjected, stroking Hercules's silky head. "Before the ladies return, we must resolve matters to their satisfaction. Stapleton, how do you propose to do that?"

Duncan looked bored, while Quinn had acquired a fascination for Stapleton's collection of jeweled snuff boxes.

"How do I—? My lord, you overstep. I haven't robbed any stagecoaches or broken into any houses, and as a peer of the realm, even if I had, the wheels of justice would not grind me under for such behavior, particularly not when undertaken to protect my family's standing."

Without turning away from the snuff boxes, Quinn muttered, "Don't be too sure about that."

Stephen rose, making certain to test his knee carefully before putting any weight on it. "Here is your dilemma, Stapleton. You have an illegitimate heir. This is of no great moment, despite the magnitude of the possible scandal. Legally, the boy's right to the title is unassailable, and he would not be the first illegitimate heir born to a peer.

"The greater difficulty," Stephen went on, "is that you have annoyed the child's mother. Your son annoyed her too. Lord Fleming has seriously annoyed her, and I daresay I myself might have tried her patience on occasion. Lady Champlain doesn't like you, she doesn't trust you, and she would be within her rights to take that child and her settlements and banish you from the lad's life. Is that what you want?"

Stapleton did not immediately reply, but then, he was not used to having to think of anybody but himself.

"My lord," Duncan said, "you raised a dunderheaded son, you recruited a dunderheaded conspirator, you are uniformly disliked by your peers, and your mistress's loyalty is to your coin rather than your person. Nobody would question Lady Champlain's decision to quit this household and shield the child from your influence."

"But the boy—" Stapleton began.

Quinn turned, a jeweled snuff box in his hand. "Is no relation to you. And a man who cheerfully sends six-year-olds into the mines, while bleating in the Lords about hard work being a Christian service to their exhausted, starving little souls, can hardly be expected to have much regard for children in general, can he?"

Stapleton put Stephen in mind of a bantam rooster, with all the arrogance of his larger fellows, nowhere near the power in a fight, and not enough brains to realize his disadvantage.

"But the boy—he's all I have. For me to remarry would be pointless, and I haven't even second cousins who could inherit."

"Harmonia will have the raising of him," Stephen said, tugging gently on a canine ear. "She will remarry and dwell where she pleases. You will not interfere with her or the child."

"Or what?" Stapleton asked.

Fleming provided the obvious answer. "Or the Wentworths will ruin us both. The duchess will put it about that I have an unmentionable disease so no woman of any standing will marry me. My father will disown me and cut me off without a farthing. In the clubs, word will spread that you are growing mentally feeble, and your temper and arrogance will lend credence to the gossip. My sister's latest gambling markers will all manage to fall into the wrong hands, and I rue the day I bloody met you, Stapleton. I'm done with this."

He rose awkwardly, though this display of meekness wasn't quite convincing. Hercules's ears pricked up, suggesting even a nibble of rare haunch of dunderheaded viscount might be his favorite snack in the whole world.

"A moment, Fleming," Stephen said. "You offended Miss Abbott. How do you intend to make reparation for the harm you caused?"

Fleming scrubbed a hand over his face. "Will she take money?"

For Fleming, that was a good try. "A signed apology, recounting your bad conduct, *and* money," Stephen said.

"But if I all but confess..."

"My, my," Duncan drawled, uncoiling from his reading chair with feline grace, "it appears you might have to leave the country for a time. Prague is a beautiful city, and not that expensive."

"Take a fortnight to put your affairs in order," Stephen said, "no more, and the sum should be generous enough to convey sincerity but not enough to be insulting. You may send your apology to the lady at the Walden ducal residence, to be received by this time tomorrow."

"Be off with you," Stapleton said, "and Godspeed."

Fleming stalked out, his gait uneven, and only Hercules looked sorry to see him go.

"He'll need a stout walking stick," Stephen said. "I really must commend Miss Abbott on her aim."

The tea tray arrived, and nobody made a move to pour out. When the butler had withdrawn, Stephen let the silence stretch. Quinn and Duncan, clearly enjoying themselves, did likewise.

"All right!" Stapleton expostulated. "Tell me how much, and I'll write out the bank draft now. The damned woman has caused me nothing but misfortune and I'm sure my son regretted falling into her snares."

"*The damned woman?*" Stephen repeated softly. "*Falling into her snares?*"

"Careful, Stapleton," Quinn said. "Lord Stephen's temper is rare and magnificent."

"Deadly," Duncan added, "when provoked. That stout walking stick is a sword cane, he has at least two knives on his person at all times, and there is not a witness in this room who will support your version of events should injury occur—to you. And by the by, that mastiff looks hungry to me."

"Your son," Stephen said, leaning across the desk, "failed to disclose to Miss Abbott that he already had a wife. He abused her trust sorely and led her to believe they'd share a castle of marital accord in Spain. When the inevitable occurred, he admitted his calumny and sent her a bank draft. She sent it back, and then nature denied her the infamy and heartache of raising his bastard. Do you still think *the damned woman* will be content with a bank draft?"

The marquess was old and small, but Stephen longed to land even a single blow anywhere on his person. A single, hard blow.

Stapleton sat back in his armchair. "Champlain would never…that is, he wasn't any different from…" The marquess tipped his chin up and looked from Quinn, to Duncan, to Stephen. "She enticed him. Women of a certain class think nothing of tempting—"

"A humble Quaker shopkeeper's daughter," Stephen said, "not a breath of scandal attached to her name before or since, and your philandering, *fucking*, wastrel of a prick of a son couldn't keep his filthy hands off her. And you—*my lord*—did nothing to stop him or hold him accountable. He broke Harmonia's heart, he all but broke Miss Abbott's spirit, and who knows how many other women suffered because you would not curb his excesses. Write out a big, fat bank draft to be sure, the fatter the better, but you are about to change your legislative priorities too."

Stapleton's hand shook as he tugged at his cravat. "Or else what?"

"Or else I will kill you." The threat was, alas, all too sincere. Quinn and Duncan did Stephen the courtesy of allowing the words to hang in the air, or about Stapleton's scrawny neck, without any polite retrenchments. Abigail frowned on violence, true enough, but Stephen frowned on nasty little men who raised their sons to be nasty, if charming, philanderers.

"He'd do it too," Quinn said, sounding almost cheerful as he took the place at Stephen's right and tugged Hercules's leash from Stephen's hand. "On the off chance that my brother required assistance, I'd happily serve. I frown on abusing the privileges of the peerage, but just the once, my duchess might overlook it. Duncan?"

"Pounding one aging windbag flat will hardly take three of us," Duncan said from Stephen's left, "but of course, I am ever available to my family when the law itself can't be relied upon to keep the wheels of justice turning smoothly and in the correct direction."

Marriage had agreed with Duncan, marriage to Matilda, anyway.

"His Grace of Walden," Stephen said, "is sponsoring a bill to reform the use of child labor in the mines. You will vociferously support that measure and any other that His Grace tells you to support. A man who can look at his six-year-old grandson and commend children of the same age to twelve-hour shifts at hard labor is sorely in need of guidance."

And a job crawling on his hands and knees through endless darkness in the mines.

Stapleton nodded. "What of you?" he asked, gaze

narrowing at Stephen. "I'll support Walden's damned bills and offer Miss Abbott handsome reparation. Tell me what I must do to ensure you leave me and mine in peace, and let's be done with it."

"From you, I want nothing. I act only as the agent of those I care about. Keep them happy, and you have nothing to fear from me. I'm off to find Miss Abbott." He bowed, such as he was able to bow, and left Stapleton to Quinn, Duncan, and Hercules's tender mercies.

"I loved him," Lady Champlain said, as she led Abigail down a carpeted corridor. "I was an idiot. Were you an idiot too?"

Abigail did not want to exchange feminine confidences with the widow of the man who'd betrayed her. Her ladyship seemed so wan and weary, though, that to snap out some acerbic rejoinder would have been churlish.

Champlain had been Harmonia's husband, and she had loved him. Both facts had doubtless caused her ladyship sadness. With some relief, Abigail realized that she had not loved Champlain. She'd been infatuated, smitten, enthralled, swept off her feet by the attentions of a dashing, worldly charmer who had made her feel feminine and desired.

She had not loved Champlain, but she did love Stephen Wentworth.

"I was easy to infatuate," Abigail said. "I knew nothing of men, I was lonely, and my father had long since stopped expecting me to get up to any mischief. I had become invisible, and at nearly six feet tall."

"While I am invisible at little over five." Lady Champlain

stopped outside a door on the third floor. "I love that sound."

A child laughed merrily in the next room, and a man's softer tones sounded patiently amused.

"The letters, if you please," Abigail said, as a vast emptiness welled in the region of her heart. "I am here only to retrieve the letters."

Her ladyship pushed open the door and stopped a few steps into the room. A large oval rug covered most of the floor, and upon the rug sat a small dark-haired boy and a handsome man of about thirty years.

"My two favorite fellows," her ladyship said, "and you are up to mischief, I see."

The man got to his feet easily. "A lad is never too young to try his hand at painting. We were making birds. Canaries, because they are yellow," he said with mock gravity, "and bluebirds, because they are blue."

"I made a green bird," the boy said. "When you swirl the paints together they make a new color." He cocked his head and turned a blue-eyed gaze on Abigail. "You are very tall, miss. Are you the queen?"

"Manners, child," the man murmured, taking the boy's hand and pulling him to his feet. "Lady Champlain, might you introduce us?"

Abigail endured the introductions, too drained by the events of the day to muster much curiosity even about the gorgeous Mr. Endymion de Beauharnais.

"If you'll wait here," Lady Champlain said, disappearing through an open door near the windows.

"Would you care to paint with us?" the boy asked. "I

like making new colors. I could paint a kite to look like birds, and the other birds might try to make friends with it. I want to make a kite that's big enough to lift me into the air. Don't tell Mama. She would worry. She worries if I merely climb a tree, so I forget to tell her when I've been climbing trees in the garden."

"The views from high in a tree are marvelous, aren't they?" Abigail asked. "And nobody knows you're there, because they don't think to look up."

The child grinned at that notion and scrambled back to the carpet. "I shall paint a tree, and I will put a little tree house in it, and all the children will want to play in the garden with the tree house. Not even pirates or bandits will be able to find us in our tree house."

"So imaginative," Abigail said softly, and that smile would turn heads when the boy grew older.

Mr. de Beauharnais was looking at her oddly and holding out a plain white handkerchief. "Are you well, miss?"

Abigail nodded, surprised to feel a hot tear sliding down her cheek. "The day has been taxing." *And that little boy is so very, very dear.*

"You tangled with Stapleton. He has worn her ladyship down to a shadow, but I am determined... Suffice it to say, she has allies. I hope you do too."

Abigail touched the handkerchief to her cheek. The scent was plain lavender, the cloth an unremarkable linen with no embroidery, and yet, the gesture had been kind.

"Lord Stephen Wentworth is among my acquaintances, and he speaks"—she cast around for the right word—"fondly of you."

"I speak of him with equal affection." The moment might have turned awkward, except de Beauharnais was smiling bashfully. "Don't believe half of what he says."

Abigail believed every word Stephen uttered, unfortunately.

Lady Champlain returned, holding a packet of documents. "I learned of these letters only because, like Papa-in-Law, I read Champlain's journals. This is the lot of them. I read some of them, because I wanted to hate you."

"You should not hate anybody, Mama. It's un-Christian." This homily was delivered from the carpet, in such bland tones as to be a mere recitation.

"Quite right," her ladyship said. "And I was not successful, in any case. The letters are nearly identical to ones I received from the same source. When I came into possession of these, you were off on some case, your companion went to visit family, and your staff took their half-day. Somebody left a kitchen window open to let in the fresh air, and your basic sense of orderliness apparently made the rest of the job easy. I did not keep my letters. I burned them in a fit of rage at some slight or other."

"There were many slights," Abigail observed, chagrined at how easily her home had been tossed. "I'm sorry for that."

"The apology is not yours to make, Miss Abbott. My mother tried to warn me, but Papa wanted the match. It wasn't all bad."

De Beauharnais watched this exchange with an expression more of concern than curiosity. "Shall I take his lordship down to the garden?" he asked, though that was hardly a portraitist's responsibility.

"I'll just be leaving," Abigail said, stealing another look at the boy. He was absorbed with his painting, his handling of the brush surprisingly deft for such a small child. He wasn't that much younger than Winslow would have been.

The empty place in Abigail's heart threatened to choke the breath from her body.

"I'll show you to the door," Lady Champlain replied, "and then I will return here, to see what masterpieces have been wrought in my nursery."

Abigail required the entire trip to the front door before she found the words she needed.

"Shall I fetch Lord Stephen to see you home?" Lady Champlain asked, a little too cheerfully.

"His lordship is doubtless occupied acquainting your father-in-law with the rudiments of the conduct expected of a peer. You may ask Mr. Duncan Wentworth to join me here."

Lady Champlain set off at a brisk walk, doubtless thinking she'd had a very near miss indeed. Abigail let her get a half dozen paces off—out of reticule range—before she brought her ladyship to an abrupt halt.

"I will give these letters to Lord Stephen," Abigail said, "because he of all people has a right to hold over this household any and all evidence relating to your son's conception. When did you plan on telling Stephen you bore him a child?"

Chapter Fifteen

Stephen gave orders to send his horse home with a groom. He wanted to be away from Stapleton's house, but more than that, he needed to be with Abigail, and to think.

"There you are," he said, as he gained the soaring foyer. Harmonia, her expression guarded, stood two yards away from Abigail.

Abigail, by contrast, had her cloak over her arm and her bonnet in her hand. Her bearing was militant, which made little sense when the battle was over and victory secured.

"My lady," Abigail said, plunking her bonnet on her head, "Lord Stephen will call on you one week from today, and you *will* receive him."

Why would I call on a woman who never wants to see me again? Stephen decided to ask the question later, after he and Abigail had enjoyed a private, celebratory hour or six.

Harmonia nodded minutely. "If his lordship calls, I will receive him. You have my word on that."

Stephen set his cane in the umbrella stand, took Abigail's cloak from her, and got the cloak situated over her shoulders. She submitted to this courtesy so passively that he was doing up her frogs before he realized Harmonia was watching them with more than a little curiosity.

"My lady," he said, retrieving his cane, "we wish you good day. His Grace of Walden is delivering a long overdue birching to Stapleton's conscience and to his exchequer. Duncan Wentworth will document the agreement reached, and I'd advise against disturbing them. You will have complete control of your son's upbringing by the time they are through." He offered a bow, though Harmonia wasn't looking at him.

Abigail did not curtsy, and neither did Harmonia. Something female and complicated was afoot between them, which was to be expected. Stephen opened the door and escorted Abigail to the waiting coach.

"That went rather well," he said, handing her in. "Wouldn't you agree?"

"I have the letters," Abigail replied, taking her place on the forward-facing seat. "I thought…I don't know what I thought."

Stephen took the place beside her, when he wanted to ruck up her skirts and share with her the most primal of joys.

"We vanquished all comers." He kissed her hand, which reminded him that she yet wore gloves. Those he dispensed with—his and hers—and after he'd kissed her knuckles, he kissed her cheek. "My mood has turned affectionate. This happens when I have a breakthrough with a design. Does solving a case have the same happy result in the inquiry business?"

"Sometimes."

And apparently, sometimes not. Stephen tucked an arm around Abigail's shoulders and she subsided against him. Perhaps she too was plagued by a niggling sense of overlooked details, or puzzle pieces that had fallen off the table. As long as the letters were in hand, those puzzle pieces could be picked up later.

"I should have focused on the dates sooner," he said, stroking her hair. "Should have known that's what had Stapleton in such a swither. The butler mentioned that the boy's birthday is next week, and that jostled something in my brainbox. Ned pointed out that Champlain wrote to you every Monday and Thursday, which was also a helpful nudge in the direction of noticing the dates."

Stephen paused long enough to kiss Abigail's temple. "By the by," he went on, "you are soon to be comfortably well off as inquiry agents go. Both Fleming and Stapleton will offer you reparation in the form of bank drafts. I know your pride will tempt you to reject these sums, but I must advise you—advise only, of course—to consider that you are owed every penny."

He was babbling, mostly for joy, because Abigail's enemies had been thoroughly routed, but also from a growing sense that something with Abigail was amiss. What had he overlooked about the situation relating to *her*?

"You aren't arguing with me. My darling Miss Abbott

never misses an opportunity to air her opinions." His darling Miss Abbott didn't take that bait, so he blundered on. "Fleming is off for an extended tour of the Continent, or maybe his papa will force him on the diplomatic corps, though he'll probably start some minor wars, given his dunderheadedness."

Abigail put her fingers to Stephen's lips. "Hush. The day did not go as I'd planned. I was sure Fleming had taken the letters."

Ah, so they were to analyze the battle maneuvers then. "I considered him too, but if he had the letters, why not use them to secure Lady Champlain's hand in marriage or a return of the gambling markers? Your letters have been missing for months and Fleming took a serious and unnecessary risk interfering with a stagecoach."

"So he did not have the letters. What made you think of Lady Champlain?"

"She was the logical next choice, having a very great interest in keeping from Stapleton's grasp anything that imperiled her standing in the household. Perhaps the old boy was growing difficult, perhaps her ladyship had read Champlain's journals and reached the same conclusion Stapleton did. I hardly care now that the problem is solved."

Later, when Abigail was smiling and once more on her mettle, Stephen would review the whole matter as he would review a rifle pattern, ensuring every part was labeled accurately and drawn to scale.

Abigail rested her head on Stephen's shoulder, the gesture weary. "I met Mr. de Beauharnais in the nursery. He's very attractive. Has all the heroic features."

Gracious. Was this what troubled her? Stephen most assuredly did not want to talk about Endymion de Beauharnais's excellent nose.

"If you must know, I think his great good looks are a problem for him. The merry widows plague him ceaselessly and the gay blades want a discreet go at him. All he longs for is to create good art and— Abigail, was that a yawn?"

"Sorry. I haven't been sleeping well lately."

"I haven't been sleeping at all."

She closed her eyes. "Have you dreamed of me anyway?"

"Yes."

"I dream of you too."

What was a fellow to make of that? Stephen let Abigail drift off, or pretend to. Her breathing was regular and slow, but he'd spent a night in her arms and knew the difference between real and feigned sleep. Abigail's reaction to a case solved and a marquess put in his place was apparently fatigue. Perhaps good spirits would come later.

Perhaps she was due for a nap.

Perhaps something had gone badly awry between her and Harmonia or her and de Beauharnais, in which case, no force on earth would pry confidences from Abigail Abbott until she was ready to share them.

When the coach pulled up before the Wentworth town house, Stephen escorted Abigail inside and sent word to Jane that the letters had been retrieved without incident. After Quinn and Duncan returned, there would doubtless be a round of brandy in the library, but first, Stephen would enjoy a private interlude with his beloved—and with whatever she was keeping from him.

Inspiration struck as he drew off Abigail's cloak: Perhaps she was the sort to have a private little fit of the weeps after vanquishing a foe. That would explain much.

"Upstairs with us," he said, when Abigail's cloak and bonnet were on their respective hooks. "We're entitled to share a tray in your sitting room."

Abigail held the packet of letters in her hand. The paper was yellowing, the ink already fading. The red ribbon binding them together was fraying on the ends.

"I want to burn these," she said. "But I can't. A tray is a good idea."

She preceded Stephen up the steps and led him into her sitting room. He locked the door behind them, and when she would have reached for the bell pull, he plucked the letters from her hand and kissed her.

"Food and drink can wait, Abigail. I have a voracious, burning need of you and hope you are similarly interested in enjoying an intimate interlude with me. I will grovel on my knees—my good knee, anyway—to win your favors, and never have I more fervently wished for the ability to literally sweep a woman off her feet." More than that, though, he wanted her to *talk* to him, to confide in him, to tell him where it hurt so he could love it better.

Those daft sentiments were extraordinary for their sincerity. Stephen had flirted with, propositioned, and been propositioned by many lovers, and it all had been so much posturing. If the other party wasn't inclined, he'd smile, wave, and design them a music box, deriving about the same degree of pleasure from that exercise as he would from a casual tumble.

With Abigail, he wanted to design the rest of their lives.

"I have missed you," she said, resting her forehead against his. "Very much. We'll take each other to bed, shall we?"

God, yes. "Take me to bed *hard*, Abigail. Take me to bed until I can't think or move."

She clasped his hand and they moved to the bedroom. "Take me to bed sweetly, Stephen." She punctuated that command with a brush of her hand over his falls. "Sweetly and *hard*."

Stephen, you have a son. Abigail had been unable to get the thought from her mind. *You have a gorgeous, healthy son with a lively mind and no worthy adult male to show him how to go on in life. Your son needs you.*

She had spent the coach ride home tormenting herself with a recalled conversation. *If I get a woman with child, decency alone dictates that I marry her, and my conscience would insist on that course as well.... Children matter, Abigail. My children matter to me...or they would if I had any....*

Well, Stephen had fathered a child and now he could marry the mother—though he wasn't anybody's husband *yet*.

Abigail untied Stephen's cravat and unbuttoned his shirt, then his waistcoat. A wife performed these courtesies for her husband, but they weren't mere courtesies, they were privileges.

"Your hooks," Stephen said, twirling his finger.

Abigail gave him her back, and he soon had her dress

and stays undone. How glad she was to be making love in broad daylight, the better to memorize the gradual unveiling of Stephen's body. He waited until Abigail had shimmied out of her dress and petticoat to drape his cravat around her neck. The silk was warm with his heat and scented with his fragrance.

"I want your cravat," Abigail said, sniffing the silk. "I want it as a token of today."

"You may have both the neckcloth and the man who wore it," Stephen said, hanging his coat over the back of her reading chair. His waistcoat and shirt followed, then he sat on her vanity stool to remove his boots.

"Did you mean what you said in the coach?" Abigail asked, taking the reading chair to remove her half boots.

He set his footwear aside. "I was babbling in the coach, but I hope I was babbling honestly."

"About..." Abigail found it necessary to roll down her stocking very slowly. "Dreaming of me? Did you dream anything in particular?"

Stephen tilted his head to the side and smiled wickedly. "I doubtless dreamed of you taking shocking liberties with my willing person. Perhaps if you toyed with me a bit, I might recall the details."

He occupied the vanity stool like the king of carnal delights upon his throne, casually naked from the waist up, legs slightly splayed, the fabric of his breeches temptingly tented. Abigail considered taking off her chemise in retaliation but instead knelt between his legs and unbuttoned his falls. His mood was buoyant.

Hers was both sad and fierce.

She wanted these memories with him, and if that made her selfish and greedy, she would be selfish and greedy for an entire week. Also bold, demanding, and—if Stephen's stamina was anything like she suspected it to be—a little sore in the most delicious places.

Stephen touched her cheek. "You do as you please with me, Abigail. If this is where you want to start, I am your willing servant. If you'd rather take me to bed and cuddle up, I will delight in your affections."

Abigail considered his offer, and considered his comfort. If they had to move to the bed in the middle of their pleasures, Stephen would need his cane and the transition could introduce an awkward moment.

"Onto the bed," she said. "On your back."

"I will spend from anticipatory bliss," he said, getting to his feet and giving her a hand up. He did use his cane to cross to the bed, and hooked it over the bedside table. "I've considered designing walking sticks that can be used to conceal bedroom toys. My family would disown me, but I suspect the results would be very profitable."

"Your family will never disown you. Lie down."

"I really must remember not to leave my riding crops around our bedroom," he said, stretching out with a sigh. "Your inherent confidence gives you a natural aptitude for—Abigail?"

She'd rested her head low on his belly, pushed his breeches out of the way, and swiped her tongue experimentally over the tip of his aroused cock.

"Behold, he is rendered speechless," she murmured.

Stephen remained silent for a long while, except for the

occasional groan or sigh after he'd peeled off his breeches. By the time Abigail's curiosity was sated, she was more than a little bothered herself. She had no sooner relinquished her prize than Stephen sat up, hoisted her back against the pillows, and draped himself over her.

"Did you like it?" she asked, tracing her fingers over his chest. "One suspects some practice is required."

"*One* damned near had me spending at the first taste, you fiend. If this is how you react to solving cases, then I hope many more difficult conundrums find their way to your door. Hold on to me."

That was her only warning before Stephen fused his mouth to hers, entered her in a gloriously sure thrust, and sent her on a breathless upward spiral.

"Let go, Abigail," he whispered. "For God's sake, I haven't a sheath, and just—*let go*."

She did not want to let go. Not of him, not ever. She wanted to hold fast and never turn him loose.

"Stay with me." She locked her ankles at the small of his back to emphasize the point. "Please."

"But I cannot—"

She kissed him and, by sheer force of will and the main strength of her sturdy female body, she overcame his determination. Their pleasure was spectacular, protracted, and vigorous.

Also... stolen. Abigail would think about that later, when the little shocks of after-joy stopped racking her, when she could breathe normally, and when Stephen's weight wasn't the most comforting bodily reality she'd miss all the way back to York.

"You are naughty," he said, kissing her nose. "Naughty, naughty, naughty. Where have you been all my life?"

"Yorkshire. Are you angry with me?"

He rolled, taking her with him, which effected an intimate un-joining and put Abigail atop her lover.

"I'm furious," he said. "Aghast at your audacity. Give me ten minutes and you may enrage me again all you please. Sweet, hard, any way you like. *Every* way you like, in fact."

Abigail curled down onto his chest. "Ten minutes?"

"Well, fifteen then. You have rendered me the veriest weakling, I admit it. A happy weakling, though. Enraptured, in fact. Perhaps I am among the celestial beings as we speak."

"Hush." Abigail raised up enough to draw off her chemise and used it to tidy them both. "Hold me."

Stephen hooked a blanket from the foot of the bed with his toes and drew it over Abigail's shoulders.

"Sleep, Duchess." He kissed her cheek. "You have earned your rest. A sweet and hard loving is satisfying but exhausting. I believe it's my new favorite."

"You are my favorite," Abigail said, cuddling close.

He drew patterns on her back—naughty walking sticks?—while she drifted closer to sleep. Her last thought before she slipped into dreams was that no short week of pleasure with Stephen, no matter how wild, would be enough to comfort her against all the years she would endure missing him.

"I consider myself a tolerant woman," Jane began, "but your brother has been carrying on like a stag in rut for the better part of a week." She paced the length of the sitting room, her skirts swishing in a way that made a new father start counting days.

"Stephen is a Wentworth male in his prime," Jane went on. "Certain allowances must be made, but Quinn... I believe his enthusiasm for Miss Abbott's company exceeds even my devotion to you at the outset of our marriage."

"*I* am in my prime," Quinn interjected, and who was to say brothers more than a decade apart in age could not both be in their primes?

Jane speared him with a glower. "Of course you are, as the state of our nursery will attest. Try to focus, Quinn. This is important."

Stapleton supporting the mining bill was important. The talk in the clubs was one part amazed, one part disbelieving, and all parts in awe of Quinn's *negotiating ability*. The credit belonged to Stephen, of course, and Stephen would disown Quinn if he mentioned that. Stapleton was as good as his word, offering clear if terse support for Quinn's bill. Fleming's titled father had enjoyed a similar shift in perspective.

"Stephen has fallen in love," Quinn said, patting the arm of his wing chair. "He's behaving like a Wentworth male in love. This Wentworth male would enjoy a snuggle with his duchess, if she's so inclined." A snuggle doomed to the platonic side of the marital continuum, alas.

"But must Stephen be so passionately in love under our very roof?" Jane countered.

"Miss Abbott is under our roof, and thus Stephen is underfoot as well. He has asked if I would finance the sale of his munitions works."

Jane's pace slowed. "He's selling off his gun manufactories?"

"And his foundry, which he uses mostly to make cannon and gun barrels. I know of some American investors who would love to get their hands on a British munitions works, and they have the means to acquire one too."

"This is not good," Jane said, coming to rest on the arm of Quinn's chair. "Stephen loves his weaponry. Cranes for the navy and circulating saws and the like are all well and good, but he delights in the intricacy of firearms."

Quinn took her hand and kissed her fingers. Never had a woman been more fiercely devoted to family, and never had a family benefited so greatly from a lady's loyalty.

"Stephen loves his weaponry, but he loves Abigail Abbott more. He can now delight in the intricacy of the female mind, or one female mind in particular."

"He seems content to delight in Miss Abbott's body, Quinn. I heard laughter when I passed by her sitting room last night."

Quinn tugged on Jane's hand, and that was enough to bring her down into his lap. "Jane, what is this about? Stephen never laughs. He is ironic, sarcastic, and droll, but he doesn't laugh. If Miss Abbott provokes him to laughter, we should rejoice. Napoleon has been reduced to a bad, soon-to-be-glorified memory, and the military has more soldiers and guns than it needs. He should be selling off his military investments. I've been telling him that for three years."

Jane scooted around, which did nothing to quiet Quinn's doomed longings. "A composer doesn't stop hearing orchestras in his head," she said, "just because symphonies have gone out of fashion. Stephen is selling off his firearms businesses because Miss Abbott has Quaker leanings. She isn't above carrying defensive weapons, but the taking of human life always violates a Commandment in her theology."

Quinn waited for Jane to settle, which she eventually did, her legs over the arm of the chair, her bottom nestled against his... lap.

"You think Stephen is selling up to placate his future duchess?"

"Stephen doubtless thinks that's what he's doing."

"Jane?"

She rested her head on Quinn's shoulder and quieted against him. "I miss you, Your Grace."

"We can last another three weeks, Jane. We've managed before." Though they would be the longest three weeks in marital history.

"I feel like a heifer. I'm suited for nothing of late but grazing and *production*. I will never fit into my dresses again, and that child has the appetite of a dragoon."

Oh, how I love you. "You are beautiful to me, Jane, and you always will be. That our baby is healthy and thriving is my second greatest joy after being your husband." As a younger man, Quinn had been too shy and backward to give his wife the words she needed. Thank heavens Jane was, indeed, a patient woman.

"It's not fair." Jane sighed against Quinn's neck. "With every child, you grow more handsome and distinguished. I become fat and irritable."

Quinn kissed her cheek. "You talk this way when you're tired. It's very bad of Stephen to be courting his Abigail while you are recovering from childbed. Duncan is grumbling because Stephen hasn't spared him even a single game of chess."

"Stephen will have time for chess again soon. I do believe I am about to steal a nap."

"Jane, what aren't you telling me?"

She was silent for a moment. Quinn had learned to wait for her replies.

"Ned is fond of Miss Abbott."

"We all are." Quinn did not understand exactly what drew Stephen and Abigail to each other, but the lady was clearly a match for Stephen's intellect and for his heart.

"She asked Ned to procure her a ticket on the Wednesday night Northern Flyer. Ned had sense enough to make it an inside ticket. She booked two seats all the way to York—one for Hercules, if you can imagine that—and asked Ned to tell no one."

But Ned, like Quinn, was entirely the Duchess of Walden's creature, and had thus apparently tempered his silence with a judicious slip of the tongue in Jane's hearing.

"And Stephen has no idea," Quinn muttered. Neddy's slip of the tongue neatly placed upon Jane the burden of telling Stephen this news.

She yawned delicately. "This is not how I envisioned their situation resolving, Quinn. You had better have a word with Stephen."

Well, of course. "Go to sleep, my dear. I will *have a*

word, and love will prevail, if I have to rap Stephen over the head with his own canes to ensure the outcome my duchess prefers."

Jane dozed off, a warm, beloved weight in Quinn's arms. Her naps were deep and usually brief, and this one gave Quinn a chance to ponder his brother's situation with Miss Abbott. They were profoundly in love, of that Quinn was certain. Stephen would not part with his manufactories for any other motivation, but as for Miss Abbott…

Quinn would have a word, and not with Stephen.

Chapter Sixteen

"You are abandoning my brother," His Grace of Walden said, taking the place beside Abigail on the garden bench. "Why?"

One did not tell a duke to take himself off, not in his own garden, but Abigail dearly wanted to.

"My reasons are my own, Your Grace. I am very appreciative of your hospitality, but my errand here in London is concluded. The time has come for me to return to York."

She would have called for Hercules and retreated to the house, but His Grace went on speaking as if she'd remarked nothing more significant than the mild weather.

"I have four daughters." The duke offered this observation with the sort of relish that suggested he stood to inherit the crown jewels.

"Lovely little girls," Abigail said. "Very dear. I'm sure you're quite proud of them."

"I am besotted with my womenfolk, and Stephen is besotted with you. Yet you turn your back on him. Is this your Quaker heritage taking a stand against firearms, Abigail?"

She should scold him for using her given name, but with His Grace of Walden, etiquette worked in reverse. If the duke condescended so far as to use familiar address, the person so addressed was honored, and, besides, Abigail liked that he'd not stand on ceremony with her. Stephen would make the same sort of duke, adept at navigating social subtleties, devoted to his wife and children—blast him to Hades.

"I do not approve of warfare," she said. "Particularly not aggressive warfare. Stephen is welcome to involve himself in whatever business he pleases. His commercial undertakings are no concern of mine."

The duke was a larger specimen than Stephen. He was more heavily muscled and took up more of the bench. His scent was pleasant, though not as enticing as the beguiling fragrance Stephen wore. Abigail would not have noticed these differences, but becoming Stephen's lover had changed how she experienced the world.

Men were either Stephen or not Stephen, and those who were not Stephen could never match the standard he set. For wit, loyalty, fierceness, passion, tenderness...

"Stephen," His Grace said, "whose affairs are no concern of yours, is arranging the sale of any interest he holds in ventures related to making or repairing firearms of any stripe. I have been urging him to diversify for three years. You come along, and in little more than a fortnight, he's set about dismantling an empire that could re-arm the French military."

Oh, Stephen. "His lordship has a flair for drama, and he is a man of dispatch. He will make a fine duke, should that day ever come."

"Be assured, Abigail, the day will come. I am determined on that score and even my duchess won't talk me around again. Stephen, however, will make a terrible duke. He will embody all that is loathsome about the species. He will neglect his duties in the Lords, he will be obnoxious and arrogant. He will grow bitter as his leg pains him more later in life, though in fact, it's his heart that has suffered the severest blow."

Abigail sat up to glower at the duke. "You insult your brother, and I will not allow that even from you, Your Grace. Stephen is the most estimable of men and a credit to his family."

Walden bumped her gently with his shoulder. "If you are scolding me so thoroughly, Abigail, then I think you should call me Quinn. Stephen has the potential to be a wonderful duke—he's already a wonderful person—but that potential is so much smoke in the wind if you desert him now. Mayfair society is not that difficult to manage. Jane excels at it, and she's a mere preacher's daughter. Pluck up your courage and marry my brother."

His Grace was finding new places in her heart to break, the wretch. "My courage is quite plucked up, thank you. I am neither charmed nor intimidated by Mayfair society, and Stephen hasn't much use for it in any case. He humors Her Grace in that regard, though as a younger man he was apparently more sociable."

"As a younger man, he was more difficult, if you can imagine such a thing. And speaking of my difficult brother, where is he and does he know you plan to leave London tonight?"

If anybody had told Abigail that she would be discussing her personal affairs with a duke, she would have concluded such a person was addled. She instead concluded that she herself was addled, because not only was she discussing her personal affairs with a duke, she was about to confide in that duke as well.

"I will bid Stephen farewell when he returns from his call on Lady Champlain." The words hurt, and should anybody inquire, Abigail would inform them that *doing the right thing* was no deuced comfort at all, not even after a week of desperate, hopeless self-indulgence.

His Grace grew subtly alert. "Why would Stephen bother to call on such a vapid, shallow—"

Abigail glowered at him *again*. "Do not judge her ladyship. She protected her child. I am trying hard to respect her for that, and I predict Stephen will be making the same effort very shortly."

The duke gazed over the garden, to outward appearances a man at peace. "I want to hear the rest of this tale, Abigail, but anything you tell me will be shared with Jane."

"Stephen has warned me that you and Her Grace are in each other's confidence." Why must the day be so pretty, and why must Stephen be such a decent, dear man? "I expect Stephen will acquaint you both with the situation soon enough, but it has already become apparent to me that the child in Lady Champlain's nursery is Stephen's son, and that her ladyship went to extraordinary lengths to hide the boy's paternity from his natural father."

Abigail rose, unable to sit calmly while she recited the terms by which her heart would finish breaking. A rustling in the bushes suggested Hercules would soon return to the terrace.

"Above all things," she said, "Stephen is haunted by the possibility that he will live down to Jack Wentworth's standards, as a human being and most especially as a father. Jack was a vile, bullying, selfish reptile. I suspect Stephen is selling off his munitions factories because he grasps the difference between a defensive war and one waged purely out of greed. Jack Wentworth would approve of the latter, while even I can grasp the need for the former."

The duke was watching her closely, and not with any particular expression of dismay. "Stephen has a son?"

"A beautiful, healthy, smart, and charming little boy. As it happens, the child's mother is widowed and of suitable rank to marry a ducal heir."

For the privilege of raising the son who should never have been hidden from him, Stephen would make that union cordial and successful.

"A son." His Grace rose easily. "You're sure?"

"I saw the boy with my own eyes, Lady Champlain confirmed his patrimony. Surely you can see—"

The duke approached and did not stop a cordial distance away. He instead wrapped Abigail in a gentle hug.

"Dukes lead the way into battle, Abigail. Stephen will be a duke one day."

Quinn Wentworth's embrace was different from Stephen's.

Abigail did not have to think of anybody's balance or where a cane could rest without being knocked over. There was no escaping Quinn's hug, and for the space of several breaths, Abigail let him simply hold her.

"Stephen will be a very f-fine duke, but I cannot be—"

Quinn patted her back. "A wise duchess once told me that dukes ride into battle at the head of armies, Abigail, not alone. Only a fool rides into life's battles alone when good comrades are on hand to share the challenges. Do you know why a duke is willing to take on the fights that need fighting, even the hard, thankless fights?"

Stephen would do that. He had arranged for his brother's mining bill to become law and asked nothing for himself.

"I know I must be on that stagecoach tonight," Abigail said, "and that I detest weepy women." Which she was very soon to become, if the duke did not give her immediate privacy. She burrowed closer and tried for a steadying breath.

"A duke rides into battle because he must be worthy of the lady riding at his side. Harmonia hasn't the heart to be Stephen's duchess, and you do. You are his choice. Let him be yours."

He kissed her forehead, tucked a monogrammed handkerchief into her hand, and sauntered back into the house. Then and only then did Abigail descend into the garden and call for Hercules.

When the beast trotted out of the rhododendrons, she sank down, wrapped her arms around him, and let the tears come.

* * *

"He's your son." Harmonia tossed the words at Stephen as if she were calling out the paces at a duel, not presiding over a tea tray.

"Well, that explains it," Stephen said, setting down his teacup slowly. The meaning of Harmonia's revelation was plain enough, but for some reason, Stephen's heart felt trapped in the pause between thunder and lightning.

"Explains what?" Harmonia asked.

"Why Miss Abbott insisted I call on you. Did she know of this?"

Harmonia sat back without pouring herself a cup of tea. "She took one look at him. *One look.* I didn't want that woman in my nursery out of, I don't know, maternal instinct, but I never dreamed she'd see a resemblance between you and your son that easily."

"Miss Abbott has keen powers of observation. Why didn't you tell me?" And why wasn't Stephen angrier? More surprised? Pleased? *Something?*

"I didn't want him to be yours," Harmonia said, "but he is yours. I cannot deny that. When you and I were dallying, Champlain was off in France fiddling with some violinist, or more likely a whole quartet. Champlain congratulated me on conceiving—congratulated me!—and I think he was honestly relieved."

Still, Stephen could not grasp how he was supposed to feel about this development. "Champlain knew he'd been cuckolded?"

Harmonia poured herself a cup of tea, the hot liquid

nearly missing the cup. "He once said that the reason I wasn't conceiving might be that we didn't suit in that regard. I could carry another man's child, he could impregnate other women—and what wife wants to hear that casual admission?—but we were not a *mating pair*. I hate that term."

"Doesn't sit well with me either." *He's your son. He's your son. He's your son.* "Does Stapleton realize who the boy's father is?"

"The marquess will doubtless guess, particularly as Nicky matures. He cocks his head as you do, and he is much cleverer than Champlain or I could hope to be. You have every right to be wroth with me."

"Do I?" What would Abigail make of this development? More to the point, what *had* she made of it? What had the most glorious week of lovemaking in Stephen's generally self-indulgent life been about?

"These things happen in the best families," Harmonia said primly, as if some venerable uncle had grown a bit vague. "You still had a right to know."

"We were *dallying*, Harmonia, each out to prove something by taking our clothes off and falling into the same bed. We were foolish." Maybe *pathetic* was the better word. "We need not be foolish now."

She took a sip of her tea, the cup rattling as she returned it to the saucer. "What were you trying to prove?"

A fair question. "Perhaps that I could swagger around like all the *real* courtesy lords who hadn't been born in the gutter? Perhaps that my knee was useless, but my pizzle was entirely in working order? Nothing of any moment."

Harmonia set her teacup back on the tray. "I wanted Champlain to *notice* me. To pay some blasted attention to the wife who loved him. I was so angry, and he was so focused on his next debauch. I might as well have been an aging lapdog for all he recalled where he'd last put me."

"Take some shortbread," Stephen said, holding out the plate. "You've had a trying time of it."

She took a piece, had a small nibble, and set it on her plate. That sequence, of following a polite order, never questioning its appropriateness, struck Stephen as some sort of metaphor. Harmonia ought to be throwing the plate against the wall or at the very least delivering a few pointed opinions on the perfidy of her late husband.

Abigail would certainly not be sipping tea and nibbling shortbread simply because convention called for it.

"Andy says I must marry you." Harmonia's hands were fisted in her lap. "Stapleton will likely take up the same notion by this time next week. Nicky is your son, he needs a father, and I am a *proven breeder*."

"Harmonia, the man who called you that will soon be far, far away. Put the term from your mind."

"It's the truth," she said miserably. "And Her Grace of Walden was brought to bed with another daughter, and you are the heir, and Andy is right."

"You've discussed this with de Beauharnais?"

She pulled an ornately embroidered handkerchief from a skirt pocket and dabbed at her eyes. "Andy isn't like you lot. He's not a lord, he's not fascinated with ever-greater sprees of debauchery, and he's good with Nicky. I like him and he likes me, and I have never had anybody simply like me before."

I liked you. As soon as the thought popped into Stephen's head it was followed by the admission that he'd barely *known* Harmonia, and the woman he'd slept with all those years ago had barely known him.

"I will not be parted from my son," Harmonia said, sniffling. "If that means I must marry you and be your duchess, then I will marry you. We can be civil about it. Being a duchess can't be any worse than being the widowed mother of a marquess."

Of a marquess's heir, strictly speaking. And of Stephen's son.

"Andy was slightly debauched with me," Stephen said, apropos of nothing in the whole entire world. "I like him. You're right. He doesn't put on airs, and he's a decent man."

Harmonia peered at him over her handkerchief. "With *you*?"

"A passing fancy on my part. I'm not sure what motivated his interest in me. We have remained friends." Why hadn't Stephen remained friends with Harmonia? Oh, right. Because she'd been hiding his son from him, and he'd been too busy…playing with guns?

"But you're…I shouldn't be surprised. Champlain was indiscriminate with his favors. I hadn't pegged you for that kind. I truly do not want to be married to another profligate rake, my lord."

"That's doing it a bit brown, Harmonia. I was never in the exalted league of rakes Champlain occupied."

"You were dashing," she said, with no little asperity. "You

were charming, and you made more advances not dancing than most men can manage in an entire quadrille."

"My apologies." *He's your son.* Though that wasn't quite right. The boy was Harmonia's son *and* Stephen's son—*our* son. This fact floated in the same sea of unreality that Stephen had been swimming in for the past quarter hour.

"Harmonia, what do you want to do about this situation? You are the child's mother, and you are clearly devoted to him." Blindly so? But what small boy didn't need a blindly devoted parent or two?

She rose to pace, which was surely a measure of considerable upset, for ladies did not pace—though they apparently dallied, stole letters, and cuckolded heirs to the peerage.

Some ladies did, and Abigail paced.

"I want to raise my son," Harmonia said. "I want to be left in peace to raise Nicky and maybe find a fellow who doesn't mind about me being so old, and not having much in the way of settlements or a bosom. I want my own house, a little manor somewhere in Kent and not in the freezing bedamned north because it's convenient to the perishing, rubbishing grouse moors."

She put a hand to her mouth. "I said bedamned. I am quite vexed. I do apologize. My mama will be overjoyed to have a duchess for a daughter."

"To summarize, then," Stephen said, taking up his cane and pushing to his feet, "you do not want *me*."

Harmonia's dread was written in her teary eyes. She dreaded to offend the man who could all but force her to the altar, and she dreaded equally to speak her vows with him.

"What matters," Stephen said, "is the child. The situation must be resolved with his best interests in mind. I'd like to meet him."

All the righteous wind dropped from Harmonia's sails. "I was afraid of that. He's in the nursery, and Andy is with him. Come along, and don't think to introduce yourself as his father. This isn't the time for that. Nicky won't understand what it means."

"My dear Harmonia, I barely understand it myself."

Abigail chose to spend her last London afternoon in Hyde Park, watching the swans glide on the leaf-darkened water. Her ears warned her of Stephen's approach, so attuned had she become to the cadence of his gait.

"You could not brood on a handy back terrace, could you?" he muttered. "You had to secret yourself in the wilds of the largest park in England and force a poor, lame fellow to track you down. Well, know this, Miss Abigail Abbott: You could disappear into the Scottish Highlands and I would yet find you if finding you were my objective, which it doubtless would be. What is this dreadful rumor I've heard about you boarding the Northern Flyer this evening?"

Abigail hadn't expected him to hunt her down, but then, when had Stephen Wentworth done the expected?

"My errand in London is complete. I have a business to manage. I meant to bid you farewell before I departed." And thank him. Thank him for so much.

Stephen lowered himself onto the bench two feet from her, and Abigail's heart sank straight to the muddy bottom of the cold, dark waters of the Serpentine.

"This errand you speak of," he said, laying his cane across his knees. "You are not yet murdered, and I distinctly recall you asking me to fulfill that office."

She dared a glance at him, but could not read his mood. He was perfectly attired for social calls, the picture of sartorial elegance. He gazed upon the water, his expression calm. But for a slight tension in the way he clasped his walking stick, he might have been sitting for a portrait: *Gentleman at His Autumnal Leisure*.

"You arranged a happier outcome for me," Abigail said. "Thank you for that. I want you to have the letters."

"Abigail, I do not care bollocks or bedamned about the letters."

His tone was mild, but Abigail would have bet the glass paperweight in her reticule that his lordship was peeved, perhaps even furious.

"The letters do not entirely establish your paternity, but they establish that the child is not Champlain's issue. As the boy's father, you should have that evidence to destroy or safeguard as you see fit."

"You have this all sorted, do you? I am to keep *the evidence*, while you are off to York to resume peeking in windows and impersonating a man. Harmonia will be my duchess, and she and I will somehow contrive to produce more sons—on purpose this time and not out of heedless, rutting stupidity. So glad the itinerary is cast in stone, for I wasn't likely to find the way on my own, avowed dullard that I am."

This was the scene Abigail had dreaded, a parting in anger and sorrow, harsh words exchanged for no reason.

"You are that child's father, and I will not stand between you and a chance to finish the raising of him. The boy has no stepfather, Stapleton sees him as some sort of hereditary prize, and Harmonia will reconcile herself to the terrible burden of being your duchess the moment you show her the Walden jewels. Besides, you would make a wonderful papa."

Those last words cut like glass, but Abigail managed to speak them in civil tones. The vast, green preserve of Hyde Park wasn't big enough for all the sadness her heart held, but she would not keep a child and his father apart. Not this father, and not that child.

"You are being noble," Stephen said, "and unforgivably stupid. Harmonia and I took revenge with each other for mostly imagined slights. Our dalliance was of no moment to either of us. That's the nature of a dalliance. You are too virtuous and stubborn to imagine such a thing, but seven years ago, I quite had the knack of the casual encounter. The Wentworth jewels, or at least my little portion of them, were on display in all manner of untoward locations."

"Are you ashamed of that?" Abigail could not decipher his tone, suggesting perhaps he was in somewhat of a muddle himself.

"For God's sake, Abigail. I have slept with both Harmonia and her current swain. He has slept with both the lady and myself. Champlain got you with child, but he could not impregnate his wife. I managed that feat handily enough, and now you and I... the situation is *ludicrous*."

Well, yes, it rather was, when compressed into a few sentences. "The child is anything but. He's a little boy, and the last thing you will do, Stephen, is turn your back on your own son."

And for a time that was the final word. The breeze stirred the dead leaves and reminded Abigail that in York, the season would be more advanced and appreciably colder. She gathered up her reticule and parasol, and prepared to walk with Stephen back to Park Lane.

"Don't you dare run off, Abigail. I am maneuvering my mental artillery into place."

"I refuse to argue with you. I know how I felt about Winslow—how I still feel about him. I know how determined you are to put Jack Wentworth's ghost to rest. I commend you for your integrity and wish you every joy."

She shifted to the edge of the bench, rose, and readied herself to begin the process of leaving London, and leaving Stephen.

"Sit down, you dratted female. You know all manner of vital information, but you apparently don't know the fact that matters most. I have not imposed the words upon you, thinking to wait for some cozy, private moment when I could ply you with spirits and tempt you with my manly charms, but to hell with that. Spirits imperil my balance, and you've sampled my manly charms. I love you, and I don't care if the whole rubbishing park knows it."

Abigail sat back down.

Winter storms in Yorkshire could blow with such ferocity that wind, cold, and snow obliterated any sense of direction. Gravity alone remained constant in the face of such a gale, and Stephen had survived this tempest of a day by clinging to one equally steadfast constant: He loved Abigail Abbott.

Well, two constants: He loved Abigail, and he hoped to hell she loved him back. Otherwise…

Otherwise did not bear thinking about.

"I'm selling my gun manufactories," he said, which wasn't an announcement he'd planned to make.

"I hope you aren't doing that for me. You love the intricacy and complication of a precisely made firearm."

I love you more. How simple life became in light of that singular organizing principle. "Do you know what the most complicated, intricate creation in the whole universe is?"

"You?"

"Close, but not quite. A child—my child, to be precise. If the boy isn't to grow up very confused and disappointed, the adults around him will have to manage an elaborate dance. His mother claims his brilliance is unprecedented in the annals of English boyhood, but all I see is a busy little fellow with a big imagination and a kind heart. He's a person, Abigail. A dear, unique person."

Abigail was looking at Stephen as if he'd taken leave of his senses. "I know that."

"To Jack Wentworth, children were *chattel*, possessions. Little beasts of burden put on earth to fetch him gin, placate his temper, beg for him, and flatter his arrogance. He was pleased with himself for arranging *the sale* of his young daughters into a life of misery, brutality, and disease. *Pleased with himself.* He was the lowest parody of manhood, but to his children he was more awful than the Almighty. He could literally kill us with impunity and laugh while doing it, and he gloried in his power over us."

"Is this why you made Stapleton support the duke's mining bill? Because children are not chattel?"

"I made Stapleton support Quinn's bill because... I don't know why, and that is not the topic under discussion. Nicky is not a thing, a *possession* that belongs to me because his mother and I shared some passionate moments. She carried him under her heart, she knows his every fear and dream, and she has had the raising of him. Who am I—*Who the hell am I?*—to strut into his life years later pretending I have a right to order his existence?"

"You are his father." Abigail's brow had acquired an encouraging crease, and she spoke with less certainty than she'd enjoyed previously.

"In a biological sense, I am his father, but I will not take the path Jack Wentworth would take and exploit such a relationship for my own convenience. I want to know Nicky, I want to be a father in any sense that contributes to the child's welfare, but that does not have to be a public undertaking. Then too, there's the whole business of Harmonia's wishes. She brought that boy into the world, and she's the only parent he's known. Her welfare matters too."

Abigail was quiet for so long that Stephen's bum took exception to the hardness of the bench, and yet he waited.

"What did Harmonia have to say about all this?"

"A very great deal. She wants a small estate in Kent and Endymion de Beauharnais's ring on her finger. She does not want me."

"She's daft."

How I love you. "Perhaps, but de Beauharnais truly has her best interests at heart, and he's protective of Nicky."

Abigail gathered up her reticule again. "Harmonia is passing up your tiara to raise sheep in Kent?"

"And perhaps to give Nicky some siblings to boss about. Are you abandoning me yet again?"

"This bench is making my backside ache. I have much to think about."

Stephen rose and shrugged out of his cloak, then laid it on the bench. "Move closer to me. You'll be more comfortable."

Abigail sank onto the bench, and Stephen came down immediately beside her. The next time she tried to bolt, he would seize her by the hand if need be.

"This is complicated," Abigail said slowly.

"It doesn't have to be." He ventured an arm along the back of the bench. "I love you, and I would like to spend the rest of my life with you. I will play whatever role in Nicky's life best suits his needs, but that in no way precludes me from being a loyal, faithful, and passionate husband to you."

Abigail's head came to rest on his shoulder. "You're sure, Stephen? I have strong opinions, I will not be told what to do, and God help anybody who speaks ill of those I care about."

He shifted closer and took Abigail's hand. "Do you know why I hate society balls?"

"Because of the dancing?"

"That too, but mostly because they are just too damned long. Standing about in the buffet line, trying to manage two plates and a cane, standing in the reception line, struggling through a promenade...But when I was your escort, I could lean on you."

"Lean on me?"

"Physically." He demonstrated. "*Lean* on you, and sturdy creature that you are, you don't even notice. My leg barely hurt at all the morning after the Portman do. Harmonia showed me to the nursery today. It never occurred to her that navigating stairs would be hard for me. She tore around that house like a whirlwind, and I could barely keep up. I don't have to ask you to slow down. You are inherently considerate, and I treasure that about you."

Abigail's fingers closed around his. "Your brother said something to me today."

"If Quinn was impolite to you, he's a dead big brother."

"He was very kind. He said a duke fights the hard battles, the thankless battles, because he wants to be worthy of the duchess riding at his side. He's a good man, your brother."

"He's a good man in part because he found the right duchess."

Abigail curled closer, scandalously, marvelously close. "I want to be the sort of woman who can inspire a duke to fight the hard battles. The battles in the Lords, the battles for the children, for decency, for wounded soldiers, and so much more. I want to be the sort of woman who can love my husband's son, even if nobody knows he's my husband's son, and who can ride into battle beside the man I love."

A peace settled over Stephen, and a profound joy warmed his heart. "Say that last part again, please."

"I love you."

"Do you know what's wonderful, Miss Abigail Abbott?"

"You are."

"Mayhap I am, but what's wonderful is you don't expect me to propose on bended knee, and if I were ambitious enough to attempt such a feat, you'd help me up at the conclusion of my soliloquy."

She peered over at him. "Would you *like* to propose on bended knee?"

Stephen thought about it, thought about getting mud on his breeches, and making a complete cake of himself in the middle of the afternoon, and of all the times nobody had thought to treasure Abigail for the wonder she was.

"Here we go," he said, bracing his cane and sliding off the bench to take a knee. "Your hand, Miss Abbott."

She drew off her glove and gave him her hand.

"Miss Abbott, our association has not been long, but my feelings for you are deep, constant, a trifle naughty, and very sincere. More than a trifle naughty, if we're to be honest, and we must be or I do hope you will spank me. Will you do me the unfathomably great honor of becoming my wife, the answer to my every prayer, and the fulfillment of my dearest dreams?"

"Spank you?"

"Only if you want to."

She enveloped him in a hug. "Yes, I will marry you. Yes and yes, and *yes*."

Stephen kissed her, and the knee of his breeches grew damp, and he kissed her some more until a goose honked indignantly, and Abigail laughed and helped him back onto the bench. They stayed in the park for a long, lazy hour, discussing parasols that could conceal peashooters and riding crops that could conceal knives. When they made their way back to the coach, they did so arm in arm at the dignified pace of a future duke and duchess.

Epilogue

"Mama needs looser dresses," Nicholas announced. "Papa Andy says I'm not to notice."

Stephen had chosen a bench halfway across Berkeley Square from Gunter's, and thus the boy's announcement hadn't fallen on gossiping ears.

"Between us fellows," Stephen said, "my own dear Abigail might soon be needing looser dresses. Do you know what that means?"

Abigail and Jane were on the opposite bench, and Stephen's two oldest nieces were kicking a ball across the grass. These afternoon outings with Nicholas had become a weekly ritual when all parties were in Town, though Nicholas had spent most of the winter with his mother and new stepfather on a small estate in Surrey.

On short notice, Stephen hadn't been able to locate a suitable property in Kent, and Harmonia had fallen in love with one he'd found in Surrey. The immediate neighborhood boasted a marquess, a baron, an earl, and a viscount. De Beauharnais had decided the matter when he'd seen the windows on the northern side of the top floor.

Across the walkway, Abigail took a spoonful of raspberry ice and licked her top lip. She did it on purpose as her slight smile and the small lift of her empty spoon confirmed.

"Ladies wear looser dresses when they are going to get a baby," Nicky said. "The baby grows inside them and then pops out like a calf or a foal. Papa Andy says Mama will have a baby this summer and we must pray that she comes safely through her travail. Is her ladyship to have a baby too? Will she get a boy baby?"

"Any healthy baby will be a blessing without limit." And the wonder and terror of that eclipsed anything in Stephen's experience. His respect for Quinn and Jane—parents to *four* children—had grown with each passing week. And oddly enough, the succession absolutely did not matter and never would, alas for the peerage's priorities. Being Abigail's devoted husband and the loving father to his children of any description counted for everything. "Is vanilla still your favorite flavor, lad?"

"Yes, my lord. Might I go play?"

Stephen ruffled Nicky's dark hair. "Of course. You're outnumbered by the ladies, so give a good account of yourself."

The boy was off the bench like an arrow shot from a longbow, and his laughter soon joined that of his cousins. Abigail changed benches, coming down beside Stephen.

"What were you two fellows conspiring about?"

Stephen took a bite of melting vanilla ice. The plane maples were leafing out into their spring glory overhead, pigeons strutted on the walkway, and shrieks of childish glee punctuated the air.

"Every time he calls me *my lord*, I want to howl, Abigail, but then I think about you, who lost a child, or Champlain, whose life was a protracted farce, and my tantrum dies aborning. Nicky and I were talking about babies, and why ladies sometimes have to wear looser dresses. I gather Harmonia is on the nest."

Abigail set aside her spoon and bowl. "We will keep her in our prayers, of course."

Abigail and Harmonia had reached some sort of understanding, much as Stephen and Endymion had. The past was the past, an unhappier time that had borne some challenging consequences. The present, however, was a joyous contrast, simplified by a shared desire to see one little boy thrive.

"You know I love you madly," Stephen said, kissing Abigail on the lips.

"Shameless man. Kiss me when your lips won't give me frostbite." Frostbite was apparently an occasion for smiling. "How is today's experiment working?"

"Surprisingly well, Abigail, but the ultimate test will be whether I can manage to kick a ball, don't you think?"

Her smiled faded. "Here, in public?"

Stephen had been refining knee braces since last autumn, and some of them had malfunctioned spectacularly.

"Hold my ice, beloved wife. Nicky is defending the

honor of young manhood on the playing field, but I daresay he could use some reinforcements."

Abigail accepted the bowl and spoon. "If you insist."

Stephen's wife let him fall on his arse from time to time in pursuit of a more effective knee brace design. She always helped him up, dusted him off, and went on about life as if his infirmity were of no moment.

Increasingly, it was of no moment to Stephen as well. He took up his cane and crossed the grass just as little Elizabeth aimed a kick that sent the ball barreling straight for him.

Stephen trapped the ball between his foot and grass. "Battle stations! Incoming enemy fire!"

The girls squealed, Nicky darted to Stephen's side, and the ball ricocheted between opposing factions for five loud minutes. Only when Jane called for the girls did three panting, happy children declare a truce.

"That went rather well," Abigail said, passing the empty bowls to a footman. "Really rather well."

"You put me on to the essential design element," Stephen said, setting Nicky's cap on the boy's head. "Do you recall asking why I could ride a horse with my bad knee when I can't reliably walk without canes?"

"You said the horse's side prevented the joint from dislocating. That the horse provided the support your knee needed."

"Stabilizing the joint laterally while allowing it to bend in only the required direction became the objective."

Nicky readjusted his cap. "You use big words, my lord."

"Come to the parasol factory," Abigail said, kneeling to

button the boy's coat. "You will hear big words and see tiny, tiny parts. The ladies assemble our products using quizzing glasses because the mechanisms are so small."

"Parasols are silly," Nicky said, with the complete assurance of a small boy.

"Parasols that hide swords are not silly," Abigail said. "We're working on one that conceals a tiny gun. Ladies must be able to defend themselves from brigands."

"Bad men," Stephen said. "Highwaymen and the like."

"When can I see the parasol shop? Will Elizabeth come too?"

Stephen took Nicky by one hand, Abigail got him by the other. The boy could out-chatter a flock of starlings, and his every word fascinated Stephen.

"We will arrange the outing with your parents," Stephen said. "Abigail and I must be getting home. We need our rest, for we've a ball to attend tonight."

Nicky shook free and scampered up the walkway. "Balls are where you dance and drink punch and play cards. I am very graceful." He minced around and bowed to imaginary ladies. "Papa is teaching me some steps. We will surprise Mama."

"She will be very proud of you," Stephen said. Abigail sent him a smile as Nicky came back to his side. Her gaze held understanding and humor, which was balm to a man's soul when he was neither graceful nor a papa of record.

They saw the boy home, and Stephen stole a hug before turning Nicky loose at Harmonia's front door.

"She looks happy," Abigail said, when Stephen was again situated in the coach at her side.

"De Beauharnais looks ecstatic. He's taking commissions for children's portraits now and gaining quite a reputation. Are we happy, Abigail?"

She peeled off her glove and took Stephen's hand, a habit of theirs when they were private. "Tonight looms as something of an ordeal."

"For me too. We shall contrive, my love." The tailors had been called upon to sew Stephen's trousers more loosely than was customary. He would eschew the required knee breeches in favor of attire that hid his brace, and he had asked that the dance floor not be chalked.

The rest was in God's and Abigail's capable hands. She had agreed to this post-nuptial ball, and if they put it off any longer, her condition would be apparent. Jane had lobbied vigorously for tonight's date, and taken a firm hand in the planning.

And after a goodly nap—and some time spent in bed not napping—Stephen was taken in hand by Quinn and Duncan, and Abigail was whisked away by Jane and Matilda. For this occasion, Stephen's sisters, Althea and Constance, had come down from Yorkshire, their respective husbands in tow.

The hour arrived, the receiving line wound down through the foyer, and the Walden ballroom was finally opened.

"Are you nervous?" Abigail asked as the orchestra tuned up.

She had remained at Stephen's side through the interminable ordeal of the receiving line, her arm frequently linked through his. He could and did lean on her, and not entirely to spare his leg.

"I ought to be nervous," he said as they lingered at the

side of the dance floor, "but I am married to the most stalwart female in creation, and she will not let me fall."

"Yes, I will, if your hands wander inappropriately. I will also step on your toes, so see that you behave."

"Or you will spank me. Have I told you lately how profoundly I adore you?"

"Yes."

"I have?"

She smiled a very, very mischievous smile. "Not with words."

Quinn caught Stephen's eye. Stephen nodded, and the first violinist held up his bow before the rest of the ensemble.

"My lady," Stephen said, taking Abigail's hand. "May I have the honor of this dance?"

Abigail was the epitome of serene feminine composure, but for a hint of worry in her eyes. "You won't let me fall on my bum?"

"Not unless I get to land atop you."

She turned toward the dance floor, her hand over Stephen's. "Well, then. The pleasure is mine, my lord. Shall we dance?"

Stephen led her out, passing his cane to a footman at the last opportunity. The instant the music concluded, his cane would be returned to him. The entire occasion was to celebrate Stephen's marriage to Abigail, months after the fact. The bride and groom thus had the dance floor to themselves. The Wentworth siblings and their spouses would join in eventually, but shortly thereafter the music would conclude.

Stephen and Abigail would thus never have to navigate

amid a crowd of dancers, and Stephen would be without his cane only for those moments when he and Abigail were in each other's arms.

The introduction began, a slow triple meter. Abigail curtsied, Stephen effected a minimal bow, and they assumed waltz position. The German waltz was stately compared to its more vigorous English cousin, but it was a waltz, and the melody a lilting benevolence over the hushed crowd of guests.

"We are waltzing," Abigail said, softly. "Stephen, we are waltzing."

He managed the steps, though on the turns he had to rely on Abigail for balance. His brace did its job, the maestro resisted any temptation to increase the tempo, and soon, Stephen was waltzing—actually waltzing—too.

"We are indeed waltzing," he said, when they'd managed another turn. "Nothing in all the world could prepare me for the joy of being your husband at this moment, Abigail."

"Or the joy of being your wife."

The other Wentworth couples drifted onto the floor, a pair of nieces giggled from the minstrels' gallery, and before all of Mayfair, Lord Stephen Wentworth waltzed with his wife, and without his cane. When the final strains died away, and Abigail had again sunk into a curtsy, he drew her to her feet and kissed her soundly.

And she kissed him right back.

Don't miss Ned Wentworth's story in

NEVER A DUKE

Coming in Spring 2022

About the Author

Grace Burrowes grew up in central Pennsylvania and is the sixth of seven children. She discovered romance novels in junior high and has been reading them voraciously ever since. Grace has a bachelor's degree in political science, a bachelor of music in music history (both from the Pennsylvania State University), a master's degree in conflict transformation from Eastern Mennonite University, and a juris doctor from the National Law Center at George Washington University.

Grace is a *New York Times* and *USA Today* bestselling author who writes Georgian, Regency, Scottish Victorian, and contemporary romances in both novella and novel lengths. She enjoys giving workshops and speaking at writers' conferences.

You can learn more at:
GraceBurrowes.com
Twitter @GraceBurrowes
Facebook.com/Grace.Burrowes

Looking for more historical romances?
Get swept away by handsome rogues and clever ladies from Forever!

HOW TO CATCH A DUKE
by Grace Burrowes

Miss Abigail Abbott needs to disappear—permanently—and the only person she trusts to help is Lord Stephen Wentworth, heir to the Duke of Walden. Stephen is brilliant, charming, and absolutely ruthless. So ruthless that he proposes marriage to keep Abigail safe. But when she accepts his courtship of convenience, they discover intimate moments that they don't want to end. But can Stephen convince Abigail that their arrangement is more than a sham and that his love is real?

THE TRUTH ABOUT DUKES
by Grace Burrowes

Lady Constance Wentworth never has a daring thought (that she admits aloud) and never comes close to courting scandal... as far as anybody knows. Robert Rothmere is a scandal poised to explode. Unless he wants to end up locked away in a madhouse (again) by his enemies, he needs to marry a perfectly proper, deadly-dull duchess, immediately—but little does he know that the delightful lady he has in mind is hiding scandalous secrets of her own.

Follow @ReadForeverPub on Twitter and join the conversation using #ReadForever

SOMEDAY MY DUKE WILL COME
by Christina Britton

Quincy Nesbitt reluctantly accepted the dukedom after his brother's death, but he'll be damned if he accepts his brother's fiancée as well. The only polite way to decline is to become engaged to someone else—quickly. Lady Clara has the right connections and happens to need him as much as he needs her. But he soon discovers she's also witty and selfless—and if he's not careful, he just might lose his heart.

A GOOD DUKE IS HARD TO FIND
by Christina Britton

Next in line for a dukedom he doesn't want to inherit, Peter Ashford is on the Isle of Synne only to exact revenge on the man responsible for his mother's death. But when he meets the beautiful and kind Miss Lenora Hartley, he can't help but be drawn to her. Can Peter put aside his plans for vengeance for the woman who has come to mean everything to him?

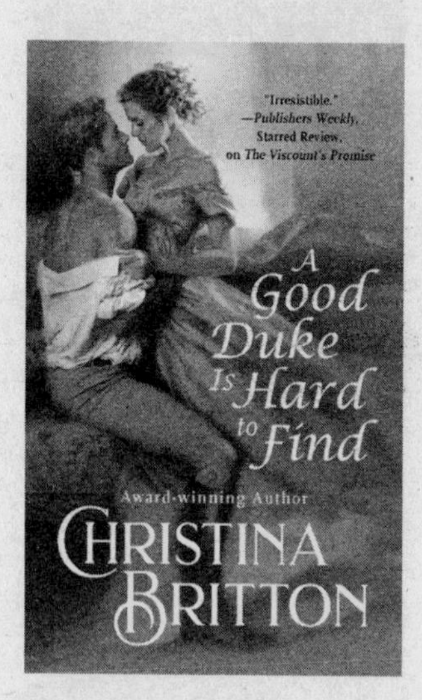

Discover bonus content and more on read-forever.com

Connect with us at
Facebook.com/ReadForeverPub

THE DUKE HEIST
by Erica Ridley

When the only father Chloe Wynchester's ever known makes a dying wish for his adopted family to recover a missing painting, she's the one her siblings turn to for stealing it back. No one expects that in doing so, she'll also abduct a handsome duke. Lawrence Gosling, the Duke of Faircliffe, is shocked to find himself in a runaway carriage driven by a beautiful woman. But if handing over the painting means sacrificing his family's legacy, will he follow his plan—or true love?

A ROGUE TO REMEMBER
by Emily Sullivan

After five Seasons of turning down every marriage proposal, Lottie Carlisle's uncle has declared she must choose a husband, or he'll find one for her. Only Lottie has her own agenda—namely ruining herself and then posing as a widow in the countryside. But when Alec Gresham, the seasoned spy who broke Lottie's heart, appears at her doorstep to escort her home, it seems her best-laid plans appear to have been for naught…And it soon becomes clear that the feelings between them are far from buried.

Find more great reads on Instagram with @ReadForeverPub

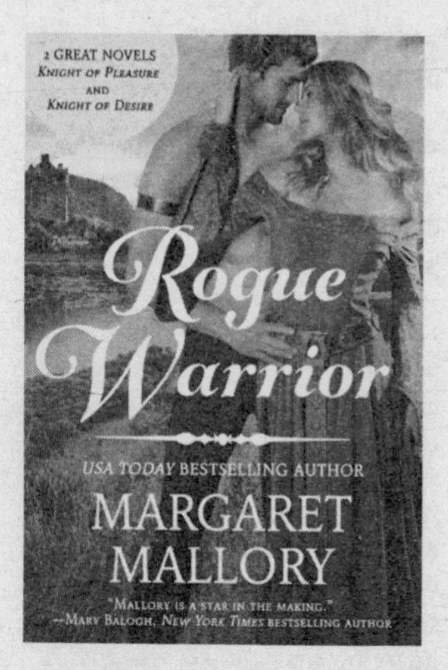

ROGUE WARRIOR
(2-IN-1-EDITION)
by Margaret Mallory

Enjoy the first two books in the steamy medieval romance series All the King's Men! In *Knight of Desire*, warrior William FitzAlan and Lady Catherine Rayburn must learn to trust each other to save their lives and the love growing between them. In *Knight of Pleasure*, the charming Sir Stephen Carleton captures the heart of expert swordswoman Lady Isobel Hume, but he must prove his love when a threat leads Isobel into mortal danger.

ANY ROGUE WILL DO
by Bethany Bennett

For exactly one Season, Lady Charlotte Wentworth played the biddable female the *ton* expected—and all it got her was Society's mockery and derision. Now she's determined to take charge of her own future. So when an unwanted suitor tries to manipulate her into an engagement, she has a plan. He can't claim to be her fiancé if she's engaged to someone else. Even if it means asking for help from the last man she would ever marry.